CN01459331

RACING HEARTS

HOLLOWS GARAGE
BOOK 3

KATE CREW

CONTENT WARNINGS

Sexual content (Consensual), acts and references to domestic violence, references to car wrecks, violence, & explicit language, dog attacks, gun violence.

Copyrighted Material

Racing Hearts

Copyright © 2023 by Kate Crew.

ISBN: 979-8-9885300-2-2

All Rights Reserved.

No part of this publication may be reproduced, stored in a retrieval system or transmitted, in any form or by any means— electronic, mechanical, photocopying, recording or otherwise— without prior written permission from the publisher, except for the inclusion of brief quotations in a review.

This book is a work of fiction. Names, characters, organizations, places, events, and incidents are either products of the author's imagination or are used fictitiously.

Cover Designer: Books and Moods at booksandmoods.com

Editor: The Author Buddy at theauthorbuddy.com

To the unapologetically grumpy girls who navigate the world with a scowl and a side-eye, but have hearts of gold beneath the surface.

RACING HEARTS PLAYLIST

Headlights - Alex Warren
Nightmare - Halsey
Blvck - Bryce Savage
I Know Places - Taylor Swift
Fred Astaire - Jukebox the Great
Middle of the Night - Elley Duhe
gold rush - Taylor Swift
Lips of a Witch - Austin Giorgio
Bad Blood - Taylor Swift
Heartbroken - Diplo, Jessie Murphy
I Wanna Be Your Slave - Måneskin
Delicate - Taylor Swift
Minefield - Nic D
I Guess I'm in Love - Clinton Kane
Daylight - Taylor Swift
Power Over Me - Dermont Kennedy
Call It What You Want - Taylor Swift

Sweet Dream - Bohnes
Monsters - Ruelle
Money on the Dash - Elley Duhe
Vigilante Shit - Taylor Swift
Look What You Made Me Do - Taylor Swift

ONE

JAX

I TRIED CONVINCING myself that I was out driving for fun, for practice on the turns, for the fresh air...anything but the real reason. That I was only trying to escape my friends.

It's something I never thought I would say considering how close we all were, and it wasn't their fault, but I could barely be in the same room as them lately without envy gnawing at me. The irony is that I was the one who had always wanted a relationship, and now I was the only one left currently who was single.

Well, aside from Kye, but I didn't even know if that counted anymore.

I had tried to find someone. I was always looking for the person who I could be with long term, but somehow dating had only made my self-esteem worse. The last relationship ended because I wasn't as much of a jerk as I supposedly led her to believe.

It was as though being decent-looking and having a fast car must mean I'm going to be a constant asshole to whoever I'm dating.

I had spent all summer debating giving up on dating since it was so hard to find anyone I even wanted to get to know in the first place, much less to know who to trust to take a relationship further.

Now, I was fully giving up. I was done putting myself out there. I kept finding the wrong person, and each one knocked me down further until I'd lost hope of ever finding someone who would like me for who I really am.

It had gotten so bad that I was constantly anxious and on edge, to the point that I couldn't feel comfortable around my friends and I could barely sleep anymore.

I thought I was completely fine with the decision to not date. That was until I woke up and realized summer was over. The leaves were slowly changing now, each day getting colder, and soon the crew would want to go do all the dumb couple shit that people do when it's cold.

Now, here I was, driving aimlessly all night because the thought of being surrounded by couples, lost to being sickeningly in love with each other, felt like my personal hell. It felt like I was an outsider at a party I hadn't been invited to. Even though I loved the addition of Quinn and Ash, I was starting to hate being surrounded by all the happy couples. Even Scout seemed to be wrapped up in her new boyfriend.

The road wound through dense forest, this part of the area more secluded, untamed, and beautiful. It was the main pass from our town to the next, but at this time of night, not many people were out, so I could speed my way through the hills and back again before I headed home to pointlessly attempt to sleep again.

First, I needed to get my own personal pity party out of the way so I could get back to my life tomorrow and act like nothing was wrong. And really, nothing was aside from not being able to figure out my own life or relationships.

I wasn't sure why I had to think about wanting more in life, but it was there nagging me. I had what I wanted, the garage, my work, the races, the crew. It was all there for me, but somehow it wasn't enough. It didn't seem fair to ask for more when I knew my life wasn't bad at all.

A flicker of green caught my eye up ahead. I slowed, an old truck coming into view on the other side of the road.

An involuntary groan escaped my lips. Helping a stranger wasn't exactly what I had in mind, but leaving someone stranded here all night with a broken-down truck wasn't an option either. Especially not when the chances that this was some old farm truck being driven by an equally-old man were pretty high. I pulled across the road to it, to park in front of the truck, my headlights bathing the truck in light as I hopped out.

"Hello?"

The dull light inside the truck was still on, and I could finally make out someone sitting in the passenger seat.

At least, I thought it was a person.

Until it barked, and barreled out of the truck, right at me.

I spun, ready to get out of there, but shock tore through me when I came face to face with a beautiful girl and a baseball bat, pulled back and ready to swing.

TWO
CARLY

SOMETIMES YOU GO to sleep and think that was the most terrible day of your life, only to be surprised when the next day is even worse.

I thought yesterday was it. I thought it would be marked as the worst day of my life. But then this morning, my stepdad and his best friend, Tristan, proved me wrong.

I spent the last eight hours locked in my room hiding, but I was sure they were gone now. I pulled open my bedroom door and peered out. The house was quiet, everyone gone or asleep, and it was my only chance to grab what I could and run.

Run as far as I possibly could, and hope that they didn't come looking for me.

I rolled my eyes. Of course they would come looking for me. Somehow their idea of family was becoming a little gang, and they thought they needed me for that.

I hadn't realized they had been tricking me for years, encouraging me to learn about computers, praising how smart I was when I'd help them. It started small, switching little things in the records for the cars at their shop. There was always a good reason for it, and my mother's unwavering faith in my stepdad made me never question a thing.

Did I like him? Not even a little. I hated him and his gross friends, but I was told that he was taking care of us and I should help him whenever he needed it, so I did.

Until yesterday. When I walked into their dirty, creepy garage after months of staying away, all the pieces fell into place. First, I had walked past the guy grinding a VIN number off of a door before adding a new, what I realized was fake, VIN plate in it's place. Then, we turned the corner, overhearing Tristan and one of the guys talking about the next round of cars and parts they were sending out of town to sell. There was no hiding what we heard as my sister had run over, throwing her arms around Tristan as he glared at me.

It was a mess, just like all the information in my brain, but then it all clicked together.

I had been inadvertently helping them steal cars.

I felt so stupid. I should have known, I should have made myself pay more attention, but whenever my stepdad was around, I couldn't think straight. He honestly terrified me and I learned fast that quiet and out of sight was best with him. So every time he asked for help, I put my head down to quickly do what he needed before going to hide back in my room.

I did exactly the same thing yesterday. I went back home, shut myself in my room, and laid in bed while I tried to figure out what I should do now that I knew what *they* were doing.

I thought I'd have more time, but this morning, I found out I was wrong.

When my stepdad and Tristan sat me down and made my options very clear. I was going to help them steal new cars. They planned to take new cars off the manufacturer lots and I was going to adjust their VIN numbers to make them *look* legal, along with creating fake titles for them. Then, they could sell them for full price, and be long gone before anyone caught on.

They had gotten this idea that I could help them by casually hacking into some national database to change legal numbers.

As scared as I was of both of them, I couldn't help but laugh in their faces. I could build websites, organize their accounts, run their programs, and suddenly I was supposed to hack into secure databases. In their delusional state, they really believed I could do this.

It didn't matter if I could or not, I wasn't going to.

That made it clear that if I stayed to help them, they would ease up on me and make sure I was taken care of, and if I didn't do this for them, they would make my life hell. More than they already were, apparently. They had thought that everything was wrapped up so nicely, but they forgot to account for the fact that I finally opened my eyes and realized this was it. If I stayed, there would be no turning back to a life outside of their illegal lifestyles.

I slipped into the small garage attached to our house and opened up Slaughter's laptop. He had one at his garage too, but last I knew, he kept copies of most of his files on this one.

I only hoped it was enough information.

I moved every single file I could find over to the thumb drive, my hands tapping against the table the entire time. My dog, Riot, came up, whining and knocking into me, probably annoyed at my sudden anxiety.

"We are really going this time," I told him, trying to calm my racing heart down as I watched the files load. "No doubting ourselves again. We are leaving."

It wasn't the first time I had daydreamed about leaving, telling Riot that we could have a better life, but it was the first time I was actually doing it. My life had transformed into a living hell, and yesterday was the last straw. It had become unbearable, pushing me to desperate measures like this.

It hadn't always been like this, but at some point, Slaughter saw my mom struggling and took his opportunity to snake his way into our lives. He took over the uninvited role of the man of the house, claiming that my mother shouldn't have to do all of this alone, and that he could help her as my new stepdad. It wasn't long before his "help" quickly escalated into a dictatorship, turning our lives upside down in a matter of days. Somehow, my mother thought this was better than handling this on our own. I tried over and over to talk to her, but she was adamant that she was happy and things were not changing.

But now I knew that I would rather be alone than stuck here. The relentless questioning, the demands, the arguments, the nasty comments about my weight or outfits, the days or even weeks spent locked in my room as if I were still a child – like I wasn't a grown woman. For so long, I thought that I owed them something, but I don't. That was just the weight of their manipulation on my shoulders.

The laptop pinged, showing that the thumb drive wasn't working. Something was corrupt on it or on the laptop.

Of course it wouldn't work. Why would this be easy?

Riot whined again, making me more anxious.

"Alright, nothing stopping us, right?" I said, slamming the laptop closed and taking the entire thing with me.

I ran back to my room, grabbing my packed bags, trying to take as much as I could carry. I had my bags, my truck, my money, and Riot was already next to me. There was nothing stopping me.

Tristan and Slaughter were headed to the neighboring town to pick up – or more likely steal – car parts because I couldn't think of any parts store that's open past 10 PM. My mom was a heavy sleeper, so that was no issue. Luckily, my sister had finally moved out and lived down the street with Tristan. It was the perfect opportunity for me to go in the opposite direction. I had been saving money for months to eventually move out and now I only hoped that I would have enough to make due until I started a job and got a paycheck.

I threw the last bag into the back of my truck and helped Riot up, his big Rottweiler body apparently too heavy for him to get himself up to the seat. Every minute that went by shrunk my window to leave, and the anxiety was starting to get to me. I didn't know how long Tristan and Slaughter would be gone, but they would know I had left as soon as they saw my truck gone. With everything that happened today, I knew they would be hunting me down immediately, especially when they saw both me *and* the laptop were gone.

I turned the truck over, not letting myself panic when it didn't crank the first time.

Or the second.

I almost cried until, on the third try, it finally turned over and roared to life.

I held back a sob as I took one more look at the house and prepared myself to let go of the only life I knew. It wasn't like I would miss it, but leaving behind such a deep part of who I was felt strange. It was freeing and scary, and I realized just how long I had been waiting for this exact feeling.

I tried to not jump every time a car passed, but it was hopeless. Every set of headlights made me worry that they had caught onto what I was doing and was following me.

I made it almost five miles down the road before the truck started to sputter. Then it popped, the entire thing shutting off and the power steering going out, making me cling to the wheel to try and pull onto the side of the road.

I cursed as the truck came to a stop and Riot perked up.

"No, you stay here," I said, jumping out. "This can't seriously be happening."

I popped the hood, laughing at myself that I thought I would be able to diagnose it. I knew how to change the oil, change a flat tire, and check fluids. I couldn't figure out what was wrong with an engine that decided to stop going down the road. I still tried, checking all the fluids and finding them a little low, but I couldn't imagine that made it shut off.

I leaned back on the bumper, looking out into the dark. There were no cars, no sounds, and nothing even remotely within walking distance.

There was nothing.

If this was the universe telling me I wasn't going to get to leave, it wasn't funny. Or maybe it was telling me that my life was what it was, and that I just needed to accept it.

It was hard to believe there could be this many roadblocks without it being some sort of sign to turn back, go home, and live out the rest of my miserable life.

I don't know how long I sat there. It could have been five minutes or hours but the sound of a car approaching finally caught my attention.

The familiar sound of an engine revving before shifting down, the curves here too dangerous to take at full speed.

My body tensed at the sound, the tears threatening now, but I pushed them away. Now was not the time to fall apart. If I was a crying mess, I would have no chance against whoever it was.

I grabbed the bat out of the back and opened the passenger door, unclipping Riot's seatbelt and ducking down to hide.

Just as I expected, the car came to a stop. If Slaughter, Tristian, or their friends were already looking for me, it wouldn't be hard to spot this old green truck if they passed. My grandpa gave me the truck, and I was grateful for it every day, even if it did stand out so horribly. There was no way I would be able to afford any other vehicle right now and it gave me the chance to save to leave instead of having to save for a car.

My plan had obviously been flawed, though, based on the truck's inability to even get me out of town. But even acting up, I still loved it.

The car pulled in, the headlights bathing us in light, but I was still hidden behind the passenger door. Riot whined from his spot in the passenger seat, and I tried to shush him, pushing his big body back into the truck more while I carefully peered at the car.

"Hello?" a man's voice that I didn't recognize echoed.

The guy walked towards the driver's side as I crept around behind him from the passenger side. I'd never seen him or the car before, but that didn't mean he wasn't helping Tristian and Slaughter find me. They had so much reach with these car guys that I wouldn't be surprised if there were already a dozen of them out looking for me.

Riot barked again and jumped from the truck, going right towards the guy before putting himself between us. I lifted up the bat, ready to swing. If the world was going to force me to go back to that damn house, I wasn't going to go without a fight.

"What are you doing?" I asked.

The guy turned, jumping back at the sight of me.

"Fuck. What are *you* doing?" he asked, taking another step back and holding up his hands.

"No. You tell me what you are doing. Why did you stop?"

"To help?" he asked, sounding bewildered. "I thought some old man would be out here. Is this your truck?"

"Do I look like an old man?"

"Obviously, not. I assumed it was an old man based on the old truck and would feel bad all night if I didn't stop."

"Are you out looking for me?"

His face scrunched. "No? What does that even mean? I'm

not actively going out trying to find women broken down on the side of the road."

"Not women, *me*. Did someone tell you to come out and look for me?" I asked, slower now.

"No. I don't even know you. What is happening?" he yelled. "And is your dog going to attack me?"

Riot was sitting at my side, not taking his eyes off of the guy.

"No, not unless I tell him to."

"Do *not* tell him to. I would like to keep all of my limbs." He shook his head and looked back at the road and then the truck. "Do you need help?"

"No," I said.

"Great then, have a good night," he said, stalking back to his car without another glance.

I couldn't imagine someone that was helping Tristian and Slaughter would leave that easily. Unless he was going to tell them that I was broken down. I was obviously a sitting duck in my current situation, and more of them showing up wouldn't help. Maybe letting him check it over wouldn't hurt.

"Wait!" I yelled, making him turn back. "Actually, I do need some help. Do you know anything about fixing a truck like this?"

His deep frown flashed in the headlights as he turned back to me. "Yeah. I know everything about fixing a truck like that."

"Would you possibly mind looking it over? Something made a big banging noise and then it stopped as I was going down the road, but I really need to get going again."

"Because someone is out looking for you?"

"Yes. I think so. Now, would you mind looking?"

"Since you asked so nicely, no, I wouldn't mind." He grabbed a bag out of his car, coming back and clicking on a flashlight. His face had calmed as he looked it over and that settled me a little more. Maybe he really did just stop to help me.

"Not the kind of car I'd expect someone like you to be driving."

"Someone like me?"

"Under seventy years old."

"It was a gift," I said, realizing that I wouldn't be able to go see my grandpa for a while, either.

He moved to step around me, but Riot growled as he got closer.

"That," he said, taking a step away. "Still looks like an angry Rottweiler."

"Protective, not angry. Enough." I said, watching as Riot visibly relaxed at my side with the command.

"And well trained." His eyebrows jumped, but he turned back to the truck, ignoring both of us.

"Yes, so while I appreciate your help, please don't make me send Riot after you."

He shook his head and reached into his bag. "You named your dog Riot?"

"I didn't. Someone else did. He was horrible as a puppy. He basically named himself."

"I can only hope that I won't be doing anything to warrant you sending him after me."

"He'll keep his distance. He's not fond of men, and I can't blame him for that."

"Ah, so both of you are jaded."

"Isn't everyone?" I replied.

"For tonight, I can agree," he said.

"What was your name? And is there any chance this will be quick?"

"Jax, and I don't know. You'll have to give me a minute. On the run from the police? Or an ex?"

"Neither," I said, looking from him to the road.

"Are you going to tell me your name?"

"Carly."

"Alright, Carly, tell me what happened to the truck."

I ran over what happened, the truck stalling out as I came around the corner. "I know the basics, but past an oil change or a new battery, I'm out."

He made a sound and peered back over the engine. It gave me a second to look him over finally. He was hot. The hard lines of his jaw and messy hair peeking out from under the now backwards hat made him look like he was straight out of a magazine.

I knew his type, but I couldn't help but think he looked sweet. Even the way his jaw tightened when I looked him over still looked cute.

I turned away, scolding myself to stop. I didn't know why he was here and him being hot could not distract me. Technically, he could still kidnap me himself, or be here to kidnap me for Tristan and Slaughter.

He took a few more minutes, tinkering with things and trying to turn it over, but none of it was working.

A car revved in the distance, making me jump. "Any luck?"

"Not yet. I'm ruling a few things out," he replied, his voice taking on a more serious tone.

The sound of the engine reverberated around us and I couldn't hide the tremble that went through me. Whoever it was had to be close to coming over the hill.

"Any chance it will be running in the next minute?"

He gave a harsh laugh. "I'm good, but not that good. No, I'm thinking it has a bigger problem than I hoped."

"Ok. Then leave it. I'll get it later."

"Give me a few more minutes. I can call someone to bring it back to our shop if you want."

"Shop?"

"I'm a mechanic."

"How surprising, another mechanic who owns a garage and

drives a fast car," I mumbled, thinking how similar it all was to my life. I shook my head, it didn't matter who he was. "No. You need to go. Take your stuff and go." My nerves were getting to me as a car finally crested the hill, it was still at least a mile away, but they would cover that ground fast. I grabbed his tools, shoving them back into his bag.

"What?" he asked, looking around the truck to me, but I was already grabbing my backpack and the most important suitcase. "It's really not a problem. I don't mind waiting out here with you."

"Just go. I'll get it later. You need to go. *I* need to go." I looked back, my heart thundering as I waited to see what car was coming over the hill.

"What's going on?" Jax said, sounding pissed off now. "What trouble are you in?"

"I need to go and I'm worried that car coming is one of the people that I am trying to get away from."

"So you really are running from someone? Who?"

"My stepdad and his goons. If they see me out here, they are going to drag me back. I need to go. Get out of here. I'll hide until they leave."

I whistled for Riot and he came to my side, but I realized Jax wasn't moving.

"Go! Grab your things. Just go," I yelled again.

"I'm not a dog to dismiss. What are you going to do? Hide out in the freezing woods all night?"

"Pretty much."

He groaned and went to grab more bags out of the truck, a serious frown on his face as he pulled them out and headed to his car.

"Get in my car. *Now*."

THREE
JAX

I FIGURED she was trying to get out of town fast, but now it seemed she actually had someone hunting her down.

Carly wasn't some sweet old man in a broken down old truck, she was apparently one step away from a fugitive.

"Go away," she said through gritted teeth as she tried to grab her bag out of my hand. It didn't work. Instead, I grabbed another bag from the bed and threw them both in my car.

"Get in. Come on, grab your stuff. I'll have your truck picked up."

She grabbed the bag in my hand, trying to pull it away again.

"Listen, you just met me, but you are obviously in trouble, and I swear I'm not a murderer or anything. So please, get in the car and we can sort the rest out once you aren't about to be literally kidnapped right in front of me."

"I can handle it fine on my own."

"By hiding in the woods? No, get in the car."

She looked at my car, then me, and then in the direction of the approaching car. Her pretty eyes went wide and nostrils flared, in what I could only guess was anger. Finally, she spun toward my car as the other car pulled off the road. Luckily, they didn't seem to see my car right away as they parked behind the truck.

"That's him," she said, grabbing a bag off the ground and throwing it in the car.

"Alright, I got it. You can stay there."

She did, but Riot did not.

I heard the loud growl as Riot pushed past me. His hackles rising up as he let out a nasty snarl, teeth bared at the guy stalking towards us.

If I thought Riot had been angry at me, it was nothing compared to this. She was right. He had been protective, but now he was out for blood.

She yelled for him, but Riot's eyes were completely locked on the guy. There was no changing his mind now.

"Tristan, back up. He's going to bite you," she said.

"No, he won't. The damn dog is all bark."

As though Riot was offended, he jumped forward, lunging and snapping his jaw.

"Come on, Riot," I said with a whistle. He looked back at me but didn't move, still pissed.

"Who the fuck are you?" Tristan asked.

"None of your business. Seems like she's none of your business, too."

That pissed him off more. He stepped up to me, his chest all puffed up as he yelled.

I didn't know what it was about guys that liked to get so close before fighting. Do we need to chest bump before it starts? Why get close enough to get hit unless you're already throwing a punch? It's become such a pet peeve that it only made *me* pissed.

His hands came up, and he pushed at my chest with a huff.

Fuck. No part of me was in the mood for this.

I leaned down, throwing my shoulder into his stomach to

push him back before swinging my fist up and into his nose. I could hear Riot barking next to us, but he didn't get any closer.

The guy was equivalent to a cooked noodle trying to fight, waving his fists and not landing a single solid punch. I hit him again, this one landing on the side of the head, making him fall to the ground with a yell.

I turned back, heading to my car and pulling open the driver's side, trying not to laugh as I saw Riot still standing over him.

"Riot. Come on," I yelled, surprised when he stopped and listened. He snapped one more time before trotting over to my door and jumping over me into the backseat.

"Tristan's going to follow," she said, her tone even and quiet.

"Then we are going to lose him. Plus, the bloody nose is going to give us a few minutes' head start."

"He races cars. I don't think you can outrun him. Even with the bloody nose. Maybe I should go with him. I can try to leave another time."

"Did I not mention that I also race cars? I have been street racing since I could drive, and considering the crew I race with, I should damn well be considered a professional now. So, no, based on how hard you're trying to get away from him, you aren't going to go right back. I can take you where you need. Then again, based on your bags, you were headed pretty far."

"As far as I could get."

"Where did you come from?"

"About fifteen minutes up the road."

"No offense, but you didn't get too far," I said, laughing until I saw her face. The angry scowl not showing any humor.

"Wow, thanks for pointing out the obvious."

"Sorry," I said, wincing. "I was trying to lighten the mood. You didn't have a destination in mind?"

"Nope, just trying to get far away and find a fresh start."

"Good for you. A lot of people want to run away from life sometimes, but most people don't actually do it."

"It's a lot easier when you run out of reasons to stay."

"Yeah, I guess it would be."

I sped back to our building. The old firehouse my friends and I converted into our personal apartment building was the only place I'd ever called home, and the only place I could think where she'd be safe this late at night.

I could easily get her to the nice hotel across town, but I was going to assume she wouldn't want to spend a couple hundred dollars to stay for a few hours. And there was no way that I was dropping her off at the gross motel.

I looked over at her, her face still in a hard frown as she stared out the window. I was a little hesitant to bring a stranger right back to our place, especially with whatever people were after her, but she didn't exactly strike me as a problem herself. The guys after her, maybe, but we had security systems already set up anyway, so it's not like anyone else would be able to walk in. I didn't think one night would cause any issues.

"Do you just want to stay at my place tonight? It's a little late to drop you at any safe hotel, and then I can get your truck to our shop in the morning. Maybe have you back on the road before the end of the day tomorrow, depending on what's wrong with it."

"I don't really have money to fix the truck and leave still. I might have to go back."

I couldn't help the laugh that escaped me. "You packed up your bags, your dog, and took off in the middle of the night. If you want to leave, don't let this stop you. The truck might be an easy fix. Let me look at it in the morning and we can see how fast, or cheap, it can be fixed."

"I appreciate it, but I really can't pay you for your work or for staying at your place for the night, and I don't want to owe anyone anything. That never ends well."

I didn't exactly disagree, but I hated to make anyone go back to such an awful situation just because of one inconvenience. I didn't know if I could actually let that happen when it might only be a simple fix needed to get her back on the road tomorrow.

No, I knew I couldn't let that happen.

"Okay then. What are you good at?"

"What do you mean?" she asked, shifting uncomfortably in her seat.

"I mean, what skills are you good at?"

"Nothing as useful as a mechanic."

"You don't have any job or hobby that you feel you are good at? Something you just like to do?"

"I don't know," she said, one eyebrow cocked up, looking me over again with that suspicious glare. "I like to cook."

"What kind of cooking are we talking about? What do you cook?"

"Mostly Greek and Italian recipes. My grandparents' recipes, but I like to try all sorts of things."

I groaned, realizing how hungry I'd become. "Perfect. Cook me lunch and dinner tomorrow while I look over your truck and get it fixed. And before you ask, I will buy the ingredients. I'll also throw in free parts if you feed my friends too," I said, trying to give her a charming smile, but she only seemed suspicious.

"Why are you being so nice?" she asked, glaring at me.

"Honestly? Because it would be harder to be mean right now. It's not like I'm doing much. Working on cars is my job. I own a garage with my friends. And don't forget, I thought I was helping some sweet old man, not an angry girl with a baseball bat, and a big, pissed-off dog."

Finally, her lips tipped up the slightest amount. "Surprise."

I shook my head with a laugh. "Really, none of it's a problem, especially if you're cooking. There's a team of us who don't, and honestly can't, cook much. We have like five staple items we make at cookouts, and that's about it. Everyone would be happy for some new food for the day."

"And somehow that would be a fair trade?"

"To me? Absolutely."

"I can't go home with some random guy."

"I'm not forcing you. But I did just have to knock a guy out who was after you, so you are obviously the one who's trouble here. I'll drop you off somewhere if you want. I don't really know how to convince someone that I'm not a creep or murderer? Although, I have three very nice, also very angry, women that can vouch for me if you come to my place, and who would personally ruin my life if I hurt you."

"You live with three women?" The shocked horror in her tone made me purse my lips harder, trying not to laugh.

"My friends and I have a building that we renovated into apartments for all of us. So, I technically live with all of my friends, three of which are women, but in our own apartments. I would never have another peaceful day in my life if I hurt you."

"I don't know if that setup makes me feel better or worse," she said with a deep breath. "Fine. I'll go back with you. It's not like I can think of anywhere else to go, and I can't sleep in my truck now that Tristan knows where it is. And honestly? I'm so exhausted I don't know if I'd care if you were a murderer. Are you sure you're fine with both of us there for the night?"

I didn't even have to look back at Riot since he was resting his big head on my shoulder.

"As long as no one bites," I said, looking at him out of the corner of my eye.

"Only if you give us a reason, too."

"I'll do my best not to."

She gave a tight smile and looked back out the window, seemingly fine with the silence as we drove back.

"Alright," I said, parking and getting out. "Let's get your bags up and try to get some sleep."

She took the bag out of my hand just as fast as I had picked it up.

"I only need this one for the night."

"Are you sure? I don't mind bringing up the rest."

"No, it's fine. No need to carry them up, only to bring them back down tomorrow. Let's get inside. Where would I be sleeping, by the way?"

"One of us gets the bed, one gets the couch."

"I will take the couch. I don't want to kick you out of your room."

"Whatever makes you more comfortable. I do have a lock on my door if you need."

"A lock that I'm sure you could get into if you wanted. Locks do not make me feel safe."

I pushed open the door, letting them both in, and trying to figure out what could have happened to make her say that. It sounded...terrifying.

I wasn't surprised when Riot began inspecting every inch of the apartment. Luckily, I was one step away from being Monica Geller with my level of cleanliness. I had watched all the seasons with the girls and hadn't heard the end of my obsessive cleaning since.

"Wow, this was nicer than I expected," she said, stopping to look around.

"What were you expecting?"

"Honestly? A cave of an apartment with various mattresses on the floor that you share with your friends."

"And you still came back here? All I can picture with that description is a murder dungeon."

"That's what it looked like in my head. This looks normal. Nicer than normal, actually."

Riot jumped onto the couch, flopping his body down and growling as he rubbed and rolled against it.

"Riot, no!" she yelled, running over to pull him over. "Get down."

"It's fine. Let him get comfortable." I grabbed him water from the kitchen before heading to get some pillows and blankets. It was only for one night. I hoped the dog wouldn't rip the entire apartment apart in less than 24 hours, but he was the size of a small horse. I could imagine the damage from him would add up fast.

She didn't need another reason to feel uncomfortable, though, so I held my tongue.

"Are you hungry?"

"I could eat. I was too nervous to eat all day."

"I can imagine why. I'm no cook, but I have chicken nuggets."

She sat back on the couch as Riot settled next to her. The dog was obviously obsessed with her, every motion from him seemingly out of pure love or protection. She still seemed uncomfortable. Not that I blamed her. It's probably better that she was on guard a little. I would be pissed if any of the girls went home with a random guy they met on the side of the road.

By the time I sat back next to her with the food, they were both almost asleep.

"Still want to eat?"

"Yes, please. My growling stomach will wake me up if I try to sleep now."

She grabbed for her plate and for the first time, I took in her features.

Long dark hair, flawless skin with a spatter of freckles across her nose, emerald eyes, and a body that I was working hard to try to ignore.

"So," she said, interrupting my thoughts. "When you pick up girls with giant dogs broken down on the side of the road, do you always bring them home for chicken nuggets?"

"So far? 100% of the time."

She laughed, the sound soft and honest, which I liked. I hated it when someone had a fake laugh. The sound was the equivalent of someone scraping a fork on a plate.

"Riot looks like he wants to take my plate," I said.

"He does. What dog wouldn't want a plate of chicken?"

"Will he?"

She laughed again, looking at the dog. "No, unless you hand it over, he'll stay put. I've never been able to stop the begging for food, not that I can blame him much, but he won't get any closer."

When she looked away, I slipped him a piece of chicken and he nearly swallowed it whole, but hopefully he understood the peace offering.

We ate, and by the time we were done, I was the one nodding off.

"Alright. Get some sleep. I'll bring the truck over first thing in the morning and we will both get to work."

"What about the food I need to cook?"

"One of us will run to the store. Do you need to go to pick everything out?"

She nodded, her face pinching like going to the store would be another nightmare.

"No problem. We'll see who can go tomorrow with you. No one here will bite, unlike you, even if they all look like it. Promise. And I highly doubt any of the people looking for you will be looking at a grocery store first thing in the morning."

"Okay. And thanks for all of this. This is a lot better than trying to walk anywhere or going back." She had leaned back, looking exhausted as her eyelids grew heavy.

"Or sleep in the freezing woods while scared to death? No problem. You're safe for the night. Security in our building is great, and any noise you hear is probably one of my friends."

"Did you need help cleaning your hand or anything? You punched him pretty hard."

"All good." I held it up, my knuckles already red but not split open.

She nodded hard and turned away. "Thanks for doing that."

"I would say anytime, but I try not to go around punching people."

"I'll keep that in mind. Goodnight," she said, her lips pressed into a tight smile.

I shut myself in my room and laid down. I hadn't been sleeping right for weeks, but I figured that sleep would come easily from pure exhaustion from the nights events. I still laid awake for what felt like forever, and the moment I did start to fall asleep, I heard Riot start walking around.

I assumed he was nervous in a new place, but it gave me time for my thoughts to run wild, thinking over Riot, Carly, the night, and what she was going to do next.

It was fine.

The big dog, the pretty woman, the broken truck, the food that I hoped would be good.

It was all fine.

I could handle the disarray for a day until it all went back to normal.

―――――

BY THE TIME the sun was up, I was ready to get moving. I showered, changed, and snuck out as quietly as I could, leaving a note with my number and where I was going. There was no point in lying awake in bed to stare at the ceiling, and the sooner I picked up her truck to get started on it, the sooner she could be on her way.

Riot watched as I grabbed a drink and something to eat before sneaking out quietly while Carly slept.

The guys were already waiting for me downstairs, ready to come with me in case any of the people after her were waiting by her truck.

"So why did I have to be up this fucking early to go pick up a car, and why did all of us need to come?" Kye asked, leaning against his car and looking half asleep. Fox and Ransom stood next to him, both interested in the answer. They had been my friends since we were kids and I knew they would come with me, no questions asked, but there was no point in hiding it now.

"Long story short, I found a girl broke down on the side of the road. She has someone, or apparently multiple people, looking to bring her back home where she doesn't want to go, so I brought her back here, and agreed to help her fix her truck today in exchange for her cooking us all dinner tonight. I need you guys to come pick up her truck in case the people after her are waiting there. *If* it's still there."

Eyebrows shot up in surprise.

"You brought a random girl in trouble back here?" Ransom asked.

"Yeah, but no one followed us or anything. I punched the guy that was there, and if there were more with him, they didn't keep up with us."

"Where exactly did she sleep?" Fox asked with a giant smirk on his face. Of course this somehow wouldn't be a shock to them, and even less surprising was Fox only worrying about the gossip.

"Why? Need to know so you can run and tell the girls all the updates?"

"Already texting them," he said, pulling out his phone with a grin. "But you know the question has to be answered."

"She slept on the couch and nothing else happened."

"Really? Interesting," Fox said, already tapping at his phone.

"Do you really think I'm going to sleep with a random girl I found on the side of the road and brought home?"

"Stranger things have happened," Fox said, still tapping away. "Next question from Ash. Do you think she's good looking?"

I rolled my eyes, ignoring him. "Please tell the girls not to go invade my apartment to meet her yet. It's way too early for that. I was going to ask one of them to bring her to the store anyway."

"Okay," Fox said, quiet for a minute. "They are *all* bringing her to the store. They want to meet her."

I could only shake my head. I should have known it would take all of ten minutes to have everyone know exactly what was going on.

"Come on. She only wants to stay for the day, so we need to get this truck and get it fixed. Are you all still coming?"

They all nodded, climbing into my car to head to the garage and get our tow truck.

"Good choice since that's the only way you're getting invited to dinner," I said.

"Perfect. I want real food. I've been warming up pizza for days now," Kye said.

Great. One day. One dinner. Granted, it would be one large, loud, messy dinner in my apartment, but then life would be back to normal.

Everything would be back to normal.

With how hung up I was already getting on those gorgeous green eyes of hers, I knew that getting back to normal was the best thing for me.

FOUR
CARLY

IT WAS BARELY five hours later, but I still forgot where I was as I opened my eyes. The warm blankets wrapped around me were cozy. This wasn't even close to the same lumpy bed I had at home, and the woodsy pine scent was nothing like the lavender scent I usually smelled. The only normal thing to bring me back was Riot's nose inches from my face, as he stared at me.

"Stop being a creep."

He whined.

"Yeah, yeah. Give me a minute."

I got up, finding the coffeemaker, but no coffee grounds, and the only thing in the fridge was flavored water and energy drinks. I think him saying that he didn't cook much was a huge understatement. I snooped through the rest of the cabinets before realizing he really had the bare minimum.

A scribble of my name on a notepad caught my attention. Jax had already left and was heading to get the truck. There was also a horrible drawing of a truck and a wrench that I stared at a full minute before laughing.

Jax seemed nice enough, and for going home with a strange

guy, he hadn't tried to make me feel uncomfortable yet, which was a shock. I had honestly expected him to suggest we share a bed or make a joke that I pay him back sexually, but so far, all he had done was feed me and agree to get my truck. I didn't really know what to make of it.

I had slept so hard that I had no idea when he left, but it was well past nine now. His number was written across the bottom of the note and let me know that someone would be taking me to the store.

My stomach rolled at the thought. What was worse than having to go home with a strange guy because you have nowhere else to go? Having to go out with his friends that you didn't know. All the while making sure I didn't run into anyone that I did know.

Jax had made it clear that him and his friends were in the street racing world, and I knew the type of people that went with that. Disgusting, crude guys, and mean, bitchy girls. Men that wanted to grope anything that moved and women who would yell at you for getting groped by their boyfriend. It was repulsive and exhausting, and I wasn't sure I could take anymore of that right now. There was no world that I was going to get along with girls that hung around with street racers.

"I was kind of looking forward to us being alone today," I said to Riot, who only stared. "Now we have random women coming here to interrogate me. I wouldn't be surprised if I somehow stepped on someone's toes by sleeping here last night."

I couldn't imagine at least one of Jax's friends not having a crush on him or having a relationship of some sort. The guy was hot enough to make me look more than twice. There was no way these other women weren't noticing.

"I hate this," I mumbled. "I hate meeting new people, especially if they might already hate me."

I grabbed his harness, clipping it on and heading out for a walk to hopefully clear my head.

As for the number, I had left my phone behind when I ran off. There was no way I was going to be found only because I wanted my phone, so his number didn't help me much.

Not that I had any use for it anyway.

When I stuck my head out the door, I didn't see or hear anyone, but I was still quiet as we stepped out the door and crept down the stairs. The entire place wasn't that big, but I was surprised at how well they did turning the old brick building into their very own apartment complex. A set of stairs led up to another landing with two apartment doors, and the other brought me down to two more doors before I could turn right and go to the garage that we came in last night, or take a left and go outside.

We walked around the block a few times before heading back in. Riot seemed to be having a good time, but I couldn't stop looking over my shoulder, worried Slaughter or Tristan's cars would show up any minute. Worried that somehow the world would turn against me one more time and lead one of them right to me.

I was quiet heading back in, slipping inside Jax's apartment without passing anyone. When I turned to the kitchen, my heart dropped as I screamed.

"Whoa!" the small red-headed girl said, turning and raising her hands.

The other two jumped back and yelled out.

Riot barked and pulled forward, more surprised at my scream than by them.

"Sorry! I'm Quinn. This is Ash and Scout. Jax said you needed to go to the store and we all do, too. We didn't mean to scare you!" she said, her eyes going wide as she yelled over Riot's barking.

"Usually it's the guys getting this reaction. I'm not quite sure what to do," the blonde girl, Ash, said as she shut the fridge. "I mean, you are Carly, I assume?"

"Yeah, that's me. Sorry, I was outside and got myself all paranoid, and I wasn't expecting anyone here."

"We knocked but didn't hear anyone, and we were dying to meet the random girl that Jax brought home in the middle of the night," Ash said, wiggling her eyebrows. "But then we were starting to worry that you left."

"No, Riot has a very strict schedule for himself, so I had to take him for a walk," I said, trying to relax.

They all looked at Riot, who was now sitting and panting, a smile across his face, looking ready to jump all over them.

"Sorry, he's not a big fan of men, but seems to think every woman will fawn all over him. Do you guys mind if I let him go?"

"Not at all," Quinn said at the same time Scout's eyes went wide.

"Is he friendly?" she asked, the shock and horror in her tone making me stifle a laugh.

"Yeah, he's a big teddy bear. Like I said, it's men he doesn't like much."

Ash dropped down and Riot bounded over, nearly rolling into her lap.

"We can all agree on that, buddy."

Quinn got down to pet him, but Scout stayed on her stool.

"If you're scared of him, you can ignore him. He'll get the hint."

"I mean, I'm not scared of him, maybe a little…wary."

I smiled at her hesitancy. "Understandable, but he really is a big baby."

He was on his back, taking the attention and basking in the petting.

"So is Scout. You two will love each other," Ash said, sticking her tongue out at Scout. "I saw that Jax has *quite* the selection here. Do you want coffee or food or anything before we go?"

"Actually, coffee would be great. It looks like he has none."

"I have plenty downstairs. We'll get some and then head out."

"Already?"

"Yeah, we all have to get to the garage later this morning, so now is best."

"Of course. That will give me time to cook, anyway."

I went to change, pulling on leggings and a shirt, trying not to think about how pretty his friends were. It wasn't that I was jealous. I liked how I looked most of the time, but some part of my brain could never stop comparing myself to other people. No, not other people, other women. It had become a habit, always comparing myself until I felt bad. It wasn't their fault, it never was, but I could bring myself down so far that I ruined my own day. I couldn't let it happen this time. I needed to force myself to stop before I let it get out of control.

Luckily, they started pulling me downstairs to another, similar apartment before I could spiral. Ash talked about who was in what apartment and more about the garage as she made us coffee, and then I was being pulled further downstairs to the garage to head to the store. I was happy they didn't expect me to do much talking about myself. They seemed fine filling in the silence, telling me about themselves and the garage.

"My family owns Holt racing," Ash said. "So we can go to the track if you ever want to. I'm not sure if you like driving and all that."

"Oh wow," I said. I had been staring out the window, taking in their excitement and stories. "I wasn't expecting that."

She flashed a smile. "No one ever is."

"That's really nice, but I don't really like driving fast cars. More of a slow truck kind of person, which I hope will be done before I have time to even go to your track."

She shrugged. "You never know. It's a lot of fun when you're on a track. And not nearly as scary as the road."

"I might have to try it one day," I said, not really meaning it. Not believing that I would be around long enough to do that. I was pretty sure after today, I would never see them all again.

————

AFTER SHOPPING, we got back into Scout's little green car. I had come to hate these fast cars, but she seemed like a better driver than most people I had known, so I tried to keep my mouth shut and not complain.

"So, I have to ask because I'm not quite sure what the entire dynamic is here. I'm not causing any problems staying there with Jax, right? None of you have a problem with it and are planning on punching me or anything? I want to clarify that I'm sleeping on the couch, not *with* him."

They all looked around and laughed.

"I'm already dating one of his friends, Ransom, and so is Ash, who is dating Fox. As for Scout, what do you think? Any feelings towards Jax?"

"I will pull this car over and kick both of your asses if you try to convince her that I do," Scout said. "No, Carly. The only feelings I have, or have ever had, for Jax are the annoying older brother feelings. I love him, for sure, but there's no romance there, promise. There's no romance for any of the guys."

I nodded, relieved that none of them seemed to have a problem. I didn't want Jax, but I also didn't want any of the girls coming for me.

By the time we made it back from the store and they dropped

me off, I even felt a little more comfortable about the idea of having to sit and eat with the entire group later.

I was surprised at how nice they all were. I mean, they joked and gave each other some shit, but it seemed to all be friendly. It was so different from what I knew. I gave up on friendships, on any type of relationship, and learned to keep to myself. It had become easier than trying honestly, and it felt so much safer than handing over any part of myself to someone.

After walking Riot again, I went right to work. I started with making the pasta and prepping dessert before I would start putting it all together when the time came.

I lost myself in cooking, not paying attention to the time or to my worries. It was one of my favorite parts of it all. I had too much to focus on in these moments to worry about my life. I could turn on music or a podcast and be zoned out for hours.

The door shut, and I froze.

"Hello?" I asked, the edge to my voice sounding annoyingly nervous. I liked to think I was tough, but I didn't feel that way right now. I was so nervous that every little thing seemed to put me more on edge.

"Only me," Jax said, walking in and throwing his stuff down. "How's it going?"

"Oh damn. What time is it?"

There was no clock in the kitchen and without a phone, I was useless at keeping track. Although, to be honest, even with the phone, I was terrible.

"Almost five. Everyone will head home to clean up, then come over. Is that fine?"

"Fine? Like an hour?" I wasn't nearly as ready as I wanted to be. I mean, the food was ready, but I wasn't. I wanted this entire dinner done and over with, then I could at least make it to the next town before midnight then, and hopefully avoid any extra small talk.

Jax only laughed. "I'm going to shower quick and then I will help you."

"No, you don't have to do that. You worked on my truck all day. Dammit, you did get my truck, right?"

"I did. I figured you would at least text, but here." He turned his phone around, showing me a picture of the truck in what I guessed was their garage. "We'll talk at dinner about its diagnosis, but it's locked up there now."

"Thank you. It really means a lot that it's at least safe."

He grimaced, but shook his head in agreement. "I'll be back in a few."

The next hour went by fast as I put the food together and tried to push Jax out of the kitchen.

"The whole point is I do this in exchange for the truck getting fixed, so stop helping. Shouldn't your friends be here soon?"

"Yeah, they should. I get you are trying to kick me out, but do you think I need to wait at the door and greet them?" he asked with a smirk. "You did meet the girls, right? There's no formalities here. They will just let themselves in. I can help you in here."

As soon as he said the words, the door burst open, a line of people filing in.

I could only step back, the apartment getting smaller as one after another came inside.

I hated get-togethers, hated parties. Honestly, I hated anything that had more than two people around me lately. I would be content here alone for weeks if I had Riot, fun food to cook, and a few books or movies.

Not only that, but big tattooed street racers made me nervous after hanging around Slaughter and Tristan, their illegal activities always bringing some sort of trouble around. Their gross, inappropriate friends always coming around to drink and grab at me.

I could barely hide away in my room without them bothering me constantly.

Now I seemed to be in a room full of them.

"You okay?" Jax asked, stopping to look me over.

His hair was still damp, his shirt clinging to him in all the right places and making me forget what I was worried about. I could see more of his tattoos now, a band around his forearm, a few others littered on his biceps. They weren't overwhelming, each one smaller and well done. I assumed there was more, but none that I had a chance to see yet. I, surprisingly, *really* wanted to see if there was more.

"Carly?" he asked again, pulling my attention back to his face.

"Yeah, I'm not great with groups, and yours is a bit too familiar and intimidating."

"Damn, yeah, I forget that all of us together can be daunting. They are really great, though. They won't give you too much shit or anything. What do you mean, familiar?" He was still smiling, stealing bites of food where he could.

"I already know all of your types. I know what they will give me," I said, straightening my shoulders. "It's fine. It's only a dinner. Can you help me carry everything out?" I asked, trying to tell myself that I'd made it through many dinners with these types. One more wouldn't kill me.

"Whoa, whoa, hold on. What are you talking about? You know what they will *give* you? Who?"

"The racer type. The *street* racer type. I know the rude, gross comments, and grabby hands. I can handle it for one night," I said, trying to give myself a pep talk more than actually explain it to him.

His eyes went wide. "None of my friends are going to be *grabbing* you. That's wild that you would even think that would be okay with us. I will personally hit anyone who thinks they could grab you when they want. As for the rude, gross comments, unless we are talking about open wounds or something, there should be none of that, especially if you're insinuating it would be sexual. I don't know if you could tell yet, but Fox or Ransom would quite literally get their asses kicked if they said something like that. You really were hanging around shitty people, huh? Just give them a chance for the night and then make your decisions." A scowl came over his face as he looked back at the crew and then at me. "Where you were before, did they… hurt you?"

The clear concern on his face was surprising… and cute.

"No, nothing like that. Aside from a smack from my mom once in a while or a twisted arm from my sister, I was okay. Luckily, I'm rude enough that no one crossed the line into anything too extreme. But it made me hate groups of people like this."

He leaned back on the counter, furrowing his brows. "So you have to tell me now. Who are you running from, exactly? I've been wracking my brain all day, but I can't place the guy I hit last night."

I could only stare, not knowing what to say. Telling him could have two outcomes.

One, he knows them and hates them too, so he would understand why I left.

Or two, he wants to send me right back, and have no involvement with them.

I guess the third option was that he actually likes them and will be on their side of this all.

He was still staring back. "I don't know how long you can stare at me, but I will sit here all night waiting for your answer. Your eyes are beautiful anyway, so it's really no problem for me." His smile grew as he wiggled his eyebrows.

I could feel the heat creeping up my neck and looked away

fast. He didn't need to see how red that was going to turn my cheeks.

"I am running from Tristan. The guy from last night, but it's more that I'm running from Slaughter. He's kind of the leader of the group, and my stepdad."

"Slaughter?" The shock in his voice made me look back over.

"You know him?"

"Unfortunately. I know of Tristian too, but I haven't had the honor of meeting him formally. You're kind of related then? Why are you running from him? I mean, aside from him being an asshole."

"Slaughter is my stepdad, so please don't consider us related. Tristan is his best friend, right-hand man, and is dating my sister. They want my help. Or more like he wants me to join whatever dumb gang they think they are starting so I don't ruin their plans. Right before I left, I was with my sister and we went down to their garage. I always try to stay away from it, but my sister is with Tristian and she wanted to stop by, so I agreed." I was quiet, thinking through it all. It was barely two days ago and it had changed every second of my life since.

"I'm assuming there's an 'and' attached to this?"

"And I got a glimpse of what was actually happening. They are taking cars and tearing them apart to sell." I didn't want to add how I had been kind of helping them, and that I had taken the laptop.

I still needed to look at it, but was almost getting too scared to actually see what was on it.

"Damn. And what? They wanted your help or wanted to keep you quiet?"

"Both? They obviously don't want me to rat them out, but they also want my help to grow their operations."

"And you refused?"

"In not so many words. I just ran away instead," I said with a tight smile.

"There was no way to stay and not help more," he said, more as a statement, but I still felt guilty enough to elaborate.

"No, I would be locked in my room until I was on their side."

His blue eyes were trained on me, and I was struggling not to stare again, but then he gave a tight smile. "Looks like we have a bigger problem than I thought. Come on, let's eat and figure this out."

"Figure out how to get me out of here faster?" I asked, with a small, nervous laugh.

He stopped and turned to me, grabbing the platter of food I had picked up. "No, just figure out how to help you. Now relax and come on before all of this gets cold and I pass out from hunger."

I watched him go, trying to wrap my head around his words. What I told him didn't seem to faze him too much, maybe a bit surprised but no anger, no outrage that I didn't say anything sooner.

Now he only wanted to help me more?

FIVE

CARLY

JAX WAS ALREADY SITTING down by the time I made it to the table. He nodded to the seat next to him and I reluctantly sat down, seven sets of eyes on me as I did.

It was as bad as I thought it would be, each of them smiling and looking me over, and I was almost holding my breath in anticipation for the comments. I already knew the girls so Jax introduced the guys. Ransom, a dark haired guy with more tattoos than I could count. Fox, who was tall, muscled, and had a nearly perfect face besides the scar running through it. And then Kye, who was possibly the most intimidating of them all but only because of the angry glare on his face. The tattoos and piercings didn't help that either.

Jax knocked my hand and leaned in, making it even harder to breathe as I caught sight of a tattoo partially hidden under the collar of his shirt. It was still too covered to read the small lettering, but I was suddenly more interested in that than the table of people staring at me.

"Remember, you're the one that bites," he said, smirking. "Take a real breath."

I met his eyes and listened, taking a deep breath.

"Good," he said, the deep, pleased tone making a shiver run through me. "Now please keep doing that and eat."

I nodded, trying to remember what we were talking about as I looked back up at him.

"I'm starving and this smells amazing," Fox said.

"Wow," Scout said, looking over all the food. "Did you seriously make all of this? There's like ten different things!"

I laughed as Scout came up next to me. For being the girl who grew up with these rough guys, and raced, she seemed the opposite. Happy, bubbly, and welcoming. "There's only three, but I doubled up the recipes. I assumed you all ate a lot?"

"You assumed right," Jax said. It wasn't exactly a dining room table, two fold-up tables pushed together with one nice tablecloth covering the entire thing. The small table that made up his real dining room table only had enough room for two.

I sat staring, a little surprised that everyone was piling their plates.

"Seriously, Carly, this all looks amazing. Are you a chef?" Ash asked.

"No, nothing like that. Want to be, maybe, but not yet."

Fox groaned as he started eating, and Kye made a similar sound.

"This is the best focaccia bread I've ever had," Jax said. "And this sauce. I want to bathe in it."

I knew my eyebrows jumped higher than they ever had. "You know what kind of bread that is?"

I really didn't take him for a guy that would know the difference between breads.

"And you want to take a bath in pasta sauce?" Scout asked, trying not to laugh. "That sounds disgusting."

"And like it would burn?" Quinn said, her nose scrunched.

"Eww, now the only image I have in my head is Jax is a big bathtub of sauce."

The table erupted in laughter and groans as Jax turned to me.

"Yes, by the way, I know what type of bread this is. I can also tell you that this is bolognese sauce." His smile grew, apparently proud of himself.

"Wow, I'm impressed. I thought all you street racers only knew cars and getting in trouble."

All eyes turned to me and I shrunk back at the sudden attention.

I shouldn't have said anything or brought more attention to myself. I knew the temper guys like them could have, and I knew what it was like to draw too much of their attention, or anger.

Suddenly, everyone broke into a smile.

"I'll have you know, Quinn has worked hard to make sure we aren't barbarians," Jax said.

"And now you have to tell us what racers you are hanging around that make you know so much about them," Scout said.

I tried to shrink back further, even though no one seemed mad about my statement.

"Carly?" Jax asked. "Care to answer the question?"

"I have some people in my family that are into that."

"Really? Who? We might know them," Fox said.

I let out a deep breath as everyone waited. "You apparently do," I said, knowing how much of a fan everyone was of my newest stepdad.

Jax knocked my hand again. "Come on. We have to tell them."

I tried not to notice the jolt that went through me as his hand lingered against mine for a few extra seconds. Or the way he said *we* instead of *you*, like I wasn't sitting here alone to tell them where I came from.

But I was. I was alone, and it was me on my own with this. I could tell them who I was, and it didn't matter how they felt, I would need to get going *alone.*

"Umm, my mom was alone for most of my life. You probably know my stepdad as Slaughter. Somewhere along the line, Slaughter met my mom and decided forcing his way into our lives would help him get ahead in life. Him and his friend, Tristian, are big into this stuff. He kind of took the role as head of our house after that, and my mom let him."

The room went quiet as everyone looked at each other and then back at me.

"You have got to be kidding me," Scout said, her mouth falling open.

"That's who you were trying to get away from?" Fox asked, looking at me first, and then around the table.

"Yeah, him and Tristan. Ever since Slaughter took over, it's been one thing after another going bad and I couldn't take it anymore. I came across some things I shouldn't have and my options were running off, or staying and helping them. I couldn't handle being around them anymore."

Quinn's face scrunched as though she was in pain. "I don't blame you."

Ransom threw an arm around her, pulling her into him. "We know him and have had our own problems with him," he said.

"Problems?" she asked, obviously pissed off. "He ran you off the road, tortured you, and tried to kill you. I don't think that's just having problems."

"Serious?" I asked. "I mean, I'm not shocked he did that, but I'm surprised you guys know him that well. Of course I managed to run right into people that would have had such serious issues with him."

Jax was shaking his head as he looked at me. "He thought we took some cars and went right to trying to kill us. We haven't had trouble with him since it was proven that we weren't the ones who took them."

"You know that's thin ice, though," Fox said. "If he has the chance, he's going to come right back after us again. He made that clear before."

"Yeah, I know," Jax said, his lips tight as he leaned back. His arms flexed as he crossed them, and I watched as his jaw clenched.

"Which would include finding out that I am hiding out here with you," I said. "After I learned all about the things he's doing, they wanted me to help them change serial numbers on cars to steal. I didn't agree and left instead," I said, not ready to add in that I took the laptop. I wasn't sure how much I could trust all of them yet. "I will immediately be a problem for them. He's not going to be relaxed about me running out. He takes the family thing seriously even though we aren't even related, and they won't be happy letting me go with what I did learn. I really should go. I don't want to bring my trouble to you all. Is my truck ready? I don't mind leaving tonight to save anyone from run-ins with him again."

Jax rubbed the back of his neck. "No, not quite. I think I found the problem, but it's not as quick of a fix as I hoped."

"What's wrong with it?"

"It's a bit of a two-fold problem. Maybe more like tenfold? Kind of a domino effect. One thing went wrong and then a few other things."

"Then a few more," Scout mumbled.

"What is wrong with it?" I asked, trying not to let my anxiety boil up. My options became very limited again if my truck wasn't ready.

"The head of your engine cracked, then your radiator cracked, and since you kept driving it they got worse and worse, which led to —"

"I don't know mechanics that well. Give me a normal person's explanation."

"Your engine is about a minute from blowing up. It's all fixable right now, but I would basically be rebuilding an entire engine unless we found a good one to drop in there. Best bet, a week to wrap it up."

"And worst bet?"

"I would say two weeks to account for parts being shipped and put on, plus testing. And that's if all the other cars I'm working on go smooth in the meantime or they help out more when they can," he said, nodding to the others.

"So I have no chance of driving for a week or more, at least?"

"I would honestly give it two just to be safe. Then all the parts will be in and I will have time to put it back together."

"*Back* together?"

"I had to tear it down to find the problem," he said, scrunching his face. "It doesn't matter either way. You wouldn't have been able to drive it far even if it was put together."

"Two weeks," I mumbled. The words echoed like a curse as I tried not to cry while everyone looked at me. "I have to go back for two weeks, and then somehow leave again?"

"Go back?" Jax asked.

"Well, I have to go somewhere and I'm definitely not getting far by walking."

Jax sighed, running a hand through his hair. "No, I don't think you can go back. It would only be worse now. If they are how you say they are, they wouldn't give you another chance to leave. What about a hotel?"

"And waste every cent I have? There would be no point because I wouldn't be able to pay for anything after I had my truck back."

"I could help you out. A loan or something to help you until you're working."

I thought it over. It wouldn't be terrible, and I would probably be safe enough from Slaughter. At least for the time being. I had no idea how I would start to pay him back hundreds of dollars for the hotel costs. I knew staying in a hotel that long would not be cheap.

"Are you serious?" Scout asked, her angry glare looking around at each one of us.

"What's wrong?" Jax sighed, the care in his tone genuine.

"She's not staying in a hotel. How is she going to feel safe from him alone in a hotel?" She honestly looked outraged, and I realized it was outrage *for* me.

"Scout, I can't risk Slaughter finding out she's here and coming for us again. That was hell before and almost got Ransom killed. Almost got us all killed trying to save him. We can't risk that."

Scout looked to me, and back to Jax. "And she can't risk sitting at a hotel in town waiting for Slaughter to find her there. There are only two hotels in this town. Hold on, there's actually one because the other is a creepy motel. Do you really think he isn't going to look for her at those places?" She turned to me. "How much do you know exactly? Like 'get him in trouble' type of knowledge or just 'piss people off' type of knowledge?"

"I don't know for sure yet, but maybe more the *get him in a lot of trouble* type."

She looked around the table again, her face hard. She was small, but I assumed she wasn't as sweet when she was pissed.

"If she did nothing wrong and doesn't want to go help Slaughter, then why wouldn't we be the first to help her?"

"Because Slaughter isn't our enemy right now and we need to keep it that way," Ransom said. "It has nothing at all to do with you, Carly."

"No, I get it. I don't want any problems for you guys," I said, and I meant it.

"That's not the point," Scout said. "We are always willing to help people and I don't know when we got so scared of Slaughter. We dealt with him once and can deal with it again. Why wouldn't we help her? We help everyone else?"

"I think it's different, Scout. You guys don't know me," I said, surprised at how much I could hug her for being so sweet right now.

The room went quiet as they looked at each other.

"I'm with Scout," Kye said. "We didn't know Quinn and helped her. We didn't know Ash, and that brought some issues around. Slaughter had a problem with us from day one and we're the ones that made it worse trusting the wrong people. Why wouldn't we help her? Scout is right, she didn't do anything, and the last place Slaughter is going to be looking for her is with us. Bringing her to a hotel would be next to useless. They know her truck broke down. They will be looking at mechanic shops and places she could be staying."

My jaw almost dropped open that Kye was on the side of helping me. He was the last one I would have expected.

"Exactly. They will be looking at shops. Ours would be on that list," he said.

Scout rolled her eyes hard and Kye leaned back. "So? We can keep it in the back bay. It would be out of the way and out of sight from the street. We can get it done, and she's on her way again."

I didn't even know what to say. I felt like I shouldn't be here for this conversation and should also tell them that the hotel was fine, but I was too stunned to speak. I never had anyone stick up for me like this, and wasn't sure how to show my thanks for them being so thoughtful. I could only look at Jax who looked right back at me. His face was calm, but I didn't miss the pinch to his lips before his face softened.

"Would you feel better staying here?"

I thought of the hotel. While I would be alone and that would be nice, Kye was right, Slaughter would definitely be checking for me there.

"Yes, but I don't want to be a problem for you," I said, still watching him. He looked around again, everyone making some silent agreement, but I caught the sharp nod of Ransom's head and Ash's annoyed glare at Jax.

"You're not a problem. And they are right, you staying here is safer. I live alone so we can figure out room for you to stay comfortably for the next two weeks."

"Seriously, I can make the hotel work if you're not okay with this," I said, barely meaning it. I don't know when staying with a group of street racers became the better choice, but it was.

"If everyone is good with you staying, then I'm good with it. Any sliver of a sign that Slaughter or Tristan found you, though, tell us immediately. That's not negotiable at all."

I looked at each one of them, from easy smiles to nods, they really all seemed in agreement now.

"And Riot?"

At the sound of his name, he ran over, sitting and looking up at Jax, hoping his name meant he was getting some food.

"As long as he doesn't eat me alive in my sleep, he was included."

"What if he does find out I'm here?"

"How would he find that out? I doubt Tristan had any chance to get a good look at me or my car before I broke his nose, and we'll all be a little more aware of our surroundings for now."

"I don't know. Like I said, if he does, I don't want any problems for any of you."

"There won't be any problems. Plus, where else are you

going to go that's as safe?" Jax asked. "The truck is already starting to get fixed, and I'll be looking for all the parts tomorrow. Just hang out until it's done."

"But Jax—"

He cut me off, leaning close that only I could hear. "Enjoy the dinner that you worked hard on and we can figure it all out later. You stayed here one night already. You can at least stay one more."

I nodded in agreement and saw the relief on his face.

"Perfect, you're staying for now, then. And a bonus for you, you'll be staying long enough to taste my cooking now," Jax said.

"You're cooking?"

The table groaned.

"Don't eat it," Scout said. "Whatever he cooks, do *not* eat it."

"You know what, my microwave mac n cheese is a delicacy. She will love it," he said, smiling at Scout before turning to me.

The tightness to his jaw was gone, replaced with a grin, and his dark, messy hair was cut back to not hide his ruggedly handsome face. It all gave him an effortlessly charming look that pulled me in. A shiver moved through me as he looked at me again. To make it all worse, every time he spoke, the easy, calm tone he always seemed to have made *me* feel calm.

I didn't know if that made me feel better or worse, but as I ate and listened to everyone talk, I tried not to think about what came next for me.

SIX

JAX

I HATED that I had to hesitate so much to help her, but I know what we went through with Slaughter and I couldn't make that decision for everyone. I hated it even more to learn that Slaughter was almost related to her, and after her for a good reason. We all knew him well enough to know that he had a one track mind and when he made someone an enemy, he would go after them until he got the outcome that he wanted. It's what he did to us when he thought we were stealing his cars, and now Carly was his enemy.

I couldn't imagine living with someone like that or having to deal with the people and problems that he brought around. I knew each one of us here got ourselves into some trouble in the past, but it was nothing compared to the things Slaughter and his group were still doing. After he got arrested for everything with us, all we've heard is that things spiraled even further out of control for him. He was also kicked out of the weekly races for betting too high on races and never paying for them. When someone is that low, they usually get desperate.

I looked her over. Her shoulders were pinned back tight, and

while she didn't look upset exactly, she didn't look comfortable
still. Which I guess shouldn't be surprising considering an hour
ago she thought she was going to be dealing with a room full of
Slaughter-like guys.

She smiled at something Scout said and then looked at me,
her eyebrows furrowing as she noticed me watching her. It was
hard not to, though. To say she was pretty was an understatement. Her dark hair was wound up in a bun and her head tipped
up, high and proud as she looked back to the table, but her green
eyes kept darting back to me until I finally looked away.

I could not keep thinking about how good she looked. I was
going to get twenty steps ahead of myself and I needed to
remember that I did not want to go down the road of a relationship with the wrong person again. And Slaughter's step-daughter? That was definitely the wrong person.

After eating and cleaning up, everyone filed out, telling
Carly thank you over and over.

"It really was amazing food. Do you always cook stuff like
that?" I asked, carrying more trays to the kitchen.

"Not so much anymore. Can you believe that Slaughter
doesn't have a very refined palette? He says that sauce was the
worst thing he's ever eaten. I believe his words were something
along the lines of 'I would rather eat Riot than eat that food.'"

"He must be dining at the best restaurants in the state then,
because I can't imagine where I've had better food than that." I
put another dish in the sink and turned to her. The freckles across
her nose and cheeks moved as her lips turned up. Between the
angry scowl and how uncomfortable she has been since I met
her, it was nice to see that she was smiling a little easier now.

It wasn't as nice to realize how much I liked it, and wanted to
keep making it happen more.

"Also, that's disgusting that he even made a joke about that,"

I added, trying to hide the fact that I had been staring at her lips for way too long.

"I agree. And that's really nice of you to say about the food. It was really nice of all of you to say such great things about it. My grandpa was the only one who ever seemed to like my food, but he's older now and a little...out of it, so he might think any food is fine dining."

"Well, based on him thinking it's delicious, I would say he is not that out of it."

She laughed, but didn't say anything more about him.

"Are you really working on being a chef, then?" I asked, trying to help her finish the last of the clean-up in the kitchen, even though she kept trying to push me away.

"I mean, I've never really thought I would get the chance to work on it honestly, but that would be the dream."

"What were your plans, then? Just drive until you see a 'Help Wanted' sign and sleep in your truck?"

"Yeah? I mean, I can hopefully get a hotel room after I start getting paychecks, but before that? Yes, I would have to stay in my truck until I made more money."

"What are you going to be doing with Riot while you're at this job? He can't sit in the truck all day. And I assume affording a doggy day care would get expensive fast."

Her eyebrows shot up as she looked down. "I don't know how I didn't think about that. I'd been so worried about just getting out and getting on my feet that I didn't think about Riot during the day. I'll add that to my never-ending list to figure out."

I wanted to offer more help, but I didn't actually know what help I could offer. She still seemed on-edge around me, and not happy about the arrangement with staying here. There wasn't much more I could think to do.

We finished cleaning up, and I knew we were both exhausted.

"For tonight, no running away anywhere. Just get some sleep."

She only nodded as she flopped back onto the couch and threw the covers over herself. Riot didn't hesitate to jump up and lay down at her feet.

"Your dog is spoiled," I said, making sure my tone was light. I really didn't have a problem with him, but I was quickly realizing that she seemed to love this dog more than anything else.

"He deserves it more than any of us. He was Slaughter's dog before he came to live with us. He left him outside in all types of weather. I know he hit him. He's got scars all over him. They have healed now and get hidden in the hair, but there are plenty. When they moved in, he just attached himself to me, and me to him. Then I found out how much he didn't like Slaughter and he came to be my little protector. He deserves to be spoiled and will live out the rest of his days like that."

I looked over at Riot, who seemed to know that we were talking about him based on his head swiveling back and forth between us.

I had noticed faint lines on him, but hadn't asked about them yet. "Fuck that guy," I mumbled as I walked to the fridge and grabbed a piece of cheese. "If he kept you safe, then he does deserve it."

I handed him the slice, and he seemed pleased to chomp away at it before flopping back down.

"Get some sleep and we will get everything else figured out tomorrow." I stopped at the door to my bedroom. "Come get me if you need anything."

"I won't," she yelled as I laid down.

"But if you do."

It was barely two minutes later when I heard a light tap come from my door, and my heart leapt, making me hit my own chest with a cough to shut it up before my imagination got away from me.

"Hey Jax?"

"Yes?"

She stuck her head inside the door. Her long, dark hair fell, and her green eyes locked on me.

"I kind of packed in a hurry and didn't really think through my options. I usually like to sleep in big T-shirts but can't seem to find any." She let her voice die out, apparently hoping I would get the hint.

"And?"

"And I was wondering if you have one I could borrow."

"I have a whole closet," I said with a small laugh before getting up and walking over to open the closet door. "Take your pick."

"No. I'm not choosing. Just one you don't care about."

"I assume a well-worn one?" I ran a hand over all the shirts, wondering which she would choose, trying to ignore the thrill running through me that she was taking one of mine.

Girls always seemed to want to take a guy's clothes, and I never liked it. They'd somehow always choose the ones I actually wore and didn't want to give up, but this time, I actually wanted her to have one I liked. One that *she* liked. It was obvious that she preferred...darker things. Not only were the shirts I'd seen her in so far funny, but they were definitely in the dark humor category. And I couldn't miss the little pink Ghostface and skeleton hand keychains on her keys.

"Preferably, but I won't be picky."

"I got a shirt one time that reminded me of the garage that I think you'll like. It suddenly reminds me of you more. It's been a favorite, so well-worn, and probably smells like me, which we both know is why you're really here for one of mine."

"It is not!"

"It's okay. I smell like heaven. It will be our secret."

"Jax," she warned as I pulled out the shirt. The playfully threatening tone made me smile, hoping this meant that she was a bit more comfortable around me.

It was a headless skeleton man riding a horse, a pumpkin head in his hand. A woman sat on the back with a pair of witchy heels and a smile on her face as though she was happy to be taken by the headless skeleton. It always made me laugh. The top read Fall Head Over Heels in Hollow Town with a haunted house and headstones were in the background.

Her mouth dropped open as she looked it over.

"Okay, I actually do love it. Like that might be my new favorite shirt."

"Look at that. I already know your taste."

"Lucky guess," she said with a scowl. "Just for being so cocky. I'm keeping this now."

"Good," I whispered, leaning down to her. "Just let me know if you need me to wear it a time or two. Make it smell like me again."

She stormed out fast, huffing about that never happening, and I waited until it was quiet before going back to bed.

I didn't care if I didn't get any sleep now. I was too excited to wake up and see her wearing that tomorrow.

———

INSTEAD OF WAKING up to thoughts of Carly, I woke up to a hundred pound Rottweiler laying on top of me like I was a dog bed. He was dead weight as I opened my eyes and rolled to my side, making him roll off of me. He didn't seem to mind, spreading out on his back next to me on the bed with his head resting on the pillow.

"Carly? Are you up?" I groaned quietly, pushing Riot off the rest of the way and sitting up. "Wow. You're a bed hog."

The living room was quiet as I walked out until Riot ran up behind me, jumping right on top of Carly.

"I was trying to keep quiet, but it looks like he had a wake up call for you, too," I said as he licked her face and crawled on top of her.

"Too?"

"Oh yeah," I said, making coffee. "I apparently got some Rottweiler cuddles last night. He snuck in at some point."

"That spoiled part includes him liking a nice big bed to sleep in. Not a couch. I would like to add myself to that list, too," she said, stretching and laughing as Riot licked her cheek.

When she sat up, I could see she was wearing the shirt, the no bra look leaving little to the imagination, but mine seemed alive and well because even looking away, I couldn't stop picturing what was underneath.

I tried to stop the thoughts, but it was inevitable. I hadn't been with anyone in months and that seemed to be getting to me. Or maybe it was just her.

"If the couch is really that bad, we can share my bed," I said, the image of waking up next to her a little too vivid. "Coffee?"

"Yes, please, to the coffee. I bought my creamer when we went to the store."

I grabbed the pumpkin creamer from the fridge.

"What in the awful drink is this?"

She frowned as she looked at me. "That is the most delicious creamer in the world. Don't be stingy."

I poured the cups but didn't hide my head shake.

"Try it before you judge it."

I poured some in my cup and walked over, handing her a full mug.

"Thanks. Also not a chance to sharing a bed. Good try,

though. And for a guy who claims he's not a murderer, you sure do bring it up a lot."

"I don't know how else to convince you to not be scared of me. And I meant for comfort, not because I'm trying to sleep with you," I said, noticing how she looked away immediately. "Also, if you are counting yourself so spoiled that you don't want to sleep on a couch, how are you planning for you two to sleep in your truck?"

"Good point. Although, that would be the only option, so I guess we would both just have to suck it up and deal with it for a while. Just like I have to suck it up staying here for a while."

"I'm not that bad, I promise."

"Really?" she said, her eyebrows jumping up. "Weren't you on the side of me not staying? I'm pretty sure the only reason I'm here is because of Scout and Kye."

My chest tightened, making me wince. "I'm sorry. It really had nothing to do with you. I promise. I just can't ask the crew to do something like that without knowing the risk. There's not a lot I wouldn't do to help someone, but putting any of my friends in danger, especially without them knowing, isn't something I'm willing to do."

"Sorry, I didn't mean it to sound so harsh. Sometimes my words sound a lot more bitchy than I mean for them to," she said, her lips pursed as she looked down at her cup.

"It's alright, I can take some harsh criticism," I said, grinning at her sudden shyness. "But I really want you to know it had nothing to do with you."

"I get that. I don't exactly like this arrangement of relying on you for a place to stay and to fix my truck. I would prefer if we worked something out that I could pay you back."

"Pay me back for fixing the truck or the staying here?"

"Both. Do you want me to pay you for rent or something? And your time working on the truck?"

"Yeah, I was thinking about that. You said you didn't want to owe me anything and lucky for you, I don't sleep much these days, so I came up with a solution last night."

Those green eyes moved back to me and all I could think about was how bad I wanted them on me like that all the time.

"Which is?"

"We trade. I use my skills to fix your truck, and in exchange, you use your skills to cook."

It was pretty clear from the sudden arch of her eyebrows that she wasn't sold on the idea.

"I can't expect that me cooking is a fair trade for me barging into your life and taking over your apartment with my giant Rottweiler."

"Fixing your truck comes easy to me. Cooking does not. I assume it does to you, though. And I like good food more than most things, so I think it would be fair."

"What about rent? And how much would all the parts be?"

"I don't have a rent. We own the place, and I'll let you know on the parts, but I'll be doing things the right way, not the cheap way. There is no point in you breaking down again."

"So what about payments for that, then? You give me the parts bill after you're done and I'll make sure it's all paid back."

"Fine with me, but don't stress yourself about it. And again, I want to emphasize that the cooking is the exciting part to me. Sandwiches, pastas, more of what you made last night, desserts. All of it. Money is definitely second to that."

"So, I will basically be your personal chef for the next two weeks, and you let us live here, safe and unbothered?"

"Yes," I said. "Personal chef for your personal mechanic."

"And you're sure?"

"One hundred percent sure."

"Well, my options are limited. Not even limited, they are

nonexistent, so I guess we have a deal. I will be paying you back for all of this with interest."

I rolled my eyes and leaned my head back on the couch. "Deal. Now onto the real problem, why didn't you text me yesterday? I was planning to send you pictures of the truck. I figured you would be worried about it."

"*That's* the real problem?" she asked, giving me that look of disbelief again. "And it's because I don't have a phone."

"How do you not have a phone?" I asked, sipping the coffee that was surprisingly delicious.

"I mean, I did, but I didn't bring it with me when I left. I didn't want them to have any way to contact me."

I shook my head, surprised I hadn't asked sooner.

"Smart move. Although, I can't believe you were out on that road with no phone, too. I can see who is going out today, and they can stop to grab you a new one."

"That's not even a little necessary for you to do," she said, eyes wide. "I really can't afford anything like that right now anyway, especially now that I'm going to owe you all this money for staying here, and the parts."

"You also shouldn't go without a phone, especially when you leave."

"But you aren't responsible for that. I'll get one later. You don't have to go out of your way to be so nice."

"Listen, I'm going to be nice to you. I'm probably going to be super fucking nice. Might even be really sweet sometimes. I'm going to make sure you have everything you need right now, and for when you head out on your own after the truck is done. I'm plenty comfortable with money. Whatever payments you want to make to me have no due date, so we are just going to make sure you have what you need. You might as well stop fighting it."

She rolled her eyes and leaned back. "I'm seeing that it might be a losing battle. It's really nice of you, but I don't want me owing you even more hanging over my head."

"Is it your birthday soon or something? You can consider it a gift from all of us. Ash just texted me back. She will be going out to the track today and can pick one up for you while she's out. Problem solved."

"Why are you so determined to be nice now? Last night you wanted me gone."

"Because it's who I am. I'm not going to sit back and watch you struggle if I have solutions. And before you start thinking I'm being weird, I would do it for anyone. I was hesitant at first for everyone else, if they're okay with you here, and they are, then we're good. You'll get the help you need."

"Hence, stopping in the middle of the night to help me and look over my truck."

"Exactly."

I leaned back, sipping my coffee and smiling at her. In seconds, she was scowling hard at me and I couldn't stop smiling. The scowl was cute, especially when that second came where she couldn't help herself anymore and a smile broke on her face.

"Do you have something else to say?" she asked. Her lips were pushing tighter and tighter as I sat quietly watching her.

"No." I lied. There was a lot I wanted to say, but I couldn't decide what was the right and wrong thing to say. I wanted to tell her to stop overthinking all of this, but I knew the words wouldn't change her mind. I wanted to tell her that it would all work out. I wanted to tell her how much I was already enjoying her being here, but I couldn't imagine she would believe it. Most of all, I was tempted to tell her how pretty she looked, but I assumed that might scare her all the way out of the apartment.

"Then why are you looking at me like that?" Her words were

so clipped as she crossed her arms, shrinking back into the couch further.

"Such a temper," I said, shaking my head, not hiding my smile and watching as her scowl deepened.

"I don't have a temper."

"No?"

She looked away fast. "No. You're just....You keep smirking at me and it's annoying."

"So no smiling at you, noted."

"That's not what I meant."

"It's alright. I'll stop," I said, still smiling. "I mean, I'll try to stop. Aside from the crew, I haven't really had anyone to talk to in the morning before work. It's fun."

"You are very happy in the mornings."

"It's all this *delicious* coffee. Which makes me wonder why you are not. Is the couch that uncomfortable?"

"No. Not at all. It's completely fine. I'm just not a morning person."

"I can see that. That's alright, I still enjoy the company, but I do have to get ready for work. I have this new customer that is demanding I finish her truck immediately."

"I am not. Do you want breakfast?" she asked with a soft laugh, making me stop in my tracks.

"You make breakfast too?"

"I mean, yeah? Isn't that the agreement? I cook while you fix my truck? I feel like adding breakfast to that is fair."

"Then hell yes, I want breakfast. You mean to tell me I'm going to eat something other than coffee and a Pop-Tart? I could kiss you right now."

She rolled her eyes. "Maybe I was just going to warm up Pop-Tarts."

I laughed, heading into my room. "A warm Pop-Tart? Not a

cold one? I'm still thrilled," I said, wishing I stayed out there to see the scowl cross her face.

It seemed like she was more comfortable now, but it still felt like she was waiting for me to get angry or change my mind about her staying. I had been hesitant at first, but the idea was settling with me now. The disarray of the apartment, and my life, wasn't as bad as I assumed it would be, and honestly, someone here to talk to all the time was nice.

I was already looking forward to tomorrow morning.

SEVEN

CARLY

THE KNOCK on the door after Jax left made me jump, and I wondered if I would feel comfortable and not worry that it was Slaughter or Tristan on the other side.

"Carly? It's Ash. Jax said you needed to get a phone."

I pulled open the door, the relief that flooded through me that it was only Ash. "More like he's forcing me to get a phone," I said with a tight smile.

I was beginning to really like Ash. Quinn and Scout, too. They seemed like a close-knit group, but didn't act like I was an outsider. They had been happy to bring me with them before and hadn't treated me any differently than they treated each other. There were no snide comments or rude attitudes towards me. And surprisingly, I didn't spend every second comparing myself to them.

It was nice. Really nice.

I had always wanted girl friends, but high school was not the place to make them for me. After high school, I never really gave myself a chance to find new friends.

"Ahh, I thought it was a little weird when he said I better get you a phone no matter what you say. Why wouldn't you want a phone?"

"I'm working on not being found. A phone makes that easier."

She grabbed a drink and sat back at the counter. "Been there before. We will get you a new number and put it in my name. No one will know anything about where you are."

"Are you serious? You would do that for a stranger?"

"It's not a problem. If it's in my name, no one will connect it to you. Win-win. You get to stay hidden and get a phone."

"I also really can't afford one."

"Of course not, Jax is paying," she said, fishing out a card from her pocket. "He said you two already agreed to that, but I'm now assuming you did not agree, based on your face."

"No, we definitely did not agree with that. I can't let him buy me a phone."

She sighed. "I will be the first woman to say women's rights, make your own money, don't need a guy's money, but I'm also not stupid. If a man hands you a credit card, you go shopping." She grinned hard. I didn't think Ash and I were much alike, but I decided right then that I really liked that.

I pulled out what money I did have on me. "I can at least pay for half. What is with you guys? You're like one big, helpful family."

Her smile brightened. "Pretty much. And seriously, don't stress about the phone. I have my phone through Holt Racing's account and can add yours to it. Make the giant racing company buy it," she said, laughing. "We are stopping for coffee, though, and Jax will absolutely be paying for that. But really, don't worry about the phone. We look out for one another."

"I'm learning that fast. It's weird for me. That hasn't been my experience with groups of people like this, especially when I am not a part of your crew."

"While you're staying here, consider yourself a part of the group. Keep an open mind with us. We're all a little strange in our own ways, but we care about each other. So, let's get going so we can get you a phone. You are coming with me, right?"

I didn't remember Jax saying anything about me going. "I wasn't planning on it. Riot is already annoyed with me that we aren't going on as long of walks as he's used to. I'd hate to make him stay here all day alone."

She went to lean over the couch, petting him as he rolled over.

"Jax said I should just pick it up for you, but I figured you would want to get out of the apartment more. Why don't you both come with me today?"

"Really?" I asked, watching Riot drool all over her. "You know, you are not what I was expecting."

"Now I need to know. What were you expecting?"

"Bitchy, cold, annoyed. The typical girl that runs with street racers."

"Well, I don't know about your typical type that runs with them, but you won't find that type here exactly. Quinn is a sweetheart and Scout is a bit of a rough street racer herself, but is an even bigger sweetheart. I mean, don't be fooled, they will both cut someone if needed. I'm not a girl that has run with any street racers. I am a racer, but since I grew up at Holt Racing, I'm more of a 'contained on a track' racer. The street makes me nervous."

"Any racing makes me nervous."

"It's at least fun to watch. Come with me. I was heading there now for a few things. Riot can come, and there's plenty of room for him to run around." She patted his head again, and he looked up at her with love.

"I don't know. I don't know how much I should go out."

"It's completely safe. Full security and I can tell the guard not to let anyone unknown in today. Plus, are any of these people looking for you really going to be looking at Holt Racing?" Her hands went to her hips with a smile.

"Very true," I laughed. "That wouldn't even make it on the list of places to look."

"Exactly. So come on, it will be fun, and I want to get to know you more, anyway. If you're going to be living here for a bit, we are all going to want to get to know you more."

"Honestly, getting out of here would be nice for the day, but getting to know so many new people at once sounds terrible."

Ash made a little cheer, and Riot barked at the sudden noise. "Oh sorry, Riot. You want to come for a ride with us?" Riot barked again in response.

"I have never wanted a dog before, but now I need one. A big scary teddy bear like this." She grinned harder as I laughed.

I changed quickly and grabbed my bag. "Don't even tell Jax that he was right, but I am so happy to get a phone. I still feel lost without it, like I'm always forgetting something."

"Then let's get that fixed. We will stop for the phone first and then head to the track."

We made it to the car before Ash gave me a sly smile.

"Okay, time to tell me everything. How is it living with Jax?"

If I questioned it before, I didn't now. These girls were not shy and definitely not uncomfortable being best friends immediately. I barely knew how to react. If I should tell her everything that was on my mind or keep things to myself. I was barely sure how to be a friend, let alone be close enough to act like a best friend.

I decided on somewhere in between.

"It's alright. We both seem okay dealing with each other, and he's obviously nice enough to be around."

She made a groaning sound before looking at me with a big grin. "I'm not here for the boring roommate stuff. Tell those things to Scout. Give me the good stuff. I meant, how is it living with a tall, hot, muscled tattooed man who is the sweetest thing in the world?"

"Oh. I mean, that part isn't terrible."

"Not terrible? Jax without a shirt on is more than *not bad*."

I looked at her, not able to stop my laugh. "Aren't you dating Fox?"

"Yeah, but I also have eyes. And Jax is basically my best friend. I have to help him out where I can."

"What do you mean, help him out? How is pointing out how hot he is helping him out?"

"So you do agree that he is hot," she said, laughing harder now.

"Okay, yes, I also have eyes and can see that he is good looking. Does that even matter? Nothing is going to happen."

"Why not? He's a good guy."

"I don't know that, and I really doubt I'm his type."

"Beautiful and funny isn't his type? Pretty sure that's right up his alley."

I looked at her, trying not to roll my eyes.

"Whatever you say," she said, that sly smile back. "I guess we'll just have to see how it goes."

Two hours later, I had a new phone that I was setting up as I watched professional racers move around a circle track with ease. It was intense, each lap making me look longer and longer at the track. Ash was looking something over with her friend Cole as they talked about the upcoming rally races.

"Speak of the devil," Cole said as another guy walked up.

"Hey now, how am I the devil?"

"We all know you're the worst of the worst, Raf." Ash said with a smile that showed she didn't mean it, but I took a small step away.

"Oh come on now, you're scaring off the pretty girl."

"Don't even start," she said to him before turning to me. "He's a nice guy, but an endless flirt."

He turned, giving me the first full look of his face. It was perfect, the hard jaw, piercing gray eyes, and smile that let me know he knew how to be charming. "Before you start listening to her lies, let me at least tell you my name. I'm Raf." He reached out his hand, but I didn't take it. He seemed nice enough, entirely relaxed and happy, but I was too skeptical of anyone right now. If Ash was fine with him here, though, I would be nice enough.

"Carly."

"Pretty name for a pretty girl. Plus, it has my favorite thing right in it, car. Nice to meet you."

I only stared. It wasn't that I was horribly self conscious. My day-to-day life didn't change because I was a little heavier. My hips and ass were a little thicker, and I knew I wasn't a perfectly petite woman, but it really didn't bother me.

Except for times like this.

I hated when I had eyes on me like this. Something about the undivided attention made me start worrying about every inch of my body until I wanted to hide. It was a big reason why I never got too far in the sex department. A guy's undivided attention on you was hard enough, but adding the layer of intimacy *and* him touching all those parts that you're feeling insecure about was hell. How could I be okay when suddenly all those parts I was worried about became the main attraction?

"Sorry," he said, wincing. "That might have been too corny of a joke. What are you up to today?"

"I came to hang out with Ash."

"Oh yeah, has she had a chance to show you around?"

"I think I've seen enough, but I'm assuming you are going to offer to show me around yourself?"

He laughed. "I was actually. Not impressed?"

"Not quite," I said, my response a little more rude than I meant it to be.

"Alright, give me another shot. Maybe I'm just flustered with a hot girl here. You don't really come to expect them when day after day it's a bunch of sweaty guys hanging out here. And Ash, of course. What are you doing? New phone?"

"Yeah, and I can't get it to log me in," I said, still trying to mess with the dumb login screen.

"I'm surprisingly good at technology. Want help?" I shrugged, handing it over.

He clicked through the phone, asking for my email and then smiling.

"All done. I better make a test call," he said, hitting more buttons until his phone started ringing. "And look at that, it works. You can save that under Raf if you want."

"You think you're really smooth, don't you?" I asked, trying not to smile as I took the phone back.

"Come on, that was pretty smooth, and I did actually set up the phone."

"Fine, you get a few points for that." I knew he was flirting with me, and I realized I might be flirting back. For the first time in a long time, it was actually fun. There were no expectations, it could just be sitting here flirting for a few minutes with no other strings attached.

I finally glanced down as a text came through.

"Did you seriously put your name in here as *hot Raf?*"

He flashed a smile that should have made my knees weak, but only made me want to put a stop to all of this. "Yep. You never know. What if you meet another Raf and have to be able to tell the names apart? Plus, the chances of him being better looking than me are slim to none."

"Alright Raf, that's enough. Come on Carly, we should get back before it gets any later."

We said our goodbyes, and I gave Raf one more curious look over before heading with Ash back to the car.

"Shit," she said. "Jax has called me like ten times. He doesn't know you came with me, does he?"

"No, I never said anything. I don't even have his number."

"Shit," she said again. "Come on."

"What's wrong?"

"I forgot to text him earlier, and now he's freaking out that you are not at home."

"Freaking out, why?"

"Because there's crazy people after you and he doesn't know where you are?"

"I don't get it. He barely knows me, but acts like it's his job to take care of me now."

"Pretty sure Jax really thinks it's his job. That's just how he operates. How the entire group operates, actually. Like I said, you're a part of that now."

"Do you want to text him and let him know?" I asked, hopeful that I wouldn't have to deal with whatever freak out he could be having about this.

"And take the wrath of Jax? No way. I'll leave that up to you."

My heart beat was suddenly out of control. "The *wrath* of Jax?"

"No. Oh no, babe. I was kidding. Wrong wording. There's no wrath with Jax. You might get a boa constrictor that can't stop hugging you, but that's about as far as his wrath goes. Don't look so scared!"

"Okay. Alright then," I said, taking a steadying breath. "We aren't far, anyway. I'll just talk to him when we get there."

I looked out the window at the setting sun. I didn't know if I wanted to be included in this group. I had never wanted to be part of any group again, knowing that it can change to a toxic group in the blink of an eye.

We pulled in and I headed up with Ash, taking the next set of stairs up to Jax's apartment as slow as I could.

The lights were on when I walked in, but Jax was nowhere to be seen. I almost yelled out for him, but Riot ran into Jax's room as soon as I unclipped his harness and I went after him.

"Riot, no!" I hissed, peeking inside, worried he was either out or asleep.

By the time I made it in, Riot was draped over Jax's knees as he sat on the bed, petting and hugging him. A book was set out next to him, but Jax moved fast to put it in the nightstand drawer before I got closer.

The fast way he hid it only made me more curious now.

"Sorry, I didn't know he was going to bolt in here like that."

"It's fine. I missed him anyway." He kissed his head and then stood facing me. I tried not to stare. He was only wearing a pair of sweatpants, and the sight of his bare chest was leaving me breathless.

Tattoos covered his body, with small random tattoos across his stomach and arms, with one bigger one across his chest. There was so much of him, and I wanted to reach out and run my hands down each muscled inch. I stepped closer, finally seeing what that little word at the bottom of his neck was.

"Forever? Why that word?"

"I'm a bit of a romantic."

"You got *that* tattooed for a girl?" I said, the horror in my tone not hidden.

He shook his head with a laugh. "No. I got it because I believe in forever. I didn't have any girl in mind when I got it, besides hoping I would find it one day."

"Wow, that is a very romantic thought. Borderline delusional to think that there's a forever with someone."

"Delusional? No. Hopeful? Yes. But I see that you are very anti-romantic. Of course, you can have forever with someone. That's not a made-up thing."

"Right," I said, breathless. There was so much of him, and each muscled inch made me want to reach out and run my fingers across that word before moving down the rest of him. He was close enough now that I could.

The thought surprised me.

Enough that I had to step back, and he noticed, pulling us both back to reality.

"Ash said you were with her at the track all day."

"Yeah."

"Obviously you're not some prisoner here, but until I know you're not in danger of being kidnapped, can you please update me if you leave?"

My brows furrowed. "Aren't you going to get mad at me?"

"I am mad. I'm mad that I spent the last two hours worrying about where the fuck you were and no one thought to let me know that you weren't taken by Slaughter today. Ash wasn't picking up her phone, and no one knew that you went with her."

"Sorry, I thought Ash let you know, and she thought that I let you know."

He looked down at me, his eyes roaming over my face. "No one let me know. I thought you were taken, and I didn't even know where to start looking. I was about five minutes from going to find Slaughter myself, but Kye advised me to calm down first."

"Is that a joke? You can't go looking for him even if he did take me!" My breath quickened, and I knew how wide my eyes were. "You barely even know me, definitely not enough to put yourself in that much danger."

"So? I was going to come find you. I wouldn't let him take you and get away with it."

The panic that he was about to flip out only got worse as he reached out, making me duck from his hand.

"Whoa," he said, jumping back. "I wasn't going to hurt you."

"Reflex, sorry. It's not usually a good thing when someone is mad at you and reaches out like that."

"No need to apologize. I wasn't trying to freak you out. I'm also not mad at you. Not really." He took a deep breath and smiled. "I'm going to do something now, and I need you to stay calm. I am not going to hurt you."

I was ready for a fight, my body on edge as he stepped closer, invading my space as he wrapped his arms around me.

"You smell like lavender, and dirt from the track," he said. "It's an amazing combination."

"What are you doing?"

"It's called a hug. It's where I hold on to you for a minute, and you," he grabbed my arms, pulling them around his waist, "hold on to me. I'm glad you're okay."

I froze for a second before leaning in. He had obviously showered, his hair damp, and everything around me smelled like the clean mint soap he had in the bathroom.

"See, no knives, no needles, no pain."

"Speak for yourself," I said into his chest.

He pulled away. "Fine, grouch, hugs over."

"Wait, no it's not." I pulled him back in, and he didn't hesitate to wrap his arms around me again. I couldn't remember the last hug I had that I enjoyed. One that I wasn't counting down the seconds before I could make it stop. They were always so uncomfortable, and if it wasn't a quick hug to my mom, it was a hug with someone that smelled, or I didn't like, or was really just trying to feel me up.

Slaughter's friends were the worst.

This wasn't like that, though. I took a deep breath, sinking further against him, until it felt like he was holding me up. He

CARLY   73

didn't make any attempt to move away, but held on tighter, taking everything I needed to let go of.

In a split second, reality crashed. He was not here to take my burdens, to hold me when I was down, or to help me at all.

He was nothing more than a stranger to me and I was somehow standing in his bedroom, holding onto him as he hugged me. All while he didn't have a shirt on, and for some reason that was making me like this even more. My thoughts wandered back to running my hands down him, the heat spreading across my face as I thought about touching *all* of him.

I pushed away again, trying to catch my breath.

"But really? Grouch? That better not stick," I said.

"Depends on how grumpy you are."

"I'm going to clean up and go to bed. And I better not hear that nickname anymore."

"Sweet dreams…Grouch," he said, as I slammed the door in his face.

EIGHT
CARLY

ANOTHER FEW DAYS went by as I learned more and more about my roommate. I learned that he likes things clean, *really* clean, which surprised me considering his job included him getting so dirty. He was constantly joking and laughing about things, and I could barely figure out how to handle such a sunshine personality.

Even before coffee? Who was that happy before coffee?

Not that I didn't like it. I just didn't know what to do with it. I was used to being grumpy and everyone being grumpy back, but he seemed unfazed anytime I was that way with him, and I couldn't understand why.

On top of it all, he kept helping me in the kitchen even when I said he didn't have to, and trying to make me laugh the entire time.

My temporary roommate was an enigma to me, and I wasn't even sure if I had enough time to begin to understand him.

I winced as the front door shut and that organization-obsessed roommate walked in. His mouth dropping open as he took in the state of the kitchen and living room.

"What. The. Fuck," he mumbled.

"I did *not* realize what time it was. I thought I had more time to clean up," I said, moving things around the covered countertops.

Not only was every surface of the kitchen covered in things I was using for cooking, but the living room was covered in my clothes. "I had been working to sort through those," I said as he looked it over. "That's when I realized I needed to get started on cooking, then needed to walk Riot, and I almost burnt some things I was prepping for dinner, so I came back in here and honestly forgot about the clothes."

He picked up a corseted top that was hung over the back of the couch and his eyebrows jumped up.

"Well, seeing this makes me a little less annoyed. And what is this one?" He asked, holding up a bra that had straps crisscrossed to my neck. "Seems a little flimsy for a Rottweiler harness?"

I grabbed it out of his hand. "That's for me, not the dog."

A smile crept over his face, but I could tell he was trying to hide it.

"Oh, you have some real kinks then, huh?"

"Not kinks. I just have good taste."

"I think that's the same thing?" he asked, eyeing the leather in my hand.

"It's clothes, Jax. I wear this."

"In *public*?" he asked, stunned.

"Yes. In public."

"Fuck," he mumbled, still staring at it. "Did not realize your kinks included exhibitionism."

"It's clothing!"

"Right, right."

I went over, shoving clothes down the couch into a pile. "Forget about that. I'm sorry. I'm sure you hate the mess, but I lose track of time once in a while. I also lose track of what I'm doing, but I'll clean all of it up."

He shook his head. "It's fine. I don't really understand how you forget an entire living room of clothes, but it's fine. I'll be out in a few minutes."

I nodded, assuming that was my cue to clean up and clean up fast, so I moved. I started throwing all of my clothes back into suitcases and then ran back towards the kitchen. I was still cooking, so I wouldn't be able to clean it all, but at least he might not have a heart attack when he came back out.

"What are you doing now?" he said, his eyebrows shooting up as he returned, the living room almost empty again.

"Trying to clean up before you came back out?"

"Where did all the clothes go?"

"Back in my suitcases."

He looked over and went for them, dragging the big one back into the bedroom with him.

"Come on. And grab that other bag."

I didn't move, not knowing what he was doing, and too afraid to find out.

"I know you're still standing there, and if you don't get in here with that bag in the next ten seconds, I will start digging in these to find all the lace and leather things I saw laid out on the couch."

I groaned, grabbing my bag and heading into the room. "I'm only coming in because I know this is a threat you would follow through with."

When I walked in, he was reclined back on the bed with a smile.

"I did not think about the fact that you were living out of a suitcase. Sorry. The dresser is yours. I did keep the one drawer if you don't mind, but I will see what I can do about making room in my closet, too, if you need it."

"What? No way. I'm not taking over your space in here, too."

"Why?"

"Because you're already mad about me taking your space out there."

"I am a little surprised at how…scattered you are, but you're not taking the space. We are sharing it."

"But you're mad we are sharing it."

"No, I just haven't shared my space with another person in years and when I did, it was with three other guys who each only had a mattress and one backpack of clothes. There was nothing to make a mess with. Now I have a big ass dog living here and a woman who seems to be a tornado." He threw me a charming smile. "Please don't come attack me. You're a beautiful tornado that I really enjoy being here so far. And he fits his name, but I like Riot here too. It's actually nice not always being alone."

"Even when I make a mess and forget it?"

"Even then. Although, I do not know how you forget about a mess right in front of you."

"You know, out of sight, out of mind? Mine is more like, right in my line of sight and I know for a fact I will maybe clean it later when my brain can process that it's a cleanable mess."

"That sounds…exhausting. I would rather just clean it up and forget it."

"Me too, but I can't. I let it sit and drive me out of my mind first," I said with a laugh, the knot in my chest easing.

"Well, I can't promise not to follow after you with a mop and bucket, but I will not be mad about your mess. Although, I would also love to know more about how you manage to forget everything while you are doing it."

"It's easy. I start one thing, remember the other thing I have to do, and start that immediately. Then it's a domino effect."

"Well, regardless, I won't get mad about it. I might get annoyed, but not mad."

"I'm beginning to think you are a bit of a softie. I'm surprised."

"I told you, I like to consider myself a romantic."

"Isn't that the same thing?"

"Not to me. One means I'm a pushover to everyone, the other means I'm only a pushover for certain people."

"I guess if that's how you take it."

"It is. As for tonight, let's do things in an order. *Please.* Finish cooking, feed the animals that are sure to show up when they smell whatever delicious food you are making, walk your little rhinoceros, and then come put your clothes away while we watch a movie."

"We going to cuddle too?" I said, joking, even though I was enjoying the view of him, leaned back and relaxed.

He only smiled harder.

"I thought you would never ask."

"Kidding."

"Damn. I like to cuddle while watching movies. Who wants to just sit there?" he asked.

"Who wants to be constantly touched?"

He pointed two thumbs at himself with a laugh.

"And fine," I said. "We will do things in your order. No guarantees that I won't get sidetracked, though. And thank you. This was really nice of you."

He got up, ruffling my hair as we headed towards the kitchen. "I have to keep the peace if I want the company and the food."

"You're really just using me for the food," I said, motioning to the meal I was putting together on the counter.

"You're really just using me for my apartment, my mechanical skills, and my body."

"Your body? I've barely touched your body." I couldn't help

my eyes wandering down him. Not that I hadn't *wanted* to touch him.

"No, but I'm your bodyguard. You need my body."

I rolled my eyes. "I think you're giving yourself that title, not me. Which means I haven't used you for your body at all."

He leaned down a little, his face closer to mine now. "I had to punch someone just to get you here safe. I'd say you needed my body."

"But I didn't ask you to do that."

"*Oh*, got me on a technicality. Do you think you're not going to need my body again?"

"Stop talking about me needing your body. I won't be needing it for anything, and when you say it like that, you know it sounds dirty."

"It's not my fault if you have dirty thoughts about me. I just meant you're going to need my bodyguard services again."

"You're fired."

He laughed, but whatever comeback he had was interrupted when my new phone started ringing on the counter. I froze.

It was such an immediate reaction, the fear shooting through me so fast at the thought of it being Slaughter or Tristan on the other end. It wasn't logical, but I couldn't help the way my body tensed. Jax was still looking at me, his hands already going to my arms, rubbing them to get my attention again.

"Would your friends be calling me now?" I asked.

"No. Everyone is here. If they needed you, they would come in." He looked over at the phone, his eyebrows shooting up as his hands dropped from me immediately. "Hot Raf? As in Raf from the race track?" he asked, not hiding the shocked tone.

"Oh, shit. Yes. He put his number in my phone."

"And you didn't bite his head off? You haven't even put my number in your phone and you live with me."

"I live with you temporarily. And no one said that I didn't bite his head off a little."

That made him smile.

"Are you worried that I'm only mean to you?" I asked, laughing.

Half his mouth twitched. "Maybe."

"Don't be. I'm mean to everyone."

"Well, at least I'm not special. Did you want to call him back?"

"With you standing right there? Not a chance. I could only imagine what would come out of your mouth."

"Raf would understand. We're friends."

"You are?"

"Hang around the track enough, you'll be friends with everyone at Holt. Does he know you're staying with me?"

"No."

"Interesting. And do I get to put my number in your phone yet?"

I rolled my eyes with a huff and grabbed the phone, handing it to him. "Hurry up before I change my mind."

"Grouch," he mumbled, adding his number and smiling proudly when he turned it back to me.

"*Even hotter Jax*," I read.

"Maybe you need a rating system," he said. "One through five on the hot scale. Raf is about a two, and I'm obviously a five."

"Is that how girls are in your phone? Like a five is 'I would sleep with her again,' and a one is 'only sleep with her when desperate.'"

He went quiet, and I immediately felt bad when I saw his face. I was used to being bitchy to people around me. I didn't care if I hurt them, but the sad look on Jax's face made me feel horrible.

"Not quite. I'll be in the living room, *annoyed*, so feel free to call your boyfriend without me around."

He grabbed a plate of dinner and walked out.

"He is not my boyfriend," I said, grabbing my plate and following him into the living room, sitting back on the couch where my makeshift bed was. "I met him one time."

"No, but knowing Raf, he will want to be. At least for this month."

"Are you saying he's an asshole?"

"Not at all. Raf is a great guy, but he likes short-term relationships. Many short-term relationships. Apparently you already think both of us do, though. But if you like him, he's no one to fear or worry about. Just don't get attached."

"I'm not really the 'get attached' type," I said.

"No? I am so shocked. You seem like a sweet little angel that falls in love with anyone."

I rolled my eyes. "Right. I think that's the exact vibes I give off."

He flipped the lights off and fell back down onto the couch. "What type of movies do you like?"

"Scary ones, funny ones, a little of both?"

"Does this mean that we have to watch some gory horror movie where the clown is laughing the entire time?" he asked, the deadpan look on his face bothering me.

"You like that movie, too?" I asked excitedly, already knowing he probably hadn't even seen it.

"That was a purely made up suggestion, but of course you have an exact movie in mind. Is that really what you want?"

"Your apartment, your movie choice," I said, irritated that he still wasn't smiling. There wasn't even a hint of the humor that I had already grown used to in his tone.

"Comedy it is." He clicked through options.

"I was just kidding about the rating girls and sleeping with them thing," I said.

"No you weren't. Would you be surprised if I had something like that?"

I thought it over, my mind immediately comparing him to Tristan and his friends who were around Jax's age. "No, I guess not."

"So you weren't really kidding, and if that is your attempt at an apology, you failed."

"Ouch," I said, trying to lighten his mood.

"I get you've been around super shitty people, but I don't like all the assumptions that I'm a shitty person, too. If I do something that makes me one, by all means, treat me accordingly, but I don't think I've done anything to make you think I'm anything like Slaughter or Tristan or any other asshole."

"No, you haven't. Not even a little."

"Then treat me accordingly."

"Okay, I think that's fair. I will try," I said as he clicked into a movie.

"That isn't a comedy. That's a romantic comedy."

"And? My fragile eyes can handle it if they make out."

"I figured as much. I'm just surprised you would pick something so…"

"So? Romantic?"

"Yeah."

"Do you have a problem with my movie choice?"

"It's not that I have a problem. I guess I just don't understand it? The tattoos, the cars, the group of racers you hang out with. It all makes you seem like one type of person, but now you want to cuddle and watch a romance movie?"

"Okay, was *that* one an invitation?"

"It was not," I said with a laugh.

He groaned. "Fine. And yeah, I don't know. This is just what

I wanted to watch. And if you have an issue with it, I can move to my room."

The sudden harshness in his tone made me freeze. Considering he wanted to cuddle a second ago, I didn't think he was still mad about the phone number thing.

"Did I upset you again?" I asked, wishing I didn't care.

He turned to look at me, his eyes roaming over my face, and whatever he saw he seemed happy with because he finally continued.

"No, I've just had some people in my life lately tell me how terrible it is that I'm like that. Maybe I'm a little pissy about that, but you didn't do anything."

"What do you mean? Like your friends are telling you that they don't like you?"

"The crew? Not at all. I dated someone who decided that I had false advertising. I apparently made it seem like I'm some mafia-style hitman that races cars and she was *very* disappointed when that wasn't the case. As you can see, I like romance and cuddling and whatever other shit goes with it."

"And she was mad about that?"

"I think it was more disappointment for her, but yeah, she wasn't happy about it. In her mind, guys aren't supposed to be like that."

I couldn't help it. I started laughing.

"That's funny to you?" he asked with an amused laugh.

"Yeah, because the night we met you punched Tristan without hesitation and I assumed you were going to be a brute. I figured you would be all violence and anger, but then I found out that you're just...not. Not completely. I've lived the life with a mean, violent person, and it's funny to me that someone is out looking to have that in their life on purpose."

"I'm sorry you had to live with someone like Slaughter. And

that's possibly the nicest way anyone has ever told me how perfect I am," he said with a grin.

"I did not–"

"Shhh, relax. I won't tell anyone how sweet you are. Our little secret. Since we aren't cuddling, can I at least lay down here? Are you okay if I'm within a foot of you?"

"It's your couch," I said, waving my hand.

He grinned as he laid down, propping his head on a pillow just inches from my thigh. His couch was big, but between my makeshift bed and how tall he was, he wasn't trying to get close to me on purpose exactly. There just really wasn't more room.

He didn't seem to think anything more of it, only shifted to his side to watch the movie.

It only gave me uninterrupted seconds to look him over without his eyes on me. It was obvious that I couldn't compare him to Slaughter or Tristian, but he wasn't exactly a sweet, innocent guy either.

My brain kept trying to put him in the right category, and as soon as I thought I had it, he did something to make me question where he belonged. From romantic movies to punching people, he felt like such a contradiction. I hadn't had many guys that I truly liked in my life. Even less that I had liked *and* spent time around. I felt so far out of my element that I wasn't sure what to do next.

I knew what I wanted to do, but those ideas seemed out of the question.

I didn't know exactly who Jax was, but I knew that I should keep my distance until it was time to go. In just over a week, I would leave and probably never see him again.

And that's exactly what I wanted.

NINE
JAX

It was ridiculous how much I was thinking about her.

There was no way I should be constantly wondering about what she was doing or wearing or thinking. I barely knew her, but I somehow wanted to know everything I could. This morning, like the last few, was spent watching her wake up with her coffee and messy hair, and somehow, less and less of me cared that I should be avoiding Slaughter's step-daughter.

I was pathetic. I was supposed to be heading back to the apartment soon and would see her, but I had to wrap up the car I was working on first. I still pulled out my phone and hit her name.

JAX

How's your day going?

Minutes went by before I got three angry faces back.

CARLY

I messed up dinner and you're supposed to be back any time now. I don't have enough ingredients, or enough time, to start again.

More angry faces followed. She was funny even when she wasn't trying to be, and I could only laugh as I texted her back.

JAX

That bad?

CARLY

Yes.

JAX

No problem. We can go to the store after I'm done or just pick up food?

CARLY

Store.

I smiled and decided that my day was done. There was no way I wasn't going to wait longer to head home. Twenty minutes later, I was parked outside the apartment with the biggest grin as she ran to the car.

"Rough day?" I asked.

"The worst. My brain is a mess, and I couldn't focus on anything, so I kept getting sidetracked. Let's just go to the store and I'll find something else to make. I messed it up beyond repair."

"Or…" I said, pulling out and heading to the diner. "We skip the store and grab some food so you don't have to cook."

The diner wasn't far, maybe ten minutes on a bad day, but with the heavy rain today, traffic was light so I could make it in five.

She started to protest, but I patted her leg. "If you had a bad day, there's no point in pushing it. Relax."

I could feel her eyes on me as she pushed my hand away.

"What about people seeing me?"

"Listen, it's cold, it's pouring sideways rain, and I'm starving. Put this hoodie on and hide that mane of hair until we sit down. I will make sure you are okay. I come here all the time and have never seen Slaughter or anyone like him. It's more like eighty-year-olds and college kids, not car thieves with bad taste in food."

It's not that the diner was bad, the little place was more like a hole in the wall for locals. Nothing fancy, but everything was clean and comfortable. The older green vinyl booths weren't exactly good looking and the wood on the walls looked about 20 years overdue for an upgrade, but it didn't matter. They were basically open 24/7 every day of the year and never seemed to judge us whether we paid in pennies, like we used to do, or hundreds.

I was surprised she didn't protest, but instead quietly pulled it on. At least she trusted me a little now.

She hid her face as we ran in and stayed close as I walked up back to the farthest booth. From here, she could sit and be hidden to anyone else in the room without a problem.

"Get in first. We'll sit like that so there's less chance of seeing you," I said and she listened without hesitation. I could feel the rumble of my chest more than I could hear it and hope that she wouldn't notice. Carly angry and ready to hit me with a bat was hot, but so was this side of her that trusted me enough to listen.

I watched as her eyes scanned the menu. Every few seconds her nose would crinkle like something sounded gross, but then it stopped as she bit at her lip. This girl was adorable, and it was making me lose my mind.

"Find what you want?"

"Yeah, I think so."

I heard the rev of the car as her head whipped to look out the window. Her body jumped and her hand clamped down on my thigh. I waited, looking as the car passed in a blur.

"It's not them," I whispered as she leaned into me harder. "I know the guy that drives that car and he doesn't hang out with Slaughter."

"Right. Of course. I can't think that every car will be them."

"It's okay. I can understand why you're worried. You can stay alert, but I promise, I can kick their asses any day. Didn't I prove that already?" I laughed, trying to help her calm down.

She bit at her lip more before laughing. "Yeah, I guess you have."

I wrapped my arm around the back of the booth behind her, way too aware of her hand as her fingers flexed on my thigh and I thankfully stifled another groan as she moved in closer, her head nearly resting on my shoulder.

"Did that freak you out so much that you need your bodyguard, or just suddenly decide you don't hate me?"

Her eyes moved up to meet mine, but her head stayed tilted until she was glaring up at me.

"Just freaked out," she finally said.

"So you do hate me then? I've been wondering, but you're so hot and cold I couldn't figure it out."

"I tried to hate you, but honestly, I'm struggling to find something to hate. It's annoying."

The waitress came over to take our order before I could answer. She smiled down at me and I guessed she had to be around our age. Her eyes lit up as she leaned down, showing off her low cut shirt as she stared at me. We came here often enough that I knew her, and knew that she was constantly flirting with one of us, but that had dwindled down to only flirting with me since Ransom and Fox were taken and Kye made his disinterest very clear. I wasn't interested either, especially not now, but I didn't have it in me to make it as clear as Kye.

She flirted more as she took our order, and it wasn't until she walked away that I looked back at Carly.

The flush of red across her cheeks was vibrant, and the deep furrow of her brows let me know that I fucked up somehow.

"Does this just happen everywhere you go?"

"Does what happen?"

"Women hitting on you. So blatantly flirting?"

"She was just being nice. She acts like that with all of us"

"You're kidding, right?"

"No?"

"She's flirting with you, Jax."

"Fine, but I wasn't flirting back."

"Are you serious? You absolutely were," she said, the furrow of her brows gone as a small, knowing smile graced her lips.

"Is this a problem?"

"Not at all. I just think it's funny that you're cozied up here with me and she has no hesitation about flirting."

The smile on my face grew more, and I took advantage of her slip of the tongue to pull her close. "I did think it was getting pretty cozy. I'm glad to know it wasn't just me."

"Knock it off," she said, pushing back away from me, getting even farther this time. I had been joking, but the sudden loss of her tucked next to me was leaving me with an all too familiar empty feeling.

Not that this was the same thing as what's happened to me in the past. We weren't here on a date and she wasn't rejecting my affection because I was too much to deal with.

Well, maybe a little because of that, but I didn't think Carly honestly didn't like me. She just didn't like me flirting with her.

The waitress came back with our food and Carly didn't hide her scowl.

"Thanks," I said. "Could my girlfriend here get a refill?" I asked, not daring to glance at Carly again yet.

"Oh, your girlfriend. Of course. I'll grab that."

The second she turned, Carly smacked at me.

"Why did you say that?"

"You wanted her to stop flirting, I wanted her to stop flirting, and I wanted to see your face turn that shade of red when I said it."

"I don't care if she kept flirting!" she whispered the words so angrily that I laughed more.

"Right, that's why you looked like you were contemplating violence. It's alright, it's all very entertaining."

"I was not contemplating that!"

"What were you thinking about, then?" I said, grinning as she stared daggers at me.

"I don't want to say."

"Then I'll believe it was about violence, and how much you like me."

"No, I was just annoyed that she didn't think we could actually be here together. Like, I get it, you're hot, but we are literally sitting right next to each other. She could at least pretend not to think I'm that beneath you."

The vivid picture of Carly beneath me flashed through my mind. I knew it wasn't what she meant, but that really didn't matter.

"Beneath me? Do you think that woman thinks that I wouldn't be with you? Don't you mean that you wouldn't be with me?"

"Don't even play that cutesy game with me. You're obviously good looking."

"I mean, I don't think I'm terrible to look at, but you're gorgeous. Why would anyone think we couldn't be here together?"

She only shook her head. "We're dropping the subject. I'm not going to sit here and talk about this with you, of all people."

"What's that supposed to mean?"

"You're too hot to understand what the issue is and too nice to think that other people are not thinking as kind of thoughts."

I didn't think there was any winning here. Scout had been the equivalent of my little sister for most of our lives, and I knew how this conversation went. I said the wrong thing, and she gets more upset. I didn't understand people. Scout had been bullied for being too skinny and I was assuming Carly had been made to feel bad for being too curvy. I didn't think there was anything I could say right now to help make her feel any better.

"I personally think you're the one out of my league. If I had to paint the perfect woman, she would look like you. I mean, granted, you know that I can't draw for shit, but you get my point."

Her lip twitched, but she still didn't smile. "I thought I said I want to change the subject."

The food came, and we started eating. "Alright, grouch, then tell me. Are you trying to be a chef in a fancy restaurant, or own something like this?"

Her nose scrunched as she looked around. "I don't think I want the stress of a fancy restaurant, but this place is a bit... outdated. Can I pick a middle option?"

"What is the middle option?"

She shrugged and turned, leaning back into the corner to face me more. "I don't know. I want to make cooking videos, create new recipes, maybe a cookbook. Something like this place would be cool if the regulars don't protest about new food items and updated decorations."

The smile on her face was so genuine that I wanted to keep it there. "They would. You know they would, but the change could be nice. And as much as I don't complain about the food here, yours is better."

"What about you?" she asked.

"What about me?"

"Well, obviously you're a mechanic, but is there anything else you want to do?"

I usually gave some boring response to this, but with her I didn't want to. "I don't know. I always feel like I want to do something more, but I don't know what that is. I like being around cars, so I don't want to give that up. I guess I haven't found anything else I want yet."

"Well, I've heard a life of crime is really popular with the racing crowd, so I guess there's always that," she said with a tight smile.

"Yeah? I was hoping for something a little less illegal and a little more fulfilling, but I will keep that in mind. I would already have some experience at least," I said, grinning at her. "Speaking of racing, we need to go."

"Go where?"

"To go race my friends, in the rain. Probably spin the car around in circles, too. Come on," I said, throwing money down and pulling her out of the booth with me. "It's fun. I promise."

"But the roads are wet, and it's dark out," she said, not hiding the panic.

"And I'm a good driver with headlights."

She got up, pulling the hood back over her hair and walking out with me. The rain had let up, but I could still feel a mist coming down on us as we got in.

"I can bring you home or you can come with me. I take you being safe pretty seriously though, so I wouldn't let anything bad happen to you."

She was quiet for a minute as I started the car, but then her hand wrapped around the crook of my elbow.

"Okay. I'll go with you," she said, the unsteady tone reminding me how unsure she was.

I nodded, pulling out and not saying another word. I don't know what made her decide to trust me, but I wasn't going to question it. Especially not when her hand stayed there, the entire time I drove. Her fingers biting into my bicep as I pushed the car faster. We hit the empty road out of town that led to an empty lot we liked to race each other at. I moved through the gears until we were at ninety, but she still didn't make a sound.

I knew her trust wasn't given lightly, but the warmth that filled my chest made it undeniable – I loved that she trusted me.

TEN

CARLY

I SPENT half of the next morning baking brownies and enjoying the peace that came with an entire kitchen to myself.

It was so calm, relaxing even, and I didn't have to worry about people barging in and making me feel uncomfortable or unwelcome. It happened so much back home that I ended up never leaving my room unless I had to. Most of the cooking I did ended up only being at my grandpa's house.

By the time I was done, I had another feeling nagging at me.

I wanted to see Jax.

So much for wanting to keep my distance.

"What am I supposed to do about that?" I asked, looking at Riot.

He whined and kept looking at me.

"Yeah, I know it's dumb. Why would I want to see Jax already? We live together."

At Jax's name, Riot perked up.

"Don't even tell me that he got to you, too?"

He came over, tapping me with his nose. His universal way of telling me that he wanted something.

"Fine. We'll go walk these down there and then we are coming back immediately."

At the word "walk," Riot ran to the door, waiting as I wrapped up the brownies before clipping him up and heading out.

I knew the garage was down the street. Jax had shown me the location on his phone the other day, but it would take me a while to walk there.

I spent the time talking to Riot, giving him a long list of reasons why we weren't going to stay with Jax any longer than necessary. By the time I turned into the garage parking lot, I was pretty confident in my reasons I was giving to Riot.

That was until I saw Jax.

He was standing next to a car, talking with Kye, and my mouth watered at the sight.

I saw him leave every day, but this was a whole different experience. His button-up shirt hung open, sweat coating him, the tattoos on his chest on full display. The always-happy sunshine boy looked dangerously hot.

It only got worse when he looked over and saw me, his face lighting up like it was Christmas. I groaned. "This was a terrible idea. We shouldn't have come down here."

Riot didn't seem to care, though, pulling me harder to get to Jax. He immediately crouched down, hugging Riot.

Up close, he only looked better, and I was trying not to stare, but it was too hard to look away from him. His hat was hiding his dark hair, and when he looked up at me, I was immediately caught up in bright blue eyes and the dimpled smile on his face.

"What are you two doing here?" Jax asked, getting up as Riot ran to Kye next. I was surprised when Kye sat down, letting Riot roll into his lap.

"Carly?" Jax asked, trying to get my attention.

"Oh. I was bored and made these. I thought you all might like them."

He looked in the container and smiled again.

"Might? Pretty sure they will be gone in a few minutes."

I hated that it made me smile. They all seemed to love what I made, and it kept making me feel so good, so special.

It felt like being around Jax was bringing out too much softness too often. I needed to remember that this was temporary and these people would not be in my life long. I was going to be on my own again soon.

"Alright, I'm going to head back now."

"You just got here. Why leave so soon?" He stepped closer, flashing a smile. "Plus, we just got lunch. Come on."

"But I didn't get food, so it would be better if I just head back."

Before I could argue more, he threw an arm around me, pulling me further into the garage. I sucked in a deep breath at his touch. I didn't know that him touching me should have any effect at all, but it definitely shouldn't have this much of an effect every time.

"I'll share. I don't mind."

"Do you ever?"

That made him laugh. "No, not with anyone here."

"Ugh, you are so happy and nice. You're like the sun."

"Really hot and hard for you to get close to without melting for me?"

"I should have said that you're like sunshine. Blinding, and happy, and warm. And I prefer cold, rainy days."

"And you're like the moon."

"Dark and mysterious?" I asked, holding in my laugh.

"No, well yes, but I meant my sunshine-like personality seems to rub off on you. You suddenly can't stop smiling back at me."

"Okay. Calm down sunshine," I said. "I'm smiling because you're ridiculous, not because of some sun beam science."

"Aww, you're calling me sunshine now? Does this mean I get to call you moon?"

"Jax," I warned.

"Yes, moon?"

"Knock it off."

"You said you didn't like grouch. What am I supposed to call you?"

"Carly?"

"Boring," he said, opening the office door and pulling me inside.

My mouth dropped open. "You can't say that my name is boring."

He only laughed. "I meant calling you by your name is boring when I have a thousand other things I'd rather use."

"Carly!" Scout yelled. "You missed us!"

She was sitting back on the couch, a smile on her face, and already smacking the spot next to her.

Jax pulled me back with a scowl. "She's sitting over here with me."

"You live with her, Jax. You can't take all the time with her during the day, too."

I could feel the shock on my face showing as my eyebrows shot up.

"I'm sharing my sandwich with her, so unless you want to share yours, she's with me."

"It's already half gone, so that's a hard pass," she said, grinning as she took a big bite.

"That's what I thought." Jax sat back, motioning for me to come sit next to him. "Will you relax a bit?" he whispered. "You look like you might start swinging at one of us."

"Sorry, old habits. Garages haven't always been the most fun places for me."

The door swung open, Fox, Kye, and Ransom walking in, spreading out, and grabbing food. I tried not to stiffen as they filled the room, but I couldn't help it. Jax knocked my arm, smirking as he pulled food out of the bag.

"Hey Carly," Fox said, sitting down across from us. "How is living with Jax? Driving you up the wall yet?"

I laughed. "I think I'm the one driving him up the wall. I'm a little more messy than him."

They all laughed, poking fun at Jax. "I think everyone is. Not ready to move to another couch yet?" Kye asked.

"Not a chance," Jax said. "I'll have you all know, she calls me sunshine now so she must like me a little." He smiled hard at me. "You don't have to admit it. I know living with me is amazing."

"You know, you say those cocky things and it makes me want to go to someone else's place."

"The only person here who lives alone is Kye since Scout has her boyfriend there more than she doesn't, and I would bet money that I'm better to live with than him," Jax said.

I rolled my eyes and looked him over. "And by the way, I do *not* call you sunshine now. I said it one time."

"One time was enough. I'll never forget it."

"Are you sharing your food, or should I get back to the apartment?" I rolled my eyes as he leaned into me, his lips only inches from my ear.

"Brat," he whispered the word softly, the heat tickling my ear and sending a shiver down my spine. "Here you go." He slid half of his sandwich to me before leaning back and taking a bite of his own.

"*Ohhh*, my favorite nickname so far," I said quietly with a laugh.

He choked, coughing, as he set his head down on the edge of the table. "Fuck, Carly," he said, so quiet that only I could hear. "I don't know if you know what you're doing and you like it, or you're just that oblivious," he said, taking a deep breath before raising his head.

"You good?" Fox said, eyebrows up as he looked us over.

"Oh, I'm great. Never better. Not rethinking my entire life at all."

Fox laughed and looked at Jax. "Hey, do you remember all the times you gave me shit when Ash was around?"

"Yes," Jax said as his face fell.

"Payback's a bitch," he said, smiling as he grabbed a brownie. "And these are amazing, Carly. Thanks for bringing them. Hey now that you're down here, do you want to look over your truck?"

"Actually, yeah, that would be —"

"Alright, knock it off," Jax said, cutting me off. "I was already going to show it to her after we were done."

"Am I missing something?" I asked, looking between them, my brain immediately assuming this was all some sort of trick.

"All you're missing is two guys who want to constantly taunt and piss each other off," Scout said. "Don't take any of it personally, and don't even be surprised when fights break out between them. *Boys*," she said, shaking her head.

I was surprised when that put me at ease. Obviously, I was missing something, but based on Scout's reaction, it wasn't about me and was more about them.

I had been the brunt of so many jokes that now I felt defensive at the slightest hint of it. I ate in silence as they all talked about cars and racing, and was surprised that it only calmed me down, not annoyed me further.

"Come on," Jax said, finishing and getting up. "Let's go before that fight does break out. *Fox*."

"Oh, need me to come with you? Yeah, of course."

"Sit down or I'll make you," Jax said, his hard stare making Fox sit back down with a smirk.

"Fine, fine. But you deserve every second."

Jax pushed me out the door and back into the garage.

"What was that about?" I asked, following him around tool boxes and cars.

"That's Fox being an ass. I do deserve it, though. I was an ass to him when Ashton started coming around."

"What does that have to do with anything?"

He turned, eyebrows furrowing. "I guess that answers my earlier question about obliviousness. Are you sure you want to see your truck? It's in pieces."

I groaned as he brought me along the side of it. "But it can be fixed?"

"Definitely."

"Then yes, I want to see it."

He grabbed my hand, pulling me to the front of the truck to look under the hood.

"There's nothing there."

"I pulled the engine out. It's behind you." I turned to see it on a stand, more pieces torn off of it.

"And you really think you can fix this in two weeks?"

"Yes. I know what I'm doing, Carly. I promise I'm not just tearing it apart for fun."

"No, I know. I mean, I trust that you know what you're doing. This just seems like a lot of work. Like a *lot* of work."

I glanced back at him, looking just as good as he did when I walked in, shirt still open, showing off that beautiful tattoo and slick set of abs. And this guy was doing all of this for me?

"It is a lot of work, but it will be fine. Seriously, I can handle it. You look like you're freaking out."

"I believe you, but like I said, this is a lot. Why are you doing this?"

"Because you need your truck?"

"It's not that simple, Jax. This looks like a huge job. This is not a good exchange for getting some food made for you."

"Says who?"

"Me?"

"Well, no offense, but your opinion on this particular subject doesn't matter to me. I like the company and the food. It's a fair trade to me."

"I have family members that I've known my entire life that wouldn't even be this nice to me. I don't know why anyone would think I'm worth doing all this for when you don't even know me."

"So? I have family members that don't care if I'm dead or alive. I also met people in my life that do care if I am or not," he said, waving his hand around the garage. "It's not any reflection on me, or on you, in this case. You have had some shit people in your life and I decided I didn't want to be one of them. Simple as that."

"But it's never that simple."

"I get your hesitation. Seriously, I do, but it really is that simple this time. Promise."

"Do you...want help?"

His smile grew. "You want to help me work on it?"

"Not particularly, but you did help me cook, so it would be fair."

"I'm going to take you up on that, but not today. I still have to get a customer's car done today, so the truck has to wait."

"Then I think I should head back to the apartment," I said, not liking any of the emotions bubbling up inside me.

He only smiled. "Alright, run away. Riot is still in the office. Don't forget him before you flee."

"I'm not –"

He stopped me. "It's okay. I don't need any explanation as long as you're running to the apartment, not away from it."

I nodded, heading right to the office for Riot and then right out the door. I'm glad he didn't ask for any explanation, because I didn't have one.

I was halfway out the garage bay door when he caught up to me.

"Want me to walk you back?"

"No. I'm alright. I'll see you in a bit."

"Alright. Call me if you need anything."

I nodded again and took off, not looking back as I rounded the corner of the garage and hit the sidewalk. The only thing I needed was to stop thinking about him. I wasn't going to be running from the apartment, not today, but I did need to run away from these emotions. Jax brought out too many of them, each interaction with him making me feel more in minutes than I've felt in months.

I needed to run to the apartment where I could catch my breath and find a way to hide all of these emotions away forever.

ELEVEN
JAX

CARLY HAD LEFT, but was still distracting me. I was trying to get this transmission into a client's car so I could work on her truck more, but it was not cooperating.

I saw Kye's boots step up next to the car. "I got some news."

"About?" I groaned, not having a clue what he was talking about.

"Carly and Slaughter."

The transmission slipped, my shock making me lose my grip as it slipped through my hands, directly onto my chest.

"Fuck," I yelled. A string of curse words followed the first one as I rolled the transmission off of me with a groan.

Kye had dropped down. "Why aren't you using the jack for this?"

"Scout was using it," I wheezed.

"Oh shit. You good?"

"Never better." I rolled out, trying not to curl up in a ball from the pain. "What about Carly?"

"Slaughter was at Jake's parts asking about her truck, and if anyone had come in for parts matching that year and model."

I tried getting up, pain ripping through my chest and arms. "Well, I haven't bought any specific parts there, so at least we are clear on that. What did Jake tell him?"

"Nothing as far as I understand. He told Slaughter that he can't give out information like that. It's not like Jake is ready to jump to help Slaughter. Remember, he ripped Jake off a few thousand dollars years ago? Now, Slaughter still walks in there like it never happened. Jake was pissed. He did ask why I was asking about Slaughter, though."

"Did you tell him?" I trusted Kye, but as much as I liked Jake, he wasn't a part of our crew and that meant I didn't trust him knowing about Carly being here. The second Slaughter caught on that she was with us, things would blow up.

"Do you really think I would tell anyone our business?" he asked with a hard eye roll. "I told him that Slaughter might be giving us trouble again, and that's it. I told him to let me know if he heard anything else."

"Fuck," I yelled again, shoving my hand into my hair before realizing it was still covered in fluid, and then swearing again because lifting my arm felt like ripping my chest open. "What am I going to do if Slaughter finds out before I'm done with this thing?" I asked, pointing at the torn apart truck in the corner.

Kye shrugged. He was the wrong person to ask, considering nothing like this seemed to bother him. "We deal with it. Kind of how we deal with everything else. You have six of us keeping an eye out, and keeping us one step ahead of him. I just wanted to let you know what I heard."

"Yeah, and I appreciate it. You're probably right. This is just stressing me out." I rubbed at my chest, feeling the bruise already forming. "I'm heading home. I can't deal with anything else today and have a feeling I will be if I stay."

Kye nodded. "Go ahead. I'll finish one up."

I grabbed my stuff and my keys to head out. Some days I

loved working on cars, most days I cursed the things endlessly until they ran right. Today was definitely a 'cursing it endlessly' day to begin with, and now that I had Carly on my mind, I had to see her.

———

THE APARTMENT WAS quiet when I walked in. No Riot running around and no Carly in the kitchen. I kicked off my boots and looked into the bedroom, but she wasn't there either.

This time, I took a deep breath before I let myself panic, and told myself that they were probably out for another walk. It wasn't exactly helping that I just found out that Slaughter was asking around town for her, but I couldn't panic yet. Last time, I might have overreacted, but the thought of her back with Tristan and Slaughter made me sick to my stomach every time I thought about it.

I carefully set my stuff down and headed to the shower, not wanting to touch anything until I washed off the fluid that still covered me from the transmission.

I walked into the bathroom as I pulled off my shirt, but froze when I opened my eyes. The tub was overflowing with bubbles and two long legs were propped up on the side. The only other part of her showing were two perfect breasts that rose up from the sea of bubbles.

I tried to back up without making a sound. Her eyes were closed and headphones were in, so she hadn't noticed me yet, but then my foot tangled in a shirt as I took another step back.

I swore and her eyes flew open, but before she could say a word, I was already falling, slipping on the scattered clothes. My back hit the floor with a thud, knocking the breath from my already-sore chest.

"Jax!" she yelled. "What are you doing in here?"

"Didn't know." I gasped for a full breath, each pull of air painful. "I didn't know you were in here."

I fought for shallow breaths, wondering if one fall could make my lungs collapse.

"And then decided to stay and watch when you saw that I was?" she yelled. I heard water splash as she moved around frantically.

"If you don't move, I can't see you from here," I said. "Your mess of clothes tried to kill me and I need a minute before I can stand."

The room was silent except for the faint noise of her angry music coming from the headphones. "Are you okay?"

"I think so. Just can't breathe."

"I am not getting out to help you."

I gave a painful laugh. "Thank you for the concern."

"Well, it's hard to care when you just walked in on me naked."

"And wet," I said, regretting it the moment it came out, but she looked so hot it was hard to miss. Pain pinched between my shoulder blades, making me groan and helping to take my mind off her very wet body so close to me.

"Jax!" she yelled.

"You screaming my name is not going to help the situation."

"What is that supposed to mean?"

"It means I just walked on the absolute hottest view in the world and I am trying to not make you more uncomfortable, but I will fail if you start saying my name like that."

"How much did you see?"

"Listen, I'm not going to lie. I tried to be a gentleman and look away, but there was plenty to see before I did."

Silence surrounded us again, and I didn't fill it.

"Yeah, I know there is," she said, her voice so low it almost sounded sad.

"That sounds like you took my comment the wrong way."

"Nope. I got it."

"I meant that those bubbles weren't covering everything, so while I didn't mean to, I saw some parts, and at risk of sounding like a pervert, the things I did see were pretty fucking great. None of what I said was a dig at you."

She groaned. "Not helping."

My lips twitched, but I hid my laugh. "Fine, then. How was the rest of your day? Where's Riot? He wasn't slobbering all over me yet. I assumed you were out on a walk."

"He's in the bedroom because he tries to get in the tub, and the rest of my day was fine. I didn't realize you would be home so soon. I guess I lost track of time after I got back. I lose track of time so easily now with nowhere to go."

"You aren't entirely wrong on the time. I dropped a transmission on my chest. It hurt to breathe, so I decided to end the day a little early." I decided right there that I wasn't going to tell her about Slaughter asking around. There was no need to freak her out more right now.

"Are you serious?" she said, and I heard the bath water splashing around. "Are you okay?"

In seconds, she was next to me, a towel wrapped around her, covering everything now.

It was hard to cover up her cleavage, though, and it was currently in my face as she leaned over me.

"That doesn't look good. Do you need to go to the hospital?"

"No. I'm good. It's just going to be a bruise."

"A very large one and it could hurt the muscle there. I'll make you a salve for it. It won't heal it, but it will hopefully cut down the time it will take to heal."

"You're going to make a salve?" I asked, trying not to laugh and cause more pain. "What does that even mean? Are you some sort of witch?"

"Maybe. You should probably be more careful around me just in case," she said with a smirk. "In the meantime, I have a recipe for the salve and lucky for you, I grabbed all my weird ingredients at the store the other day."

I stared up at her, determined to get the full smile that was threatening to show up.

"What kind of weird ingredients are we talking about? Like olive oil and tomatoes, or worms and dead bugs?"

She laughed, her hands still on my chest, and I didn't want it to end. "Olive oil and tomatoes? I'm not rubbing an Italian dish all over your chest. And I don't know what store you are going to that sells worms and dead bugs, but I meant more herbs, oils, and stuff."

"Honestly, you could rub any of those things on me right now, and I would still be a happy man."

She pulled back, dropping her hands from me as I groaned.

"Okay, this is done. Are you ready to get up and go?" she asked, seemingly trying to hide how red her cheeks were getting.

"I'm suddenly enjoying myself."

"Enjoying laying on the bathroom floor?"

"Talking to you."

The scowl that crossed her face was one that was becoming burned into my brain.

"Too bad," she said.

"I'll go. I'm going to close my eyes and get up. If I die slipping on more of your clothes, are you obligated to carry me out of here?"

"No, but I will be nice and let your friends know where you are as I run away. And close your eyes tight, no more looking. I'm already self conscious now."

She helped pull me up, my eyes closed, and I tried not to open them as I felt around, while also trying not to comment that her body was a dream come true.

"I can promise that you should not feel self conscious. I didn't see it all, but I have a very strong imagination and you definitely have nothing to feel self conscious about."

"You're saying that to be nice and I hate it. Now leave."

Unless I started crawling across the floor to beg to see more, I couldn't think of any other way to tell her that I liked what I saw in a way that wasn't going to be weird.

I mean, I was suddenly fine with the idea of crawling back over to beg, but I didn't think she would be.

I closed the door behind me, trying to calm myself with a deep breath, but pain pinched in my chest again.

Damn, I see one pair of boobs half covered in bubbles, and I was ready to drag her out of the tub and into my bed.

I had to stop. I was going to ruin my own life all over again by falling for the girl who had already made it clear she would be leaving me as soon as possible.

I groaned, realizing she locked Riot in my room, which meant my bed and blankets would be torn apart like he did every time he found a spot where he wanted to make himself comfortable.

But when I opened the door, all I saw was Riot on the bed, flipped onto his back, sleeping on perfectly straightened blankets.

"Apparently you like my bed?" I said, stripping off the last of my clothes and grabbing a towel. His head rolled to look at me, but he didn't move, happy and content.

I sighed as my shoulders sagged. I was so tired, and still needed to clean myself up, but at least I could look forward to seeing what she was planning to put all over me. I was running myself into the ground at this point. Trying to make sure I was keeping up with work, her truck, life in general, and now Carly. The thought of coming home made me more excited each day, and I couldn't find a way to stop it.

"I'm going to use someone else's shower," I yelled, knowing no one else would care.

"No, wait," she ran out in the towel. "It's all yours. I was just trying to clean up. I wasn't trying to take it from you."

I furrowed my face in confusion. "What? You weren't. You're allowed to bathe when you want."

She looked up at me. "Yeah, but I didn't want you to get mad that I was still in there when I knew you wanted to be. I just didn't want to leave it a mess, too."

I kept all my swear words to Slaughter to myself. Apparently, he made life hell for her, and that was more obvious by the minute.

"You aren't second to me, Carly. You can use the bath before me, even if you are in there for hours, it's fine. Even if I do want a shower," I said with a laugh. She was trying to keep her head high and eyes hard, but she honestly looked upset.

Her face finally softened, and I made a small, careful step closer.

She was still staring, and I smiled more when I realized she wasn't staring because she was freaked out. She was staring at me, and I was suddenly pleased that the towel was wrapped a little lower than normal around my waist, giving her plenty to look at.

"Carly, my eyes are up here," I said, keeping a playful tone and hoping she would play along with me.

She jumped, a red covering her cheeks as the scowl set in. "How the hell does that happen? I have seen your fridge. You eat burgers and frozen food, and wash it down with energy drinks."

"How does what happen?"

"Abs!" she yelled.

"Oh. I don't know, good genetics? Working out, and constantly working on cars all day sweating my ass off?"

She made a sound of agreement before finally looking up at me. "I'm getting dressed and cooking. What do you want?"

I stepped closer, only a foot between us now. "Anything."

She rolled her eyes. "Seriously? That seems like a trick somehow."

"A trick? No. I will eat anything you cook."

"Anything?"

"Yes. And don't even test me, you will lose. You can cook any type of meat or cuisine and I'm eating it. Unless you purposefully make it disgusting."

She looked back down at my chest, her lips pursing together and I couldn't look away from them.

"Your bruise is already looking bad. I'll make that salve right now, too. It will help it feel better in a day or two."

"A chef and a witch? How did I get so lucky?"

"And here I thought you were still disappointed that I wasn't some old man on the side of the road."

"At first, it was really hard to come to terms with," I said, shaking my head. "But then I realized there is nothing to be disappointed about with a roommate who knows how to cook, make potions and salve to heal me, and looks —" I stopped as her eyes trailed up my body, a hard, hooded, glare meeting my eyes. "You know? I'm going to go shower. I'll help you after I'm done."

She nodded, her face scrunched. "Good choice."

I couldn't figure out how I managed to find the hottest, angriest girl around sitting on the side of the road, and somehow convinced her to come back to my apartment, but I didn't think I could push my luck.

I showered as fast as I could, still taking way too long to scrub off fluid and dirt. By the time I threw on shorts, grabbed a shirt, and came back out, she was cursing in the kitchen.

"You good in here?"

"No. Wait, no." She turned to me, a bowl in her hand. "Don't put on a shirt."

"Happily, little witch."

She rolled her eyes before reaching into the bowl and slathering my chest with a green, sticky goop.

"What does this stuff do exactly?"

"Basically just helps the muscle. The bruise won't disappear immediately, but it should hurt less after tomorrow."

I looked at her as she worked, slathering her potions across my chest.

"Thank you," I said, enjoying the feel of her hands on me again, already wondering how many times I could ask to have this reapplied.

"That was very nice of you to make for me, and I will try to believe it was only because you wanted to help, and not because you wanted to run your hands all over my bare chest."

Her mouth dropped open. I should have expected it, but I didn't see it coming as her hand came up and smacked the sticky salve all over my cheek.

TWELVE
CARLY

"You didn't," he said, frozen in place.

I pulled back my shoulders and froze, ready to fight, but not sure what Jax would do.

"I absolutely did."

His nose scrunched and, for a quick second, I almost expected him to get mad, maybe yell, but he only leaned forward, wrapping his arms around me and sticking his cheek right against mine.

"Jax! Get off of me!"

"Can't. We're stuck now," he said, making no attempt to move.

"We are not! Get off!"

He peeled away, and I was glad to see he at least kept most of his chest off of me.

Riot barked, jumping up at Jax to get between us, but Jax dropped, letting Riot smell the salve before petting him until he rolled over.

Suddenly my phone went off, pinging over and over, making my heart rate pick up with each new incoming text.

"Oh shit, I forgot to tell you that I gave Ash your number for the group chat," he said, grabbing his own phone to glance at before setting it back down. "Sorry, I had no choice. She was going to come for me if I didn't."

"What? Why would she want that?"

"Check your phone and good luck. Please remember that I am not the one who inflicted this on you. It's all my friends' fault."

I opened my phone to see a group chat that was already ten texts deep.

ASH

Hi Carly!

SCOUT

Finally.

KYE

Do you really think she wanted to be in on this? Say goodbye to your phone battery.

SCOUT

Why wouldn't she? I keep trying to tell you guys that we're delightful. Stop making people think we aren't.

KYE

Speak for yourself

FOX

I'm pretty fucking delightful.

I looked up at Jax. "What is happening?"

He gave a tight smirk. "Welcome to the group chat. Like I said, good luck," he said, laughing now. "They wanted you added. I can't tell them no. Sorry."

"Why would they want me on this?"

"Maybe because they like you? They want to talk to you?"

"Jax, I can barely handle texting one person back. What am I supposed to say?"

"You can be a grumpy little witch and tell them to shut up, or say nothing, or just join in the conversation. Whatever you want. The point was that they wanted to be able to tell you stuff, not to make you all anxious and feel obligated to respond. I go days without saying anything. Ransom just adds pictures. Kye only makes smartass comments. You can say hi or even send a middle finger emoji if you're feeling extra feisty today."

> QUINN
>
> We wanted to see if you guys were going to the races tonight?
>
> SCOUT
>
> I will be.
>
> FOX
>
> Shocking, Scout. And yeah, Ash and I are going. Leave in an hour?
>
> KYE
>
> I'll meet you guys there.
>
> QUINN
>
> Sounds good. Carly? Jax?

"They are asking if we are going to the races tonight?" I said, not looking away from the texts coming in.

"Oh yeah, I forgot about that. Yeah, I'm going. Did you want to come?"

"Should I? Won't there be a chance of Slaughter or Tristan there?"

"I doubt it. I haven't seen Slaughter at races in months. I assume Tristan would be with him usually? They aren't as interested when no one will bet them money. When everyone knows you don't pay, but want to get paid, no one is interested in betting with you. I don't know if you knew or not, but they got unofficially kicked out of Thursday night races. This one is even smaller than that, and is only happening because it's supposed to rain on Thursday when everyone usually meets up," he smiled up at me, still on the floor with Riot. "Plus, I'll be there. Your dedicated bodyguard."

I rolled my eyes. "Of course. How could I forget? So, what should I say then?"

He got up laughing. "You are overthinking this. You could literally only send an emoji and they won't care. Do you want to go?"

"Actually…yeah, I do," I said, surprising myself. I would normally choose to hide away, but for the first time in a long time, getting dressed up and going out sounded fun.

He moved behind me, wrapping his arms around me, and tapping at the phone. I tried not to move, the feel of him flush against me was both wonderful and tortuous.

CARLY

We are going. We'll be downstairs in an hour.

"Now hit send," he said, waiting as my thumb hovered over the button before hitting send. "Ahh, that's my girl, being brave and texting a bunch of street racers all at once that you want to go hang out with them." He started laughing hard, his body shaking behind me as he pulled away. "Not only hang out with them, but you want to go *race* with them."

I stayed still, trying to hide the shiver that ran through me at him being so close. As soon as he stepped away, I stepped even further, needing that distance as my body flushed.

"Let's eat then and get ready."

I sat back, picking at my food, and thinking about what I was doing. He was right. I had just texted a big group of them that I wanted to go out to the races with them. And I think I was even looking forward to it.

A sudden wave of grief rolled over me. I wanted to text my sister.

She always tried to tell me to go out more with her, but I started to go less and less until I never went at all. She still did, always asking me to go with her, but I never liked her friends, so it was hard to have any fun when I did try to go.

She would laugh if I told her what I was willingly doing tonight.

The weight on my chest wasn't easing, and I lost my appetite all at once.

"I'm going to go get ready," I said, cleaning up, shaking off the sadness and trying to stay excited to go. At least Ash, Scout, and Quinn would be there. Maybe I could try talking to them more. They might understand why I missed my sister more than Jax could.

"I need to grab my clothes and then I'll change in the bathroom."

He nodded, following me into the bedroom.

As I turned to go to the dresser, Riot ran in, hitting my legs and throwing me to the side.

Jax grabbed me, pulling me hard against his chest and keeping me upright.

"Thanks." I breathed, not looking any higher than his collar-bone. The tattoo on his chest was full of intricate details that I was pretty sure I could stare at for hours, but the small block lettering that only said 'forever' was the only thing keeping my attention right now.

"You're welcome," he said, still holding onto me.

"How are you already naked again?"

"I only took my shirt off. I'm not naked."

"Mmm, right," I said, my hand splaying out across his abs. I really was only doing it to push away from him, but the minute I felt them, I lingered. They were so solid. One part of me could only think about dropping down and running my tongue down them.

The other part of me was horrified that I even thought of that. "You can let me go now."

He pulled away with a knowing smile before heading to the closet as though nothing happened, but my entire body was on fire.

Jax was attractive. It was hard not to notice, especially with that smile that seemed to never leave his face, but I wasn't expecting to notice quite so much.

I couldn't get any ideas that anything was happening and expect him to be interested in me. He could have any girl he wanted, not one with literal truck loads of baggage, about twenty extra pounds on her body, and not anywhere near the sweet, cuddly woman that would better suit his constant sunshine attitude.

I knew all this, and knew that it wouldn't change, so every time I noticed just how good he looked, I would have to find a way to ignore it.

Since I never really cared about noticing guys and their looks, this could easily be controlled.

I glanced at the dresser, knowing the laptop was hidden away there and trying not to feel guilty. I still hadn't had the guts to open it up and look through everything on it. I was too worried about what I would find and too worried that they would be able to track me somehow if I did. If there was evidence to get Slaughter in trouble, I would have to pursue it, and right now, I didn't know if I could do that. The entire thing felt so over-whelming.

Worse than that, I wasn't sure if I could tell Jax what part I had played in it all. If they knew that I helped, even inadver-tently, they might worry that I was on Slaughter's side of all this and not want to help me anymore. And if I didn't have Jax's help right now, I had no other options.

I grabbed my clothes and headed to the bathroom, hoping that all of my body would calm down by the time I came back out, including my brain.

I had chosen one of my favorite outfits. I could probably get away with wearing whatever I wanted tonight, but after days in the apartment, and years hiding in my old room, I wanted to feel good and go out, even if it was only to drive around.

I slid on my skirt, the zipper off to the side and a harness garter on one leg. I pulled on my bra, which was half a harness too, the straps wrapping around my neck before trailing back down. Last, I grabbed my shirt, the low cut top showing off so much of the bra that it looked like an accessory. It took me ten more minutes to fix my hair and put on some makeup before I was ready.

I thought I looked good.

For the first time in a while, I felt good.

I walked out, finding Jax leaning against the back of the couch, scrolling through his phone. He was in his dark jeans and t-shirt, a leather jacket thrown on the couch next to him, and hated how good he looked with his damp hair and defined muscles. I shouldn't care about this. I shouldn't worry about how cute that ridiculous smile was going to be.

But I cared. Every part of me cared.

"Ready?" he asked before finally looking up. "*Fuck.*"

His stunned gaze roamed up and down my body, inspecting every inch of my outfit.

"Well fuck," he said again, getting up and coming closer. "What the hell is this? This looks like some sort of bondage outfit. It's that kink thing from before, isn't it?"

His eyes were wide as he mindlessly ran his fingers over the straps around my neck. The touch put me right back to where I was before.

So much for not bothering to notice him.

"It's a part of my bra."

His lips parted, and he pulled his hand back.

"Right. Wow."

"I really can't tell if that's a bad wow or a good wow."

"That's a good wow. I didn't know people wore these things in public. And wow, I also didn't know I was going out to get into fights all night. I should probably change out of my favorite shirt to avoid blood stains."

"And why would you be getting into fights?"

He waved his hand over me. "I don't think I have to say anything. Look in a mirror. You aren't going to be able to walk five feet without being hit on. *Repeatedly*. Have you been to any race night? Unsurprisingly, it's a hopped up testosterone and adrenaline party with men clawing to take a woman like you home." He grabbed his keys and headed to the door. "Fuck, I need to meet a girl," he mumbled, but I heard it clear enough. I didn't like that my heart fell at the words.

I didn't realize that I had been looking forward to hearing his compliments. That I was waiting for his face to light up like it seemed to do at everything else, but he was only frowning now. The deep curve of his lips was unnerving when I was so used to his smile.

I pulled my shoulders back and tried to forget it.

Not that it mattered. What he thought of me didn't matter. I repeated that four more times as I slid my shoes on.

"Ready?" he asked again, waiting as I stared at the open door.

"Yeah," I growled, stomping out the door in front of him. I went to the garage, not bothering to wait for him as I headed to his car.

Quinn and Ransom were still at their car. "Whoa, who pissed you off?" Quinn asked. "I guess that's a rhetorical question, considering you are staying with Jax. What did he say?"

"How do you know he said something?"

"Because Jax is gifted with saying and doing the wrong thing at the wrong time. We don't know how he does it, how he senses it, but it never fails," Ransom said.

"I can tell," I replied as Jax came down. Quinn gave him a pointed glare before getting in the car with Ransom.

"What was that about?" he asked, watching me over the roof of the car.

"Nothing. Are we going?"

"Are you riding with me?" he asked, making rejection shoot through me.

"Should I not? I can go with someone else."

"No, you should. I planned on you staying by me, but I didn't know if you were going to fight it based on the sudden attitude."

"I wasn't planning on it, but maybe I should," I said, getting into the passenger seat.

He got in the car with a smile. "Grumpy?"

"Annoyed."

"With me? How is that possible? I'm perfect," he said, the joking tone annoying me further.

"You are a perfect ass."

"I do have a perfect ass. Thank you for noticing. Most of the time, I understand what I say wrong, but this time, I really don't know what I did."

"Nothing."

"You know I was kidding, right? I'm not actually going out to fight. We are just going out to race a bit."

"Yeah, I figured as much."

"Then, I have no idea what I did, but you're stuck with me

all night, so you either better get over it, or tell me what's wrong."

He pulled out, following behind the rest of the crew as they turned onto the main road in a line before taking off. One by one, they sped up until we were right there behind them. No hesitant braking, no questions, just them driving together like I'm sure they had done a thousand times before. The calm confidence of it all brought me comfort and kept my anxiety at bay.

At least my anxiety with the fast cars.

"Nothing is wrong," I said, trying to take one deep breath for a more confident tone. "But I'm not sure what I'm supposed to do if you bring a girl back to the apartment. Do I stay with someone else? Do I have to ride back with you?" I asked, my nose scrunching at the thought. "No, that's not even an option. I'll get a ride with someone else, and I will absolutely stay with someone else. Scout is a little afraid of Riot, but maybe Kye will be fine with us for a night?"

He cocked his head towards me but didn't take his eyes off the road. His eyebrows were furrowed so hard that there was a crease between them. "What are you talking about? Bring a girl back? And why are you even insinuating you would stay with Kye? I know for a fact that I didn't say something so bad that you would want to go stay with him now."

"For a fact?"

"Okay, well, fair point, the confidence in that is wavering. I'm about eighty percent sure now," he said, smirking.

"You said that you need to find a girl, and I want to be clear on what I'm doing if that happens."

"I said that?" he asked, the crease forming again.

"Yes?"

"Oh. *Ohhh.*" He shook his head as we slowed down. "Shit, no. I didn't mean I was coming out to find a girl tonight. I just meant..." He shook his head harder. "I didn't mean it like I needed to run out and find someone to bring back to the apartment. I promise, I can handle not bringing a girl back while you are here. I don't really do that anyway. And in my defense here, your damn outfit got to my head."

"Do you really have a problem with my outfit? I thought it was cute."

"I never said it wasn't. Although cute is not the word that came to mind."

"What word came to mind?"

He was quiet, and my imagination ran wild with what he could say. None of them were good.

"Seductive. Tempting. Hot. Everything besides *cute*."

My eyebrows shot up, and I was speechless as we drove. I really didn't know what to make of him saying that, especially after he said that he would prefer someone other than me.

He pulled into an abandoned parking lot that was now overflowing with people, and came to a stop between Scout and Kye's cars.

"Stay around me, and if Slaughter or Tristan are here by some chance, we are leaving immediately."

"That part, I will not fight."

"Good, because I'm already prepared to piss you off if you don't want to listen."

"How exactly are you pissing me off this time?"

He parked and turned to face me. "I'll put that damn harness to good use and force you to come with me."

He looked so proud of his threat, but I wasn't falling for it.

"Prove it," I said, leaning in closer.

I was surprised when his finger hooked under the strap at my neck and pulled.

"Don't even think for a second that I won't follow through on what I say. I'm protecting you tonight and unless you want this to be used as a damn collar to drag you back to the car. Be a good girl and don't cause trouble."

"Don't patronize me."

"Don't act like these demands wouldn't keep you safer." He was so close now, his lips only a foot from mine, and I could smell the clean musky soap he used.

"*You* are a jerk."

"And *you* are a brat," he said, his lips twitching with a smile.

He was still holding on me, his finger hooked under the strap. My body flushed with heat and I couldn't help but bite down on my lip to find any other sensation besides…hot.

"Fuck, now I don't know if I'm threatening you or flirting. Come on. I need to race."

"And I need to get away from you," I mumbled as we got out of the car. Really, it felt more like I needed to get away so I wouldn't crawl all over him. I didn't know what was wrong with me, but I needed it to stop.

"That's not happening," he said, grabbing my arm. I tried to pull away, but he only held on tighter.

"Stay by me all night. Please, Carly, don't make me worry about you all night."

The problem was that I didn't want to be away from him, especially in this mess of street racing, but I hated my body's reaction to him. I looked him over, the concern in his eyes clear, but the genuine need to keep me safe only annoyed me further. He shouldn't want to do all these things for me, and I hated how cute I thought it all was. This strange attraction was one sided, and I needed to remember that. I let out a deep breath and relented, stepping closer to him.

"Fine. I'll stay by you all night."

"Thank you. Now, can we please go have fun?"

THIRTEEN
CARLY

I STAYED STUCK to Jax like glue as we looked around. I hated crowds, and this one was big enough to put me on edge.

"I thought you said this was a small race night?"

"It usually is. It looks like everyone had the same idea, and is out tonight since Thursday night probably won't happen with the heavy rain."

We barely made it another ten feet before someone stopped Jax.

The guy smiled and reached out, grabbing his hand in some dude style hand shake. I never understood how they all seemed to know what to do. Then again, it could only be my social anxiety, because I could make a regular handshake awkward, and there was no way I could be smooth about something as detailed as this.

"Looking to race?" he asked.

"Of course," Jax said, stepping back next to me.

"Perfect. We're mapping a new route here. Round the park here and follow it back. One lap to win."

"Sounds good. I'll be ready when they are."

The guy nodded. "Get ready. I'll check."

Jax turned back to his car, popping open the hood and shrugging off his jacket. I watched his arm flex as he leaned over the engine to check it over. There was something about the way each muscle moved that made me step closer, tempting me to reach out and touch every inch. Not that I could.

The crew headed our way, and I knew I had to snap out of it.

"Am I supposed to ride with you for racing, too?" I asked, trying to get my mind straight.

"No. You don't have to. Stay here with them," he said, stepping closer and leaning down with a grin. "You can watch me race. Sorry, my windows are tinted. I would love to have you staring at me like that more."

"I wasn't staring at you."

"You were, and practically drooling while doing it."

"I was not."

"Don't worry. I don't mind. If anything, I'll be on the edge of my seat waiting for it to happen again."

"It won't."

"Don't make promises you can't keep."

I only glared up at him, and he leaned back down. "I'll be gone for a few minutes, so stay close to the crew. Also, before you start comparing me to other racers that you know, even if I shamelessly win, it doesn't mean anything else is going to change about me or my attitude. I know you look for any comparison, but unlike the racers you know, I will be racing, and I will not be a huge asshole to you after. Or ever."

I rolled my eyes, looking annoyed, but I wasn't going to admit how badly I needed to hear those words.

Jax took off, heading to his car as Scout pulled me back to hers. She looked effortlessly cute in jeans and a shirt tonight, and I was surprised to find that I wasn't already lost in a rabbit hole of comparison between us. I didn't know if it was Scout's easy, friendly attitude or that I was finally getting better with my own insecurities, but there was some deep relief that I could just enjoy hanging out with her.

"Come on, we will have a good view here. Are you nervous watching races?"

"Not the races, but I do hate the crowd. I've been around the racing, so it doesn't bother me much."

"Perfect. Quinn was all uptight when she started watching Ransom race. She still gets worried about all of us, so I wasn't sure. Ash had been racing since she could walk, so it was all normal to her. Did you go to a lot of races with Slaughter and them?"

"As few as I could, but even that was still enough for me. I was really starting to assume it was all assholes and criminals that did this type of thing."

"But you're good with us and believe we aren't criminals because we race?" she asked, laughing.

"I wouldn't go *that* far," I said with a smirk. "But honestly, no. I'm trying not to. Jax has been nothing but amazing, but it's hard not to believe he won't become an asshole all of a sudden. Not when you have dealt with the type of people I have for so long."

"I will say that all of us can be assholes. Ransom can be a prick. Quinn gets a temper and so does Ash. Fox gets to be such a grumpy asshole we avoid him. Kye is worse than all of us, and I'm the first to get an attitude about anything, but Jax isn't like that. He never has been. Jax is just…good? Kind? Nothing truly pisses him off, at least not much that I've seen. You wouldn't think it with his dumb comments, but I don't know that there's any part of Jax that is, or could be, a true asshole. Not for more than five seconds, at least. And some of his comments are almost rude, but I really don't think he ever means them to be. I think he's really doing it to try to make us stop being assholes. Like our own buffer between being happy people and being grumpy jerks."

I watched as Jax's car idled at the starting line and I really wished he didn't have the tinted windows, because I suddenly wanted to see his smile. I was turning into such a sap.

"Yeah, he seems to like things calm and happy as much as possible. I think I get in the way of that," I said with a laugh.

"I think we all do," Scout said, laughing with me.

"Do you think he's going to win?"

"I think with you here there isn't a chance he's going to lose," she said as Quinn and Ash slid onto the hood next to us.

"No. Not a chance of him losing. He's dying to impress you. I think these guys compare their racing skills with their ability to give orgasms or something. If they win, somehow that means they impress you enough to get you," Quinn said.

"I really don't think that's what is happening here," I said with a nervous laugh as I watched Jax pull forward. "Is that what happened with Ransom?"

She gave a groan that said it all, but she wasn't going to stay silent. "He wishes. He basically bet me as a prize. I can't believe I fell for him."

"Maybe the winning races thing really does work? They did get both of us," Ash said.

"Lies," Scout said. "I've been watching them race and win for years and haven't fallen for any of them."

"That's because you see them as brothers. Watch a hot guy you could possibly like win a race and then prove us wrong because now I'm a little worried," Ash said, and turned to me. "Also, Jax trying to impress you is exactly what is happening here. Have you two not been flirting constantly? You're always smiling at each other."

"I haven't been flirting," I said, knowing it was a lie, but wishing it wasn't.

All three of them looked at me with eyebrows raised. "Are you sure about that?" Scout asked.

"Well, all I'm saying is that Jax is giving you a lot of attention, and I believe you are giving it back. Maybe we should be a little cautious about what these races do to our brains," Quinn said with a laugh.

"He might be giving me attention, but I don't know why, and honestly, I don't even know what to do with it."

Ash snorted. "He's giving you that attention now because he likes you. And attention from a hot, sweet guy like that? You take it. You *revel* in it," she said, making us all laugh as her head tipped back and she held out her arms.

"Okay, if you would have asked me when I first met Ransom, I would have felt the same as you, but now I'm with Ash on this. You definitely take the attention."

"I don't get how you know that, though. I'm sure I'm not Jax's type and I really don't think it's flirting. Maybe he's just being nice."

They looked at each other and then at me.

"It's flirting," Quinn said firmly. "Jax is nice to all of us, but there's a difference in how he is nice to you. Promise."

"And the difference is that he is absolutely flirting with you," Ash said.

"Even so. I don't know what to do about that. I'm not exactly experienced in the flirting department and don't know what to do with his attention."

"Alright, why am I getting the feeling there is more to this than what we are talking about? What do you mean exactly that you don't know what to do with that attention?" Ash asked.

They all looked at me, waiting for an answer.

The answer that I didn't like to tell anyone.

Then again, I never had a group of girls to hang out with that seemed so friendly, and it's not like we were going to be friends forever, so why not tell someone.

"I mean, that I have never had that much…attention anywhere near the bedroom. I have pretty much kept to myself and honestly, I have never wanted that type of attention from the guys I've been around."

"But you do now?" Quinn asked.

I looked back over at Jax's car. "I'm not sure yet, and anyway, I don't even know if that's an option."

"The man has eyes, Carly, and he hasn't stopped looking at you. I *promise*, it's an option."

I could feel the deep scowl come across my face. "It's hard to believe that."

The loud rev of engines caught all of our attention and we all looked over as the race was starting. Seconds went by before he took off, getting out in front of the other guy with ease.

"Watch out, Carly, might need to cover your eyes or something, just in case," Ash said.

I barely heard her as Jax went around the first turn, the back of it broke loose and, for a second, I was worried he was going to spin out, but it moved gracefully around the turn until he made it to the straightaway and took off again in a burst of speed. He hit the next turn and did the same, letting the car drift around it like it was the simplest thing in the world. The other car kept up, close enough that I wasn't sure who was going to come out in front after the turn.

"I don't think she's as superstitious as you two," Scout said.

"I'm pretty superstitious, but this is hard to look away from," I said.

"Uh, oh," Ash mumbled, but I ignored it. I already liked looking at Jax, and I liked talking to him. Being happy if he won his race wasn't going to suddenly make me fall for him.

The last curve came, and this one didn't look as easy. He

hooked the car again, sending it around in one smooth motion. The makeshift track turned farther into a curve, and it seemed to surprise both drivers as they moved quickly to correct their cars. As they straightened out, Jax sped up again, pushing the car faster until he was ahead of the other driver. This time, it was far enough that I knew he would win.

"Do you know how you can believe it for yourself that Jax is flirting?" Ash asked, looking at Quinn, her lips pursed in a grin.

"How?" I asked, scolding myself for how eager I sounded to find out.

"You go over there right now and see him."

"Why would that help?"

"Just see what he says. I bet you could have your answer by the end of the night."

They all looked at me, sly smiles on their faces as I got up.

"I'll talk to you all in a while," I said, walking away before they could say anything else.

"If this doesn't confirm our theory, I don't know what will," Quinn said as I walked away. I hadn't been to this exact place to race, but I knew the general idea of it. He was going to stop at the other end and check who won before heading back over to park.

I made it to the car as he stopped and rolled down the window with a smile.

"You won."

"Did you come over to celebrate?" he asked, eyebrows shooting up in surprise.

"No," I said, crossing my arms. "I only came over to say good job."

"You walked all the way over here to tell me something that could have waited until I drove back over?"

"Forget it," I huffed. I had been right, Jax hadn't been flirting with me. If the girls wanted proof, we had it now.

"Wait, I'm kidding. Come here," he said, moving the car up a few feet.

I spun back, but didn't match his smile.

"Why?"

"I was just messing with you because you're usually a grumpy little witch so I was excited that you came to see me."

I walked over, leaning down onto his window. "Well, I only walked over because you won your race."

He looked down, glancing at my chest that was inadvertently on display as I leaned over.

"You being nice might be just as bad for me as you being mean," he groaned. "Does this mean that if I'm a good boy, I get attention? What if I win again? A treat when we get home?"

I couldn't help but smile back at him. "No, that seems generous. Maybe a pat on the head or something."

His head tilted back, and he laughed, his eyes quickly finding mine again. "Come on, get in."

"I told you I can walk back."

"I know, but I don't want you to."

I didn't know if it was talking to the girls, or Jax's attitude, but I realized they could be right. I don't know that Jax was only being nice. It was a hard thing to wrap my head around, and while he made me feel confident, the moment I turned away from him, doubt crept in.

"Are you going to desperately miss me for the next three minutes?" I asked, trying to keep my tone light.

"Yes, I absolutely am. And if you're going to be all sweet and flirt with me while looking like that, there's plenty of room on my lap," he said, his ridiculous grin growing.

"I am not flirting, and I was only trying to be nice because you did good and won your race."

"Then I am about to be a very, *very* good boy and win you

another race to see what else I can get," he said with a wink. "Are you really trying to say that you aren't flirting with me?"

"I don't know. Are you?"

"Way more than I should be."

His answer was so fast that even my brain couldn't find a way to make it be a lie. My chest tightened, but I think it was from disbelief more than worry.

"Are you getting in?"

I shook my head no, not sure what would happen if I did get in. I was a little worried that being that close to him right now might lead to wanting a *lot* more.

"Fine, be stubborn. Just know my lap is very open and very comfortable," he said.

"Right. Super comfortable. So nothing is going to be poking into me?" I said, laughing as he started to pull away.

He stopped fast, his mouth falling open. "I can't believe you just called me out like that. And here I thought you were completely oblivious."

I only smiled, waving at him to go.

"Get over there and meet me at my car," he said, his face deadpan as he took off to circle around me and head back towards the crew.

Excitement shot through me. Maybe flirting with Jax before I left wasn't a bad thing, and maybe he was flirting back. Either way, I think Ash was right. By the end of the night, I was going to have my answer.

FOURTEEN
CARLY

I T WAS NO MORE than a hundred feet to get to the crew and the cars, but I knew he would still beat me there with how thick the crowd was now.

I made it halfway through the crowd when a pair of eyes locked onto me. He was around my age, but no one I could place. He did look a little mean though, his nose a little crooked and a faint bruise around one eye. My first thought was that he had to know Slaughter and Tristian.

Or he could know who I was.

That's why he was staring at me. He had to know me to look at me like that.

I tried to look around for Jax, but between the guy's height and the thick crowd, I couldn't see him clearly enough.

This could be nothing. He could be looking for someone else or just confused.

"Do I know you?" I finally asked, trying to look annoyed and hide the fact that my heart was about to explode with fear.

"I don't think so. You should, though."

"Why?"

"Pretty girl like yourself? Why wouldn't you?"

I took a big step back, my stomach churning. There was no way to know if he knew who I was or if he was looking for me. I moved to step around him and he blocked my path.

"Wait, don't go yet. We haven't officially met yet."

That gave me some relief. Maybe he didn't know who I was. I got up on my toes, trying to see Jax, but I could still barely make out his car from here.

I reached an arm up, trying to look for him. I knew Jax hadn't been joking when he called himself my bodyguard, but I really hoped he would be looking for me already.

Panic tore through me as the guy grabbed my raised arm. "What are you doing? Have somewhere to be?"

"Yes, let me go."

His arm slid around me, jerking me closer to him, as my arm dropped.

Before I could fight back, I was being ripped away.

"Get the fuck away from her," Jax's voice cut through the noise of the crowd and my pounding heart.

I could finally take a deep breath. Jax was there, pushing the guy back and ripping me away from him. His eyes were wild, and I could tell he was ready for a fight. Every muscle tensed and pulled back, ready to spring forward. He was terrifying and comforting. I knew he could be violent. Hitting Tristan was proof enough of that, but so far, he had only been violent for me, not against me.

"What the fuck? Why are you pushing people like that?"

"Get away from her. Why are you bothering her?"

"Hell, I don't know. She looked hot and all alone. Figured she wanted some company."

"Yeah, well, she doesn't, so go."

"Oh, come on, dude. She was fine before you got here."

Jax stepped forward. "One more fucking comment and your

nose will be broken. *Again*, I assume," he said, waving at the guy's *very* crooked nose.

"Damn man. I'm going."

The guy walked off and Jax turned to me. "Shit. Are you okay?"

I stepped back in the direction of the car. "Yeah. Maybe."

I could hear the unease in my own voice, but I couldn't find the words for why I wasn't okay. It was seconds of being left there, wondering if the guy was coming to find me, trying to figure out what he was doing, and wondering if I would be dragged back to Slaughter, kicking and screaming.

Seconds of having no control over my life again.

I hadn't realized the freedom that had come with staying with Jax, the safety I had felt around him and his friends for the first time in a very long time. The feeling that it could all be over in seconds, and I couldn't do anything but look for Jax.

It had only been a week and a half of my life, but somehow all the good Jax was bringing was erasing the bad so fast that I forgot that it wasn't real. That it would all be over and I would once again be alone and running from that danger by myself.

It was too comfortable. I needed to end it before I lost my sense of survival any further.

I made it back to the car before Jax caught me. He grabbed my arms, spinning me to face him as he backed me against the car.

I could still see the angry pinch to his lips and wild eyes.

Tears were threatening me and all I wanted to do was be wrapped up in his arms, but I couldn't be that pathetic.

The guy hadn't done anything to me, really, not compared to the horrible things I had been imagining.

"What's wrong? Did he hurt you?" Jax asked. "If he hurt you, tell me now before he gets any farther away."

"No, he didn't. I think he was trying to hit on me."

"Fuck. I'm sorry. I figured you would be okay for the short walk. Then again, I did know that outfit was going to cause a few people to stop you," he said, trying to smile, but I didn't reciprocate.

He moved to hug me, but I stepped back. I didn't know why. I wanted him around me, but I couldn't count on him to comfort me. I needed to keep doing that myself.

"Carly?" he asked. His face had fallen, softer now, sweeter, with every trace of the angry, ready-to-punch-someone look gone.

"It's fine. I just want to get in the car." I pulled at the handle, but the door was still locked. "*Please.*"

He stepped closer again, moving to open the door, but a loud popping broke out behind him.

I jumped, mindlessly moving closer to him, and he didn't hesitate to wrap his arms around me, pushing me against the car.

"It was backfire from a car. You are all jumpy now." He moved to touch my face, but I pushed at his chest before he had a chance, angrier at myself.

"I know. I just want to get in for a minute." I wanted the safety of the car, not him.

The anger that crossed his face made me more upset.

"Yeah, of course." He hit the button and reached to open the door. Every part of me was scolding myself for relying on him. He was handing me everything I needed, and I was taking it. Now it wasn't only a place to live and help with my truck, it was relying on him to protect me, to comfort me.

Somehow I couldn't remind myself enough that I barely knew him. That I shouldn't be flirting or wanting him to flirt with me. I didn't want love or need it. What I wanted was to get away from everyone and go back to the safety that comes with being alone.

I slid inside and took a deep breath, the peaceful silence washing over me before Jax got in too.

"You have to tell me what's going on," he said, grabbing the steering wheel but not moving.

"Nothing. I just want to leave. I'll sit here until you're ready to go."

"No. We aren't moving until you tell me what's wrong. You said he didn't hurt you, but you're acting like he did."

"I can't tell you what's wrong."

"Why not?"

I was quiet, still holding back tears. I was never this emotional, at least not in front of people, but now this seemed to be a common occurrence around him.

"I don't know how."

"Try," he said, and I could hear the anger in his tone. I don't care what anyone said. Jax could get angry. Everyone could.

"I'm freaked out about Slaughter finding me, obviously. I thought I would be okay tonight, but then that guy stopped me, and that's not a big deal on its own, but I froze. I was looking for you instead of doing something about it myself."

He gave a harsh laugh. "And what were you going to do about it if you were alone? Fight him?"

"I don't know, but shouldn't I know that? I need you to stay back and not be my safety net. I feel like I can't even handle things myself because I'm counting on you. I didn't do anything when that guy stopped me. I only looked for you. What am I supposed to do when I *am* alone again? I need to leave and not forget how to be on my own. I need to keep my distance."

"So, what are you saying? You like me being there for you too much? Like being around me, being safe? Like living with me?"

"Yeah…kind of," I said.

He was silent, but I could see the anger there.

"You can't leave yet. I'm not done with your truck, but fine. Considering what I was just planning to do, it would probably be best for both of us to keep our distance."

My heart sank, and I didn't know why. He was allowed to want that too, but the sudden idea that I will be losing his easy smile and that one day soon it would all be gone was depressing.

He grumbled about something, but I couldn't make out the words.

"What?"

"I said, I'm going to race again, so decide if you're staying in the car or not."

"Not."

"Then *actually* stay with the crew this time. If another guy tries to touch you, I *will* break his face this time, regardless of how strong and independent you want to be."

I got out, rushing to sit back with the girls.

"You good?" Scout asked.

"Yeah. Yeah, I'm okay. Pretty sure you were wrong about Jax not getting mad, though. I think he's really pissed off this time."

They all looked, watching as Jax made it to the starting line again, seemingly cutting in the line to take a turn.

I knew I pissed him off.

I knew I needed to follow through and keep my distance from him, but it didn't stop the racing in my chest as he lined up, or when he won again, or when he parked and brushed past me.

My heart stopped as he leaned against the hood of Ransom's car to talk before a girl walked up. She immediately wrapped a hand around his arm. I watched as each finger moved around his bicep, making me want to rip them off, one by one.

Before I could do anything, though, Jax was pulling her hand off and shaking his head, saying something that had her rolling her eyes and walking away.

Then he looked at me, his eyes hard as they met mine, before turning back to Ransom.

As upset as I was at him, as much as I remembered we were staying away, I was excited knowing that I would still be going back to his apartment with him tonight. That it would be us alone in the car going home, even if we weren't talking. That he blew that girl off and looked at me.

I was telling him to keep our distance, but I was still excited that he would be staying with me tonight.

And for that, I didn't hate him. I hated myself.

FIFTEEN
CARLY

JAX and I had barely spoken since the night at the races. We had made it two days now with only one word answers, and both of us stopping ourselves when we went to talk more.

At one point last night, he went to put on a movie and only pointed at the tv to ask if I wanted to watch it. I had nodded back, and that had been our entire conversation.

I had spent years in my house talking as little as possible, but now, not talking to Jax was one step away from torture. I wanted to tell him about what I wanted to cook. I wanted to ask about his chest. I wanted to hear how my truck was and hear him tell me about the crew or what ridiculous thing one of them said that day. I was getting so used to sitting together every morning that I actually missed it. My truck still wasn't done, but I was asking about it less and less.

Especially considering he brought me a cup of coffee every single morning, which was pretty much a dream come true.

I wanted to hit my head against the wall as I realized that I missed the person that I was living with.

My phone chimed as more texts came through on the group

chat, but I couldn't bring myself to say anything on it. I *had* noticed Jax was texting on it more, though. Sending photos and funny comments throughout the day, and I was pathetically hoping they were actually for me.

I didn't think we were fighting each other necessarily, but we had both agreed to keep our distance and seemed to be sticking to that.

It sucked.

It took me the entire day yesterday just to unravel my thoughts and all morning today to realize how badly I handled my freak out. I wasn't wrong in knowing that I needed to put a little distance between us, but he wasn't doing anything wrong. It's more that he was doing everything right.

I still hadn't told him about the laptop, and each day that went on only made me feel more guilty about it. I thought I knew most of what was on that laptop, files and files of paperwork that would show the cars they stole, and who they sold them to. It was Slaughter's way of keeping track of his 'business' and his clients. It was information he wouldn't share with anyone else, even the guys at his shop, because it was too incriminating.

I was putting them all in a position that could get them hurt, and I hated it. Then, when I thought I could possibly be forced back to help Slaughter, I freaked out and took it out on the one person who seemed willing to do anything to help me.

And the forever-helpful Jax even gave me the space I asked for, and I hated that part more than I expected.

I was hoping that an apology and a really, really good dinner might make things go back to normal for us, but it all went to hell halfway through cooking.

I had opened a can of tomato puree to make sauce when it slipped and crashed to the floor, covering it in red. Of course Riot heard the can drop and came in, grabbing the can and running around the apartment. Before I even had a chance to catch him, he shook his head, red splattering over the front door and everything in a five-foot radius. I watched in horror until he slowed, knowing that chasing him would only make it a game.

I thought it was over when he finally dropped the can, but then he ran to the couch, his sauce covered feet leaving perfect sauce footprints across it.

"Riot!" I screamed, finally able to grab him and drag him into the bathroom, slamming the door.

The apartment was a wreck, sauce everywhere, the couch stained in red along with what looked like a crime scene at the front door.

I knew Jax hated the mess, and this wasn't going to help my whole 'lets be friends' apology. I knew he would be home any minute now, so there was no way I was going to get it all cleaned up before he saw it. So much for making things better. Somehow, I managed to make everything worse.

I raced for the bucket and rags, trying to get the couch cleaned first, hoping it wouldn't permanently stain the brown leather. Seconds later, the door swung open, and I ducked behind the couch.

The room was silent for a second as he walked in, and I squeezed my eyes shut.

"What the fuck? Carly?" Jax yelled into the apartment. "Carly, you better answer me, or I'm going to assume this is all blood. Please tell me this isn't blood."

"Not blood. Tomato sauce," I said, popping up from behind the couch.

His jaw dropped open. "Tomato sauce?"

"Yeah. I was cooking and...dropped it."

"Dropped it or threw it around the apartment?"

"Dropped it, but then Riot grabbed it and, well...this happened."

He finally moved, and I froze, watching as he dropped his

keys into the tray and took off his button up mechanic shirt. I was expecting a shirt on underneath, but once again there was nothing except a tattooed chest and abs. The sight of it made me lose my train of thought for a second before reality hit again.

"I'll clean it. I am now. I'll make sure you can't even tell what happened."

"Yeah," he said with a huff, trying to navigate around the sauce to the stool to take his boots off.

I went back to scrubbing and moved to the floor before either of us spoke again. He had grabbed a rag and was wiping down the door.

"I know we aren't talking and all that, but I don't need help. I'll take care of it. Please. I was trying to be nice and make dinner, not make you clean up."

"No, but apparently Riot was," he said with a quiet laugh. "You were trying to be nice and cook me dinner?"

"Yeah," I said, not looking away from him. I didn't want to lose my nerve. "I wanted to talk to you."

"About what?"

"Anything."

He finally smiled, the dimples showing. "Are you trying to say that you missed me?"

I scowled harder. "No, because missing someone that I live with is ridiculous."

"Then call me ridiculous because I've wanted to talk to you all fucking day." I knew my face softened, but I refused to smile. Maybe he only wanted to tell me to leave.

"Really? Why didn't you?"

"Because you wanted your space, and I know that it's better for both of us if we do keep that distance."

"I know why I want to keep my distance, but why do you?"

He went back to scrubbing the door. "Because you are going to leave and I don't think I am going to want you to," he said, not looking at me. "I didn't even like going two days without talking to you, even though I still got to see you. Unfortunately for me. I get attached to my friends and I like keeping them around. Hence, the apartment building we share."

"So we *are* friends now?"

"I like to think so," he said. "Do you really think I'm going to be happy when you leave?"

"No, I guess not," I said, taking a deep breath and wanting to look anywhere but at him. "So what do we do?"

"We clean up."

"And then?"

"Maybe we deal with that after? I currently want to pass out because of how disgusting all of this sauce is," he said with a smile.

I finally smiled back. "Yeah, we can do that, but seriously, you can sit down. I will clean this all up. It's my fault."

"It's technically Riot's fault," he said with a small laugh. "And you think I'm going to sit there and watch you clean? Should I start calling you Cinderella, too?" He turned, wiping more of the red sauce off the white door.

"Jax, you really don't have to," I said, trying to stop him. He seemed to ignore me, carrying on.

"Although with your dark, strange clothes and black hair, I really don't think you can pass as Cinderella. Maybe a seductive Snow White? And what would that make me in the story? I'm obviously choosing to be the charming prince," he said, his easy tone back again.

"Seductive Snow White?"

"Yeah, I would say you could be the villain witch, but they are usually not nearly as hot."

"Thanks. I think?"

He laughed harder as I started mopping the floor. "It's meant to be a compliment."

I wasn't going to add that I probably weighed close to two Snow Whites, and that fact probably disqualified me from being compared to any princess.

We finished up quickly between the two of us. Jax sat back on the stool, his jeans still hanging low on his hips, and I could see the bruise on his chest had lightened but was still there.

"Do you want me to put something on that later?" I asked, nodding to his chest.

He looked down at it, and back at me. The corners of his mouth turned up, but I could tell he was trying to stop it. "That would be amazing."

"I was a little worried this was going to be the final straw for you. I assumed me and Riot would be on the street by the end of the day."

"You think I would kick you out over sauce?"

"No…Okay maybe, but only because we already seemed to be on thin ice."

"Come here," he said, leaning forward and reaching for me. As soon as I was close enough, his arms wrapped around me, pulling me between his legs until I was against him.

"It's okay," he said. "It's just a mess. It's not a big deal."

I stayed frozen in his arms, feeling a little self conscious, and honestly still a little worried. "You aren't mad?"

"No. Not mad, just tired and I'm sure as hell not going to make you leave over sauce. How could you even think that?" he said with a laugh. My body relaxed, falling against him with a deep breath, but he held on. "Forget it. I already know why. And I wasn't mad at you before this either. Maybe a little upset at the races, but only because what you said made sense."

"So you think that we should keep our distance?"

"We can try."

I nodded against him, my body finally relaxing. "I didn't mean to make the apartment a crime scene."

He laughed again, the sound soothing, after all the bad ways this could have turned out. "I'm still glad it wasn't blood. That part gave me a heart attack."

"Did you really think it was?" I asked.

"I had a full thirty-seconds of worrying I was going to find you killed in here," he said with a shudder. "I don't know how I could live here any more."

"A bit of bleach and you would never know."

"You're morbid."

It was my turn to smile. "I should finish cleaning and cooking dinner."

I went to move, but he leaned on me further. "I'm ready for bed."

"Isn't everyone coming here to eat?"

"Yeah, they are literally begging for your food, so instead of going to bed I am going to help you clean Riot, and cook, and then hopefully eat. Where is Riot exactly?" he asked, before a bark came from the bathroom. "Ahh."

"I haven't even looked in there yet."

He groaned, kissing my forehead before dropping his arms.

"Dinner can be saved, right? I'm starving."

"It's all still usable. But we might have to use a difference sauce," I said,

"Fine by me. After this, I don't think either of us will want anything with tomato sauce for a while. To add to that, I would prefer a less disgusting sauce being thrown around the room next time."

"I don't think I can handle a next time," I said, making him smile more.

An hour later, Riot was bathed, Jax had changed, and I headed back into the kitchen to finish dinner as Jax finally sat down.

He laid his head down on the counter. "You know, I get why

you freak out about fights. Everything in my life growing up would cause a massive fight. One wrong move and a full on screaming match broke out. Is that why you haven't talked to me since the races? You thought I would blow up at you?"

"Kind of? The girls did say you rarely get mad, so when you did actually get mad, I figured I pushed you too far. I mean, part of me understands that you aren't a violent or angry person, but the other part of me is just waiting for that shoe to drop, you know? Like, what is going to set you off to become that person?"

"And you were mad that I pushed that guy away and threatened him?"

"No, but I was mad that I was counting on you to do that. I was also mad that you feel like you have to be my bodyguard all the time. I need to be able to take care of myself. And you weren't doing it because the guy was hitting on me. You were doing it because you thought he might have something to do with Slaughter. Not that I blame you, I was a little worried about that myself at first, so I really had no right to be rude to you."

I didn't catch my own words until I looked over at Jax's growing smile. The pure joy on his face making me contemplate what I said.

And before I could take it back, he was already starting in on me.

"You were mad that I saved you from that guy because I was worried, not because I was jealous?" He was up, coming around the counter and cornering me in the kitchen. "You wanted me to do it because I was jealous that another guy was hitting on you?"

"What? No, that's not it at all. I was just meaning —"

"You said that you were mad that I was doing it out of bodyguard duties, and not because I was jealous."

"I didn't exactly mean it like that."

He stepped close enough to touch me but didn't reach out, the winning smirk still on his face. "Who said I wasn't jealous?"

"You did?"

"No, I never said anything like that. If you would have asked, I would have said that the way he was gawking at you was pissing me off more than anything else. And the way he grabbed you made me want to cut his arm off. For someone who really doesn't like resorting to violence, that being my first thought really says a lot. And I get that you might have never had someone that wants to keep you safe, but me doing that doesn't mean that you suddenly can't defend yourself. I would argue that you can defend yourself a little *too* well. It just means you get a break while you're with me. That I will look over your shoulder and have your back so that you can enjoy your night." He shook his head, the grin spreading back across his face. "I already knew my entire night was going to be filled with getting jealous when you chose that stupidly hot outfit. Then my grumpy little witch came over to flirt with me? You were smiling and flirting with *me*, and I was losing my fucking mind. By the time he came up, I was already about to use that harness thing to drag you away, and then he touched you and I saw red. This is amazing. You were mad because you thought I wasn't jealous? Meaning that you liked that I was."

"No, I —"

He leaned down, cutting me off as his face came close to mine.

He was about to kiss me. He had to be.

I almost leaned in, but the front door slammed open before I could, making me jump away.

"Sorry, I —"

"Don't be. I'm in no rush," he said, smiling as the apartment filled with noise.

And without another word, he walked out, talking to everyone as they sat down, leaving me to finish cooking in my own silence as I tried to calm down.

SIXTEEN
JAX

MY DAY HAD SUCKED, and coming home to that mess sucked even more. I was exhausted. Two days of barely talking to her had me sleeping like shit and feeling even worse all day. I couldn't stand the underlying tension every second until she finally said something. There was a reason I always tried to defuse tense situations. I couldn't handle them. Years of living in a tension-filled home always made any strained situation immediately fill me with dread.

It made it worse that I had agreed to it. I told her that we needed to keep our distance and I knew I was right, but I was already failing. The crew was here now, all of them sprawled out on the couch, talking as they waited for Carly to finish. Everyone had offered to help, but she was adamant that she didn't want anyone else in the kitchen. Not that I blamed her. It wasn't that big of an area.

As I walked back into the kitchen to grab more dishes to carry out, she gave me one more reason why I couldn't stay away.

I stood frozen, watching as she pulled her finger into her mouth, sucking off whatever sauce she had on it before sliding it back out. My dick jumped in response, and I was beginning to think that everything she did was to torture me.

"Can you stop staring at me and come taste this?"

"No, I can't stop staring at you, but yes. Taste testing is my specialty."

"I thought body guarding was your specialty."

I moved behind her, her long hair thrown over one shoulder, showing off her neck. Great, now necks were turning me on.

"I'm a man of many talents," I said, leaning down to taste whatever it was she was stirring. "I don't know what it's supposed to taste like, but it tastes amazing either way."

"It's a garlic sauce, and perfect. Everything is done then." I stayed right behind her, and it was the wrong choice.

I knew it the second I leaned back in and let my hands move down to her hips. I leaned down further, running my nose along the side of her neck up to her ear, careful that my lips didn't touch her yet. I could feel her freeze for a second before she moved back just enough that I could tell.

It was enough of an opening and I dropped back down, pressing my lips to the side of her neck. I heard her sharp intake of breath and did it again, moving up an inch and kissing her neck again.

"Jax," she whispered. "Should you really be doing that?"

"No," I whispered back. "I definitely shouldn't be, but I don't want to stop."

I flicked my tongue out, running it along her ear before pulling the lobe in between my teeth.

"Jax," she gasped, the cry of my name only making me harder, but I knew it was loud enough that everyone probably heard.

Loud enough that I remembered that everyone was right on the other side of the little wall that hiding us in the kitchen.

"You're going to get us caught," I said.

She ducked under my arm, spinning to face me as her chest heaved. "Then we won't do anything that we could be caught doing."

Her phone pinged, pulling my thoughts back to reality as I looked at her. She was in another black t-shirt–this one had light purple lips with vampire teeth and said *feelings suck*—and black leggings that made me stop and lose my focus.

The phone went off a few times, and I glanced at her. "You getting that?"

"I wasn't going to."

"Why? Who is it?"

"The only person that has my number and isn't in this building."

"Raf?"

"Raf."

The jealousy erupted, but I didn't move or make a sound. I couldn't believe how jealous I was again. It's not like I didn't already know I was a jealous person, but now it was showing in the ugliest ways and the most inopportune times. I couldn't be jealous of another guy talking to her.

She wasn't mine.

Even if I had just been kissing her neck and making her say my name.

"Playing hard to get?"

"More like playing impossible to want. My indifference to dating and love has become an art form."

Kye walked in, catching the last of it. "Hey! Me too!" he said as he grabbed a drink from the fridge. "If you ever want to exchange notes on how to keep people away, let me know."

She laughed and grabbed plates, still ignoring her phone.

"Can I silence that? The pinging is going to drive me out of my mind."

"Sure. You can just turn it off," she said with a shrug, telling Kye what to carry and walking out.

Her phone didn't have a password on it so I reached up, snapping a photo of myself and quickly setting it as her lock screen before shutting it off.

She walked back in, eyeing me as she grabbed more stuff to carry out, and I did too.

I set everything down and quickly filled up a plate, Scout coming up next to me to look over all the options.

"Mmmm, that smells delicious."

Carly smiled at her. "Good, because I made enough for all of you and didn't want it wasted."

Scout looked over my overflowing plate. "Are you sure about that?"

"Hey, I'm hungry. I didn't even eat lunch. And I'm tired too, so lay off."

"Alright, don't bite my head off. I just want to make sure there's enough for me."

"I was hoping you guys wouldn't show and I would have this all to myself," I said.

"You wanted this all for yourself?" Fox asked. "This could feed the whole fucking block."

I shrugged. "I would obviously make it last me a day, maybe even two."

I sat back on the couch with my plate and Kye sat down next to me. "We have a chef move in and you think you get her all to yourself?"

I shot him a glare, biting my tongue before I called her mine. But hell if I didn't *want* her all to myself. I was starting to worry that there would be no keeping my distance. That I would be falling for her faster than I could stop myself, and even after getting burned so many times in the past, I was worried I wouldn't even care now. She wasn't afraid to tell me what's on her mind or if she thought I was being ridiculous and that somehow made it all feel better.

"Please, you guys have to understand that I'm not a chef," Carly said.

"Your food begs to differ," I said between bites. A thrill ran through me as she sat down close to me. I shook my head, scolding myself. I was being pathetic now. She wasn't even touching me. It was as close as anyone else in the room would have sat, but yet I couldn't stop thinking about it.

"Hey, I wanted to talk to everyone. I had an idea," Ash said, half of us responding in groans immediately. "Oh shut up, you will like this one."

"You guys should be thankful for our ideas," Quinn said. "You all had no manners and at least now you can sit through a dinner without turning into heathens. And Ash was right about that time she said you needed some new clothes. Plus, I didn't hear any one of you complaining when the girls at the store couldn't keep their eyes, and *hands*, off of you all."

"Very true," Ransom said. "I didn't mind that part at all."

"You didn't mind another woman rubbing all over you?"

He threw an arm around her. "I didn't mind you all riled up and jealous."

"What do you want now, Ash?" I said, not needing anymore of this loving couple shit when I wanted so badly to pull Carly against me.

"I want to go away for the weekend. I thought with Carly all locked up here, it would be fun to get away, plus we really haven't gone on a vacation together. We could rent a cabin in the mountains and we could go. No one will recognize Carly there so we could actually hang out, go into town, be normal for a long weekend."

"I'm in," Scout yelled with a smile.

"Me too. I need a break from life, and that sounds perfect. Carly? Want to come hang out with all of us in another house, but this time in the woods?" Quinn said.

I looked at her, waiting for her to say no, but she smiled. "That actually sounds amazing."

"Perfect, and don't worry. I'll book one with a hot tub," Ash yelled, dancing as she pulled out her phone.

"And us guys are invited, right?" Fox asked.

Ash patted his arm. "Of course, babe, although now that you mention it, a girls' weekend could be fun."

He groaned. "No, it wasn't a suggestion. We are going."

I didn't say anything, but had to agree with him. Leaving Carly to go to a romantic cabin in the woods without me seemed...depressing.

The thought of being alone in my apartment again was even more depressing.

She had been worried that getting closer to me was going to make it harder to go out on her own again, but I hadn't really thought of what it would be like here when she leaves. Not until right at this moment.

Going back to no Carly and no Riot again, being alone at night and every morning? It sounded miserable.

I tried not to look at Carly, but failed, catching her green eyes that I was surprised to find were looking at me like she was waiting for more of an answer, but I couldn't give one.

Even if she could find a way to distance herself from me, I wasn't sure if I could do the same.

"Great," Ash said. "Keep the garage closed for a long weekend and we will leave in the morning. We're going on vacation!"

———

KYE STILL LINGERED HERE, sitting on the couch with Carly as they talked about watching a movie.

It shouldn't be, but him sticking around was starting to annoy me.

"I'm going to shower. I didn't get a chance earlier," I said, grabbing a change of clothes and shutting myself in the bathroom.

I had been so close to kissing her, so close to crossing that line, until everyone interrupted. I was hoping we would pick up right where we left off, but now Kye was staying, and by the time the movie ended, she was going to be passed out.

I know I needed to stick to my word and keep my distance, but it was hard to care about patience when she looked at my lips and licked her own.

I showered and changed fast, but froze when I heard Kye's voice.

"*Finally.* I have someone else around here who likes horror movies," Kye said. "Trying to get them to go see the last one in theaters was like pulling teeth and I'm not even going to tell you who left the theater midway through."

"I'm guessing Jax?" Carly said, and I smiled. Even if she didn't want to admit it, she knew me pretty well already.

Kye laughed. "And Quinn. They would cut someone in a heartbeat but not watch a scary movie? I wasn't even going to attempt to watch this with any of them."

"With the comments I've heard, I'm almost worried if I will sit through this," Carly said, and that shocked me. I figured she would watch any scary, gory thing she could get her hands on.

"Let's hope. If you liked the first one, I think you could handle this one."

"I'm surprised you wanted to watch this tonight. I figured

you would have a date or be out racing or something," Carly said and I smacked my own chest, the jealousy rising up. Was she hinting at learning more about Kye's dating life? Kye rarely dated, so it hadn't even occurred to me that there could be something with them. Although, now I could see that they had things in common.

"Waiting on a part for my car, and no, I don't date, so no problems there."

"Date, sleep around. You know what I meant."

"Don't sleep around either. I'm not a big touchy person," Kye said.

He wasn't kidding. The guy hated to be touched unless necessary. We all could hug him and whatever, but he even tried to avoid that. I really couldn't wrap my head around not wanting someone's touch, but I knew how he grew up was different from me.

"Yeah, I get that. I'm not either."

"No, like, I can't stand being touched. I mean, I'm fine with the crew around and touching me sparingly, but even that makes my skin crawl sometimes. I can't stand it when it's someone I don't know."

"Oh," she said, and I was mad that I couldn't decipher the tone, and my horrible mind went right to thinking she could be disappointed. "That's really not what I was expecting."

"Yeah, it makes sleeping around a little awkward. Like, please don't touch me, but sure we can sleep together. A logistical nightmare. Surprisingly, girls do not find that to be a turn on." His tone was light, almost joking, and I was surprised Kye didn't mind her asking. He didn't really talk to anyone about it. He knew his issues got in the way of relationships, but he really didn't seem to mind at all. We've all asked and offered what help we could, but he made it clear that he truly doesn't care and doesn't need it fixed.

The room was silent before Carly burst into laughter. It only made me smile. I knew Kye would appreciate her not feeling sorry for him, and it only made me happy that she could be herself.

"I'm sorry. I'm so sorry. It's not funny, but the mechanics of that. Have you ever been able to even do that?" She asked. "No, sorry, you don't have to answer that."

"I have, but thank you for the concern," he said, but I could tell he was smiling. "I've only told a handful of people, but I can honestly say that no one has ever started laughing that hard."

"I'm really sorry. But I never expected that from you. You're the tall, dangerous, handsome type with all the tattoos and piercings, and I know some guys like you, they are complete womanizers. I was assuming you were, too. Sorry for laughing and making assumptions."

"No problem to both. I know what I look like. It makes it easier to stay away from people when the way you look makes people want to stay away from you."

Hearing her call Kye handsome was enough for me to pull open the door and stalk out. I left my shirt off on purpose this time, knowing she liked to stare and didn't miss when her eyes flew to me half naked.

"What are you guys watching? Wait, let me guess. Serial killer at a cabin in the woods?" I asked, seeing the title.

Carly's smile grew as she turned back to the TV and I saw Riot was draped over Kye's lap.

"How did you know?" she asked.

"You are a dark little witch and Kye almost exclusively watches horror movies. Most people would not want to watch a slasher film based at a remote cabin when they are the ones going to a similar place, but here you two are."

She leaned back, getting comfortable. "Well, I think Kye

could scare off most people and I'm different. I have a personal bodyguard."

"True. Although, I don't know how to feel about having to now protect you from serial killers. That seems like a whole different level of bodyguard."

"You're the one who volunteered for the position."

Kye shook his head. "That was your first mistake. It's every man for himself in these movies."

I fell back on the couch next to her, trying to get close enough that I could smell the lavender scent she always had.

"In my defense," I said, keeping my voice down. "I was hoping you would actually be touching my body more."

She looked over, her mouth falling open with a grin. "I suddenly don't think you understand what a bodyguard is and now I'm concerned."

I laughed, shaking my head. "I do, but I thought there would be more clinging to my body and crawling into bed when the nightmares came," I said with a wink.

I could see the red bloom across her nose and cheeks and I wished I was close enough to see it mix with her freckles and kiss every single one of them.

She turned back to the movie fast, not looking over at me again, but I still watched her.

Kye asked her something about the movie, and another one they both loved. I was relieved when that didn't make me jealous, only happy. I wanted her to like my friends. I wanted her to feel comfortable here. Granted, I was a little surprised that she was getting along the most with Kye, of all people, but I shouldn't be. He was a pretty weird person, and she seemed to like that.

I moved until I was close enough to lean against her, my lips inches from her ear. The small, sharp intake of breath got to me again, and I leaned in even more.

"Leaving for the weekend might set me back a few days on your truck."

"And?"

"And that would mean you would have to stay longer."

"Oh," she said, not looking over at me. I wanted her to though. I wanted to know what she was thinking as her face pinched. I couldn't imagine that staying here was *that* bad. "I don't want to invade your space any longer than I have."

"What if I said that I like my space being invaded?"

That got me an annoyed eye roll, but I would take that reaction over the pained one she had a moment ago.

"I wouldn't believe you."

"Why would I lie?"

"If you two don't stop whispering about things, I'm going to turn it up to drown you out."

The door slammed shut behind us as Scout walked in. "Hey. Kye said you were watching a movie."

"Yeah," I said, as Scout rolled onto the couch. I was about to be annoyed that they were still there, but it made moving closer to Carly about ten times less obvious.

"Can we stop talking and watch the movie?" she whispered.

"Yes, but for the next hour and a half, you are *my* bodyguard because I have to watch a serial killer chase people around the woods, all while realizing that will be me tomorrow."

"Always dramatic."

"Where would the fun be if I wasn't?"

"I'm watching my movie, Jax, and if you're going to invade my space, you are going to do it quietly."

"Alright, brat," I said, moving in closer as I leaned back.

I could hear her suck in a harsh breath before blowing it out slowly, and I loved every second.

I wanted to make her breath unsteady like that a thousand more times.

I also loved the way her eyes drifted from the movie to me, over and over

"Jax, I told you —"

"Shhh, I'm watching a movie."

I knew she was staring daggers at me, but I kept my eyes on the TV, smiling the entire time.

SEVENTEEN

CARLY

I TRIED TO FALL ASLEEP, but the thunder rolled endlessly, shaking the building, which I couldn't imagine was an easy feat. We didn't have horrible storms often, but when we did, they came through with a vengeance.

I told myself I was fine, but streaks of lightning lit up the room, making me think of every horror movie where the killer is seen in that sliver of a lightning strike. It would be the perfect night for a serial killer to show up and drag me away, the thunder covering my screams.

I was losing it, sitting in the quiet as I ran through every horrible thought.

"Jax?" I hissed into the dark living room. I knew his door was open and if he was awake, he would be able to hear me. I sat up, the thunder rolling again.

"Jax," I hissed again.

"Are you moaning my name in your sleep or do you actually need me?" he asked, the deep rumble of his voice sending a shiver through me.

"I am fully awake. I wanted to know if you were."

"I haven't been to sleep."

"What are you doing?"

"Reading."

"Reading what?"

"None of your business," he said, and I could almost hear the smile that I knew was on his lips. "What's wrong?"

The thunder rolled and lightning cracked, making me shriek.

"What's wrong little witch, that scary movie getting to you?" he asked, the lightning illuminating his form as he filled the doorway to his bedroom.

"No, geez, you look like the killer in the slasher movie. Hanging out in the doorway on a dark and stormy night," I said, waiting seconds before the room lit up again. This time I could see that he was shirtless, a pair of sweatpants hanging off his hips.

"Should I assume you're into that type of thing? Do you like me even more now?"

"Even more? Who said I liked you in the first place?" I said, smiling into the dark room.

"Playing grumpy witch tonight? I guess I'll head back to bed and shut my door, since you don't like me at all."

Another roll of thunder came as he called me out on my attitude. "Wait! I do like you. So, *so* much. So please don't leave me out here all alone when I'm about ninety percent sure there are serial killer clowns waiting in the hallway for me."

"Serial killer clowns? Alright, you have to stop watching those scary movies."

"It's not my fault that the loudest storm I have ever heard came through on the same night I watched the movie."

He laughed, walking over to me. "So, who do we blame? Kye?"

"Definitely Kye," I said laughing. "Would you maybe want to sit out here with me for a while? I'll be quiet while you read," I said, hoping I wouldn't have to sit out here alone all night.

"We went from you not even liking me to wanting my company all night very fast," he said, stepping closer.

"What can I say? All that charm is wearing me down."

"Good, because I've really been giving it all I have, and I was worried it wasn't working."

"It was. Unfortunately, it works really well."

"Wow, you really are scared if you are trying to sweet talk me this hard. Lucky for you, I'm falling for it."

The thunder rolled, and I reached out, grabbing his hand. He was still standing in front of me, the line of his sweatpants perfectly at eye level. We said we were keeping our distance, but somehow that had included kissing my neck and touching me constantly. I thought it was fair that I allowed myself to touch him, so I pulled on his hand, forcing him to step closer.

I was quiet as I finally looked up at him. The lightning flashed again, and I could see his chest rise before it went dark again.

There was a safety in the dark that gave me a sudden burst of confidence. Letting me do something that I had wanted to do since I first saw Jax without a shirt on.

I reached out, running a hand down from his chest to his stomach. My finger hooked under the waistband before running back up his stomach.

"Finally," he groaned, the quiet sound rumbling under my fingertips.

"Jax," I said, moving him closer until his legs hit the couch.

"*Fuck*," he whispered before dropping down over top of me, forcing me to lie back. His hard body pushed down on mine and I was glad he couldn't see how red my face was. His lips hovered over mine, the small hesitation making me worry, but his hand started running down my side, over my hips and thigh before going back up.

"Do you like when I touch you?" he whispered.

"Yes," I breathed, my hips pushing up against him.

He groaned, apparently that was enough of an answer. He dropped down further, his lips pressing lightly against mine.

I could barely register what to do next. Jax was kissing *me*.

"I have wanted to kiss you every second I've known you, and it's even better than I imagined."

I went to respond, but his lips found mine again, kissing me harder now, each swipe of his tongue more demanding.

His hand moved down my neck to my chest, and I was suddenly aware that I wasn't sure what I was supposed to do now. His tongue slid against mine, running along the roof of my mouth and back to my tongue. I wove my hands into his hair and pulled his mouth back to mine. He groaned as I bit at his lip and moved my hands down his neck and shoulders. Each groan from him only encouraging me to do more.

His hand trailed down farther until he was pushing between my thighs, teasing me as his fingers moved along my shorts.

"Maybe you won't be as scared if you're busy having an orgasm," he whispered, his finger pushing a little harder as it moved back and forth along the hem of my shorts. I could only nod against him in agreement. He kept getting closer to the one place I needed him, making me lose my mind a little more each time.

His finger hooked under my shorts, pulling them to the side as a crash of thunder shook the apartment. I jumped, pushing closer to him.

"I find it funny that of all the scary things my little witch *isn't* scared of, it's thunderstorms that make you jump. I don't think you even flinched during that scary movie," he said, laughing as he pulled his hand away and wrapped his arms tight around me.

"Yes, but this storm is bad, and that movie did leave me with a few concerns."

"A few concerns?"

"Like, what if someone comes into the building?" I asked.

"Unless it's one of us, they won't. We have it well secured. Relax. It's only the storm making noise. No one else is here."

Lightning cracked and something boomed, the electric going out with a pop. I pushed harder against him, grabbing onto his shoulders.

"I don't know that you can actually get any closer to me and I think if you dig those nails in any harder, you're going to draw blood," he said, a hint of laughter in his tone.

"There is no way I am sleeping out here by myself tonight. I already feel like serial killers are watching me and now things are blowing up."

He laughed quietly, kissing my forehead. "I assume it's a transformer blowing up or something. We're fine, just no power. As for the serial killers? Is it possible that I was right about the movie?"

I was quiet, wrapping my arm around him further. "It is possible," I mumbled.

Riot jumped up on the couch, laying at our feet.

"Would you be okay if we stayed in the room with you tonight?"

"I was already prepared to beg for that so yes, it's okay."

We were quiet for a second, but the nagging feeling that something was wrong kept bothering me.

"What if someone is in the hallway?"

"No one is in the hallway," he said. "Come on. Riot is calm. He wouldn't do that if someone was creeping around. Do you want to go get into bed?"

More thunder rolled and another snap of lightning came. "Yes, and you're back on bodyguard duties tonight."

"I really didn't realize this was an on-call type of job."

"It is. Break-ins, thunderstorms, hateful family members who probably want me dead. Of course it's an on-call job."

He pulled me up, wrapping his arms around me again and immediately pulling me towards the bedroom.

"No one is going to hurt you." He stopped, grabbing my shoulders and turning me until we were face to face. "I would miss you too much."

"You would miss food."

His hand moved from mine and rested on my hip, unmoving, but it didn't need to be to make my entire side turn to flames.

"I would miss you. Coming home to food is great, but I could get takeout if that was the problem. I like coming home to see you. I like waking up and knowing your sleepy, grumpy face is out there to spend the morning with. Having a roommate is more fun than I expected."

Before we made it to the bedroom, Riot was up and growling.

"Riot. Settle down," Jax said, but he jumped down, barreling to the door before either of us could stop him.

"What is he doing?"

"I don't know. He's not scared of storms like this. He only does this when he's guarding," I said.

"As in, he heard or smelled something to guard us against?"

"Yes," I hissed, lowering my voice. "I told you I thought someone was out there."

"Here," he said, pulling his phone out. "Hold on to this and if I tell you to, text everyone to come out immediately."

"Now you're freaking me out. I thought you said that you had a good security system."

"Yes, but the power is out, so I have to check."

He got up and moved towards the door, Riot still growling endlessly.

Jax pulled open the door, peering out before stepping out completely, Riot right behind him. I moved closer, trying to hear as Jax cursed and said something. Fear coursed through me and guilt nagged that this was my fault. Someone broke in to find me, or find the laptop I was hiding, but either way it could be my fault if they were here, and ended up hurting someone.

Jax had been right to hesitate in the beginning, because I was already putting him and his friends in danger.

"Jax?" I whispered, going closer to the door and was met with silence. I didn't even hear Riot moving around.

Seconds went by and I was nearly ready to cry right before Jax stepped back inside, running right into me.

"Shit. I can't see anything," he said, holding onto me as he grabbed his phone from my hand and turned on the flashlight making us both wince at the sudden brightness.

"What happened? Is someone really out there?"

"The only one out there is Kye, who is currently bleeding on our floor because he got his hand and arm cut open from a fight," Jax said, sounding annoyed. "And now, he fell outside the door from wet boots, and power being out. Can you grab the first aid kit out of the bathroom?"

I stood frozen for a second, letting the relief wash over me that it wasn't Slaughter or Tristan. That I hadn't put anyone in danger.

Yet.

I couldn't actually believe I was safe from them, and this should be proof of that. Maybe I was letting myself get too comfortable in a place that was too close to them. Not only too close, but with people who *knew* them, and had problems with them in the past.

"Are you okay? It's not them, it's Kye, but he needs some help."

"No, I'm okay, just relieved. Yeah, sorry. I'll get that now."

I ran to grab the kit in the bathroom and headed back out to Kye, who was now leaning over Jax's kitchen sink, washing his arm and hand.

"What happened?"

"I got in a fight."

"And lost?"

Kye smirked. "No, but it was close."

"What were you fighting about?" I asked, pulling things out of the kit. It's not like I was used to this, but it wasn't that strange to me. Slaughter would often come by with his friends and have my mom or me clean up a cut like this.

"Does it matter?"

"I guess not. You're okay other than this?"

"Yep. The mix of blood and rain made me slip on the stairs and then I couldn't see shit. Sorry if I woke you guys up."

"You didn't," I said, snapping my mouth shut before I implied anything else.

Kye didn't say anything, but I could see his smirk in the glow of the phone.

"Here," Jax said, handing him things. "Put this on first, then the bandage."

"Did you want me to do it?" I asked.

They both shook their heads at the same time, and then Kye got to work, patting the cut dry and covering it before turning to us with a smile. "Thanks so much. It's like my own little hospital stop on the way up to my apartment. You two have a *great* night," he said, smirking as he headed to the door. He stopped for a second, petting Riot before leaving.

As soon as the door shut, Jax turned to me. "Kye is a trouble-maker. That's a common occurrence."

"Him getting slashed is common?"

He smiled as he cleaned up. "Common enough that you

shouldn't worry. It has nothing to do with what is going on with you."

"But I thought it did. I thought one of them found me and came here."

"But they didn't."

"But they still could. I let my guard down *again*."

"Yeah, maybe we both did. But nothing bad actually happened, Carly. Everything is okay, and let's hope that they aren't so hell-bent on getting you back that they try breaking in here in the middle of the night, even if they did find you."

"They might," I said, thinking about the laptop again. The one that held all their secrets. The one I still couldn't find the words to tell Jax about. The one that would make me admit to everything I did.

"In the event that actually happens, we will stop them."

I nodded, wanting to believe him, but struggling to.

Ten minutes later, I had finished cleaning up and Jax had gone to reboot all the security systems on the small generator, so now the entire place was locked down again. It didn't do as much as I hoped to ease the tightness in my gut.

 The thought of following him into the room now felt a little awkward, so I avoided his eyes as I walked over.

"What are you doing?"

"Going to bed?" I said, pulling back the covers.

"No, you're going to the couch, but you should be going to bed. Didn't we already agree on that?"

"With you?"

He groaned and leaned down, kicking my legs out from under me and picking me up. I yelled, trying to fight him, but he only held me closer.

"Stop struggling."

"Put me down. I'm too heavy. You're going to drop me."

He lifted me up and down. "Nope, it's fine. You were trying

to go to the couch and I want to at least pretend I sleep, which isn't going to happen if you're out here freaking out."

"I wasn't freaking out."

He threw me onto the bed with a laugh and crawled over the top of me.

"Don't lie to me. You were going to lay there forever worrying. An hour ago, you were worried about serial killers."

"And I was right!" I yelled with a laugh.

"There are no serial killers, it was just Kye." He leaned down, pressing a kiss to my forehead.

"I thought we agreed that we both were going to keep our distance?" I said.

"I don't want to say that I lied, but I have to admit that I never thought that I was going to do well with that," he said.

"We should probably try."

He laughed, rolling off of me until he was on his side of the bed, not touching me at all. We laid in silence for a while, but I wasn't tired now.

"Why don't you sleep?"

"No idea. It's why I was out driving the night I met you. It just hasn't come easy. I will for a few hours hopefully. You're okay, though. Thunderstorms and serial killers will not be a problem."

I snuggled back into the pillows, surprised how comfortable being here with him really was, even more surprised that nothing bothered me again as I drifted off to sleep.

I KNEW it was still the middle of the night, but the small glow of the light next to the bed was on. Jax was laid out next to me, asleep, with his book on his chest.

He seemed to read a lot, but I could never see what it was

when it was on his phone. I reached over, trying not to take note of how cute he looked asleep, as I picked the book up carefully.

I don't know what I was expecting, but it wasn't this.

This was a full-blown romance novel.

It was a popular one. I hadn't read it, but I knew enough about it to know that it was a little darker, but more romance than anything.

All I could think was that my sweet little street racer, who is the first to step up and protect me, is now laying here, trying to make me feel calm while also reading a romance book.

I don't know how he had the right to be this adorable.

I flipped to the first page, starting it when he rolled over, throwing an arm over me and hitting the book. He jolted awake, looking at the book and then at me.

"What are you doing?" he asked fast before letting out a groan. "Shit, I actually fell asleep."

"Yep, and left your romance book out for all to see."

"Don't read that. Pretend you didn't see me reading that and go back to bed."

"Why would I do that? I like learning dirty secrets," I said, flipping through the book. "And it looks like I'm finding out exactly how *dirty* this one is."

"Carly," he warned, grabbing me and pulling me close.

"Jax," I warned back, flipping the pages as I briefly caught words and scenes. "I have to admit. I'm already intrigued and will be reading this."

"So you're saying I have good taste at least?"

I smiled over at him. "So far, yeah, it looks like you do."

He grabbed the book out of my hands. "Fine, but you can't start it until I'm done and you cannot make fun of me."

"Oh yes I can," I said, propping myself up next to him on my arm.

He tried to frown, but the smile was inevitable. "I swear if you talk about this with anyone else I will—"

"What? I would actually like to know what you would do?"

He reached out, wrapping an arm around my hip, pulling me against him until he was rolling me onto his chest. His other hand plunged into my hair, forcing my head back until I was staring up at him.

"Brat," he whispered. "Always calling me out."

My mouth fell open, but I couldn't find words. The grip he had on me was sending heat through my body and making me instantly turned on.

And not the turned on I had felt in the past. There was no question what to do next now. I knew exactly what I wanted to do and I could even think of a few things that I wanted him to do, too.

He didn't let me go, but instead leaned up to me. His tongue came out licking along the roof of my open mouth before he laid back again with a playful smirk.

"You tell everyone my secrets and the next time you get into bed with me, I'll have you over my legs getting spanked before you know it."

My mouth fell open again, shocked at the image that his words created, but I snapped it shut, biting down on my lip so it didn't happen again.

"Well, I might not be getting into bed with you again."

"Right," he said.

It was the right thing to say. Reminding us both that in another week I wouldn't be there.

But it being the right thing to say didn't explain why it made me feel so bad.

Or why it made his playful smile fall and grip loosen on me.

Or even why both of those combined made me suddenly upset.

He flipped me over until I was on my back, my head back on my own pillow, then he leaned down.

"Goodnight, my little cold-hearted witch,"

He went to move back, but I stopped him. "Jax, I'm —"

"Right. You are right," he said softly. "Go back to sleep. We have to be up soon to leave."

I laid back, staring up into the dark room, remembering that I had agreed to go stay the weekend away with all of them.

A weekend away with Jax.

It shouldn't feel any different than living together, but it suddenly felt *very* different. And I agreed to it all.

What had I been thinking?

EIGHTEEN

JAX

I DIDN'T KNOW what I was supposed to do now.

It was already pretty obvious to me that I liked Carly. *A lot.* But waking up next to her only made it worse.

She had rolled over this morning to look at me, and I was convinced it ruined my life. Her perfect green eyes had gazed up at me with a look that made me want to make my entire world that color. Paint my walls, my car, make everything in my life that exact color green.

And then I realized I might have to if I wanted to keep seeing it forever.

We got up and quietly packed before heading down to the car. Both of us avoiding any conversation about what had happened.

As much as I loved driving, sitting in the backseat with Carly sounded better, so when they asked me yesterday, I had decided we would just ride with Kye and Scout, but that was before last night.

Now I had to sit in the backseat with her, and remind myself constantly to *not* reach out and touch her. She was leaving and falling for her now would only put me in the exact situation that I didn't want to be in.

Kye started up the car, waiting for Scout as Fox and Ransom pulled out in their cars. We had to take the Jeep that Fox and Ash had bought since it was the only car we owned that Riot could comfortably fit in the back of. I had asked Kye to drive, giving Scout the front seat. I didn't miss her knowing smirk as she got in and looked back at me.

Carly leaned over, reaching for her phone that had fallen, and her hair brushed against my arm, making me forget what I had been doing. All I wanted to do was pull her close and spend the entire ride with her right against me. Her hand grabbed onto my knee to brace herself, and I coughed, trying to hide my groan.

"Do you guys want music or a podcast?" Scout asked, pulling me out of my desperation.

Kye and Carly answered together, both agreeing on a podcast, but I sat quietly.

"Three against one Jax, we're listening to true crime."

I rolled my eyes. "Is that really a good idea after last night?"

"Yes, it's a great idea."

Kye smacked Scout's arm. "I finally have someone to watch scary movies with."

"I'm all for true crime. Scary movies? Not so much." Scout said. "That one last night freaked me out."

"Well, that makes two of you," I said quietly enough that only Carly could hear me.

"I'll watch scary movies whenever you want," Carly said, glaring at me. I didn't know if it was a challenge to show how independent she wanted to be or a hint that she wanted me to be there when she was scared, but I was hoping for the second option.

"You guys had to choose a slasher movie about people getting killed in a cabin in the woods. You're seriously going to sit there and tell me that you won't be freaked out again tonight?" I wanted to keep my voice light, but the strain of knowing I probably wouldn't be next to her all night again was making my throat tight.

"Serious," she said with a smirk. The eyeliner she had on today made her eyes look so cat-like that I couldn't look away.

I couldn't even care that she was lying with the way she was smirking at me.

"Carly, I —" I started, but Scout had turned around asking her about another scary movie that I had not seen.

Then they moved to the podcast, talking over whatever the crime was, but I didn't want to join the conversation. I wanted to figure out what was going on with us and if we were drawing a firm 'not going to happen' line between roommates and anything more. But I couldn't do anything but sit and watch.

I clicked my phone on, pulling up my book to tune them out, and try to focus on anything other than Carly. It worked for a while, the ride passing without a problem until my phone vibrated with a new text.

CARLY

What are you reading? More of your romance book?

JAX

I don't think I should tell you.

CARLY

I know your secret, and I could already tell that it's your book.

JAX

Snooping?

CARLY

Well, I had to do something. You seem mad.

JAX

Why would you think that?

CARLY

Because you've barely made one joke or
ridiculous comment since we woke up.

I smiled down at my phone, but didn't look at her.

JAX

I wasn't sure what to say and didn't want to
fuck up more by saying the wrong thing

CARLY

Well, I don't like it. Did you have anything you
would like to say to me?

JAX

You don't like me not talking? I thought that
would be a relief for you.

And I always have things I want to say to you.

CARLY

Tell me.

JAX

They don't fall under the 'keeping our
distance' or 'let's be friends' category, so I
can't.

I heard her sharp intake of breath, but still only looked down
at my phone, worried that I wouldn't be able to resist touching
her when I did look at her again.

CARLY

Tell me anyway.

> **JAX**
> Why the sudden interest? I thought we agreed on you being right that we should keep our distance.

> **CARLY**
> Maybe that agreement only applies to when we are living together. Maybe it doesn't need to count when we are on a vacation.

I groaned, kicking my legs out more and finally looking at her. She caught my eye before quickly looking away.

> **JAX**
> I like the sound of that. What did you have in mind?

> **CARLY**
> I told you that I wanted to hear your thoughts.

> **JAX**
> You've obviously been thinking about this. What is it that you want?

> You look ready to kill me half the time. Why get shy about your feelings now?

Her lips pursed, and she texted back fast before looking back out the window.

> **CARLY**
> Because I don't want to say something and you reject it.

> **JAX**
> I don't know what I have done to make you think I would reject anything you say, but that's almost impossible. If you want it, I'll give it to you.

> And I stand by giving you literally anything you want, but I might need a written list of your wild kinks just in case I have to google anything.

She looked over at me, biting at her lip and looking at mine, and I was suddenly mad I hadn't driven so we could be alone.

CARLY

> I was only hoping that we could pick up where we left off. I didn't prepare a list.

I closed my eyes and took a deep breath. Now I was pissed off that we hadn't taken my car.

JAX

> Tell me more.

CARLY

> How much more?

JAX

> Every damn detail you will give me.

CARLY

> Serious?

I laughed, for how confident she was about other things, she seemed so shy about sending a few dirty texts, but I had no problem getting this started.

JAX

> You can tell me how wet you are thinking of me. You could tell me how much better you would feel if I slid over there and got you off. I guess you could also tell me to fuck off.

Her eyes went wide as she bit at her lip again.

JAX

I need that damn lip between my teeth

CARLY

Oh.

I would like all of that.

This really had to be the first time she's done this.

JAX

Would you? I'm going to need to see the words.

CARLY

Can I tell you to fuck off but also have you keep texting me these things? My brain can't function enough after reading that to come up with a response.

She was almost laughing, but kept quiet.

JAX

I will happily take control of this, but you have to be good and do what I say.

CARLY

No.

JAX

Brat.

Then you better speak up and say what you want.

She groaned, and I winked when she looked over. She looked away fast, her cheeks red and eyes glued to her phone again.

CARLY

But I want more

JAX

Fuck, you're cute when you're all shy and sweet.

CARLY

And when I'm not shy and sweet? What about when I'm mean?

JAX

Hot. So fucking hot.

CARLY

So you don't mind if I'm mean to you?

JAX

Not the way that you do it. You're hot when you're telling me off and calling me out. I'd let you take charge of me any day.

CARLY

So if I said that I wanted your tongue after your hand, what would you say?

I adjusted myself again, trying to not make it glaringly obvious that I was already hard.

JAX

Sweetheart, if you asked for that, I would already be on my knees spreading your legs before you even finished the sentence.

CARLY

So it's kind of like you will do my sexual bidding.

I made sure I hid my laugh and looked at her with a smile

JAX

I think that's pretty much exactly what it means. Wouldn't any guy, though?

CARLY

I think saying any guy would be a stretch.

JAX

Not at all. Not that it matters, I would prefer to think that backtalk and pent up anger were only for me.

I could see her eyes roll as she furiously texted back.

CARLY

Most guys are not going for girls like me.

I laughed, looking over at her. I was expecting a smile back, but her eyebrows were furrowed hard and she looked pissed.

JAX

Maybe that cute angry face is scaring them off. Which is probably for the better. Who wants a guy that you're going to scare off that easily?

CARLY

You know that's not what I mean. Please don't act like I look like the typical girl you go for. You wouldn't look twice at me if we met any other way.

JAX

What? Why would you think that?

CARLY

Because I'm sure you're going for perfect, sweet girls who don't look like me, and aren't mean to you.

I set my phone down and slid next to her, not caring what Kye and Scout had to say about this now. She stiffened as I put my arm around her, but I pulled her close anyway.

"What the *fuck* are you talking about?" I whispered, the podcast up loud enough to drown out my voice.

"Exactly what I said." She crossed her arms, trying to not look at me.

"I don't know why you are suddenly worried about this. Did I say something that made you think that there was a problem?"

"Not exactly."

"Then why the sudden concern?"

"It's not *sudden* for me. It's a constant concern in my mind."

"Oh, well, I didn't realize that. You haven't really made it seem like it was an issue for you."

"How could it not be?"

"Because you're beautiful? I guess I was assuming you knew that. Although, I guess you have made comments that I should have picked up on better."

"I mean, I don't think I'm ugly, but you can't tell me that the girls you usually go for aren't smaller than me."

I shrugged, thinking back. "I don't know how that matters. Are the guys you usually go for racers that like romantic things? Do they look like me? Act like me? I highly doubt it." I leaned back, the jealousy at other guys she's been with washing over me, and my own insecurities about who I was rearing up. "Forget it. Maybe I do get it," I said, watching her eyebrows furrow as she looked over at me. "I mean, I get the 'comparing yourself to other people like that' part. Not your exact problem."

I sat quietly for a second before pushing my own insecurities aside. Hers were different from mine, but I could understand wanting to be accepted for who you are and only that. Not what you could be. Not what someone hoped you would be.

I held her tighter, bringing my focus back to her and only her. I moved back down towards her neck, kissing it once and making my way up to her ear. When she didn't pull away, I moved again, biting at her neck until her head dropped, giving me more access.

"I have thought about you and your perfect body since the

moment we met," I whispered. "I spent the first week trying not to stare because every time I looked at you, I was losing my mind. I honestly thought I was being way too obvious about it."

"No. I didn't know that. Why didn't you say something?"

"Because if I had come up to you and said hey Carly, I know you've only been here a few days but I'm already having dreams that you come into my room and do ridiculously dirty things to me so let's make that happen, you would have kicked me in the balls and I would have never seen you again."

That made her smile, and I reveled in the small laugh that escaped her. "Okay, fair, I would have probably done exactly that."

"But can I tell you now?"

"As long as you don't expect me to talk," she said, pursing her lips in a small, cute smile.

I leaned in, my lips against her ear as I spoke, so there wasn't a chance of someone else hearing me. "I've wanted you laid out underneath me without an inch of these clothes on and panting my name as I give you orgasm after orgasm until you are begging me to stop. I want to bend you over, lay you down, have you on top of me. I want to see your face as you come and I want you so lost in pleasure that all you can do is hold on to me. I even want your demands and commands, telling me what you want, how you want it, making me do whatever you need to make you feel good. I can sit here all night, giving you detail after detail of how badly I want you. Not any girl, *you*."

She was quiet for a second as her eyes went wide. "Oh."

"*Oh,* you're still into this, or *oh,* you're going to kick me when we get out of the car?" I asked, only half joking.

She looked up front to Kye and Scout, who were ignoring us now. Hopefully they got the hint that they should continue ignoring us, even though I knew damn well Scout probably already texted the girls, and Fox, how close we were back here.

Carly turned to face me, her lips inches from mine, and when I thought she was going to finally pull back, she leaned in, kissing me.The only thing better than kissing Carly was having her lean in to kiss me first. Her tongue ran along my lip, searching for more, and for the hundredth time since we got in, I was kicking myself for not driving.

I pulled her harder against me, kissing her a few seconds longer before breaking apart.

She tilted her head, her lips at my ear. "Alright, now I really need more."

The car turned, pulling us down a long driveway to the cabin.

"And you're about to get it as soon as we stop."

NINETEEN
CARLY

JAX WAS GOING to be the death of me.

I always thought my type of guy would be someone like me. Someone not so smiley, less extroverted and friendly. But, unfortunately, I was pretty sure my type now was Jax.

Whatever made Jax, Jax seemed to be everything I liked.

The way he made me always feel more confident, and more like myself. The way I wanted to spend all my time with him. How good he looked today in his hoodie with his hat on, somehow making his blue eyes stand out even more. I hated it. I hated feeling this way at all, but even more with someone so amazing. I hated that I wanted every single thing he was suggesting.

He pushed up the sleeves of his hoodie, revealing the strong, perfectly sculpted forearms that I spent way too much time looking at. My body flushed as my eyes moved up to the small tattoo at the base of his throat again, the hoodie hanging low enough to show it off.

How could one person look so effortlessly hot? I looked like I just rolled out of bed.

As soon as Kye put the car in park, Jax was in motion. He lifted Riot out before grabbing our bags, holding them in one hand as the other strong hand around mine, pulling me with him with a smile.

"Come on," he said, nodding for me to follow as everyone headed inside.

I stopped to take it all in. The cabin was cute, more modern than the rustic cabin I had pictured, but it was still cozy. The Fall weather had taken over the mountains, the air was colder here, and the leaves were all shades of orange, yellow, and red. It was beautiful.

Ash walked in behind us. "There are five rooms, so everyone should have their own bed, but not their own room," she said, smirking at Jax and I. "You two can discuss amongst yourselves, but Carly, you're either sharing a room with Jax or Scout."

Ash walked away and Jax held out my bag.

"You can choose where you want to stay, but I can promise to pick up *exactly* where we left off, and I'm honestly the best at cuddling. Plus, I will still honor my bodyguard duties in the event of serial killers."

"Wow, you really seem to have a lot to offer," I said, grabbing my bag and walking around him into the room. "I'm really curious if you can deliver on all of that."

The door slammed shut behind us and before I knew it, I was being tackled to the bed.

I caught a glimpse of Jax's smiling face before he was kissing me. His hands moved up from my hips to my breasts, taking my shirt with it.

The self-conscious thoughts started to take over, but then he was biting my lip and groaning as his hand slipped under my bra.

As soon as his fingers moved over my nipple, I gasped, arching up for more.

"All I want to do is kiss every fucking inch of you right

now." His hand moved up my thigh and over my pussy, moving right over that sensitive spot that made my hips push up with a gasp. I was still fully dressed, but every caress burned into my skin.

His head dropped to mine. "You're going to kill me with that sound. I'm already desperate for it again."

He moved like he was about to do exactly that when a knock came from the door.

"Carly!" Scout yelled, making us both freeze.

"Yeah?" I asked, surprised she was looking for me.

"Girl gang meeting downstairs. Come on," she yelled.

"Right now?" Jax asked, pushing his hips down into me enough that I could feel how hard he was already.

"Yes, right now. We have important girl stuff. Come down or we are coming up."

His forehead fell to mine again with an annoyed groan as I laughed. "I'm guessing they are completely serious about coming up here?" I asked.

"Oh, they will kick the door down just to spite me," he said, smiling as he kissed me again.

"But we have all weekend to continue this?"

"Yeah, we do, and had I known you were going to change your mind about me this weekend, I would have gladly found us our own cabin to stay in."

My hands splayed on his chest as he pulled me up, kissing me once before stepping back. "You better go down there before they come for us. I'll find you after you are done."

Twenty minutes later, I was sitting on Ash's bed, listening as they talked about some guy that Ash knew and who he was dating now, but I was too lost in thought to care.

I was hopefully hours away from losing this stupid virginity tag that I had been unwillingly carrying around for the past few years.

It wasn't that I hadn't wanted to lose it, but it had only grown harder as the years went on and my insecurities only got worse.

But now there was Jax, and he seemed to help with that. It was hard to care about your insecurities when someone like him was all over you.

I looked around at the girls, who were still talking as Ash did her nails.

"Hey," I said, waiting as they looked at me. "I think I need your guy's help."

―――――

I WALKED out onto the back patio of the cabin, trying not to immediately turn around when I realized all the guys were farther out in the yard around a small fire.

This was supposed to be a confidence boost, but the thought of taking off this hoodie and only being in a swimsuit in front of four incredibly good-looking guys was intimidating enough. Add in the fact that I actually liked one of them, he might actually like me, and there was a huge chance of losing my virginity to him made this all worse.

I shut the door as quietly as I could, not wanting any of their attention on me. Maybe I could be half confident and slip into the hot tub without any of them noticing.

I had already negotiated for the hoodie being on. When I asked the girls for help and tried to find my confidence, their plans ranged from Quinn suggesting I drag Jax back to a bedroom and getting naked, to Ash's suggestion of walking out in a bikini, and announcing that I needed to see him.

I said I would meet in the middle and go to the hot tub, wear the swimsuit, but hide in the hoodie until I was about to get in. When Ash tried to protest, I had to boost my own confidence and say that if Jax liked me, he was going to like me hoodie or no hoodie. That made Ash relent and agree, which was great, but I wasn't even sure I believed it myself.

The plan of getting into the hot tub before anyone was ruined when Jax turned to me the second I stepped out. His hungry eyes took me in as he stalked closer.

"Hey," he said, smiling hard. "That's my hoodie."

"Yeah. I figured you would be okay if I used it tonight. Hopefully?"

"More than okay. I really want to kiss you right now," he said, stepping closer.

"In front of your friends?"

"You kissed me in front of Scout and Kye. I was assuming you were fine with it now."

"That was a little impulsive of me. I didn't think you would want your friends to know."

His smile grew. "Why would I care? They would find out eventually. You can see that secrets are hard to keep around here. And I've been waiting hours to see you. You have somehow stayed hidden away, even though we are stuck in the same cabin together."

"I had a few things to do."

"Really? Long list of chores to do at a random cabin in the woods?"

"More like a really long pep talk before I could face you again." His eyebrows shot up at my confession.

"Because you decided that you don't like the things I said and need to let me down easy, or because you want to put them into action?"

"I was leaning towards the second option," I said, as he reached over, tugging on the zipper of the hoodie down and peeking inside.

"Damn," he whispered. "You're about to get in the hot tub, aren't you?"

"Yes."

He stepped back, bringing me with him as he moved towards the hot tub. The hot, steaming water looked perfect to slip into as my feet started to freeze on the concrete.

"What are you doing?" I asked as he took off his shirt.

"Did you think that I wouldn't be going in with you?"

He kicked off his boots next and pulled me into him. "Are you taking this off and letting me fully see what you have on underneath?"

"I wasn't planning on it," I said with a hard shake of my head.

He gave a quiet laugh, leaning down to my neck to kiss it once. "How were you planning on getting in, then?"

"I was hoping you wouldn't see me until I was already all the way in. Hidden by water and darkness."

"And miss you unwrapping yourself like my own personal present? Why?"

I only glared, not wanting to say how insecure I currently felt. I already confessed enough earlier. I wasn't going to repeat it.

"Aww, come on," he said, pulling me against him. "Don't look at me like that. Scowling is one thing, but upset scowling is another. You're beautiful, Carly. Every single part of you is perfect. I dream about it. Crave it constantly. Want it all for myself." He leaned in, kissing my forehead and distracting me as grabbed the zipper and pulled, undressing me in one motion. "Now you came out here to get in the hot tub. Come on, get in."

I tried to take a deep, calming breath, but then he was pulling off his belt.

"What are you doing?" The devilish smirk as he undressed right in front of me was making me forget how to move.

"We have already established that I am going in with you."

"Naked?" I asked, my throat tight.

He laughed quietly, hooking his thumb in the waistband of his jeans and pulling them off.

"I was going to keep my boxers on if that's okay with you?" he asked, still laughing as he reached up and moved to pull the hoodie off of me completely.

"I think if you took them off right now, I wouldn't be getting into the hot tub with you."

"No? Would you be running to hide away?"

I looked him over, somehow finding my confidence again, even when he was looking at me with his cocky grin. His eyes were heavy and his fingers ran up my arm, making their way to my neck.

"I was going to say I would probably want to skip the hot tub and head right to the room," I said.

I wanted this. I wanted this all to happen so much, but admitting it was like saying all my deepest fears out loud.

He fell forward, his arms wrapping around me as he pretended to fall more into me with a groan. "Every fucking time you surprise me with that dirty mouth. Is there another way I can convince you to skip the hot tub?"

"No," I said with my own smirk. "I think that would be the only way." I moved back, stepping around him and slipping into the water as fast as I could.

He groaned again, jumping in next to me. "Fine. I should probably slow myself down, anyway. All I can think about is bending you over the side of this thing until you scream, but I'm assuming that would be frowned upon."

"Yeah, I feel like your friends wouldn't love that," I said, laughing as he moved in close. My face flushed, but I tried to stay calm and keep my cool. "Do you think about these things often?"

"More often than I should." His words were quiet as his hand moved to my thigh. "But my grumpy little witch finally told me that I could share those thoughts, so prepare to hear an endless string of possibly incoherent dirty thoughts."

"And do you always do what you're told?"

"Maybe when it's coming from your mouth."

His fingers were moving in lazy circles on my thigh. I was already so turned on that it wasn't helping me focus. "So what if I tell you to move your hand higher? What would you do?"

His hand froze before he moved, sliding higher until his fingers were running along my swimsuit. "I guess I could do what I was told, obviously. How high do you want me to move? Here?" he asked, running his hand back and forth along my pussy, the swimsuit putting way too much fabric between us.

"Close," I said.

He moved my swimsuit aside, his hand finally moving along my wetness.

"Right here?" he asked with a groan. "You're already so wet for me."

I leaned back further, trying to quiet my moan as he moved over my clit.

"Are you going to be good and stay quiet if I fuck you with my hand?"

I shook my head, knowing that I didn't stand a chance being quiet enough if he kept touching me like this.

He laughed, biting at my neck. "Such a brat, never able to do what you're told. Always talking back and not listening."

"I thought that you're the one that's supposed to do what you're told, not me," I panted as his fingers pushed against my entrance.

"Only when you're giving the commands. When you're laid back begging for more, then you do what I say. Now be quiet while I fuck that perfect pussy with my fingers."

Before he could move, the back door shut, the girls walking out and heading right towards us.

"Looks like our private party is over," he said quietly, adjusting my swimsuit back into place. "Unless you're ready to go to bed?"

Ash walked over, handing us both a cup. "These are for you two," she said, handing us both one.

"I think we're staying here for now," I whispered.

His lips moved to my ear, quiet as he whispered to me. "Fine. I'll allow one drink before I take you to the bed and make you come all over my cock."

"You'll allow it?" I said. "Looks like I'm having two drinks now."

He laughed softly, throwing an arm around me while everyone else got in and started talking.

"You know, if you don't listen, you have to be punished. I think that's the rules."

Each whispered word sent a shiver through me, and I was already debating on telling him it's time to go to bed. I had never been so ready to be naked with someone, every time in the past always making me more self conscious than excited. Now, though, with Jax's hand moving in lazy circles on my shoulder and dirty words being whispered in my ear, I was about to drag him away.

"Does that rule apply to you, too?"

He leaned back, blowing out a deep breath. "Damn. Yeah, I guess it does. It absolutely fucking does," he said, loud enough that everyone turned to him.

"Need another drink, Jax?" Ash asked as everyone else broke out into laughter.

"Yeah, I definitely do," he said as she got out to get more. He sat against me, not moving away, and talking to everyone until we finished the drinks Ash had brought back.

Another twenty minutes went by before I found the least

suspicious break in conversation. "I think I'm done," I said. "I'm going to head to bed."

They all said their goodbyes and grinned as Jax got out with me.

"Fucking finally," he said, trailing behind me as I dried myself off and headed inside. "I was starting to worry that you were changing your mind."

"What made you think that? Because I wasn't trying to feel you up the entire time like you were to me?" I asked with a small laugh as he shut the door behind us.

"How can I not when you look so damn good?"

As soon as we were away from the door and windows, he started pushing me back, walking me to the bedroom as he ripped my top down until my breasts fell out.

"Fuck, more perfect than I remember," he mumbled, leaning down to take my nipple into his mouth. His tongue rolled, and he nipped, making me stop and moan.

"Have to keep going. This isn't our apartment, so I have to get you into the room," he said.

I laughed, moving again as he grabbed my hips.

"All I have wanted is to touch you like this. It's been driving me out of my mind," he said. We made it to the room, but he kept moving until I was falling back onto the bed.

I laid back for a second as he moved around.

This was it.

I'd been waiting years to feel this comfortable with someone, and somehow that someone was Jax. Gorgeous, sweet, Jax.

I couldn't see where he was, but I felt the moment he got on the bed. He pulled up my leg, kissing from my ankle to my thigh before moving up my body to kiss my lips.

"I have thought about you like this more times than I should probably admit."

"Why not admit to them?" I asked, realizing the drinks might be taking the edge off a little too much. "I want to hear all the dirty ways you've thought about me."

"If I start telling you those things right now, this entire night might end before it begins because I'll be coming before I'm even inside you."

I never romanticized losing my virginity. Honestly, this was probably nicer than anything I imagined with a guy who was better than most of the men I knew combined, but the thought of doing this was making me nervous now. Each second that he kissed and teased me was only making my anxiety worse.

"I really like what you're doing," I said as he flicked my nipple with his tongue. "But for tonight, could we skip right to the sex part?"

He laughed, moving up until his lips were against mine. "Are you sure you like it? I'll do other stuff unless you really are just as ready as I am, and want to get to the best part?"

"The best part." The calm, slightly drunk part of me liked that. Liked that he could think sex with me would be the best part when the sober part of my brain knew I was not even close to the hottest girl he had slept with.

"You're so damn beautiful and perfect. I can't wait to have you wrapped around my cock. I've been dying all night next to you."

He sat up, the bed moving as I heard him unwrapping something.

Thankfully, he remembered a condom because, between my anxiety and the drinks, I forgot pretty much everything besides freaking out that this was happening.

In seconds he was back over top of me, wrapping one leg around him and positioning himself at my entrance.

"One hundred percent sure you want this?" he asked, leaning down to kiss me.

"Yes, one hundred percent."

With that, he pushed forward, moving slowly as my body tried to adjust to him. Each inch was slow and painful, but I tried not to make a sound.

I didn't want him to stop, and I knew he would if he thought there was a problem.

"Fuck, you are tight," he whispered, pushing into me harder.

I sucked in a hard breath. I wasn't naïve to sex exactly, but when it came down to it, I was still nervous.

He pushed his cock farther into me with another groan, and my body tensed.

"Sweetheart," he said, pushing deeper. "You already have a fucking death grip on me."

"Sorry," I breathed, trying to remember if it was in through the nose or out. Pain shot through me, and it took everything not to pull my hips away.

"Sorry? I assure you that is nothing to be sorry about. I'm sorry that I'm going to last all of a minute. Fuck, you feel so good."

He pulled out once and slammed back into me.

I squeezed my eyes shut, the pinching pain getting worse.

I was suddenly regretting my decision not to tell him the truth when he slowed again, the pace steady now. It gave me time to take another deep breath, and this time felt better, the pain easing and a wave of pleasure breaking through.

I couldn't hide my squeak as he picked up the pace.

"Are you okay?"

"Yes, I think you are just bigger than I expected."

At least, I thought he was. There wasn't exactly a long list of comparisons for me of real men. If we are comparing this to toys, though, there is a very large difference.

"You stroke my ego as good as your pussy strokes my cock," he said, slowing down. "I'll go easier."

He pushed again, moving into me so slowly, giving my body

more time to adjust. It eased the tension in me, letting a strange pleasure take over.

It wasn't nearly as uncomfortable now. His lips found my neck, kissing me with each thrust, the feel of both together only heightening my pleasure.

It was so sudden, the change from pain to pleasure, that before I knew it I was the one moving, forcing him into me faster.

"Jax," I breathed, feeling like I was walking off a cliff and needing him to hold on to.

"Does that feel better now, sweetheart? All wrapped around me, and taking me so good? Your pussy's so greedy, holding my cock so tight that I can barely move. I could stay here forever."

"Jax," I said again, knowing it was louder that time but unable to care.

"That's it. Come for me, sweetheart. Let me feel you grip my cock even harder as you come on me."

I understood dirty talk. I liked to think I could do it myself, but getting told these dirty things while he was actually inside of me was different. Each word brought me closer to the edge of that cliff.

He curled his body over me, fucking me faster as his lips came to my ear.

"I should have known you would be a good girl when you finally got my cock. Always a brat, running your mouth to me, and now you can't say anything but my name."

By the time he finished his sentence, I was falling apart. My body was tightening and I could feel how hard I clamped down on him.

My hands grabbed for his shoulders, holding on as pleasure ripped through me, sending me into darkness as I yelled his name.

His mouth came down over mine, stifling my yells and

moans as he rocked into me harder.

He groaned, slowing down until he stilled inside me.

"You're amazing," he said, finally pulling away from me.

I could barely keep my eyes open, my body light and still humming with pleasure.

Jax laughed. "You look amazing, too. All satisfied and sleepy. I'm going to get a washcloth. Don't move."

"A washcloth for what?" I said, trying to make sense of the world again.

"So I can clean you up? I'll only be a second."

He left, shutting the door behind him as I rolled to look at the ceiling.

I didn't know if it was the sex or the alcohol, but I felt so good that I didn't even want to try to move.

I was officially not a virgin, and letting that title go felt like letting go of one more shred of who I used to be in the best way.

He came back in a few minutes later, sitting next to me and pulling my legs apart.

"What are you doing?"

"Taking care of you. Would you rather take a shower?"

"No. This is okay."

He moved the cloth over me, leaning down to kiss my thigh before moving to the other side.

"Did you want to get sleep or go back out with everyone?"

I laughed. "If you think I can walk right now, you've lost it. I'll stay here. Feel free to go back out with them."

"Not a chance. I was hoping you would want to stay here. I never know if you're trying to run, though."

"After that, I don't think I'll be doing any running tonight."

He groaned, pulling me close against his chest and kissing my head.

"Perfect. So fucking perfect," he said, keeping us tangled together as I drifted off.

TWENTY

JAX

I ROLLED OVER AND GROANED, a headache hammering its way into my brain.

"I'm going to kill Ash for the drinks."

"I'm going to help you," Carly said, her groan matching mine as she looked up and over at me.

"Then again," I said, moving closer until she was flush against me. "I did get to wake up here with you, so not all bad. What do you want to do today?"

She kicked out her leg with a small whine and rolled away from me.

"What was that?"

"Nothing," she said, but a small groan escaped her.

"Are you hurt?"

"Not hurt. Just sore. More than I was expecting," she said. I reached out to pull her closer, but she only pulled away again. "I see why people say they can't walk after that."

"Wow, I was right. You are incredible for my ego. Are you okay?"

"Yeah, fine. It's nothing that I can't handle."

"Well, from 100 to 0 with the ego," I said, smiling.

She groaned again, turning into the pillow, and worry sunk in.

"Okay, I'm not an expert at the female body, but I don't think it should hurt that much."

"It doesn't hurt like I'm concerned. I'm just sore and surprised."

"Yeah, but I remember it clearly enough to know that I wasn't that rough," I said, trying to get her to smile, but she looked away.

"No, no, it's fine. Drop it." She sat up, moving even farther away, but I didn't want her to get all weird and shy with me now. I moved across the bed, laying beside her again.

"I'm not going to drop the fact that I might have hurt you."

"You didn't. I already know what's wrong, so just drop it."

"You are only freaking me out more. What is wrong, Carly?"

She huffed and laid down again, looking back up at the ceiling. She wasn't going to look at me, but seemed fine as I wrapped my arms around her and pulled her against my chest.

"I'm blurting this out and then we are never talking about it again," she said against me. "I'm sore because before last night, I was a virgin."

I couldn't tell if blood drained from my face or filled it, every part of me freezing at the words.

"Last night was your first time?" I asked, already knowing the answer but hoping I heard her wrong.

"Yeah," she said.

I untangled my arms from her and sat up, my heart racing as I looked her over.

"No." The words sounded so horrified, but I couldn't believe it. "Why didn't you tell me that?"

"I didn't think it was important to stop and talk about it, considering what was happening."

"You're a virgin and you didn't think that was important to tell me?" I knew I was raising my voice too loud, but I didn't care. "You thought lying to me was better?"

"I did not lie. I never said that I *wasn't* a virgin."

"But you omitted it. I could have hurt you."

She had the nerve to roll her eyes. "I didn't tell you because of this exactly. I didn't want to be one anymore, and it was getting increasingly harder to change that as I got older."

I got up, digging through my bag for clothes. Anger and confusion coursing through me.

"What does that even mean?"

"This," she yelled. "Exactly this. Would you have done everything you did last night if I had told you? Would you have even slept with me to begin with, or would you have politely declined? Would you have talked to me like that? Do you know what it's like being twenty-two years old and still being a virgin? If you tell a guy that, they have one of two reactions. One, they think it's great. They think it's *too* great." Her face scrunched in disgust and I think I mimicked it exactly.

"Or two, they are turned off. They want nothing to do with that, and let me tell you, that hit to your self esteem is worse than anything. Having a guy say 'I absolutely do not want to sleep with you' is something hard to forget, and I wouldn't have been able to handle that from you."

I let out a long breath. "That's fair, that's all fair, but that does not give you a pass for not telling me, Carly. I could have hurt you. I *did* hurt you. And did you really want it to be here, half drunk? You think you deserved that for your first time?"

I sounded so mad, but it wasn't just anger rolling through me.

I ruined it. I already knew that what happened wasn't ideal, but I couldn't take wanting her longer. I knew I could handle messing up the first time we were together, but messing up *her* first time? It felt so wrong. One thing I had going for me was that I was good at romantic shit, and now I wasn't even good at that.

"Okay, tell me then," she said, snapping me back to reality. "What would you have said if I told you last night, before it happened?"

"I would have said absolutely not here. It could happen on a different day. Maybe we could have talked about it and not done…" I waved my arms around. "That after drinking."

"Exactly," she said. "I didn't want flowers, or candles, or whatever other ridiculous romantic thing you are thinking that I should have had. I mean, seriously, can't someone just want to get it done and over with in a normal way even if they waited awhile?"

"Done and over with? I was someone to get it *done and over* with?"

She didn't answer me at first, her face hardening. "That's not what I meant. I meant that I've been waiting to feel comfortable enough with someone to be able to do that. I didn't need fancy. I needed to be comfortable."

"And I can understand that, but I want to feel comfortable too, and I am not comfortable with how it happened."

I got dressed as I started to pace. Everything she was saying was only making this harder, making it all the more confusing. I didn't want to be upset, but my heart was hammering too hard, anxiety rushing through me until I couldn't hear anything besides my blood rushing in my ears.

"I can't believe I just took the virginity of a girl who thought that getting it done and over with and not telling me was better. This is my own personal type of nightmare. Whatever idea you had that not telling me was better was wrong. I deserved to know that. And since I was someone to get it done and over with, I guess you are done with me then. You will want to gain more experience because who only sleeps with the first person they've been with. Especially when that person was considered a 'done and over with' person." My train of thought was going off the rails now, but I couldn't stop it.

"Maybe, and maybe not. It's not like it's your business what I do with my body."

My laugh was harsh as I leaned over her on the bed. "Guess what? Your body is my fucking business now, and it was last night. This," I said, moving my hand over her body, "is definitely my business." I pulled away, running a hand through my hair. "I'm going to get some breakfast or coffee or something that isn't in this room. I'll talk to you later."

"I'm not sorry, Jax. I am sorry that you regret it so much, but I don't."

I stopped at the door. "I don't regret what happened. I regret the *way* it happened. It shouldn't have happened like that and you know it. But there's no going back from it now."

I hated doing it, but I couldn't be near her.

I had woken up planning to spend every second with her today and now I couldn't be within five feet of her without thinking about how badly I fucked things up.

———

I DIDN'T KNOW how it went from the best weekend of my life to the worst in a matter of hours. I spent the day trying to avoid her, and she seemed more than happy to ignore me. At some point, I had wanted to talk to her, but didn't even know where to start.

And when I went to the bedroom that night, she was gone.

I grabbed my pillow and headed to the living room, knowing she was going to set herself up on the couch, but I wasn't going to let her pout out here and make me out to be the bad guy again.

I saw her wrapped up in a blanket like a burrito, her eyes focused on her phone.

"Go to bed, Carly. I'm sleeping out here."

"I'm already set up."

"I don't care. I call dibs out here. Go to bed."

"No."

"It's either go lay in that damn bed or we are going to share the couch."

"Like you would rather sleep out here than in there. Go away, Jax. You don't need to act like some chivalrous gentlemen after what you did."

I really didn't know if she meant taking her virginity while drunk or acting like an asshole when I found out, but I didn't care. I was an asshole for both.

Between spending all day busy with the crew while in constant turmoil about her, I was fucking exhausted.

I walked over, looming over her, but she still didn't look up.

"Go to bed, Carly."

"No."

"Fine," I said, leaning down and scooping her up, making sure the blanket and pillow were caught up with her.

She flailed. "What the hell are you doing? Put me down. I told you that you can't carry me."

"And I told you that's bullshit."

"You won't be able to go all the way to the bedroom. Put me down now."

"No, you are not going to act like I kicked you out of the room when I can kick myself out of the room. Sleep in here, be comfortable."

"I was fine where I was."

"I'm sure. That couch looks so fucking comfortable. And I'm sure you're going to love when all our friends start making noise at all hours of the morning. I'm already excited to stay awake all night on it."

"Exactly, you won't be able to sleep out there, so stay in the bedroom."

I pushed open the door and threw her onto the bed.

"I won't be able to sleep anywhere because I won't be next to you and I know you will be in the other room, completely pissed off at me, so sleep in here where at least one of us will enjoy the bed."

I turned, shutting the door behind me and stalking back into the living room. I knew I wasn't lying. I wasn't going to sleep, no matter what.

It was like I could feel the anger rolling off of her, flowing straight to me and eating me alive. It was completely my fault, and I didn't know what to do about it.

TWENTY-ONE
CARLY

I SOMEHOW MADE it through the rest of the weekend avoiding Jax. For the first time since I met him, he seemed to be avoiding me right back, which only made me angrier.

When it was time to go home, he even went as far as choosing to drive, and I knew it was to avoid sitting in the back with me. Which was fine. I liked sitting with Scout more, anyway. And if he wanted to be mad at me for something that was out of my control, then he could. If he wanted to treat me like that after he knew my insecurities about it, then fine.

I was *fine*.

My nose scrunched at the word. Because I was sick of being fine. I had been fine for years now, and I didn't want to be just fine anymore. I wanted to be good. I wanted to be happy, and I wanted to have control of that on my own.

I leaned forward over the console between Jax and Kye.

"When will my truck be done?" I asked, looking over at Jax. His eyes stayed glued to the road, but I saw the way his nostrils flared and his hands tightened on the steering wheel.

Good. I hoped I was annoying him.

"Like I said, this weekend was going to set me back a few days. I can try to finish it up, and maybe have it done before next weekend."

"Is there anything I could do to help that?" I asked.

"Do you suddenly know how to rebuild engines?" Kye asked with a playful smirk.

"No, but I didn't know if there was anything that I could do to help speed up the process."

"There's not," Jax said, the tone sounding like this was a final decision for him. It probably was, because I could only assume that he wanted to stay as far away from me as possible until I left.

"Fine. I was just checking," I said, sitting back and looking at Scout, who rolled her eyes.

"There's plenty she can do, Jax, and it wouldn't hurt to teach her about it so she can do a few more things herself."

"I can either get it done quickly, or I can teach you about what I'm doing. Your choice, but I can't do both."

I didn't answer. While I loved Scout for being on my side of this, I didn't think Jax and I working on my truck together was going to help anything. Although he might move quicker if I was hanging around bothering him.

I stayed quiet the rest of the drive, and the entire time we unpacked, neither of us said a word until I tried to cook. I had been so focused on being mad that I ended up burning the entire thing. It was so burnt, I couldn't even attempt to taste it, let alone choke it down.

He gave a harsh laugh when he saw the pan. "Is that supposed to be chicken?"

"Yes," I said, gritting my teeth. "But obviously I burned it."

"Yeah, I got that," he said, still smiling, but at least he was trying to hide it this time. "I'll order us food."

I could only huff and clean up, even more pissed off. Considering how mad I was, I was surprised that it was even possible. Even more surprised that I was so mad, but couldn't think of being anywhere else.

Later, when he sat down in the living room, I grabbed the remote and put on an old scary movie. One that he probably wasn't going to like. Maybe I was being petty, a little passive aggressive, but I wasn't going to break and apologize to him. I didn't want to, and if I didn't stay angry, I was going to fall victim to his stupidly cute face.

With his freak out after I opened up, I didn't think I had anything to apologize for, so I was going to sit, be angry, and wait for my truck to be done.

———

AS SOON AS Jax left on Monday morning to head to the garage, I started pacing around the apartment.

I wanted to run away and not have to deal with any more of this, but that currently wasn't an option. I had to get through another week of this and then I could disappear. It wasn't impossible. It's not like Jax was doing anything to make me feel rushed anymore than I was rushing myself, and leaving would only be easier if we weren't talking.

The thought knocked me back, because whether it happened now or in a week, I knew I was going to miss Jax. I was going to miss all of them.

It was the exact thing I had been trying to avoid. No part of me believed in forever, and I needed to remind myself of that. It had to end at some point. Why not rip the bandaid off sooner?

Aside from Jax and the girls, there was only one other person I could talk to. One person that I had talked to all my life, but hadn't dared to call yet. I had wanted to wait until I was gone to call, but now the laptop and I would be out of here soon. Then, I could open the laptop, and decide what I could bring to the police without fear of Slaughter hurting the crew.

Tears threatened me as I stared down at the phone. My sister was the only one who could truly understand what was happening right now. But as much as I trusted my sister, she was also in a house with Tristan, and I didn't know how much he monitored her phone. I took another deep breath, trying to sort through my thoughts as the door swung open.

"Hey, Carly," Scout said, heading right to the coffeemaker, Quinn trailing in after her.

"Hey," Quinn said, coming to a stop as she looked at me. "Are you okay?"

"No, I mean, I'm kind of okay. What are you guys doing here?"

"You seemed all pissed off and quiet in the car, so I told Quinn we should stop by after we were done with errands. Ash wanted to come, but there was something at Holt that she needed to take care of. She does want to have a girls only night this week though, which, obviously, I'm in."

"What about tonight?" I asked. "One less night of awkwardly hanging around Jax would be great."

"Uh-oh," Quinn said, sitting down at the counter. "What happened?"

"Nothing that I shouldn't have seen coming. I want you guys to know that as long as my truck is done this weekend, I'll be leaving."

They looked at each other before looking back at me. "It's that bad? Does Jax know you are planning to leave so soon?"

"I don't see why he wouldn't. He's barely talking to me and knows that I want my truck done as soon as possible. I even offered what help I could to finish it sooner."

Quinn laughed. "Only Jax could piss a girl off so much that she is begging to go to the garage and work on an old truck. Not that I don't agree with you on this, because Jax runs his mouth so bad sometimes that even I want to smack him. Is it possible that this could be fixed?"

"I don't think that's a question for me. I think that's a question for Jax. My contribution to this fight isn't as bad as his, at least if we're comparing the two. And I don't even think it matters now? I think the fight and my plan are set in stone, so I will be leaving next weekend."

Quinn's phone rang, and she apologized before grabbing it.

"How is that even possible?" she said. "We stopped by this morning and it was fine."

Scout leaned in closer, trying to listen in on the conversation, but Quinn swatted her away, making me laugh. "Yeah, fine. We'll head there now."

She hung up and looked between Scout and I. "So, I guess with everything going on, that it would be a no to coming down to the garage to help me right now?"

"Why? What's going on?" Scout asked.

"Apparently, the office sink had a small leak while we were gone that has now turned into a big leak. They didn't notice until the water started dripping out into the garage. The guys already turned the water off and fixed it, but I have a ton to clean up now. I know Scout has a car she needs to get done, and Ash will be at Holt most of the day now. So, maybe you wouldn't mind coming to help?" She gave a hopeful smile.

"Damn. We still have a lot of parts in the office. Hopefully, they started moving them. Do you feel bad enough for Quinn that you will come with us?"

"You only need help cleaning up?" I asked.

"Yeah, and maybe some organizing after. It sounds like it might have made a mess, so it could be an hour. It could be all day. I'm not sure yet."

"And Jax would be…"

"In the garage, and we could kick him out if needed."

I took a deep breath and nodded. "Yeah, of course I'll come help. And I shouldn't worry about Jax. I have to live with him for a few more days. Being around him shouldn't be an issue."

"No, but you're allowed to be upset with him. And allowed to be sad. If you don't want to see him, you can stay with either of us until your truck is done. We can figure out something comfortable at Scout's place. We had a second bed in there before, so we could do it again."

Even mad at Jax, it was an easy answer. "No, it's alright. There's no point doing all of that for a few days. It's fine. We can be civil to each other."

"Alright, whatever you want. Seriously, just tell one of us if you change your mind. So you'll come with us to the garage? And Riot would come too, of course," Quinn said, patting his head.

"Yeah, I'm in. But after we're done, would you mind being the one to drive me back down?"

"Not at all. Maybe some time with me will help you get your mind off of things for a while. And hopefully Jax won't bother us."

"I don't think he'll be bothering you necessarily. I think it's more like he will be there begging for forgiveness," Scout said.

"Yeah, that's pretty likely," Quinn agreed.

"I'm not looking for that, so let's hope not," I said with a tight smile before going to change. I cleaned up the last of the kitchen quickly, Quinn's words stuck in my mind.

Was I sad about Jax's reaction? Or just angry?

I barely had time to think about it as they talked the entire way there, and ten minutes later, I was walking into the garage. I knew there was a side door to the office, but Quinn parked us in front of a bay door, leaving me no rational choice but to walk through the open bay.

I don't know if he saw us coming or if it was that much of a coincidence, but Jax stepped in front of me as soon as I stepped inside.

"What are you doing here?" he asked, but he didn't sound angry. If anything, he only sounded surprised.

"Quinn asked for some help."

"I figured you would be staying a hundred feet away from me at all possible times."

"I was planning on it, but I'm not going to tell Quinn no when you have all been so nice to me."

"Quinn is being nice because she is nice, not because she expects it to be a favor that will be repaid."

"I know that, but I like her and want to help," I said. "Is that a problem?"

"Not at all. I'm glad you're here. Do you want to go get something to eat with me in a bit? I've been wanting to talk, but with the daggers you stare at me, I've been a little worried about being murdered if I try."

I looked up at him, his hair a little messy, his annoyingly hot button-up mechanic shirt pulling around his biceps. His smile that always seemed to be aimed at me.

It was hard to believe this was the guy that had been quickly becoming my best friend, and the one I had slept with. I don't remember the last time that I spent this much time with one person and gave so much of myself. Worst of all, I couldn't believe how little I hated him and only wanted to do it all again.

I was always quick to cut friends and potential boyfriends out of my life for the smallest of things, and now the thought of letting him go, letting them all go, hurt.

He was still waiting, looking me over as intently as I was looking at him.

"No," I said.

Jax's face cracked, his smile growing. "No?"

"No. You don't get to be all sweet and make a joke and think this is fixed. You don't get to go out to eat and be all charming and think I'm okay with this."

"So you do think I'm charming?" he asked with a grin.

"Are you serious, Jax?" I said, moving to push around him.

"Sorry," he said, wincing. "Joking when someone is mad at me is a habit. I don't want to make a joke of it. I just wanted to talk to you."

"I don't want to go out to eat with you. I have to go help Quinn anyway," I said, heading towards the office.

"Carly, wait. I'm sorry." He almost yelled the words, making me stalk back to him.

"I don't want to talk about this now."

"I want to talk about this now."

"And that's not your decision," I said. "You hurt me. You don't get to decide if, or when, we talk about this." The weird lump in my throat grew again. I did want to talk to him. I wanted him to fix it and make me feel better again, but I was almost too scared to find out what he had to say.

He was quiet, but didn't look away. "Fine. Are you going to tell me if you do want to talk?"

My heart sank, and I nodded. "Yeah, I will."

I turned and headed into the office, not looking back at him. Maybe I was too scared to talk to him, maybe I was too angry, or maybe, deep down, I knew this would make leaving easier.

Either way, I didn't turn back, and he didn't come after me. Everything was exactly how it should be.

TWENTY-TWO

JAX

ASKING her to lunch was a long shot, but I didn't know where else to start. Now she had been in the garage office for over four hours with Quinn, and I hadn't even gotten another glimpse of her.

"Hey, I have to finish this car up, and Scout has a few things to do on that one," Fox said, nodding to the two full garage bays. "You want to get dinner here tonight? I assume you're on truck-fixing duty."

I looked at the green truck in the corner. I had made a little more progress, and more parts had shown up today that would put it close to done when I got them on. The truck that would take Carly as far away from me as possible. Working on it was like nailing my own coffin. Not that I had done anything the other night to make her want to stay.

"Yeah, sounds good. The girls staying?"

"Scout and Quinn? Yeah, of course. Ransom will be back from the store soon, so he will be here. And Ash will be back from Holt soon too," he said with a grin.

"You know who I meant."

He rolled his eyes. "Maybe try asking her yourself?"

"I would prefer to, but I was trying to keep the peace."

"No, you want to avoid the wrath of Carly."

"I want to avoid the rage that seems to radiate from her when I am close."

Fox rolled his eyes as Quinn and Carly walked out.

"I'm starving," Quinn said. "We forgot to eat lunch with the mess in there, so I really hope food is on its way."

"Give me five minutes and it will be," Fox said, disappearing to call.

Carly leaned on the car next to Kye, asking him things that I couldn't hear. I wasn't trying to avoid her completely, but now I was worried about saying the wrong thing again. I was on thin ice. What if one more stupid thing came out of my mouth and cracked that ice completely?

I spent the next twenty minutes pretending to look at a car, but I was only thinking of what I could say. I guess there was no avoiding the inevitable–and me saying the wrong thing was, in fact, inevitable.

"Hey," I said, moving around to Carly. Kye eyed me but kept working. She didn't even look at me. "Can you come here for a second?"

"I can't. Kye is teaching me about cars."

"Yeah, well, he can continue doing that after. I just need a minute."

She looked at Kye, who shrugged, and then looked back at me. "Fine. One minute."

I was already grabbing her hand and pulling her through the back door before she finished. I wasn't going to waste any second she was going to give me. We had turned the area behind the garage into more of a backyard than anything, with chairs, a fire pit, and a place to grill. We usually ended up here once a week to cook out, but Carly's cooking, and colder weather, had everyone ending up at my apartment more often lately.

"What did you want to talk about?" she asked, crossing her arms and closing herself off immediately.

I was already off to a great start.

"I want to actually apologize. I'm sorry that I freaked out, and said those things. I'm sorry that I acted that way at all and I know that doesn't make up for what I said. I should have stepped back for five seconds before freaking out."

She stared up at me, looking over my face, but not giving anything away.

"But did you mean what you said?"

"Of course I did. You should have told me, and it shouldn't have happened that way. And I was right to be mad that it did. But it didn't mean that I should have reacted that way. That part is all on me. I shouldn't have left you there alone, and I should have at least tried to make the experience better for you."

"None of it was bad until you did that."

"Yeah, I realize that now, but at that moment, I thought I ruined everything for you."

"The only time you ruined anything for me was storming out. I get I should have told you sooner, but you know what doesn't help when someone has insecurities around sex? Storming out angry after they tell you it was the first time they felt comfortable enough to do that."

"I know. I know that, but at that moment I wasn't thinking about that. I was being selfish."

"Food is here!" Fox yelled from the garage, making Carly pull away immediately.

"It's fine, Jax. It's not a big deal, okay? We both messed up, and it's fine. This is better for both of us, so let's go eat and forget about it."

Before I had a chance to say anything more, she was gone, disappearing back into the garage.

———

TWO HOURS LATER, everyone was sitting around talking while I kept working on the truck. Even Carly stayed back to hang out, Riot sleeping at her feet now after running around all day, which I hoped was a good sign from both of them. She was still here and wasn't sending Riot after me. Not that I worried about him much anymore. If Riot wasn't next to Carly, it was because he was next to me. Not only was I getting attached to Carly, I was getting attached to Riot, too.

As I leaned back, I couldn't help but steal glances at her. She had taken over every corner of my mind, a magnetic force that made me want to be next to her, touch her, talk to her. I didn't want to sit this far, and pretend to ignore her.

"Could I use someone's car later this week?" Carly asked, looking around as everyone's heads snapped to her.

"For what?" Scout asked, probably wondering the same thing I was. Where could she possibly be going that she needed one of our cars?

"I wanted to go see my grandpa. I haven't tried to see him with everything going on, but I think it's been long enough that they'll think I'm too far away to visit. At least I hope so. I would like to see him once more before I go, since I don't know when I'll have the chance again."

The crew was quiet, and I knew they weren't going to offer their cars. Not because they didn't want to help her, but because they already knew I would do it. Sometimes having a group of friends that knew you better than anyone was annoying. And sometimes, it was the best.

"I'll take you," I said.

"I can drive. And pretty well, actually. That's not the issue. I just need something to drive for a few hours."

"I know, but I'll still take you. Better that you don't go alone. Just in case."

"Just in case, what?" She crossed her arms, glaring at me.

"I don't know. In case something goes wrong. I'll take you."

"And if I would rather someone else take me?" Her eyebrow arched and her snippy tone pushed at every button I had. She always wanted to be a brat, and she knew it. I didn't know if she realized exactly how much I liked it, though. I would always let her take the lead if it made her more comfortable but when she acted like this it only turned me on which I didn't think was her intended effect.

I got up, stalking around, and grabbing her hand to pulling her up.

"What are you doing?" she asked, as I put my arm around her.

"Talking to you," I said as we came around the side of the garage where my car was parked.

"We already did that."

"Well, we need to try again." I leaned her up against my car, caging her in. "I told you, I'm sorry and I want to fix it."

"And I said fine, but I know you're about to be all charming and cute and think that gets you off the hook."

"Then what am I supposed to be? I can't be all grumpy and glaring. That's your role here, and I can't be a complete asshole to you because that isn't going to fix this. And also, I don't *want* to be. Do you not like me when I'm all sweet and charming?"

"Maybe. I don't care either way, but I don't like that it makes it harder to be mad at you."

"I have to come with all I've got to get past your defenses. You can't take the only weapon I have."

"Weapon? Are we at war now?" For the first time since this

fight started, the scowl broke and her lips turned up the slightest amount. It was hope for me, at least.

I laughed, leaning down and kissing her cheek. "I think that's a good way to describe fighting with you. I will wave the white flag, though. I surrender completely."

"No kissing."

"Well, I hate that, but I will do pretty much anything you tell me to if it makes up for what I did. I had a bad moment, a freakout from my own insecurities, and panic that you couldn't actually like me and I hated it. It wasn't fair, but what you did wasn't fair either. I can't sit here and have you push me away. I won't let that happen without trying to do everything I can to make you not do that."

Her eyebrows furrowed, but she didn't say anything for a while.

"We can go back to being friends, then. That way you can be yourself, and we can live in peace for the last few days that I'm here."

"You want to be friends with me?"

"We only have a few days left. So yeah, friends."

"I was hoping we could have a redo of all of this. Your first time, a relationship, and maybe you stay a little longer."

"Or we can be friends, no redo, and I still leave once my truck is done."

"I really wish I had more bargaining power here," I said, and she grinned. "If we are negotiating, then we negotiate every-thing, including the leaving part."

"Then I guess we aren't negotiating," she said. "We will be friends and I will leave soon."

I leaned down, my lips hovering at hers. "Friends then. Best *fucking* friends."

TWENTY-THREE
CARLY

THE NEXT DAY, we were headed to my grandpa's house, and I was more of a mess than I expected. Maybe Jax was right. I tried to go to war when I was mad, and that apparently included war with myself. Now I was spending way too much time convincing myself that being friends with him was easier than staying for more.

But I liked the way he looked at me, the way he smiled at me, and that he always seemed to be trying to make me smile back. I shouldn't have let myself get so wrapped up in him.

As if the world wanted to remind me of that, I opened the drawer to finish getting dressed and froze, staring at the laptop. I needed to face my own fears and open it. Now, I knew as soon as I did, this could all be over. I needed to face what I had done, and stop being a coward, but going up against Slaughter still felt like too much, so I slammed the drawer shut again.

I was going to focus on one thing at a time, and today that was going to see my grandpa. Then, when I was far away from Jax, I could face Slaughter without risking any of them being involved.

I moved to the mirror. I looked different, softer maybe, although there was something in my face that never seemed to lose the resting bitch face look. I didn't think it could ever change now.

Even in the red sundress, I still didn't look exactly as soft and sweet as I hoped, but I did think I looked nice.

When I stepped out into the living room, Jax wasn't looking down at his phone or preoccupied this time. He was already staring at me, a smile plastered on his face.

"Fuck," he said, his lips parting. "You look..." His words died out with a quiet laugh that made me freeze.

"Are you seriously laughing at me for wearing this?"

"No. I mean, not really. It's just, most days, you dress like you summon demons in your spare time, little witch. Maybe even scare them off when they arrive. Now you're dressed like that and look like a perfect angel. You look cute."

"Is that supposed to be bad, then?"

"Not at all. Just different. You could wear anything and I would like it, though, so I might be biased. I was sitting here, getting more and more excited to see what you chose. It's become my own little show every day, waiting to see what you walk out in."

"You did seem ready to see me today."

"I'm always ready. It's a highlight of my day now, and you always deliver. I can't think of one outfit you've worn that hasn't driven me crazy."

"What about my leggings and t-shirts?"

"Are you kidding? Your ass looks so perfect in those things. They are a personal favorite."

"Jax! Do you say those things to all your friends?"

"No, but I normally don't sleep with my friends, and I don't want to just be your friend. I'll try to behave with the friends thing, but you aren't making it easy."

"Are you actually going to behave? My grandpa is a little weird, but I also don't want him to know about any of this," I said, waving my hand between us. "I also don't want him to know about the racing, or what happened with Slaughter, or any other bad thing you can think of, so you have to behave."

"I promise to be on my very best behavior with all of that, but there's no possible way for me to keep from flirting with you. Besides, you flirt back. Now, come on, let's go or we are going to be late."

He started out the door, not waiting for me to catch up. Riot ran after him, and for a second I could only watch them go.

Riot had always been glued to my side, my little shadow that was never more than an arm's length away, and we both always seemed to want it that way. It didn't matter who came to the house or who I hung out with, Riot was next to me. Without me even realizing, Riot had made himself at home here, and with Jax. He was always happy to hang around him, follow him where he could, and I was starting to suspect that Riot would be happy going to the garage with him for work every day based on his cries when Jax left in the mornings.

My dog had become a traitor, and I couldn't even blame him.

———

TWENTY MINUTES LATER, we were headed to my grandpa's house, tucked away down an old farm road. You wouldn't be able to see another house for miles. The landscape was a mix of fields and forest, but utterly devoid of people, which was somehow comforting and unnerving at the same time.

"Your grandpa lives all the way out here?"

"Yeah, he moved out here a long time ago for the peace and quiet. But I think it became a lot for him to handle and things, um…changed."

"How?"

"You'll see."

Jax shifted in his seat before glancing over at me. "Is he going to hate me?"

"I honestly don't know what he's going to think about you, so I guess we'll see about that, too."

"Now you're freaking me out. All I'm picturing is some hard ass, old army guy that is going to hate my guts."

"Um, not quite, but I still don't know how he will react. Turn here," I said, pointing down another road.

"Has he ever met a boyfriend?"

"Are you trying to insinuate I would introduce you as one?" I asked, my eyebrows jumping up.

"No, but I was curious how many guys he's met with you before me."

"Do you think I've had a long enough relationship with a guy to introduce him to my family?" For some reason, I assumed he already understood that I didn't really have relationships.

"Well, I don't know," Jax said. "Why wouldn't you?"

"Guys don't really last long in relationships without sex, and I don't last long in relationships at all."

"Okay, so what's the longest relationship that you've ever had?"

"I don't know, two months maybe?"

"I feel like that could be a red flag," he said, smirking.

"Add it to my list and maybe take it as a sign that being friends is the right choice."

He gave a hard laugh. "That's not nearly enough to make me think we should only be friends. I can absolutely beat two months. I'm almost there already, *and* we are living together. I would date you without sex, if that's what it took. You know, if that was an offer you were making."

"Why would I want to date someone without that now? I found out I liked it, so there's really no going back."

He groaned. "I'm going to say that I hope that means I might still have a chance again, and then I won't say anything else about it."

He finally turned into the well-manicured driveway, the trees perfectly trimmed and beautiful wildflowers lining the path. He shifted the car, letting us move to a crawl down the long driveway.

"This is it?"

"Yeah."

"This is…nice. I'm guessing he's like an old school perfectionist then? He's really not going to like me."

"Not quite. Keep looking."

Jax crept down the driveway, but stopped as he saw the first one.

"What in the *hell* is that?"

I looked closer, already knowing exactly what it was.

"A metal dinosaur."

"Excuse me?" He looked over, his eyes wide and mouth open.

"Keep going," I said.

We made it further, and it only got worse. A giant flamingo, a bicycle with a yeti. I finally put my head down on the dash as Jax continued.

"What is going on? Is this for real? Is this his place?"

"Yes and yes. He likes to…make things."

When I looked up, we were at the house. The entire place was clean, neat, and perfect. Anyone would think he was an uptight, grandfatherly type based on the house, but the yard was littered with his creations. Animals, cannons, cars, the things he created were endless.

"He got into a very specific hobby later in life. I told you that he's a bit…eccentric. Please, be nice. I know he's a little strange, but I do love him, and if you are mean to him, we are going to have an even bigger problem."

At my words, my grandpa came out, a scowl on his face as he walked over to the car.

"Wow," Jax said. "I can already see the relation."

He looked so mean, and I had always figured that's where I got it from, but he was never mean to me. I got out, noticing the sling and purple hue around his temple.

I ran over, nearly falling before I reached him.

"What is this? What happened?" I grabbed his good arm, making sure he was steady before pulling him into a hug.

"Ahh, your dumbass stepdad stopped by and that correlated with me falling over. Nothing a shotgun couldn't fix."

"Grandpa! He did this?" I looked at Jax, seconds from bursting into tears. "Why?"

"He thought you might be here. It was about two weeks ago now. I'm alright, dear, calm down."

"He hurt you because of me?" I asked, but I already knew the answer. Of course it was because of me. I had been so worried about bringing trouble for Jax and his friends that I never thought to worry about my grandpa. The words *my fault* were screaming in my mind.

"I'm fine, Carly. It was a little sprain and a bruise from the fall. He just pushed me over a little faster than I was expecting," he said, smirking now. "Then he wasn't expecting my shotgun."

I could only shake my head. "And he hasn't been back?"

"Not after I told him I would call the police if I saw him again. Funny how he thinks he is big and bad until I say that."

Jax smiled back, and I smacked him, my eyes widening as he looked at me.

"I can have a security system set up if you would want that?" Jax asked.

"Yes, we would love that. Thank you," I said, trying to pull my grandpa back to sit on his porch. He shrugged me off, finally looking Jax over.

"Who is this?" He asked, the gruff tone very unfriendly. "And no, I don't want a security system. I told you that I have a shotgun."

"This is my friend, Jax. He drove me out here today."

"I see that. He drives one of those cars like your stepdad?"

"Yeah," I said, wincing. "But I promise he's nothing like them."

"Hmm. Interesting. I would hope not if you are willingly hanging out with him." He was still scrutinizing Jax. "Do you work?"

"Yes, sir I do. I own a mechanic shop with some friends."

"He's fixing my truck for me. I broke down a few weeks ago."

"Oh, I heard. Heard you ran off, and they came across your truck, and some guy hit Tristan. They were going to call in that you were kidnapped, but I told your mother that was ridiculous till she finally listened. Then they came over after that."

"Kidnapped?" I said, my voice going high. "The only one trying to kidnap me was Tristan. Jax had to punch him just so we could leave."

Grandpa laughed, looking at Jax again. "So that's why Tristan's nose was purple? Good," he said with a firm nod before turning to me. "I knew you would be leaving there, just didn't know when. I'm glad you finally came around here, though. Are you here to stay for dinner too, or dropping her off?"

"He's staying if you're okay with that," I said, not knowing why this was making me so nervous.

Grandpa's frown deepened as he looked at the tattoos on Jax's arms and then back up to look him over.

"Depends."

"On?" Jax asked, obviously nervous.

"On if you want to come see what I'm working on."

Jax let out a deep, relieved breath. "I absolutely do."

"Good. Are you coming with us, or are you heading for the kitchen?" He asked me, but turned to Jax. "She was always more worried about what we could cook together. It wasn't until I brought that truck around that she came out to see what was going on. Then, for a long time, we couldn't get her away from that thing. I knew she had to keep it. Now she likes to make sure I eat, though. Can't get her back out here."

"It's not that I don't want to. You eat frozen TV dinners if I don't cook a ton while I'm here."

"Yeah, yeah. Always taking care of me. Those TV dinners taste fine."

"Are you saying you don't like my cooking?"

"Like it? Not at all, dear, I love your cooking. It makes me feel like I'm home every time. Just don't leave me out here with your hooligan friend for too long."

"I barely want to leave you two alone for a minute, let alone for a long time."

Grandpa turned, heading towards his big barn as Jax leaned down to whisper to me. "I hope I'm not about to be killed in the barn."

"No, but I swear if you two blow anything up, I'm blaming you."

"Blowing up? He's got stuff to blow up?"

"Jax," I said, dropping my tone.

"Come get me if you need help," he said, kissing my cheek and running to catch up.

I should have thought this through more.

Jax was wild, and so was my grandpa. He was eighty-five years old and wanted to run around like he was younger than me.

Nothing good was going to come of them being out there together.

———

AN HOUR LATER, I had prepped almost all the food, and knew I had to go check on them before I started the actual cooking.

The walk to the barn wasn't far, but I was nervous the entire way. At least Jax's car was still here, and he hadn't been run off. I went to open the door and screamed as something really did blow up.

"Carly?" Jax asked, coming around the back side of the barn to me. "Shit. We didn't know you came out here."

"What was that?"

"You are not going to believe it. Come on. Come see what we made," he said. He was so excited as he wrapped an arm around me to pull me back.

Then grandpa came around the corner. "Sorry, dear. Nothing was going to hurt you, so calm down."

Then I heard it.

Engines revving as they slowed, coming down the driveway.

I reached for Jax, my fingers digging in as I pulled him close. "Slaughter?"

"No. No, it's the crew. Your grandpa said I should invite them over, too."

My fingers relaxed. "All of them?"

Jax laughed, pulling me towards the cars. "Is there someone you don't particularly like?"

"No. Of course not, but do they all really need to meet my grandpa?"

"Yes, they do. He asked to meet all your new friends, and I wasn't going to tell him no. Plus, I had them stop and install a security camera in the metal dinosaur so we can see if Slaughter or Tristan come back."

Relief flooded me, and it took everything in me not to throw myself at him. My grandpa would be safer now.

"Are you sure they should come meet him, though? You've hung out with him. He's a little strange."

"Are you serious? He's awesome. We just built a fucking potato gun."

"You did what?" Scout said, hopping out of her car.

"We built a gun that shoots *potatoes*," Jax said, holding my hand and waving it all along with his. He looked so excited, so happy, that any nervousness I was feeling about my grandpa meeting them was disappearing.

"Come on, we made two of them."

My grandpa's eyebrows were up when everyone came over.

"Well, this is about what I was expecting." He looked them all over, from tattoos, to dirty boots, to the obviously fast cars. There was a lot to take in. "Seems like a group of criminals," he added, but then started laughing.

I went through their names, introducing them all to him.

He gave a grunt in return. "Call me grandpa or don't call me anything. Now come on, Jax, your friends are here. Let's see who's the best shot."

Jax held on to me, following grandpa back around the building. "I never want to leave. Please, let's move here."

"Oh, I'm sure he would love the company. Would it just be you and your six friends?"

"Yes, and my unruly witch and her dog."

I couldn't not laugh. "Right. Let's keep you all contained at the apartments for now."

"Fine, *for now*."

Riot went along with them, everyone disappearing as I tried to take it all in. I thought my grandpa would be hesitant like I was after knowing how much he hated Slaughter and Tristan too, but he was ready to have them over and apparently didn't mind hanging out with all of them.

It was too easy. This life with Jax fit too well and everything felt simple, even the big things. Seeing how happy everyone was only made me want to cry, wishing it could stay this way, but I knew things didn't last like that. It couldn't. I was technically lying to him, hiding the laptop, and not coming clean about what happened, not completely.

We were friends now and if I left it this way, it would be a clean break.

TWENTY-FOUR
JAX

CARLY HAD COOKED, and if I thought what she made for us was a lot, the amount she made today would put those dinners to shame.

We helped pack it all into his fridge and freezer before sitting back down to eat more. Not that I minded.

"Alright," her grandpa said, pushing away from the table. "I've made my decision on all of you."

That grabbed all of our attention, everyone looking at him. I had expected a mean, stuffy old man, and while he was a little of that, overall, he was pretty great.

"And?" I asked, every part of me hoping this was going to be good. I couldn't imagine Carly wanting to hang around anyone her grandpa didn't trust.

He looked right at me.

"Get up. All of you. Come on."

We listened, waiting as he got up and made his way to the door, where we lined up behind him. None of the crew seemed to mind. We were all too curious to see what he could want for any of us to protest.

"Grandpa, what are you doing?" Carly asked, running to his side. "It's dark out."

"Everyone's got those damn lights on their phones if they're scared of the dark."

"I was more concerned with you falling in the dark," she grumbled, trying to hold on to him. I went to her side, balancing her as she balanced him.

'Thanks,' she mouthed as we all made it outside and started across the lawn.

"Carly, honey, I live alone. You think I'm not out here all the time?"

"Fine, I get it. Why are you taking them back here? We never go to this barn." He was leading us to a barn at the back of the property that I would have guessed was abandoned. I leaned down to her ear, taking any opportunity to get closer to her.

"No? I thought this spooky old barn would be your favorite place." She elbowed me hard as I laughed.

"Yeah, and for a damn good reason," Grandpa said, taking my thoughts back to what we were doing.

"Why? What's back here? I don't think I've ever even seen the inside of this one."

"Bunch of junk," he said. "A bunch of junk that no one but your mom knew about, and I planned to keep it that way."

"But?" I asked, knowing there had to be more.

"But," he said, motioning for us to move the metal that had been piled up in front of the door. "I'm old enough to know when I'm right about things. And I've decided I'm right about you all."

"Damn," Scout muttered to Fox behind me. "He's taking us all out at once in the creepy old barn."

"I really have some respect for that," Kye said. "Very efficient."

"Or maybe just Jax for messing with Carly," Fox added.

"Will you two shut up?" I asked.

"We're going to miss you, man," Fox said. "We will take really good care of your car."

I turned, ready to hit him, but her grandpa spoke up again. "Now cut this lock off," he said, handing me a set of bolt cutters. "I lost the key years ago."

"What's going on? What is in here that you haven't told anyone about?" Carly asked, her hands on her hips now. She was looking more pissed off by the second.

"Something I got years ago. Many, many years ago now. I always thought your mom would remarry someone that I actually liked and maybe he could take it, but that didn't work out. Then I thought your sister or you might have it one day, but I saw the way you looked at that truck, and your sister Chloe was never interested in cars."

"So why show us?"

"Because I told you. I know when I'm right and I know when I'm wrong. After so many years of surviving, you just learn how to listen to your gut."

The lock broke, letting Ransom and I pull open the doors.

I don't think anyone was ready for what was on the other side, though.

"A 1968 Charger? This is what you consider a bunch of junk?"

"I like calling it that. Keeps the nosey people out of my business."

Without a word, the crew was surrounding it, brushing it off and moving things away from it.

"Jax," he said, snapping my attention away from the car. "What do you think?"

"I think it's beautiful."

"I'm glad you think so, because you're going to make it run."

"I am?"

"You fixed her truck. Might as well have you fix this, too. It shouldn't be too bad. I've worked on it through the years and started it up, but it needs attention."

"And you trust me to do that?"

"Grandpa, no," Carly hissed, moving him aside as though we couldn't all hear. "I'm not staying with them. You can't give them the car."

"I'm not giving it to them, but Jax can take it and fix it. I assume take a drive or two in it," he said chuckling.

"But I'm leaving as soon as my truck is done."

"Sure. And that's fine if you think you want to do that, but I know how happy you are. And it won't hurt to let him take this. Maybe you'll be back. Maybe you can all come over all the time and we can cook together again." Her face fell and sad eyes met mine as she looked right at me. "I wish I could, but I don't know if that can happen."

"He's taking the car, Carly, and if he would like to drive it, I don't mind. Now knock off your attitude and enjoy the night."

I hid my laugh as her eyes went wide and nostrils flared, more pissed off than ever. I doubted there was anyone else that would tell her that and not get an earful in response, but she wasn't going to talk back to him. I only laughed harder at the thought. I didn't think this was going to add any points in my favor, but I still went right to her side, all that anger turning on me.

"You can't take it."

"I wasn't going to take it, but I will take it to the garage and get it fixed for him."

"No, just leave it here."

"Not when he asked me to do something for him." I knew she was going to be more mad, but I wasn't going to let her need to not intertwine our lives make more problems for her grandpa, and quite honestly, I would rather be on her bad side for a few hours than on his forever.

"You are serious?"

"Completely. We will take it back to the garage, fix it, and return it."

"Fine, then. I'm going back inside." She spun on her heel, stomping out of the barn and leaving us to look over the car more and talk to him about it.

When we said goodbye and made it home hours later, she was still clearly annoyed, doing her best to give me the cold shoulder. But despite her attempts to keep up the act, I couldn't help but notice how she couldn't resist stealing glances or reaching out to touch me. It was becoming pretty obvious that I still might have a shot at something more again.

TWENTY-FIVE
CARLY

By Saturday, I was on edge. I had tried to stay busy with cooking, and Riot, and quite literally anything that would keep the dirty thoughts about my roommate at bay, but nothing was working.

I should have known only being friends with Jax would be almost impossible. He wasn't helping by apparently doing anything he could to remind me how much he liked me. And I couldn't get through one day without him reminding me how good he thought I looked. As someone with huge insecurities with my body, it was a shock to have someone constantly reminding you of something like that.

And to know that my grandpa seemed to love him wasn't helping. Before we left, my grandpa had let me know that he wanted us all to come back soon, and even hinted that he would like to come by the garage. Next thing I know, my grandpa was going to be out at the street races with the crew.

I was annoyed about it because I secretly loved it.

The fight with Jax, then having to be friends with him, and now wanting him close, but also wanting to leave, was putting me in such a bad mood that even standing here alone in the kitchen was pissing me off.

Jax walked back in after apparently spending the morning out with the guys at some car event. I hadn't wanted to go even though I had been invited, preferring to seethe in peace instead of watching Jax walk around all morning looking hot and untouchable.

I reached for a bag of chips, needing something to angrily snack on as I baked. As though the world was cursing right back at me, I immediately struggled to open it, trying to rip it open, and only growing more frustrated when it wouldn't.

I heard the front door shut as Jax walked into the kitchen smiling as he saw me. I could feel the annoyance and anger boiling. My life was somehow falling apart again, and this bag not opening was the last straw.

He walked over to grab water, not interfering with my ongoing temper tantrum as I turned my back to him.

"Can you hand me the scissors?" I asked, knowing he was watching my every move. He came up behind me, wrapping his arms around me and grabbing the bag from my hands.

"Here, let the big, strong man do that for you."

"Jax," I warned as he pulled away. He hadn't added any sweet nicknames, but I knew he was trying his best to be flirty and cute to make me happier.

"What are you —" My mouth dropped open as he walked to the other side of the kitchen, grabbed a pair of scissors, opened the bag, and handed it back to me.

"There you go. See, your big strong man is always here to help." His tone teasing me now as he patted my cheek.

"Jax!" I yelled again, my temper rising before he looked at me and smiled.

The playful grin on his face making me smile back at him before I could stop it. The one flaw in Jax was that there was no being mad at him. The sweet eyes and bright smile made it impossible.

"I'm glad that sunbeam science is back. A little sun on your face, and you can't stop smiling."

"You are ridiculous. Stop making being mad at you so hard."

"Oh, don't even worry. I know even with your smile, you are still mad at me."

"Good," I said, trying to be pissed off again. "Because the smiling and cute stuff like that, and the joking around, is really getting under my skin."

He laughed, leaning against the counter next to me. "There's my little witch. Back again with her scowl. I'm surprised your hands aren't always around my throat now that all my charm has worn off."

"Well, I'm sure you're looking forward to that. I know I am."

I could feel the heat of him right next to me now, the light scent of him taking over, and I tried not to let it show how much it was affecting me.

"You say the filthiest things. It's no wonder why I was so shocked to find out you were a virgin."

I spun, looking up at his smiling face. "Maybe it wasn't meant to be filthy. Maybe it was meant to be threatening."

"Then please forgive me when I get hard as your hands wrap around my throat."

A huge part of why it took me so long to lose my virginity was because of my lack of interest in most guys and my insecurities surrounding my body. Getting naked with someone was not as fun when all you were thinking about was how horrible you might look.

But with him I wasn't. Not nearly as much as I had with everyone else. With Jax, I could almost believe I was beautiful, and that was a powerful feeling.

I trailed my hand up his stomach and chest, reaching his

collarbone. His head tilted up, giving me all the access I wanted as my hand reached for his throat. I could feel him swallow as my fingers wrapped around his thick neck, and my nails dug in a little harder as he groaned before I let go, dropping my hands back down to his chest.

He pulled in a ragged breath. "I already told you what's going to happen. I won't be apologizing for it."

"Something wrong?" I asked, moving in close until I could feel how hard he was. His nostrils flared and his chest heaved.

I liked this.

A lot.

"I'm fine," he said, his throat tight.

"Great, then do you mind helping me and stirring this batter?" I dropped my hands and stepped back, losing all contact.

His breathing was still erratic as he began to stir the brownie batter. I didn't actually need his help, but I wasn't quite done with this game yet.

"That's good. Let me taste it?"

His eyes narrowed as he smirked. "Of course." He stirred once, filling the spatula with the batter before lifting it towards my lips. Right before it reached my lips, though, he dropped it down, letting some of it drop to my chest.

"Oops, my bad. Let me clean up my mess." Before I could say anything else, his head dropped and his mouth was on me, licking and sucking off the batter.

I wove my fingers into his hair, pulling his head away. "What are you doing?"

"Cleaning up after myself," he said, an innocent smile across his face as I held his head back by his hair.

"I think it's clean enough."

He was laughing hard as he stood up, swiping a finger across the spatula until it was coated in batter. "Fine, here," he said, moving his finger along my lips. "Lick."

I usually hated being told what to do, my first reaction was to always do the opposite, but every time that need to fight back fell apart when he gave those commands.

I sucked his finger into my mouth, not missing the way he groaned as he pushed down onto my tongue. I couldn't help my hum of pleasure at knowing that everything I did was affecting him.

"I thought you were in charge here, little witch. Now you're the one moaning as you suck on me," he said, the deep rasp of his voice almost making me moan again. I pulled back instead, licking my lips as he stared at my mouth.

"I was only moaning at how good my brownies were. Did you think that was for you?" I asked with an innocent smile.

A smile grew on his face as he licked at the same finger that I had just had in my mouth, cleaning the rest of the batter off. "Such a brat," he said, as his other hand reached up and wrapped lightly around my neck. "You want all that control over me, but don't even know what you want to do with it now." His thumb stroked along the side as he gazed down at me, the thoughtful look in his eyes making me freeze. "We are all going out tonight. A friend is having a party. Would you like to come with me?"

"Is this a safe-party-for-me to go to or could certain people be there?"

"Safe. Very safe."

"Then yeah, I would like to go," I said.

"Good. Be ready in two hours," he said before disappearing into his room, shutting the door behind him.

———

TWO SILENT HOURS LATER, I was dressed and ready to go. As soon as I stepped out, Jax's eyes jumped to me and he groaned.

"Again?"

"Again what?"

"You know damn well what I'm talking about. Why are you wearing that?"

I ran my hands over the white frayed and torn sweater, the sharp v in the front showing off the leather harness underneath.

"Do I really need to explain each piece again, or are you asking to get a better look? You have already seen some of this."

"Neither," he said, shaking his head. "I can already see everything I need to."

"Not true. Do you know that this specific harness isn't just a bra?" I lifted the sweater, my mesh bodysuit under it all, but I was showing off where the harness disappeared under my skirt. "It's an entire body piece."

He stepped closer, and I could see his chest rise and fall harder now as he leaned into me.

"Fuck," he said, shoving a hand through his hair. "You know, for a virgin, you dress like you tie men up and make them beg to cum."

"Maybe I do," I said. "I don't have to fuck anyone to make that happen."

"I believe that considering it's the only thing on my mind and you're not even touching me."

I stepped forward until our lips were only an inch apart, his body flush against mine.

"Would you like me to tie you up until you beg to cum, Jax?"

"Yes," he hissed. "No. I meant no. We need to go." He didn't move. "What happened to the uncertain virgin that was in my apartment before? She didn't seem to want anything to do with me."

"She's not a virgin anymore? She liked it? She's suddenly feeling very confident?"

"Fucking hell," he whispered as he moved back.

I pulled away, grabbing for my bag and phone before turning back to him. He was still staring, looking me up and down over and over.

"Stop," I snapped.

"I don't want to. You look amazing."

Heat covered me until I remembered that we were friends. Nothing had technically changed that.

"Great. Hopefully everyone there will think so too," I said, turning to leave.

I heard him cursing as we walked out and went down to the car. He didn't say a word as everyone pulled out and we headed across town, and he still didn't speak when we pulled up in front of a large house. Cars littered the huge driveway, the yard, and front porch covered with people. It was nice. No, not just nice, mansion nice.

"Are these more of your friends?"

"Yeah, I'd consider him a friend now. Someone Ash knows, Ollie. It's his birthday, so he's going all out. No one you know should be here to bother you, so I'd say it's perfectly safe tonight. I'll still be around for you, though. I won't let anything happen."

"I know," I said, not attempting to leave the car. "I was more surprised at the fancy mansion. I really don't think Slaughter would be going to a place like this."

He smirked. "Right, of course. Yeah, Ollie's one of Ash's friends so they all grew up pretty rich. He's great, though."

I nodded as he leaned in closer. "Did you want to go inside or stay out here?"

"Stay out here and do what?" I asked, my breath hitching as he leaned a little closer.

"I can keep you entertained," he said.

"More entertained than a party in a mansion?"

He groaned. "Maybe. Hopefully."

I laughed and patted his arm. "We're going in."

"Fine, hold on," he said, getting out and coming around my side of the car. He pulled open my door, and I only stared for a second.

"What are you doing?"

"Opening your door for you?"

"Why?"

He gave a hard sigh, reaching in for my hand to pull me out. "Because I want to be nice to you. *Brat.* Now get your ass into the fancy party because the faster I get you inside, the faster I get to take you home and that is quite literally the only thing I'm looking forward to about this night. Which is ridiculous, considering you will want to sleep on the couch again."

"Oh," I said as he pulled me out and shut the door behind me. "Well...you're demanding tonight."

His hand laced in mine as we made it to the door. "Because I'm losing control of all this, and I'm trying to stay nice so I don't drag you back to the car caveman style."

"What's wrong? Did I finally push the sunshine boy to his limit?"

He pulled me to a stop, spinning me to face him. "Close, really fucking close and if you choose now to call me sunshine, I can't promise not to actually lose my fucking mind," he said, leaning down to run his nose along my neck. "Plus, I think you know this, but one of *my* newest kinks is these outfits. And you wearing this out pretty much assures that I won't be thinking of anything else all night."

"Come on, Sunshine. It sounds like you need to get your mind off things," I said, dragging him inside behind me.

He started to yell my name, but the music drowned him out as we walked in. The crowd grew thicker as we walked in, and I could only push closer to him. Finally, we found some relief when we made it out back of the house on the porch.

"Where did the crew go?"

"No idea. Did you want a drink?"

"Yeah."

"Alright, just stay right here and I'll get them. Don't move or I may never find you again," he said with a smile.

I reached out to stop him, but he was already gone in the crowd. I hated this, I hated the crushing of bodies, and loud music. I pushed back towards the side of the house. I thought I was doing a pretty good job at being invisible until a girl walked right up to me, looking me over before plastering a smile on her face. I frowned harder.

There was no good reason that someone would be coming up to me, of all people, with that big of a smile.

"Hi! Are you here with Jax? I thought I just saw him."

The girl seemed nice, but the way she was looking me over seemed off.

"Yeah, I am, and you are?"

Jax walked up behind her, his eyes catching mine, before he looked at the girl in front of me.

"Gina? What are you doing here?" he asked.

"Jax! Hi! I'm here with one of my friends. She's dating one of Ollie's friends, so we all came. I wasn't expecting to see you here, though."

He handed me my drink, coming to my side. "Carly, this is Gina. My ex."

I turned to him. "Your ex?"

"Yeah, the one I told you about."

"You talk about me?" Gina asked, her smile growing.

"Not in the way you hope," I said.

Her smile finally fell, and she looked at Jax, apparently deciding to ignore me now. "I haven't heard from you in a long time. How are you?"

I don't know if it was the speech Jax had just given me or knowing that this girl was so nonchalant about hurting him.

It's not like Jax could do no wrong, but I don't know what he could have done to deserve someone making him feel so bad about himself.

"I'm fine. Did you need something?" He sounded so annoyed, upset even after the happy, sweet tone he just had with me minutes ago.

"Wow, no need to sound like an asshole. I just wanted to say hello and talk more," she said.

"Well, I have nothing to talk about with you," he said, the words clipped as he looked out at the sea of people instead.

He'd stand up for me all day, every day, his friends too, but was apparently going to take her calling him names. Apparently, Jax wasn't as good as standing up for himself.

"Don't call him that," I said.

Gina seemed more like what I had been expecting when I met the girls. The rude, bitchy type that seemed to love starting shit. These were the types that Slaughter always hung around. Gina just happened to dress better.

"I'll call him one if he's acting like one."

"Well, he's not, so don't do it again."

"Who the fuck are you? And why are you getting involved in our private conversation?" she asked, waving her hands over me.

Her perfect hair hadn't moved, and her designer clothes didn't look out of place at this party, and I knew mine did.

"Why are you coming over to me and then acting like I'm intruding? You're interrupting our date, not the other way around."

"Date? You think he's going to date you? He dates people like me."

I knew exactly what she meant, and it only pissed me off

more. I was sick of people that could tear down others and not even think twice about it. Especially people like Jax.

"What is your problem? Just go away," I said, trying to take a deep breath.

"Yeah, it's time to go, Gina. Go on before this gets worse."

"Worse? I'm not even doing anything."

"Yeah, of course not–" Jax's words were cut off as Gina stepped closer.

"See, even you agree. Maybe you shouldn't be a dick and then we can talk about things."

I stepped between them, my back to Jax, and Gina's eyes went wide.

"Stop being a bitch and calling him nasty names."

Her mouth dropped open, and before I knew she was reaching out, her long nails slicing across my neck as she hit me.

"Gina! What the fuck?" Jax yelled. He reached for me, but I kicked my foot up, my boot pulling back until I kicked, hitting her right in the stomach as she stumbled back with a scream.

"Fuck," Jax said, grabbing me to face him. "Are you okay?"

"Yeah, yeah. I'm fine.

Gina was still yelling, the people around us crowding her more, but Jax was already pulling me away.

He kept pulling until we reached a bathroom. The door slammed behind him as he pushed me back against the sink.

"Are you okay?" he asked.

"Yeah," I said, not wanting to touch the painful spot on my neck.

"Are you sure?"

"Yes, I'm—" My words were cut off as his lips crashed into mine.

TWENTY-SIX
CARLY

HE KISSED ME HARD, each swipe of his tongue taking more until we both pulled back, gasping for air. His touch felt so good, so needy, that I didn't even care enough to feel self conscious as his hands moved up my thighs to my hips.

"I can't believe that just fucking happened. Are you really okay?"

He found a washcloth, wetting it down and pressing it to the painful spot on my neck.

"I told you, I'm fine. It just stings a bit."

"She fucking cut you with her death claws. And why? Because you were standing up for me?" His chest heaved as he wet the cloth again and continued wiping at my neck.

"Maybe take a breath, Jax. Are *you* okay?"

"No. Not even a little. I've been so worried about everything else going on. Did we really have to add to that?"

"You're the one that dated her," I said, smirking, but he didn't look up to see it.

"I'm sorry. I don't know why she was even here." He shook

his head. "Are you sure you're–" I cut him off, grabbing his neck and pulling him into me for another kiss.

"I'm fine. I can handle a slap or two."

He only shook his head. "But you shouldn't have to handle that."

"And you shouldn't have to handle anyone talking to you like that. Especially the person who made you feel bad in the first place."

"So what? My grumpy little witch is now my fearless protector?"

I smiled. "Look who the bodyguard is now."

"I should have known from the moment you came at me with that bat," he whispered, leaning down to kiss my neck, right where it stung. "You're amazing."

I leaned forward until my lips were almost touching his, and the way he sucked in a breath made me smile. I loved how this was affecting him because it was affecting me the same way.

"I want more, Jax. I *need* more."

He looked at me, hesitating for a second before his hands were all over me again.

"Anything you want, sweetheart. I'll give you anything you fucking want," he said, kissing his way down my neck and pushing my hair out of the way.

He licked at the cut on my neck and then bit the other side, sinking his teeth in as he gave a soft laugh. "I can't get enough of you. You're perfect, every inch of you is pure perfection. Do you know what I was thinking the entire time I fucked you?" he asked, his words a whisper in my ear.

"No. What?" My words were so breathless, I could barely hear them over the noise of the party.

"*Mine.*"

I couldn't even hide my moans. His lips crashed into mine, his hands grabbing my hips and pulling me hard against him.

"How much more?"

"All of it," I said.

"I refuse to have to sex with you for the second time here, but I will gladly do everything else." He sank to his knees, spreading my legs as he started kissing my thighs.

"Are you particularly attached to these things?" he asked, pulling at my tights.

"No, why?"

Instead of responding, he grabbed at my thighs, ripping the seam in half. I gasped, but he was already leaning in, his tongue running hard along my wetness. "Fuck, you're the best thing I have ever tasted. I just—"

He cut himself off, pushing his tongue hard against me and making me gasp. Loud.

"Let me hear how much you like it, brat. Let everyone hear how much you like my tongue."

"The only thing you are going to hear if you keep stopping will be me telling you to quit talking and to get back to what you're supposed to be doing."

"Mmm, what a bully. I can't help it. I want to tell you how good you taste. I want to taste you on my tongue all night." He groaned as his hand came up. "I want you to know how much I do like you. How insanely attracted I am to you. How I could stay here all night. How sorry I am about what just happened."

I loved every word. Each one reminding me how much he wanted this and me. It soothed any insecurity or doubt I had as he continued. I grabbed his hair, pushing him harder against me. He made a noise somewhere between a moan and a groan, and it almost made me come right then and there. I had never had a man make that noise before and I was dying to hear it again.

His tongue pushed hard against my clit and I almost came undone completely.

Before I could reach an orgasm, he was standing up, kissing me once as I groaned.

"Jax," I said, ready to start demanding that he continue.

"I'm right here, sweetheart, and I wasn't done." His hand moved to where his mouth had just been, running along my wetness. "I've barely got started with you. There is no way that I would be done already. I could never be done with you."

He pushed one finger into me, each slow movement making me want to beg for more.

Before I could ask, he was already adding another.

"You're so wet, sweetheart. Fuck, I promise I'll take good care of you. Do you want me to lick and kiss and fuck this perfect pussy again?"

I nodded, lost as his fingers moved faster.

"No, sweetheart. I'm going to need to hear you."

"If you hear me, everyone would hear me," I panted.

"Good. Let them all know you're mine. Let them know that they don't stand a chance."

"And if someone walks in?"

"Why?" he said with a smirk. "Do you like the idea of being caught? Do you want someone to see my head buried between your legs? Or would you rather this? Have them see how much you like getting fucked by my fingers and make them dream about sinking into you. If they only knew how well you take my cock, how tight you clamp down when you cum. If they had any idea, I would be fighting every night of my life just to get to sleep next to you."

I moaned, each thrust of his fingers bringing me closer to the edge until I was closing my eyes just to keep from falling over.

"Cum for me. Cum, and scream my name right now."

I listened, panting his name as stars clouded my vision until I was screaming, my words an incoherent mess as I fell apart.

He finally pulled away from me, looking over with a smile.

"Feeling any better now? Should I take you home and get you to bed?"

"Who said that I was still going home with you?" I asked jokingly.

He gave a harsh laugh as he leaned in. "Me. I'm saying it, and if you think for one second that you aren't, I will be dragging you out of here kicking and screaming."

"Aww, you're so cute when you threaten me," I said, getting off the counter and looking up at him.

"Yeah? Now you know how I feel every time you threaten me," he said with a smile as he tapped my nose.

"I think it's basically becoming my love language."

"I guess I'll have to brush up on my threats, then. If you don't get your ass in my car right now, then I'm going to make you watch romantic comedies all night."

"Okay, I should clarify that I like threats that end up with some sort of pleasure for me. You might have a little more brushing up to do."

He groaned, leaning down to bite my neck hard. "Fine. My girl is ruthless, calling me out all the time. I really thought that was a good one, but I'll keep trying. You know, I was only kidding when I said you tie men up and make them beg to cum. I feel like you took that as a challenge, not a joke."

"I was joking too, but you were right. It sounded so fun that I changed my mind. Ready to go get tied up?" I asked as we walked out of the bathroom.

"I think for the first time, my answer to that is *yes*."

We made it halfway across the room when I stopped, backing up against him as bodies crushed around us.

"I really hate crowds," I said, leaning harder against him.

His teeth found the back of my neck again, biting down and

then kissing the same spot, making me arch into him. I was pressed against his hard cock, and his hands gripped my hips, holding me in place.

"You're trying to make me pass out in the middle of this room," he whispered before pushing me forward, bringing me to the corner of the room and caging me in.

"Me? I didn't do anything," I said with a smirk.

"No? Do you just always go around rubbing your ass all over people?"

"Maybe."

He leaned down, pressing his lips to mine. He was gentle at first, each movement slow and soft, but it couldn't last. I pushed into him, and he responded, running his tongue along mine.

"I pulled you over here to try to hide my dick being hard, but I don't think this is helping calm it down."

"Calm that down? Why? I like how turned on you get."

I moved both hands over his jeans, still impressed with the size of him.

My body flushed and my mouth watered. "You are so hot. My own perfect sunshine boy."

His cock jumped in his jeans, and I smiled at how much he loved that nickname.

"If you make me cum in my jeans in a room full of people, I will be the one tying you up."

I reached up, kissing his neck. "See, now that's a good threat. I bet these straps can really be of assistance when you tie me to a bed. You know, I'm apparently super inexperienced. What would you do to me all tied up?" My hand still moved over him, faster now.

"Carly," he said, pushing us closer into the corner as his forehead fell to mine.

"What?"

He made that same moaning sound again, as his lips pushed against my neck, the deep rumble of it vibrating through me.

I never knew how powerful this could feel, how little my insecurities mattered when this beautiful man was falling apart with need for me.

"Hey Jax?"

"What, little witch?" His words were so tight and hoarse.

I moved my hands over his cock again, moving along his length.

"*Mine.*"

He groaned as his teeth sunk into my neck. I didn't stop, my hands running back and forth along his length. I could feel his cock jump once more and he pushed me hard against the wall.

"Fuck," he growled. "What have you done to me?"

"Well, I thought it was fun, but you don't sound too happy?"

When he pulled back, I could see his soft smile. "Happy? That's the most embarrassing thing that's ever happened to me and now I am in a room full of people that I have to walk through. I can only pray it isn't obvious."

"Embarrassing? That's the *hottest* thing that's ever happened to me. Okay, maybe second hottest, you doing all of that in the bathroom might be first still."

"Hottest? So you're not even less interested in me?"

Jax was sweet and protective and the hottest guy I had ever seen, but I knew the other side to him now, and I was starting to realize he had his own mess of insecurities and doubts.

"Even less interested? Jax, don't feel like that. I've always been interested."

"You've always been pushing me away, and I know how bad you want to leave."

I chewed my lip. He wasn't wrong about that either.

"I don't have a romantic, hopeful heart like you. Remember,

mine is all cold and dead?" I asked, smiling. "But my interest in
you has made me continually stay when I knew that I should be
leaving. And right now, I'm interested in going home with you
and seeing how many times that tongue can get me off."

A smile finally broke on his face again.

"Well, you just purposefully got me off in a crowd of people,
so you better help me get out of here without everyone seeing
that now."

"Fine, but only because I get to go home and watch you
undress and shower. If I could clean you off right here, I would."

"Filthy. Completely filthy," he whispered in my ear, wrapping his arms around me from behind as I led him towards the
entrance. "I'll never figure out how you make *me* feel like the
virgin half the time."

I snorted, thankful the music drowned it out a little, but he
only leaned down to kiss my neck again as I tried to navigate us
out of the crowd, and onto the driveway.

"I can't believe she hurt you like that."

"You hurt my soft little feelings every day," he said, eyes
sparkling.

We had made it to the car, and I turned to him. "I don't hurt
you that bad, do I?"

He shook his head, pulling me closer. "No. No comparison, it
was just a joke for my grumpy little witch."

"I know I'm not nice, Jax, but I don't want to hurt you like
that."

"You wouldn't hurt me like that. You're mean," he said with
a wink, "but I already know you care about me. And anyway,
even if you did, I would probably let you." He stopped me at the
car, leaning down, and cutting off anything else I had to say with
a kiss. "Now can we please leave so I can take a shower?"

I laughed, trying not to double over. "Yes, of course, yes."

WE MADE IT HOME, and I was more tired than ever. I was tired, satisfied, and trying not to think about what came next for us. I could barely manage to walk Riot and brush my teeth before heading into the bedroom to change.

Jax was already changed and in bed, stripping down faster than I could blink.

"What all happened with her?" I asked, my voice quiet.

"Who?" he asked. "With Gina?"

"Obviously."

"I don't know, everything I guess."

"Like?"

"Like she didn't like me. She hated that I was a mechanic. It was too dirty and pathetic for her. I don't think that she thought I had enough money. Then she just didn't like how I was. She didn't like that I was a romantic, and not a huge asshole. That was apparently also too pathetic for her. She didn't really like anything about me aside from the fact that I looked decent and raced cars. I ended up not liking anything about her either, and then I found out she was sleeping with other people, anyway."

"I'm sorry."

"Don't be. By the time I found out, I was already pretty much done with the relationship."

I nodded, finally laying down, snuggling under the blankets and avoiding touching him still. I could feel him moving closer, but I needed this cleared up a little more before I could do anything else.

"What do we do now? I feel like things aren't quite as friendly now, so how would we go back to friends?"

"I will give you anything you want, but this one time I don't know if I will not be agreeing to going back to friends."

"Why?"

He rolled over, pinning me down to the bed. "Because there is no way that I will try to only be friends with you again. That was torture. Now, I know what you taste like, how you sound when you cum, how you scream my name. I'm sorry, but I will never be able to be *just* friends with you again. I would be willing to make another deal, though. Come to an agreement of sorts."

"Oh, no," I groaned, pushing him off of me with a smile. "I feel like I'm going to hate this."

"You are. I will agree to be your roommate with benefits. For now. If you agree to let me be my romantic self and you actively participate in it."

"What would that include?"

"I don't know? Me being myself? I get to do flowers, fun gifts, and dates. And you know what? My little cold-hearted witch has to read my books that she makes fun of and you have to watch more romance movies. We need to thaw out that heart."

"This is starting to sound less like benefits and more like dating."

He rolled away, looking under the bed and coming back up with a book.

"Here. You are going to start with this one. And it's not dating unless we say it is. That's my offer."

"Orgasms, and you, but in exchange, I have to accept all the romance you want to throw at me?"

"Yeah, which, fair warning, both are going to get overwhelming," he said, pulling me back to his chest.

"What if I can't handle one part of that?"

"Then the entire deal is off."

"And what if you get the wrong idea and think I'm going to stay?"

"Then the deal can be off."

"If this is going to hurt you, I don't want to do it," I said.

"Neither one of us can suddenly believe I will be able to stay now."

"This is going to hurt me either way. I might as well enjoy every second until it does."

"Famous last words?" I asked.

"Put them on my headstone."

TWENTY-SEVEN
CARLY

W HEN J AX SAID he was going to be a little overwhelming with romance, I didn't realize exactly what he meant.

There was what I thought of as romance, and then there was Jax.

After making me breakfast and handing me a cup of coffee the next morning, he said he had to leave for a few hours, but wouldn't tell me why.

Two hours later, my phone pinged.

JAX
Come downstairs.

CARLY
For what?

JAX
I'm not going to tell you. I obviously want to show you. Come on, little witch.

I got up, slipping on my shoes and nearly running downstairs. It had to be my truck. I couldn't believe it was finally done.

But when I pulled open the door leading to the downstairs garage, it wasn't my truck. It was only boxes upon boxes stacked next to his car.

"Wow, what did you order? An entire car? Wait, are these all the parts you need for my truck?"

"Hey," he said with a bright smile, walking around the stack to kiss my cheek. "Can you help me take these upstairs?"

"No way am I lifting box after box of car parts just to walk them back down."

"It's not heavy car parts. I have three strong male buffoons if I need car parts lugged upstairs. Come on, help me out."

He loaded up my arms, and I was quietly relieved that they weren't too heavy.

He grabbed a stack, both of us heading up, dropping them down before going and grabbing another pile.

By the time we made the third and final trip, I was breaking a sweat.

"Okay. What is all this stuff?"

"Open it," he said, kicking off his boots and coming over. He looked like a kid on Christmas morning and I couldn't believe how cute I thought it was.

"Me? Why?"

"Open it and answer your own questions."

I did, opening one of the medium size boxes to find a new professional knife set.

"Jax," I whispered, grabbing another box to see if this was really all what I thought it was. Maybe that was a fluke. He could get me a gift, but couldn't get me boxes and boxes of gifts, right?

The next box was smaller, holding one beautiful stainless steel pan. Riot barked, jumping up for the empty box in my hand. I handed it over, and he immediately ran to the couch, proud of his new prize.

"Jax, no."

"Oh yes. Yes, to all of it. You keep opening, and apparently giving Riot his new toys, while I throw out basically the entire kitchen."

"You bought everything new?"

"I think so. I might have missed something though, so look through it all. Make a list if you need something else."

"There's at least forty boxes here. How could you have missed anything?"

"Because I'm not a chef, and had to piece a list together online. I really tried to fill in the gaps, but don't think I got it all." He grabbed one of the boxes and started putting his old beat up kitchen stuff in it.

"Why did you do this?"

He shrugged. "I'd never really bought new kitchen stuff and didn't have much to begin with when you came. Some of it was just thrift store shit because I didn't know what to buy or what not to buy. I found a list online and thought it was the perfect checklist. So I got it all." He was smiling so hard that I wondered if his cheeks hurt.

"Jax, this has to be thousands worth of items. I know this one pan alone is not cheap and you're telling me there's more?"

"Yeah," he said, still happy as could be. "Oh, hold on. There's one other thing that isn't kitchen related. Well, not completely."

He dug through the boxes until he found the one he wanted and handed it over.

I pulled out the red thing and could only look at him. I had no idea what it was.

"This is a little stand for your phone that can hold it in all crazy positions. Now you can make cooking videos."

"Jax," I said.

"Alright Carly. You've said my name like ten times. Do you like the stuff?"

"Of course I like the stuff, but why? Why would you buy all this? I cannot pay you back for this. These knives have to be a thousand dollars, Jax, I can't."

"Well, I can swear it's for my kitchen, but it's for you. I don't even know what this thing is," he said, holding up a garlic press. "If you're going to start all the cooking business stuff, you need the basic tools. Think of me as an investor in your business. We had to put out a lot of money for our tools at first. Now you have everything you need."

"Jax—"

"Please say something other than that."

"I don't know what to say."

He waited, and I was surprised he didn't tell me that I should say thank you. It felt like the common response to that.

"There's no paying me back, unfortunately. This falls under the agreement that I get to do romantic things for you."

"No. Romantic things are like holding my hands or giving me flowers. Not give me an entire kitchen of professional cooking utensils." I opened another box. A stand mixer inside. "No, Jax, this can't be happening."

He leaned back on the counter, right back to his wicked smile. The tight T-shirt not doing anything to help me be mad at him for spending too much.

I had barely been given gifts. We usually didn't have enough money to get anything elaborate if I did, but since Slaughter came around, it's been nothing each year for my sister and I. I couldn't think of a time I had ever been given this many gifts, but not only that, gifts that I wanted. Things that I liked.

"Jax," I said, trying not to cry.

"If you say my name one more time, I'm going to buy more."

"No one has ever given me anything like this. I don't know what I'm supposed to say or do."

He smiled, the dimples coming out, and I was gone. He was so sweet and gorgeous that I couldn't even move.

Lucky for me, Jax was fine taking care of everything because he came over and wrapped his arms around me.

"You don't have to say anything."

I reached up, my fingers trailing along his jaw as I pulled him down to me. My lips found his, and I didn't hold back. I was nearly crawling up him, but he seemed fine, pulling me up and against him hard.

He kissed me again as the door slammed open.

I jumped back, trying to put any distance between us.

Jax laughed as the crew filed in, each of them looking over the sea of boxes.

"Um, what is all of this?" Scout asked, peering into one of the boxes.

"Carly took my credit card and went on a shopping spree," Jax said, grabbing empty boxes and piling them up. "There is still more to open and sort through, too."

"I did not!"

Ransom laughed. "Yeah right, you women love taking those and going shopping."

Scout snorted. "You men love handing them over and begging us to shop so we'll like you more."

"Alright, that's partially true," Ransom said.

"Partially?" Quinn echoed, her hands firmly on her hips.

"Okay completely. At least we are self aware that we can be difficult," Ransom said.

Jax beamed, coming to my side and pulling me against him. "Always worth it. Carly has what she needs to start her cooking videos and business now."

"Oh my god, please tell me that means we get to come try all the experiments. Our chef would always let me try them and, ugh, I miss it so much," Ash said.

"*Our* chef?" Fox asked. "You are so spoiled." The words were loving and I could barely take it all in. They were all so…sweet.

"Um, yeah, if I decide to do it, then I'll be bothering you all to come taste the food."

"You can do it," Jax said. "You would absolutely kill it too with your food, no matter what you do."

Everyone made noises of agreement and something inside me cracked. I was in a room full of people who had known me for barely a month and they were ready to lift me up and believe in me. I was standing next to a guy who almost literally handed me a silver platter of everything I needed and seemed so proud to help me achieve this dream.

For the millionth time that day, I was speechless, so I did the only thing I could think of. I reached up, kissing Jax on the cheek with a smile.

Red bloomed across his face, and my heart thundered in my chest.

I somehow found the cutest, sweetest guy who would probably kill for his friends. It was all laid out for me, but still felt too good to be true.

He kissed me back as the crew made aww noises.

"Damn," Scout said. "I think we all assumed, but good to know for sure."

"What?" I asked, realizing my own mistake. "No, no, it's not like that. We've just grown…close."

"Naked close," Jax said, and I smacked his stomach.

"Seriously?" I yelled. "You did not just say that!"

"What? It's not like I have women coming to live with me all the time and I really don't buy them entire kitchens. I assume my friends are smart enough to figure out that I intend to keep you here."

"Jax!"

"Carly!" He mocked.

"Both of you!" Scout yelled. "While Fox here loves the drama," she said, patting Fox's arm, the height difference only making the two of them together funnier. "We need to get going. Why are you two not ready yet?"

"Ready for what?" I asked.

"Shit," Jax said at the same time. "It's the charity race today. I agreed to work with them for the day, teaching kids to drive and ride along and stuff."

"All of you?"

They nodded.

"Wow That's so…wholesome."

"Don't get any ideas," Quinn said. "They're still heathens. Even this little one," she said, wrapping an arm around Scout. "Could you two be ready in ten?"

"Give me 20 minutes. I need a shower. We can meet you there?" Jax asked.

"Yes, perfect," Ash said. "Let's go before my dad starts blowing up my phone about where we are."

They all nodded and filed out, knowing smiles on their faces that I wanted to wipe off.

The door shut, and I spun, heading to the bedroom to grab clothes. "Great, Jax. Now all your friends think we are having sex."

"Well, we did, and we will be again, so I don't see the problem. Plus, they aren't blind. Pretty sure I can't help but make it obvious that I want to," he said, following me.

"But we aren't right now. Now they think we needed time so we could do it," I yelled, grabbing my clothes.

He came up fast behind me, spinning me around. "We could be. There's some time."

"There's also time for me to get dressed and ready." I grabbed all my clothes, turning back to find Jax looking down at me, a frown flashing across his face.

"There's time for both if you're interested," he said.

"I'm only interested in getting dressed. Thanks for the offer, though." I reached up, kissing him again. "Next time you are hoping to get laid, don't announce it to the room and you might have better luck."

I walked out, hearing him mumble something about stupid words and mouth before smiling as I went to change.

TWENTY-EIGHT
JAX

"No, no, no," I said. "Not a chance."

"What now?"

"You are not wearing one of your BDSM outfits today," I said, taking the piece of leather out of her hand. "This is a charity event and children will be there."

"And? I'm not showing off anything. I'm completely covered."

I set the leather down and grabbed her arm, pulling her to me. "No, but I have to look at you, knowing what's underneath, knowing what you taste like. I can't do this all day. I will end up dragging you into a room and fucking you senseless or passing out from blue balls."

She gave me a sweet smile. "Those both sound pretty entertaining. Although, can option number two even happen?"

"When you have been teasing me for days and wear shit like this, yes, I have no doubt that it could happen. It very well might happen either way."

She made an appreciative sound. Every inch of me focused

on her lips so hard that I didn't notice her hand moving down until it reached my hard cock.

"Please don't stop doing that," I groaned. Even over my jeans, her touch felt like heaven. "Or maybe do stop. If you don't, we will have another incident."

"You're the one who ruined it with your naked friend's comment. I was about to strip you in the kitchen before you said that."

"You were not," I said.

"Well, now you will never know."

"I feel like you're enjoying teasing me more than anything, so I think I have a pretty good idea," I said, leaning down to kiss her. I ran my hands down her sides to her back, and it was taking everything in me not to pull her into the bedroom.

"I *am* enjoying that, and now I guess it will just keep happening," she said, her hand running over my dick again. "We really are on a time crunch, so I'm going to get ready."

"You know I'm going to get you back for all of this. The teasing, the party incident, touching me constantly so I can't think straight." I groaned as I kissed her. "But fine. Let's go race. Here," I said, grabbing a shirt from my closet, "wear this shirt and leave the leather behind for today. Please."

"What is this?" She held it up, looking it over. It was one of the shirts we had made for racing, a picture of my car and my last name across the back with the Hollows Garage logo on the front.

She rolled her eyes. "You're asking me to wear this on purpose."

"Absolutely. I want everyone there to know that you're mine. Maybe certain people will get the hint and keep their hands to themselves. Now I'm going to shower." I leaned down to kiss her, running from the room before she could argue any further.

———

TWO HOURS LATER, I was sitting behind the wheel of a Holt Racing track car, waiting for another kid to slide in beside me.

I had agreed to do this today, and was honestly happy to be here, but my morning with Carly was the only thing on my mind and it was making it harder and harder to focus. I kept trying to look for her, catch any glimpse of her, and it was taking everything in me to focus on the road. Luckily, I knew this car and the track well enough that making laps had become second nature for me.

The door opened, and I didn't look over, still scanning the crowd for her.

"Ready?" I asked, as the door opened, and someone slid in next to me.

"Nope. I'm only here to check in on the driver, not actually go for a ride."

"Carly," I breathed, turning to see her smiling in the passenger seat.

My pathetic heart exploded in happiness until I looked down.

"What the fuck are you wearing?"

"Hello to you, too. A kid spilled water all over me, so I was letting the shirt dry. I didn't think everyone here needed to see my nipples," she said, her eyebrows jumping up with a smirk.

"Why didn't you come get me?"

"Because you've been in the car for hours? I couldn't wait."

"And you haven't changed back into it yet?" I asked. I had only been daydreaming for the last two hours about her in that shirt, and now it was gone.

"This one is pretty comfortable." She smiled, and I knew she was doing this on purpose.

"I know you're provoking me, and you know it's working."

"Is that another threat?"

I pulled off my harness type seat belt and leaned over to her. "Yeah, it is. You're going to be the one begging me to stop giving you orgasms. And you can fucking bet that the first thing I do when we get to my car is going to be cutting this damn shirt right off of you."

She leaned closer, putting her hand on my bicep, and I tried not to be an idiot and flex, failing immediately.

"You know I've never been interested in racers before. Never really saw the appeal."

"Great, another point in my favor," I said, the sarcasm obvious.

"If you let me finish, I would tell you that all of that was true until I had to watch you out here driving, teaching people about the cars, all hot with your hat turned back and those sunglasses on. Then you pulled your shirt up, and I saw all of this." Her hands slid under my shirt. Her fingers splayed over my stomach and moved up to my chest before her nails raked lightly back down until she reached the waistband of my jeans.

"Carly," I said. I could barely breathe and I knew she could hear the tightness of my voice.

I kept my hands glued to the steering wheel, worried I wouldn't be able to control myself if I touched her again.

"Yes, sunshine?"

I don't know what needy part of me had to react so strongly to that nickname, but it worked every time. It was like she was praising me for who I was and it immediately made pleasure roll through me, making my dick hard again.

"That's it. You are not going to tease me and tell me how hot you think I am and use cute little nicknames. We are leaving. Now." I moved to shift the car, but her hand slid down to mine, stopping me.

"We can't leave yet. You still have more driving scheduled," she said.

"I don't care. I can't stand this any longer."

"I think you'll be fine to wait a few more hours."

"And what if you decide to tease me all night?"

"Then you're about to have a very fun night," she said in her playful tone. I meant what I said when I called her hot when she was grumpy, but her flirty and sweet could bring me to my fucking knees.

Somehow, it made it all feel special, or at least made me feel special. I was the only one getting this side of her.

"You're terrorizing me, and I'm going to pay you back for every second."

"I'm looking forward to it. Now get back out there and keep looking all hot so I can decide if I really do want to have sex with a street racer or not."

That was enough. I leaned over, kissing her hard. "You already have, sweetheart, and the way you're teasing me, I can guarantee you're going to be doing it again soon."

I could hear her suck in a breath, but she wasn't going to give me any more.

"Really? Who? I think Kye is your only single guy friend? I mean, Raf is a racer, so I guess that could work."

I wound my hand into her hair, using it to pull her closer.

"I know you're kidding, but you know it's working. Say it again, Carly. Taunt me again and I will cut this shirt off of you right now," I said, my hand moving down to the hem of the shirt and pulling it up.

She smiled up at me, the devious smile already letting me know I lost.

"You can make your threats, Jax, but I already know how jealous you are. You wouldn't put me on display like that in front of everyone."

"I am not jealous."

"No? Then I'm going to go talk to Raf. I'll see you soon."

She moved to open the door, but I grabbed her, pulling her back against the seat. "Fine. I might have a jealousy issue, but in my defense, it has never been this bad. I've also never had someone driving me this far out of my mind. I just want you next to me all day."

She laughed, but I suddenly wasn't kidding. I leaned over to buckle her in and she immediately slapped my hands away.

"What are you doing?"

"Getting you buckled in and safe? You're coming with me. I need you to not flirt with Raf and I also want to continue touching you, but I have to keep driving, so now you're coming with me. Problem solved."

"No way. I'm not riding with you to race. I thought you were taking these kids for rides."

"I was, but I'll tell Kye to take a few laps with them for now. I need a break anyway."

"Then you shouldn't be driving at all if you need a break."

"I need a break with you, not from driving. Come on, we are only going around the track a few times."

"You know that I don't like the fast car stuff. And this isn't doing donuts in an empty parking lot. I saw how fast you are taking those turns."

"Because it scares you or because you've only ridden with shit drivers?"

"Probably both."

"You're in luck then. You know I wouldn't put you in any danger and I'm a good driver. It's also on a closed track, so Kye and Fox are the only other two on it right now. It's fun and at this point, I've probably done it a thousand times."

"Yeah, fun for you. Not for me."

I couldn't imagine the problems she had with Slaughter and Tristan along with their driving, but I also couldn't imagine her not liking it once we got out there.

"Try it with me once. If you never want to do it again, I won't ask."

She seemed to think it over, looking over the track. "I will go around once and if I want out, you stop and let me out."

"Okay."

She let me buckle her in this time, and I didn't miss how her fingers were already gripping the door handle.

I left my hand on her thigh, reaching over with my left hand to shift before taking off at a slow pace.

"You really don't need to hold my thigh."

"I don't mind. It brings a new challenge to shifting," I said, reaching over to hit the shifter again.

"No. I mean, you don't have to because I'm way too self conscious for you to have your hand there." She peeled my hand off, setting it on the shifter.

"Self conscious of me touching your leg? You know I have already touched a lot more of your body? And will be again?"

"That's different."

"How?" I picked up the pace, trying to keep the engine noise to a minimum.

"Because when things are like that between us, I forget to be self conscious. When we're like this, all I can think about is how huge my thigh is and I think that it's all you're thinking about."

I yanked the car to the side of the track, kicking in the clutch and braking before turning to her.

"I am absolutely, without a doubt, never thinking about you like that. If my hand is on any part of you, all I can think about is one, how long you are going to let me keep it there. And two, is how I got lucky enough that such a perfect woman would let me touch her. And honestly, three is all sexual. I'm not even going to lie. If my hand is on your thigh, I'm also wondering how long until I can move it upwards. More the first two though, I swear."

She mumbled something, but I couldn't hear her over the engine.

"I don't know what I can say to make you feel a hundred percent in believing me, but please understand that I am only thinking amazing things about you. I am only thinking about how perfect and beautiful you are. Constantly. Like so much that it hurts. As for other people, most of them are too self absorbed, and the other half are probably looking at you because you dress so hot."

That made her smile more, and I reached back over. "If my hand there really makes you that uncomfortable, I won't, but please tell me the moment I'm allowed to again."

She was quiet for a second before looking back over at me. "You really don't think anything bad about me? Ever? That seems extreme."

"No. Why would I? I like everything about you. You're funny, and smart, and mostly nice to me."

"Ugh, you are so sweet. Fine, take me around the track, touch my thigh. I don't even know how I am supposed to say no to that face."

I shifted back into gear, taking the win and pulling out.

"And, in the event you think I could possibly think you're anything but hot, please always think back to the most humiliating night of my life, the party, and what happened when you touched me. There is no part of you that doesn't turn me on."

"For someone who is always saying the wrong, sarcastic things, you really know what to say when I'm feeling bad."

"Good, if there's one thing I would like to be able to do in life, it's making you happier."

"Then don't wreck this car. *That* would make me happy."

"I can do that. I will do that," I said, taking off again. We went around once, before I slowed to check on her.

"You good?"

She nodded, a smile on her face. "Okay, that was more fun than I thought, and you were right."

"About?"

"About me having sex with a street racer. I will definitely be doing it again with the way you just showed off."

I could only laugh, pulling out onto the track again as it hit me just how deeply I was falling for her.

TWENTY-NINE
CARLY

By the time he pulled off into the pit area, I was almost ready to ask him to go again. I had been forced to ride in these stupid fast cars with reckless drivers so many times that I had only learned how not to throw up, not how to enjoy it. Until now.

Jax came around, pulling open my door and helping me out.

"Have fun?"

"More fun than I ever had in a death trap."

"Good, you did amazing. We're going to have to take my car out more often," he said, leaning down to kiss me. "But for now, I have to go park the car and wrap this part of the day up."

Scout and Ash came over as soon as I walked away from the car.

"Hey, want to go grab food?"

"Yes, please," I said, surprised I had an appetite after being so nervous. "I'm starving, and all I've seen so far is water and beer."

Ash laughed. "Yeah, they had some hot dogs out for the kids, but I haven't been able to get my hands on one."

"Ugh, it's so hard being the princess of this empire," Scout said, linking her arm in Ash's.

"It truly is. I'm so glad you don't have to have the burden of benefiting from this."

"Benefiting?"

"Scout is working her way onto a Holt racing team. It's a long shot right this second, but hopefully she's still on her way to the qualifying races. She makes fun of me for being a princess, yet she's treated like the queen of the castle. Even my dad loves her."

Scout cocked her head, leaning it on Ash. "At what point do you all bow to the Queen?"

Ash pushed her off. "Oh my god, you are terrible," she said but was laughing. "Come on, food, now. Come on, Ransom and Quinn have it all at our cars."

We made it over, Quinn already pulling bags of food out of the car and walking them over to a small table right in front of the cars.

I leaned back on Jax's hood, grabbing a burger and listening as the crew talked. They were so different from Slaughter and his friends. Where they would degrade and taunt the women, these guys seemed to worship the girls. It had all become obvious by this point, but sometimes it still felt like a shock. Tristan had been dating my sister and seemed nice enough to her, but he would still mess around with any girl that would take him. None of these guys ever made any indication that they knew women existed outside of the group, let alone do anything with one.

I went to take another bite when a head came around mine, teeth sinking into my burger and pulling away to kiss me on the cheek.

I turned back to see Jax laid out on his hood, chewing his giant bite with a smile.

"You stole my burger!"

"I don't know. My car, my girl, seems like it should be my burger, too."

"I am not—"

He cut me off, his tone low and serious. "For now, you are."

He laid back, sunglasses on, as he looked up at the sky. He looked so happy, so relaxed and it hit me how easy life was with him. "And don't fight me on it or I will literally only refer to you as my girl. I will tell anyone that walks by until your cheeks turn red like that constantly."

I covered my face, feeling their warmth. "You're the worst," I said, still smiling.

"Hey, do you guys want to go to the races tonight?" Scout asked, looking at her phone. "Apparently, there's a pretty big round of them going on."

"Right, because we haven't had enough cars today?" Quinn snorted, but rolled her eyes as soon as she looked at Ransom. His usually hardened face now softened into a sweet, charming smile.

"Oh my god, fine, yeah we will go."

Everyone else agreed, but Jax was quiet behind me. I could feel him slide up next to me, leaning down to whisper.

"I don't know. I was more looking forward to getting you home," he said, a small laugh on his lips.

"More than racing?"

"Always," he said, biting at my ear.

"Racing tonight sounds great," I said to the group, making Jax groan against my ear.

"Devil woman," he mumbled. "You're trying to test that theory of passing out from blue balls. You're in luck, it's working. I'm feeling faint."

"Eat another burger. Maybe you just need protein."

"Not quite what I need, but another burger does sound good."

We sat for a while longer, Jax next to me the entire time as I tried to not think of everything he could have been doing to me tonight instead of racing.

I thought making him wait longer would be funny, but honestly, now I was mad at myself.

His leg pushed against mine as he sat next to me, the heat of him reaching every part of me.

Then his hand was on my back, his thumb moving in slow circles, trying to kill me.

I suddenly didn't think I was going to make it the entire night.

———

IT WAS ONLY eight at night and I had never been so ready to go home and go to bed.

Why did I do this to myself?

Why did I not take the tall, dark, and handsome street racer to bed last night when he wanted to, and why didn't I rush home tonight instead of coming out?

Why did I think teasing him was so much fun?

And why was the third girl of the night hanging all over him?

I leaned back on the car and tried to take a deep breath. I had been next to Jax until I realized he was going to talk to everyone and I needed a break from…everyone.

Now I was sitting car lengths away, watching as he started grinning hard, his leather jacket hanging open to a white t-shirt underneath as he talked with Ransom, Quinn, and some girl that I didn't know.

I almost screamed as a guy came up behind me. Kye slid up next to me, kicking his boots up onto the bumper and pulling out a knife.

"Maybe don't sneak up on girls alone in parking lots and pull out a knife," I said, laughing as I tried to slow my heartbeat.

"This wasn't to use on you," he said, laughing. "It kind of seemed like you were over here plotting a murder, based on your face."

My lips twitched with a smile. "Normally, I would agree, but I think this time I'm the one who put myself in this position. I left him there to talk to everyone while I took a moment of not talking."

"So, just a fight, then?" He asked, flipping his blade and handing it to me.

"What's this for?"

"Just in case. I assume Jax didn't give you one yet?"

"No? Do I need one?"

"The girl who has some nasty fucking people hunting her down? Yeah, I feel like a knife is the least you can have. I'm assuming Jax didn't give you one? He tends to ignore the bad parts of our lives."

"The bad parts?"

"The wrecks, the fights, you know, the bad things. He does what he has to do and moves on."

"Yeah, that sounds like him. I could scream and yell and be a complete asshole to him and he will move on and be fine. Like, he forgives me immediately," I said, throwing my hands up.

"We all deal with our upbringing and lives differently. Jax likes to keep the peace. His family were fighters. Constant yelling and screaming. I think half the time they forgot he was alive, or maybe hoped that he wasn't."

"And now he wants that attention," I said, the words quiet. "You deal with it by not being touched?"

"Hard to like hands on you when they only brought pain."

"But you like fighting?" I asked, laughing.

He laughed along with me. "I guess it feels like home. I'm not going to say it makes sense. I'm pretty fucked up here some-times," he said, tapping his head.

"I feel really great about being over here alone with you now," I said, making sure the sarcasm was obvious.

He laughed harder, pulling out another knife and throwing it up in the air before catching it. "Yeah, right. I would bet you're like me enough and could put up a hell of a fight."

"You think I'm like you?"

He shrugged. "I think you're like all of us. Fit right in with your problems chasing you down and weirdo quirks. Plus, you walk around looking like you want to kill someone. I personally enjoy it, but you're not exactly little miss sunshine. I'm not either. Honestly, I'm only hoping you stick around so I have a better chance at the scary movies getting chosen on movie night. I swear if Jax offers up Pretty Woman one more time." He flipped the knife around again, shaking his head as he leaned back and looked over. Jax was laughing about something, and my stomach clenched.

"What I was getting at is since you seem to be sticking around and getting close to Jax, maybe don't go for the throat on him. One of the few people I would want by me in a fight, but between the crew he can't take turbulence and I know he doesn't want it with you. I'm not trying to say he can't handle it if he deserves it, of course, but other than that, the guy is a little pathetic about needing affection."

I smacked his chest. "Hey, don't be mean to him."

"Damn, I was right. One wrong word about Jax and you're already getting violent."

I stood up and shook my head. "I would hug you, but I don't know which one of us would hate that more, so thank you for the knife and the weird pep talk that actually worked. I'm going to go get Jax now."

Kye laughed. "And I'm going to race. Keep that knife on you and don't let your guard down here tonight."

I nodded, feeling for Jax, who was still talking with the other three. He had glanced back a few times as I talked to Kye and I could see the jealousy from there. I knew the only reason he wasn't stomping over was because it was Kye.

I wasn't shying away now. I wrapped an arm around Jax's waist, sidling up next to him. He beamed down at me, angling his body in front of mine and stepping until I was forced back.

"What are you doing?" I asked, laughing as he leaned down and kissed me.

"Taking what I have been thinking about taking for the past hour. Why did we come? I want to leave."

"Okay," I said, breathless. "Let's go."

"Serious?"

"Completely." I pulled him down, kissing him until his lips parted and his tongue slid against mine. It was a match to gasoline, lighting me up until I was panting with need.

Jax groaned. "I agreed to a race."

"Right now?"

"In a few minutes. I'm supposed to be going to get my car."

I smacked at him lightly. "Right when I was about to beg you for sex, you pull away and say you need to go race? So close, Jax, so, so, close."

He rested his forehead against mine. "Forget it. I don't want to race."

"What happens if you back out?" He kissed me again, his hands running down my sides to my hips, where he grabbed hard, pulling me closer.

"I'm forfeiting and losing two grand."

"Excuse me? You're racing for two thousand dollars?"

"Yes. I don't always do it only because it's fun. I'll tell them I'm out. Coming with me or waiting in the car? It will only take a minute."

"Whoa, not a chance. You are racing. There's no way you're losing that much money just to get home a little faster."

"It's fine. I'll make up the difference on a different night."

"You would give up the race and that much money to get home an hour or so faster?"

"Do you fully understand how bad you've been teasing me? I mean, I get you don't have a lot of experience and stuff, but you do realize how fucked up I am right now with wanting you, right?"

"Yeah and it's definitely not two grand worth of fucked up. Go race and win your money. If you forfeit, nothing will be happening tonight."

"You're serious?"

"Absolutely." His smile grew, and he laughed against my lips. "Fine, I'll go race and then we are leaving. As in, you wait at the line and get in the car as soon as I stop."

He pushed me back further into the shadows until we were at his car.

"Are you wet for me yet, little witch?"

The words knocked the breath from my lungs. "Yes, all night."

He made that low groan against my neck. "I would pay all that money just to taste you right now. Actually…" He moved until my back was against the car and wrapped his hands around my thighs, lifting my legs up until I was sitting on the hood. He shifted until I could feel him hard between my legs. "I'm really trying to convince myself that sex right here wouldn't be a good idea," he mumbled.

"Really? It's looking like a good idea to me." I cupped his jaw, pulling him back to me and he responded, biting my lip and kissing me harder.

A blaring horn went off and he leaned back, catching his breath. "Tell me now, sweetheart. Do you want to go, or should I race?"

"Race. Definitely race. At least if you're two grand richer

tonight, I won't feel so bad about all the things you bought for me this morning."

He laughed as he set me down. "Race it is then. Reluctantly, just so you know."

I moved my hand down his chest to his jeans, feeling how hard he was. "Oh, I know."

"Devil Woman," he whispered with a smile before pushing away. "I'm going to get this over with. Like I said, be ready."

I headed to the rest of the crew, who were lined up sitting on the front of their cars. Scout was on the end and smiled as I leaned back next to her.

"Is he all ready to go?"

"I think so. He better be after that high of a bet."

Scout laughed and knocked against Ransom on her other side. "They seem to get higher and higher the older we get."

"That's because a thousand dollars was a million to us back then. Now we can handle it. It makes it more fun, anyway."

"You mean it makes your ego feel better when you win," Scout said, and Ransom moved to put her in a headlock.

"Like you don't bet money on your races?" He asked, laughing. "And how many times have you hustled men that think you're a small, innocent little thing only to see you beat them by a mile and take their money?"

She was yelling for him to let her go and smacking blindly at him until he finally did.

"Dammit, Ransom, you're going to mess up my hair." Her red hair was braided into two long braids and she patted them down. One was coming loose, but she couldn't reach it to fix it.

It all felt so comfortable. No passive aggressive attitudes, no hateful tones, not even the normal toxic family moves. They genuinely liked each other.

And I hated to say that I liked them all, too. I knew part of me would always be an outsider to any group, but they didn't make that feel weird or wrong. They let me be.

"Here, move over. I can fix the braid."

"Thanks. Ash did them. I have no idea how to do them myself."

I nodded, fixing her hair and tying it up as Jax pulled up. All at once, the crew got up, yelling and whooping their cheers.

I stood up but stayed quiet, watching Jax's car line up. The track was circular, leaving part of it out of view, but it was short, which meant he wasn't out of sight for long. The revving engines reverberated through the air, creating an electrifying atmosphere that sent shivers down my spine.

As the roar of engines echoed, they suddenly burst into view around the corner. Jax was at the forefront, his car a blur as he maneuvered around the turns with ease, each motion more proof of his skill and expertise. Jax's car surged forward, overtaking the other car with one last burst of speed that left me breathless. To go that fast in such a short distance felt foreign to me.

By the finish line, it was clear that Jax was ahead, with an entire car length between them.

The cheers from the crew echoed around me again, but I couldn't stop staring at his car as he began to slow. Jax was caring, kind, constantly sweet, but he was ruthless too. Knowing when to push himself and win, knowing when it was right to fight and when it wasn't, knowing when to push me out of my comfort zone, like making me drive.

The overwhelming need for him to be mine right now hit me, and before I could think it over, I was already on my way to him, ready to take every inch of him for myself.

I was halfway there when the other car pulled over, cutting Jax off.

Jax got out of the car with a smile, but just as fast, the other guy stalked over, pulling back his fist and landing it on Jax's jaw.

He wasn't expecting it. Falling back into his car, but just as fast he punched back, hitting the guy in the stomach and then face.

It turned into madness.

I ran over and pulled open the passenger side door to Jax's car to grab my bat as the guy lunged for Jax again. He grabbed his jacket as Jax swung towards his face, hitting him in the eye.

I could hear the connection, the crunching of the guy's nose.

The anger that burned through me was so hot I wanted to scream. Jax was the last person here who deserved this. I swung the bat, landing it on the back of the other guy's thighs.

He yelled out, trying to turn, but Jax pushed, throwing him into the car.

"What the fuck are you doing?" Jax asked the guy and looked at me. "And what the fuck are you doing? Get away from here, Carly." He was covered in blood now, his eye already turning an angry red, and shirt ripped and covered in more blood.

"Are you okay?" I asked him, trying to move closer, but the other racer was still in between us.

"I'm fine, Carly. Now go," Jax said.

"Not a chance," I said, surprised he would even suggest it.

I suddenly couldn't stand the thought of anyone hurting Jax.

THIRTY

JAX

THE OTHER RACER SPUN, casting a glance back at Carly with an angry twist to his face that made my heart race. Great, not only was this guy coming for me because he's mad he lost. Now she got herself involved.

"Did you just hit me with that?" he asked, looking down at her. She wasn't short, but still barely reached this guy's shoulders.

"Yes," she said, the anger clear in her voice. "So stop hitting him or I'll do it again."

"What the fuck?" The guy turned back to me, his face twisted in confusion. "You send your fucking girl to fight your battles instead of handling this? Make her stop."

I couldn't stop my lips from tipping up as I looked at Carly. "I don't send her anywhere. You're the one that pissed her off. What do you expect me to do about it?"

The guy lunged for me again and I welcomed it. Anything to get his attention off of her. He hit once, and I swung back with a satisfying thud before he yelled out in pain. The bat had connected again, hitting him hard on the arm this time.

For the second time in my life, I was face to face with Carly and her bat. Luckily, this time, I wasn't at the wrong end of it.

"Hey sweetheart," I said, trying to stay calm. "I can handle this one on my own if you would like to set the bat down and step back."

She rolled her eyes. "Not happening, and obviously you can." She turned back to the guy. "It would be better for all of us if you leave him alone."

He spun around fast, the outrage on his face scarily obvious.

"Or what, bitch? Gonna beat me with your bat?"

"No," she said, her tone so sweet with a smile. I stepped towards him, ready to drag him away if he got any closer to her, but she stepped back. "But hit him one more time, and I'm going to start hitting your car."

"I'll kill you," the guy said, raising his hands as though that was going to calm Carly down. Even I didn't know what was going to calm her down right now. I had never seen her look so pissed, even after our fight at the cabin.

"I'll kill you first," she said, sounding offended.

Leave it to me to find a girl who looks so willing to commit murder. As though we needed another one of those in our crew.

"What the fuck is wrong with your bitch?" The guy asked me, the seriousness of his curiosity almost funny.

I didn't have time to say a word as Carly's bat crashed into the guy's headlight.

"What the fuck?" he screamed. "I didn't even touch him."

"You called me his bitch, and I didn't like it," she said, smiling, her eyebrows jumping up.

"Alright, Carly. Maybe we step back with the bat and let him leave."

"Leave? You think I'm going to let her fuck with my car and then leave?"

I groaned as Carly raised the bat, ready to drop it down onto his hood.

"Wait," the guy said. "Carly? And the red car and guy. You the Carly that Tristan is asking around about?"

She froze, eyes wide with the bat still raised.

The crew stepped closer, the girls watching her and the guys watching him.

It was five seconds of pure panic, no one knowing what was about to happen.

"Alright, I get that you are all pissed because you're a shit driver and lost, but we're done." I said. "I don't care about the race, or the money. Get the fuck out of here before I unleash the entire girl gang on you." I wasn't going to put any focus on what he said. Hopefully he was too stupid or worried about his car to dwell on it more.

He looked at the rest of the girls, each one looking more pissed than the next, and I was pretty sure that Scout was about to start handing out switchblades.

"The fuck is wrong with you guys. Who has their girls take on their fights for them?" he said, taking a step towards the back of his car, hopefully to leave, but I think it was more to get away from the girls.

I hide my laugh, my lips pressed tight. I loved each one of these girls that Fox has lovingly taken to calling 'vipers.'

"What else are we supposed to do with them?" I asked. "Do you think we're dumb enough to keep them home and leave all that pent up anger for us?"

The guy looked at me and then back at Carly. "I'm leaving. I'm leaving."

She still kept the bat raised, watching as he got farther from me and waited until he slid into the driver's seat.

Finally, she came back over to me and I realized then how badly my hands were shaking. She put herself in the way of someone apparently trying to beat the shit out of me and seemed perfectly fine.

I couldn't reach out and grab her like I wanted. I was too worried she was going to notice how bad I was shaking now. I leaned down, kissing her hard before pulling back.

"Car. Now," I said, opening the passenger side. "We're leaving," I yelled to the crew. They all nodded, and I put all my focus back on Carly.

"What, why? Now you sound mad. Are you? I wasn't trying to cause you any problems. I wanted to help."

"I know. Now get in."

"Are you okay? Are you hurt?"

"Get in the fucking car, Carly. *Please.*"

I didn't say anything more, waiting as she stared me down. I didn't really care. All I could care about was ripping her skirt right off of her, and it was taking everything in me to wait until we weren't in a crowd of people.

Nothing like a girl coming to your rescue to make your dick hard.

For all the times people made fun of me for being romantic about things, it wasn't until now that I realized the extent of it. The crew always came to my side in a fight. I had come to learn early in life that with them I wasn't alone, but the fact that Carly just did was something else.

I knew she didn't like a lot of people, and honestly really did assume she only loved her dog, but she obviously liked me, cared about me, and her wild display of that was jaw dropping.

"Jax, please," she breathed, making it all worse. "Tell me."

"For once, *once,* do what I ask and get in. Please." She frowned harder but brushed past me, getting into the passenger seat.

I slammed the door shut and went to the driver's side. My hands were still shaking as I pulled out, the quiet of the car unnerving me, but I couldn't get my thoughts straight with her this close.

I drove a few miles before finally finding a place to park and shut the car off.

"Jax, I'm sorry. I didn't know you would be so mad. I really was trying to help."

I moved and slid myself into the backseat. "Come on. Get back here. Get on top of me."

"What?" she asked, turning to face me. "Are you serious?"

"Get back here, and get on top of me," I repeated. I know how angry I sounded, but I couldn't wait any longer. I needed her.

She turned back, facing the windshield in silence.

"Carly," I said, seeing her cross her arms. She didn't get to be mad at me now.

"What?" she yelled.

"Get back here. Now," I yelled back.

"Did you just yell at me?"

"Yes, now get back here before I drag you back," I said, laughing now.

"Fine, but I don't need to come back there for you to yell at me more."

She crawled onto the console and looked up at me.

"Fucking hell," I mumbled, trying not to look at her chest too long. "Good, come on. Crawl over top of me."

"If this is some way to just yell at me, I'm going to be pissed."

"I'm about five seconds away from yelling at you more if you don't listen," I said.

"I can't believe you're yelling at me in the first place. Is this about what he said? That he recognized me?"

"No, we aren't going to talk about that tonight. We are too busy to care about what he just said, so forget it for tonight." I knew the second she thought about it more, she was going to run. We didn't have any more time to waste on her little teasing game, not when I needed her to know everything I felt. I waved her back, patting my leg.

"You can't be serious. I feel way too self conscious to sit on top of you."

"Right this second, I have no fancy, pretty words to make you feel better. Right now I want to feel better and I'm sorry that's so selfish, but I need you. I have been thinking about you and every perfect part of your body for hours. I got in a fight and all I can think about is you coming to my defense and how perfect you are. Nothing I can say will make you believe me, but I think you're the most beautiful woman I have ever met and there isn't one other fucking person in the world I would rather be with tonight. Your body is all mine and there isn't one thing I would change about it."

She finally moved again, crawling over the top until she straddled me.

"Good girl," I whispered, cupping her face and pulling her hard against me. My lips grabbed hers and in seconds I was drowning in her.

Her tongue slid against mine as she grew more demanding, kissing me harder, and pushing off my jacket.

I had to be covered in blood, but I couldn't find it in me to care when she was kissing me like this. I pulled her against my chest as my hips moved up, my hard cock pushing against her, and she ground down harder.

"You seemed pretty confident swinging that bat. How are you feeling now?"

"Less confident. Much less."

"So you feel more confident violently threatening mean racers than sitting on my lap?"

"One hundred percent."

"That sounds like a big problem. One we need to fix."

"If I knew how to fix it, I would."

"But look at you, already doing so fucking good. Pull that skirt up. Let me help."

"What?"

"Don't be a brat about this. Stay right here on my lap, and pull up your skirt."

Her head tilted, and she looked up at me, a small smile tugging on her lips. She was ready to protest, always talking back, always perfect.

I had already known it before. I had known it every second I had spent with her.

But if there was any doubt that I was completely in love with Carly, they were all gone.

I was hopelessly in love with her and I didn't think there was anything in the world that could change that now.

THIRTY-ONE

CARLY

"Jax—"

"I won't say it again."

I looked down at him, debating on not listening, but part of me was too curious. Everything he did to me felt so good that it was hard to fight it, especially when he was looking up at me with that hot, intense gaze.

"Fine, but if I don't like what you do, I'm getting out of here."

"Don't worry. You won't want to go anywhere."

I pulled my skirt up and before it was even out of the way completely, his hands were on me. His fingers moved through my wetness, the dark car leaving me feeling less on display.

"You're so perfect," he whispered.

"So are you," I said.

"You do so good for me. Are you ready to come on my fingers again?"

My throat was tight, but I managed to answer. "Yes."

"Good girl. You get anything you want." His fingers stroked me a few times before pushing into me. I gasped at the sudden fullness, my pussy clenching as I tried to get used to the feeling. He kept moving, each slow thrust making me relax more.

"That's it. You're taking it better now." He groaned. "You did so good that night, just like you will tonight. This time though, we aren't going to drunkenly rush it. Are you ready for that?"

"Yes," I said, my head falling back as his fingers moved deep into me.

"Look at me," he said, my attention snapping to him. "Keep those beautiful eyes on me and ride my hand. Show me that you're ready for my cock again."

"I don't know if I can." My thoughts going back to my body, not wanting to embarrass myself on top of him.

"Ride my hand or take my cock? Because you're currently doing one of those really well, and you've already done the other perfectly. You're beautiful and vicious and fucking flawless, and all I want to do is please you, sweetheart."

His hand sped up and I couldn't help but move my hips. "That's it, keep going. I know you like being loud. Let me hear you, brat."

I kept moving, the pleasure building and everything around me fading away. There was no self consciousness, no worry if my stomach or hips or body looked bad. There was nothing on my mind except my pleasure and Jax. The man who was always giving and giving was only giving me more now.

In seconds, I broke. Warmth and pleasure moving through me until I was falling into Jax as I tried to catch my breath. When I sat back up, he was smiling, the dull glow of the moon leaving enough light to see him.

He held up his fingers. "Taste, you good little brat. Taste how much you enjoyed my fingers."

My tongue flicked out, running along his fingers. The simple act making me feel dirtier than I ever had, and I loved it.

My mouth dropped open as he pulled his fingers into his own mouth.

His hand moved along my wetness again, before I pulled away. I grabbed his belt, undoing the buckle and button on his jeans.

"What are you doing?" he asked.

"Was that all you wanted to do?"

"Of course I want to do more than that, but we don't have to do it here. We can wait until we are at the apartment."

"I don't want to wait," I said, pulling open his jeans and pulling out his cock. I had already decided what I was going to do next, and I didn't want him to stop me.

"I understand that you want things perfect and romantic and all that, but I don't need it. I don't need flowers, or candles, or whatever other thing you think we need. And while all that is sweet, all I need is you. You are more than enough on your own without all of that, Jax." I sunk down onto the floor, licking along the length of him. I don't know what it was about Jax, but every time I was around him I felt confident. Confident enough to do something like this.

"Fuck, sweetheart. That's not what I was expecting." His hips pushed up as his hand wrapped into my hair.

I moaned against him, taking him deeper before swirling my tongue around the head. My movements were slow at first until I finally found my rhythm, loving his sounds of encouragement.

"You're going to have to decide if you want me to fill your perfect mouth," he said through gritted teeth. "Because I can't...*fuck*," he moaned. "I can't last long with you on a good day and...*fucking hell*...this is not a good day." He let out another moan, the deep grumble of it making me wetter. I wanted him, but more than that, I wanted to do this for him.

I kept moving, loving each moan and groan he made, letting me know exactly how much he was enjoying it, enjoying *me*.

I was so screwed.

He moved my hair over my shoulder, watching as I took him deeper again.

"Look at me," he said, the words barely a whisper.

I turned my head, looking up at him as I moved my tongue along his cock, my lips still wrapped around him. His mouth fell open and his hand moved back into my hair.

I figured he had to be close, so I stopped. Pulling my head back and teasing him with my tongue.

"Do you happen to have a condom?"

"No, but I do at home. In our bed where that will happen, not here."

"Do you really think either of us want to make the entire ride back?" I asked, taking him until he hit the back of my throat.

He groaned again, pushing up. "No, I don't want to, but I'm going too. After what you are doing, I'm worried if I'll even make it a full second once I'm buried in you."

I crawled back up him. The dull glow of the moon giving me enough light to see as I leaned in, kissing him, but stopped when he winced.

"Are you okay?"

"For some reason, my face hurts," he said with a smirk, leaning in further to kiss me still.

That pulled me back to reality, and I pushed back from him, trying to look over his face more. "We should get you back to your apartment and clean you up. Hopefully, nothing is actually broken."

He leaned his head back again, closing his eyes. "Our apartment."

"Your apartment," I said, climbing off of him and trying to adjust my clothes.

"You live there, too."

"Temporarily."

"Or permanently."

"Or very temporarily."

"I can promise you a lot, Carly. I can promise you everything you want or need."

"You can promise things today or even this week, but you can't promise them forever. We all inevitably grow and change. Come on, we should go, not do this."

"Then I will make sure we grow and change together."

I wanted to agree, but I couldn't now. For now, I needed to focus on one thing at a time, the next thing being getting Jax cleaned up. I got out, waiting as he fixed his jeans.

"You can stay and cook and build whatever business you want. Or don't. It's fine either way." He slid out of the backseat, getting out and turning to pin me against the car.

"Jax, this is too much for tonight. Can we just go home?"

"Fine, but you have to drive. I think I have a half broken nose and a concussion."

"Are you serious?"

"Yep. Might have to stay up all night now too, so I don't die and all."

I groaned, but already knew I would. "You know I love my sleep."

"We can find something fun to do. Maybe you can run me one of those witchy baths with all your potions, or you could read my new book to me."

"You got another book?"

"Of course I did. I have a very long list to read, so yes, I did. Don't worry, this one's darker. More stalkers and sex, less lovey dovey stuff, so you will love it."

"You might be the weirdest man I've ever met. You got into a fight, are covered in blood, gave me a great orgasm, and now you want me to go home and read your romance books to you?"

"Someone has to. My head hurts and I won't be able to concentrate on reading."

"As much as I want to help, I'm not driving."

"You are too. You can get this home, no problem."

I blew out a hard breath, and he leaned down, kissing me once. "Sorry about all the blood," he said.

"Sorry I didn't get to you sooner."

He laughed, clutching his side. "I can't believe you came to my rescue. You're amazing. A little scary, but amazing."

"You're scared of me?"

"Not at all. My little witch has a soft spot for me, but your face tonight scared a grown man looking for a fight. You're a little intense when you're pissed off."

"Well, I didn't like him hurting you."

"And I'll be grateful for that forever. Now come on, take me home."

———

HALF AN HOUR later we were finally home after one nerve-wracking drive for me. He shrugged his jacket back off, and I pulled off his shirt, the bloody mess of it making me take it right to the trash before pulling off his jeans. Finally, he was sitting on one of the kitchen chairs in his boxers, blood on his cheek and neck.

"There's blood all over my face, isn't there?" I asked, realizing the streaks across his face were from me kissing him.

His fingers moved over my cheek and jaw as he nodded.

"Yeah, sorry," he whispered, pulling me down to him. I smiled as he kissed me again.

"It's alright. Let me wash some of this off."

I moved the washcloth over each bloody inch until he looked almost normal again.

He grabbed it from me, wiping my face in turn. "You saved me a lot more pain tonight," he said. "Thank you. Even if I am a little pissed you got yourself involved, it was also really sweet."

"I'm so glad you see that as a sweet act."

He started laughing, pulling me closer until I was straddling one of his legs. "It was sweet because you cared about me."

I didn't respond, too worried about what was going to come out of my mouth. I didn't think I was ready to admit just how much I cared about him.

"I can't wait anymore," he said, kissing my neck, half lifting me off of him as he got up and started pulling me towards the bedroom. "I need you, and maybe we can finally do this right."

I didn't have a chance to say anything as he kissed me the entire way to the bedroom, pulling off my clothes as we went.

By the time I was laid back on the bed, I was in nothing but a bra and underwear, and feeling completely on display for him. He came down over top of me, pulling off my bra and groaning as he leaned down to my breasts. He caught one of my nipples, rolling it between his teeth before licking and sucking, and moving onto the next one. Heat and wetness flooded between my legs as he continued. The sensation of it making my spine tingle as my hips bucked.

He groaned again, but didn't say anything, kissing down my stomach. A self conscious thought crept in and promptly took off. The silence giving me all the time in the world to let all my worries take over.

I grew more frustrated as he continued, not saying a word as his lips and tongue moved over every dip and curve of my body. I wanted to enjoy this, but I had grown so used to Jax talking the entire time, I hadn't realized how soothing his words were to me.

"What are you doing?" I finally asked, growing annoyed.

He pulled back with a smile. "I assumed you understood foreplay?"

"I do, but what I don't understand is why you are silent. I usually can't get you to *stop* talking."

"I was trying to be romantic about it, and nothing that comes out of my mouth is going to be romantic," he grinned, going back to my neck.

"Jax, stop," I said, pushing him back again. "I can't do all of this like…well like this. I like when you talk."

"But I wasn't going to be saying anything sweet. I don't want this ruined for you."

"You are ruining it by not being yourself. I'm laying here in silence wondering what you are thinking and growing more self-conscious by the second. If you want to talk, *please,* talk."

"It doesn't ruin it for you?"

"Like I said, this is ruining it more than that. Please, stop putting so much pressure on yourself, and just be you. It makes me comfortable, and I enjoy it a lot more than this."

He groaned again, moving down to kiss me. "How did I get so lucky to find someone who likes me exactly the way I am?"

"I could say the same thing," I panted as he moved back to my breasts, pulling one into his mouth as I gasped.

His hand trailed down my body until his fingers were running along my wetness. "So ready for me already?"

I could only manage a whimper as his fingers pushed into me.

"If you're going to make sounds like that from only my fingers again, how are you going to keep quiet when you take my cock?"

I laughed, my own moan cutting me off. "I won't."

He gave an appreciative groan and pulled away. "I think I will need to hear that for myself."

I kissed his shoulder, waiting as he slid the condom on and positioned himself at my entrance.

"Are you going to take it all again for me?" His nose trailed up my neck to my ear. "Are you going to tell me if it hurts this time?"

"It felt good last time just, like it will this time. It hurt at first, but I told you I liked it."

"Then take it, sweetheart." He pushed harder into me, taking his time as my body stretched around him.

"Did you like making me cum like that? Do you like knowing how much I want you?" he asked, leaning down to kiss me.

"Yes," I breathed, pushing my hips up to take more of him. "How is there still more?"

He laughed, grabbing my hands and pinning them above me as my head fell back. It didn't hurt like it had the first time, but my body still ached at the fullness. I clenched hard, trying to take more.

"It's okay, sweetheart. Take your time." I took another steadying breath before he continued.

"Good girl. You're taking it so perfect. Look at you, sweetheart. *You* are perfect."

His words encouraged me more, until I was pushing up, taking the rest of him in one motion. His fingers dug into my hips as I yelled out, my pussy clenching as I tried to get used to the feeling. He moved, each slow thrust making me relax more.

"Yes," I said, my head falling back again, pleasure taking over.

"Always so greedy for me," he said. He kept moving faster until he was slamming into me. It pushed me over the edge, my body tightening before exploding into a thousand pieces. My vision blurred as I reached for him, trying not to yell any louder, but I couldn't stop myself as I fell apart around him. He groaned, but I couldn't make out anything else he said, the sound of my own heart racing the only thing I could hear now.

He finally slowed, my body coming down off the high of my own orgasm and turning my limbs to jelly.

"Damn," he panted. "And I thought that was good the first time."

"Were you worried it wouldn't be as good?" I asked, laughing.

"Not even close. I knew it would be amazing. And it didn't hurt?"

"No, I'm fine. More than fine."

He laughed, kissing me hard before rolling to his side. "Come on. Between the fight and the best sex of my life, I think I would like one of those witchy baths now," he said.

I nodded, taking his hand as we walked back to the bathroom. I started the bath, adding in everything I wanted before he pulled me over to clean me up as it filled.

I finally sunk into the warm water, Jax getting in behind me. I could feel him laughing behind me, the shake of his body making the water splash.

"What's so funny?"

"The last time I saw you in this tub, I was already dying to get in with you. Dreams do come true." He leaned down, kissing my neck and holding onto me.

I could only lean back against him. For the first time in a long time, I let go of any worry I had and took the rest of the night to enjoy the good things in my life.

THIRTY-TWO
CARLY

THE NEXT DAY, I was standing in the kitchen when a knock at the door made me freeze.

Jax had gone out, saying he needed to grab a few things before we left, and I knew that no one else here would be knocking.

Riot barked once and ran to the door, his little tail wagging fast when he smelled under the door.

"Hello?" I asked, not knowing who Riot would be excited to see.

"It's only me, Carly. Calm down and open the door."

"Why are you knocking?" I asked, still not opening it.

"Because you told me I get to be my romantic self, and that self wants to pick you up for a date."

I rolled my eyes. "Are you serious?"

"Completely."

I finally pulled open the door. Jax was on the other side, a bouquet of what looked like roses in his hand, the deep red a harsh contrast against his black leather jacket.

As usual, he was smiling, handing the flowers over to me and leaning down to kiss my cheek.

"This is all a little cliche, don't you think?"

He pulled me close, careful not to crush the flowers that were between us.

"Come on, little witch. I let you tease me even when I'm following after you like a damn puppy dog. Let me have this because I am already having so much fun."

It was clear he wasn't lying. The playful smile on his lips made it look like he really was having the time of his life.

"Fine, but you can't be this cheesy all the time. What is this? A dozen red roses? It really is a little cliche."

He rolled his eyes this time, letting out a dramatic breath. "Give me a little more credit than that and actually look at the flowers."

My eyes dropped, looking down at the bouquet in my hands.

There were the red roses, the deep crimson red beautiful and almost black in places, but mixed in were actual black ones. The deep gray and black color making the red ones even more crisp.

"You added black roses?"

"Yes, I thought you might like something to match that cold, black heart. Plus, I knew you were going to give me shit for the flowers, so I thought this might appeal to that darker side of you. Based on your smile, it seems to be working."

I pulled my smile back into a frown.

"Alright grump, do you want to go on a date with me or do you want to pout all night that I brought you flowers?"

I was quiet for a second, almost too stunned to speak that he did this for me. He thought to go out and get me flowers, take me out on a date, and I was already looking forward to whatever other ridiculously cheesy thing he had planned because now that I knew Jax, I knew there would be more.

And worst of all, I knew that I would love every second.

At some point, I was going to have to reel these feelings in and remind myself that I had a life to go create, but right now, I couldn't care about anything other than the man standing in front of me. The one currently running a hand through my hair and pulling me closer.

"I want to go out on a date with you," I finally said.

His smile grew, and he leaned down, catching my lips with his. In seconds, it turned from a simple kiss to him moving the flowers out of the way and helping me onto the counter. His kiss was so slow at first, so deep that I ran out of breath. He pulled back, letting me breath before brushing his lips and tongue against me again. Then he was everywhere. Stroking my tongue, my teeth, the roof of my mouth. I already knew my lips had to be turning red. He nipped at my bottom lip, pulling it between his teeth before moving back to my tongue.

"Maybe we should stay home."

"As much as I want to say yes, not a chance," I said. "I'm too curious to see what you have planned."

"I knew you were going to fall for all my charm and romance. Come on, let's go before I drag you to bed."

"Where are we going?"

"One of my favorite places, but I have something else to show you first."

He grabbed my hand, pulling me downstairs until we were out in front of the apartment.

As soon as we stepped outside, I saw it.

"My truck?"

He went over, opening the driver's side door.

"Yep. All fixed up and ready to go. Although, tonight will be the true test of that, so don't hold me to it being completely fixed."

"But you drove it here?"

"I did, and we are going to take it to the drive-in to watch a movie. The crew is already headed there, so come on. Let's go."

I laughed as I pulled myself up into the driver's seat before turning to face him. "You want to take me on a date, but are bringing your entire group of friends?"

"I kind of told them what I was planning, and they invited themselves. Is it a problem?" His face scrunched, and I realized he was truly asking, worried I wouldn't like that they would be there.

"Not at all. I love them. But I think it's funny. You guys are the definition of a package deal."

"Pretty much. It's been that way for as long as I could remember. I barely think about it now. One of us goes somewhere, there's a parade behind them."

"I actually like it. Can I start this?" I asked, turning back to the steering wheel. I loved this truck. It was old, and slow, and a little beat up, but there would never be another car like it to me.

"You're going to have to drive it, so yes, get going."

Another five minutes went by as Jax told me everything he did, and then we were headed down the road. There was so much freedom wrapped up in having my truck back. I wasn't stuck anywhere. All of my options were back.

I could leave at any moment with ease.

I looked over at Jax, a reality that I had pushed aside crashing down around me.

"Why are you looking at me like that?" I asked.

"You looked so happy. It's hard to look away from," he said.

"Thank you. For fixing my truck, for letting me stay with you, for a million other things."

"Stop," he said, his tone harsh.

"Stop what?"

"Breaking up with me before we even go on an actual date."

"I wasn't —"

"Stop, Carly. I knew the moment you had your truck back, you would be ready to leave. I wasn't going to try taking that from you, but please, *please*, don't try to run out tonight."

"I wasn't leaving tonight," I said quietly. "I'm looking forward to spending it with you."

"Okay then. You're welcome for everything else."

The inside of the truck went quiet as I turned onto the main road, shifting until I ran out of gears and it went comfortably down the road at fifty-five miles an hour.

"It's running better than ever."

"Good. I was hoping that would be the case. I upgraded a few things that should help it at least reach the speed limit easier."

We made it to the drive-in without a problem, and I pulled the truck in next to the rest of the crew's cars. The colorful lineup made me laugh as I pulled my truck in. The faded, dull green was not quite as fun as theirs. By the time I got out, Jax was already in the bed of the truck, moving things around as I peered in, Kye coming up next to me.

"For once, I'm jealous of an old, slow-as-fuck truck," Kye said. "That looks a hell of a lot more comfortable than my hood."

Jax unrolled what could only be described as a sea of blankets and pillows until the back of the truck was a fluffy, perfect bed that I wanted to sink into.

I moved to lean towards him as Kye went back to his car. "This is really sweet."

"And you hate it?" he asked, the honesty of the question heartbreaking.

"No, not at all. I love it."

The smile that lit up his face made me step back, but he followed, kissing my forehead. "I'm going to get food and drinks. Get comfortable," he said, leaning down to my ear. "*Really* comfortable."

Heat shot through me and I leaned back on the tailgate, watching as he walked away. I couldn't keep my eyes off of him. I could see him at the stand, ordering us food, and for a moment I couldn't breathe.

He was here with me. For right now, he was mine, and I guess that I was his.

Ash was saying something, making me turn back.

"What?" I asked, realizing she was talking to me.

"I asked how it's going. You two seem…cozy. We were all a little worried after the races, and *someone* didn't text us back."

I couldn't hide my laugh. We hadn't texted anyone back, deciding to spend the entire day alone in the apartment instead. "Yeah, things are good for now."

"For now?" Scout asked.

"Yeah, I mean, the truck is done, so I guess I'll still have to go soon."

Their faces scrunched. "You know," Quinn said. "You can just…not. You don't have to leave. And it seems like things are going good for you two, so why leave?"

"Because I don't know if staying is the right choice. I've never tried anything else. What if I choose this and never try anything else and then Jax gets sick of me? I would have nothing else. No one else." I was trying not to spiral into my desperate, negative thoughts, but it was all true. I trusted Jax, but that didn't mean I could suddenly trust him with forever.

"I don't think Jax is going to be upset if you build a life for yourself, how ever you want it. I mean, he did already show that he's ready to help you with building a business. Staying doesn't mean you have to do nothing else with your life."

"He seems to have more belief in me than I have in me. I really wish he wouldn't have done all of that."

"Sometimes you need that," Ash said with a shrug. "Fox had more belief than me that I would go back to racing. I would be having a panic attack from just sitting in the car, and he still believed I could do it. From personal experience, let someone believe in you."

"Plus, bonus, we all believe in you too," Scout said. "We're not quite as overwhelming about it as Jax, but we do."

"It's surprising to me that you all are so supportive when I'm not even a part of your group."

They all looked at each other and back at me.

"What are you talking about?" Quinn asked. "Why wouldn't you be?"

"Just that...I know you have all been nice to me, but I also understand I'm not exactly a part of this little family you've made."

Quinn was the first one to shake her head. "To you, it might not seem that way, but we are more than happy to let you be a part of all of it. I hate to be the bearer of bad news, but the only reason you don't feel like you are is because you are keeping yourself a bit separated. We understood why, with you wanting to leave and not get attached, but if you want to be a part of our group, you have a place here waiting with your name on it."

I stared at them, taking in what she said. I knew as soon as she said it that she was right. I was the one keeping the distance, but I didn't really know how else to be. I kept to myself so much that I never knew how to open up and have friends.

"Thank you," I finally said. "Thanks for saying that and for how nice you all have been. I don't know what I'm doing next, but I appreciate you three."

All three of them smiled and pulled me into a hug.

For what felt like the thousandth time since I met them all, I felt like crying. I thought I was doing good, keeping my distance so that I could leave without a problem, and not involve them in my mess, but it's obvious I was failing at that, too.

Now, I wasn't sure what I was supposed to do.

THIRTY-THREE
CARLY

BY THE TIME Jax came back over, I was already waiting on the tailgate. He was smiling as he carried everything to the truck.

"You're smiling pretty hard at me," he said as he set the drinks and snacks down. "It's making me a little worried."

"No need to worry. Now get in the truck."

He gave a quiet laugh. "Yes, ma'am."

I moved up to the makeshift bed he had made as he pulled the tailgate shut, closing us into our own little oasis. The stars were already out, and the night was cold enough that snuggling up in all these blankets would be perfect. The movie started, and I sank back farther.

It was heaven. I moved pillows around and he pulled me in.

"Mine," he whispered, coming closer until he was kissing me.

"What?"

"The night of the party, I said that you were mine, and you agreed that I was yours. I am yours. You are mine."

"You know that I'll be leaving. I can't —"

"Stop, Carly. I told you. Don't talk to me about leaving or

ending this. Not tonight. Give me that at least. The only thing you're allowed to end tonight would be this date, and that's only if you decide you really don't like me." His hand trailed down my stomach to my leggings, sliding in and finding how wet I was. "But it seems like you might like me a little."

"I might," I said. His face lit up again, his smile deepening until dimples showed.

"I think you would like staying with me longer."

He slipped two fingers in, the sudden touch making me gasp. I loved how he touched me. How he always knew when to take over. How he gave in to anything and everything I wanted. It felt like he would do anything for me.

"Maybe," I whispered. "And maybe not."

"Then stay. Even if it's only a maybe. I want you to. I need you to. You give me so much that you don't even know about. I hadn't slept well for months before you came and now I sleep every night next to you. I didn't care about the world around me, and now I want to do everything and give you everything I can."

He was still fucking me with his hand, the slow, methodical movements working perfectly as my body ached for more and more.

"Asking me this while you're working on giving me an orgasm doesn't seem fair."

"I don't want to be fair right now. I want to do whatever I have to do to make sure you see that we are perfect for each other."

"We aren't. You're perfect. I am far from it. Maybe you haven't had good luck in the past, but you need someone else. Someone bubbly, happy, romantic, perky."

He froze, his hand pulling away as he pulled me hard against him.

"Who are you to tell me what I need, Carly? Maybe I need you. Your grumpy, dark self that likes to talk back until I'm touching you. I like that you're bossy and maybe a little mean sometimes. I like that you're sweet and soft and kind to me when it matters. I don't need you parading around in pink with a smile plastered on your face. Plus," he said with a groan. "I can't get over how much I fucking love the things you wear. I wouldn't even be able to tell you how hot it is and how much I look forward to seeing what you pick out each day. No frills or pink are necessary unless you want it."

"I don't know."

"But I do. I didn't know what I wanted. I really didn't even know what I needed, but I do now. It's you."

I didn't say anything, too scared of what my answer would be.

"Fine," he said. "Then, for tonight, let's have our date."

"Does our date include sex in the back of the truck while the movie is playing?"

"Yes, it does," he said, pulling off my pants and rolling me onto my side. "But only if you can be good and stay quiet."

I nodded, and he moved, curling himself around me, his chest pressed hard to my back.

"All mine," he said as his cock pushed into me.

I pushed back, taking more, and groaning as he filled me.

"Take it for me sweetheart, I know you can. It's all yours."

I relaxed as he moved, taking it easy with slow strokes.

"You've never been anyone else's. No one else has ever had you the ways I have and I hope to the entire fucking universe they never will. I want it all for myself."

He picked up the pace, fucking me harder while I tried to stay quiet.

"Jax," I breathed, trying not to moan.

He slowed again, drawing out my orgasm as I stayed so close to the edge of it.

"If you don't give me an orgasm right now, I'm going to tease you for days again," I said.

"You are terrible with threats. I like the torture. I like dying with need for you," he said, laughing as he picked up the pace again.

Then his hand wrapped around me, rubbing my clit as he fucked me. Every part of my body caught fire until it engulfed me. I've done both of these things now, but putting them together was more intense than I would have imagined.

In seconds, I was falling apart, and there was no way I could hide my moans as I came. Jax's hand came up, covering my mouth as I quietly moaned into it.

"You're so fucking perfect. Do you know how good I get off with you? Your body was made for me."

I couldn't control anything that was happening, my body melting against him.

I didn't move, didn't say anything as he held me, neither of us pulling away.

"I want you to stay," he finally said. "Stay for me. Stay because I want you too, and because I promise to make it worth it."

It wasn't really a hard decision, but saying I would stay indefinitely was too scary to face.

"I can stay for another week."

"Just one."

"That's all I can say right now."

"I'll take it. Now, I'm going to watch this movie and hold you the rest of the night because I can finally breathe again now that I know this isn't the last night."

"Finally breathe?"

"I've been dying knowing you would leave. Knowing that the second I handed over the keys to this, you wouldn't need me anymore. It's selfish and I know it, but I really didn't want to go back to my life before you. At least I have another week."

I didn't say anything, trying to take in the words. I knew Jax said whatever was on his mind, good, bad, or ridiculous. He didn't mince his words or really seem to lie.

I didn't know how to react to someone wanting me to stay with them so openly.

"I've never had anyone that wanted me," I said, the words quiet with the movie echoing from cars around us.

"Never? What about your family?"

"No, I think most of them are fine that I'm gone. Aside from the concern I might snitch or go against them. I know they don't care. Honestly? They probably haven't really noticed in their day-to-day life. I spent most of my time locked in my room. My grandpa was the only one that wanted me around, really."

"You're wanted here, with me, with the crew. You're wanted, Carly."

I pushed back into him, not able to say anything else for the fear of tears spilling over.

We watched the movie for a while, his hands never leaving me.

"Thank you," I finally said quietly. "For this date tonight and for fixing my truck. And for telling me that you want me to stay, for being so clear about it. Thank you for that."

"I will always be clear about wanting you."

I spun around to face him. "And you understand that I won't? That I would never be so open and careless with my feelings?"

"I know. My little witch has a black heart and won't let anyone see it bleed." He kissed my nose and pulled back. "As long as you play along with my ideas, I'll be romantic enough for the both of us."

"I have a feeling that's a dream job for you."

He laughed. "Kind of, yeah. Even convincing you that romance and love do in fact exist has been a dream come true."

"Alright Prince Charming, let's just watch this movie now and stop talking about feelings."

"Finally," he said. "I made it to Prince Charming status. I'm still putting you in the seductive Snow White category." He was quiet for a second. "Damn," he mumbled.

"What?"

"Now I'm getting turned on by thinking about you being a villain style Snow White."

"Alright, now it's really time to watch the movie. Come on, knock it off," I said, moving until I was propped up in front of him, facing the screen. "I'm flattered though," I added.

And I was. Flattered that he always thought of me in such nice ways, flattered that he always made it clear he wanted me, and flattered that someone so perfect could think so much of me.

I didn't know what I was going to be looking for in life, but I was starting to worry that finding anything better than this would be impossible.

THIRTY-FOUR
CARLY

JAX HANDED me my cup of coffee, making it exactly the way I liked it, before sitting on the other side of the couch.

"Drink up and then get ready."

"Another date?"

He shrugged. "I guess it could be considered a date. Actually, yeah, let's make it a date."

"Are you going to make every outing a date?"

"Sweetheart, going to the grocery store feels like a date with you. Maybe stop being so cute and flirty everywhere we go."

"I do not do that!"

"Right, right. Keep telling yourself that. Now go on, get ready."

I did, changing fast and almost racing him downstairs to the car.

I didn't ask where we were going and really didn't care. I somehow enjoyed everywhere he took me. His hand moved to sit on my thigh, but he froze, ready to pull it away.

I grabbed it, setting it down, and he smiled, leaning back in silence until we reached his apparent destination.

A bookstore.

"I still can't believe you read and read romance at that."

"If you're going to start making fun of me, we can leave. I honestly hate that you know already."

I reached for his hand as we walked in and he started to look over the shelves. "You can't hate that. I like knowing your dirty little secret."

"Just for that, I'm going to pick out a book that makes you cry."

"None of them are going to make me cry."

"I bet I will have tears running down your face by midnight."

I slid between him and the bookshelf, blocking his view, but he only smiled down at me, his dimples growing as he grinned.

"There are other ways that we could have tears running down my face by midnight if you're interested," I said, running a hand down his stomach.

He groaned, leaning his forehead against mine. "Respectfully, you are the sluttiest virgin I have ever met."

"No need to be respectful about it and I am not a virgin anymore, so you have to stop calling me that."

"Do I if I'm the only one you've been with?"

"Are you saying it doesn't count unless I sleep with someone else?"

His smile fell, and he pushed against me. "No. That is definitely *not* what I'm saying."

"Then you better knock it off."

"I take it back. Would you like to leave so I can make up for my comments?" he asked, grinning.

"Why leave? You could probably figure it out here if I just–" I adjusted myself onto the small table behind me, it was hidden enough back here. I reached up, wrapping a hand around his neck to pull him closer to me. He groaned, pushing hard against me.

"I love when you get all cute and in charge, but don't even think about it," he said, laughing as he pulled me off the table. "Now, let's get our books and get out of here before you start ripping my clothes off. Who would have thought a bookstore turned you on so much?"

"Fine. You're no fun." I stuck out my tongue, and he leaned down, grabbing it and sucking it as my mouth fell open.

When he pulled back, I was almost speechless. "If you don't want your clothes ripped off, maybe don't do weirdly hot things like that," I said, breathless. He wasn't smiling, the dark look on his face making a shiver run through me. It was the same dangerous look he would get when he was jealous or ready for a fight, but this time, it was all for me.

"Should we go check out and get home, or do you want to find more?" I asked with a smile.

"Just so you know, I will be getting you back for getting me so fucking turned on when I can't do anything about it. And no, now I definitely have one more to get."

"Which is?"

"One to make you cry."

"I don't know why you want to see me cry so bad."

"It's not that I want to see you cry. It's two things. One, it proves you do in fact have a red, beating heart like the rest of us. And two, I want you to see that, while it might hurt sometimes, love and romance are one hundred percent worth it."

I rolled my eyes. "You are so sweet and sappy. I honestly don't know what to do with you. And I don't know how you say that when you've been hurt so badly before."

"Because I learned my lesson and moved on to better things. That better thing being you."

"You can't claim to like me that much. You don't even know everything about me," I said, my words growing quiet at everything he really didn't know about me. That laptop was haunting me now, and I knew time was running out to come clean.

"Stop thinking you're not special. I don't need weeks or months or years, Carly. I was falling for you the moment I saw you. I know this is going to be hard for you to understand, but loving someone does not mean that you know everything about them. It means that you are agreeing to love everything you already know and the things that you find out. Good and bad."

"And what if the bad is really bad? What if it's an instant problem for you?"

He shrugged. "Obviously, if it's cheating or lying, I'm not going to be okay with that."

"No, I mean things about me, about my past, not that I would purposely hurt you. I don't know how anyone could willingly hurt you."

He laughed. "No one will be able to when my girl wants to fight to the death for me every time."

"Or maybe I don't like people trying to hurt my friends."

"Friends? Just admit you have fallen in love with me so we can move on."

"Would you really want me to admit to something like that out of pity?"

"No, I guess you're right," he said, throwing an arm over me. "I want to watch you fall so in love with me you fall flat on your face."

"Wow, first you want to make me cry and now you want me to fall flat on my face? And you say I'm the mean one."

"Mmm," he said. "It's not meant to be mean. I'm just getting desperate to make you see how much you like me."

"Keep giving me orgasms, and you might change my mind," I said, trying to not talk about falling for him a second longer.

"Done. Prepare for the rest of your day to be absolutely wrecked.

———

THE DOOR to the apartment shut behind me and before I could take another step, I was being forced up against the door. My face pressed against the cool wood as Jax's hand wrapped around my neck.

"I've made a decision," he said, the deep rasp to his voice only turning me on more.

"Which is?"

"For every minute you get me turned on in public, is one more minute you'll be doing exactly what I say when we get home."

I laughed, his hand tightening at the sound. "What if I don't want to do exactly as you say?"

"Listen or don't listen. I already fantasize about your ass being red so I have my fun either way."

He grabbed my hands, pinning them behind my back as he pushed me towards the bedroom. We made it in the doorway before he stopped.

"Undress."

"Completely?"

"Well, I won't be licking every curve of your body with clothes on."

Heat flushed, but I didn't move. If he cared, he didn't say anything, choosing to start kissing my neck instead.

"Now, get undressed."

"I can't stand in front of you completely naked."

He pulled off my sweater, and then moved to my leggings, hooking his thumbs under the band and pulling them off. "You can because you're going to be doing a lot more than standing in front of me naked. Now bend over, put your hands on the bed."

He pulled at my shirt, taking it off until I stood naked in the room, frozen.

"You aren't listening very well, brat." He pulled my arms, pinning them to my back and walking me forward. He kept moving until I was on my knees, moving across the bed.

"Good," he said, wrapping his hand back around my neck again. "Look at that, you're here naked, and I'm harder than ever." His hand moved higher, tipping my head back against him. "I can't wait to have these lips wrapped around my cock again. I will tell you a thousand more times, you are perfect, every single thing about you is perfect and I would give my entire world to have you in this bed with me every single night." I leaned back into him, realizing he was naked against me. I could hardly breathe, each harsh whisper turning me on and I could already feel how wet I was.

"Now bend over," he said, leaning me forward on the bed until my face was against the blankets. He let me go, my hands moving to hold myself up. "Not a chance," he said, pushing me back down as his hand slapped against my ass.

I bolted up, the sting of it sending a thrill up my spine.

"Jax!" I yelled, more shocked than anything.

"Yes?"

"I…I like that."

He groaned. "Of course you do because you're a dream come fucking true." He moved closer and I could feel his cock pushing against my entrance now. "I'm going to take you just like this now, holding these perfect hips that make me lose my mind. I want to sink my fucking teeth into them, grab them every second of the day." He grabbed them now, and for the first time, I didn't care that they were a little soft, didn't care that they had some extra weight on them with how he grabbed onto me. His fingers dug in before one pulled away to spank me once more. "Fuck, please yell if this is to much," he said.

"If what is—" My words were cut off as he slammed into

me. I expected pain with the pace he was going, but my body stretched around him easier now.

He didn't stop, thrusting into me as my body responded, liking the roughness of his touch.

Soon, I was pushing back, moving in rhythm as my orgasm built.

He reached down, wrapping an arm around my hip until his fingers found my clit. I yelled as he hit that sensitive spot, the blinding pleasure almost too much to take, but he didn't stop. In seconds, I was falling apart, turning my face into the bed as I yelled out. He finally slowed, both of us staying like that as we tried to catch our breath.

He rolled next to me, pulling me against him as I tried to come down off the high of my orgasm.

"Living with you is like living in a fairytale and a porno all at once. I can't figure out which one this is," I said.

"Obviously I'm doing my best to make it both," he said, his chest rumbling with a laugh.

"Well, you are doing great. Are you always like this with girls?"

"Like…what?"

"Sweet, caring, hot and demanding. All of this."

He gave a small laugh, wrapping his arms around me and pulling me close.

"No, not quite the same. Although, I do like to think I'm sweet and hot all the time."

"Of course you do," I said, rolling my eyes. "That's why I asked."

"Ahh, worrying that you aren't special again?" he asked, rolling to his side to face me. His hand moved along my jaw and I reached up to grab it, needing an answer first."I've never been like this with someone else because I've never felt so much like myself with someone. I've never felt like someone likes me for me the way that you do, which is ironic because you don't seem to like anyone," he said with a small laugh. "You let me be me, and I already know you secretly love me for it. So no, I have only given all of this to you. All sides of myself, every part of myself, to you."

I didn't say anything, deciding to kiss him instead of admitting that I did already secretly love him. I loved everything about him.

THIRTY-FIVE

CARLY

I woke up to Jax pulling me against his chest.

"I have to get up and head to the garage. Would you like your cup of coffee before I go?"

I snuggled in closer to him, the warm blankets, soft bed, and his arms around me to enticing to move from.

"Or you could stay here and we get our coffee in a bit," I said.

His chest rumbled with a laugh as he kissed my head. "I think my heart just exploded. You're asking me to stay close and snuggle? I knew you secretly loved all of those, all of me. I do, unfortunately, have to get to the garage today, though. I stayed with you all day yesterday and if I don't go today, I don't know if I ever will again."

"One more day won't hurt."

"We could have a thousand more days like this if you stay."

I could feel my body stiffen, but I didn't pull away. "A thousand? So about 3 years and that's it?"

He laughed again, reaching down to smack my ass. "You're terrible. Thousands, forever if you want it."

"So I could have forever, but not this morning? Seems like a trick," I said, stifling my laugh.

"It is. I have to keep you guessing, so you are curious enough to stay."

"Stay forever." I repeated the word that was currently in my face. Forever was tattooed on him, but I still didn't know how to promise someone forever or believe that they could promise me that. As though he read my thoughts, he leaned in to kiss my forehead.

"Need your name tattooed above it so you believe me? It could say 'Carly forever' if you want."

"Absolutely not. You better not tattoo my name on yourself."

He shrugged. "I would do it. I don't care. If you don't want your name, we can do something else. It could just say 'little witch' above it," he said, laughing harder. "You can tattoo the rest of my body if it means you believe in forever with me."

"I do not want the pressure of choosing tattoos for someone. I can't even choose one for myself," I said, trying not to panic.

"I'll choose then. It will be a fun surprise one day for you," he said, laughing as he kissed me. "Now, I'm getting up before I take you up on your offer of staying here all day. You can come with me if you would rather."

"Go stay in the dirty garage all day or stay here with my dog and this amazing bed? I think I'll choose here."

He kissed me again before getting up. "I don't blame you."

I hung around Jax, telling him goodbye, and kissing him a hundred more times before he left.

———

AN HOUR LATER, I stepped out with Riot for his walk and pulled out my phone. Riot knew the longer path we were taking now and led me along while I watched cooking videos. It had become a routine that I loved. The calming walk each day making me feel some semblance of my life being normal.

We walked down the street towards the garage, turning down a side street to go around the block. I had thought about going to see Jax instead, but decided I might need to calm myself down and walk around the block once or twice, instead.

I could hear the rev of an engine, the sound not making me jump anymore. Their shop was so close that I knew it would be them. I was comfortable, finally feeling completely at home with Jax and the crew.

I turned the next corner, the peaceful street one of my favorites. The rev of the engine got closer, and I turned back, smiling to myself at the thought of Jax coming to see me. I had told him I was heading out on a walk, and knew that he was also hoping I would walk down to the garage. The car came to the stop sign and turned.

My heart dropped, my stomach churning as I watched the white car come towards me, the orange stripe down the side impossible to confuse with any of the crew.

It was Slaughter.

"No. No, no, no," I said, trying to remember how to make my feet move.

But I could only stand there frozen, watching as his car sped towards me as bile rose in my throat. This was it.

He was here. He came to take me back. The sound of my own heartbeat filled my ears, the overwhelming rushing sound only making the anxiety worse.

My brain finally caught up, and I turned in the opposite direction, breaking into a run with Riot helping to pull me along. My throat tightened as tears threatened me. I didn't want to go back.

I could make it, though. I could turn the corner, and then

another before heading right to the garage. The entire crew was there, and I knew Slaughter wouldn't be able to face them all alone.

The light at the end of the tunnel disappeared fast as another car turned the corner in front of me. This one was white with a blue stripe.

Tristan.

He turned down the road towards me, and I stopped. They were trapping me in, the entire yard behind me, surrounded by a tall fence. Riot realized something was wrong, his hackles going up as he watched the approaching car. I fumbled for my phone, wishing I hadn't shoved it into my pocket before they showed up.

Jax.

I needed to call Jax. He wouldn't let me get taken without coming for me.

I only had to make sure he knew where I was. I laughed, the sound coming out like a cry instead. I pulled out my phone as soon as Slaughter got out.

"Hey Carly, I've been looking all over for you," he said, the furious tone chilling.

"How did you find me?"

"Had a friend tell me about a bitchy girl he ran into at the races. I almost didn't believe him that it was you at first until he described you."

Tristan came to a stop, jumping out and blocking me in further. I hit Jax's name as Riot lunged, knocking the phone from my hand. The snarl that ripped from Riot made me pull back in shock, but he only pulled me forward again.

"Get him back or I will shoot him," Slaughter said. I already knew how serious he was, but the gun he waved in his hand gave me a second reminder.

I pulled back again, only getting him half under control as Tristan came up behind me. Riot turned on him, snapping until he took a few steps back. "What are you doing here?" I finally said, my voice so unsteady that I only grew angry with myself.

"You know why I'm here. I'm running out of time and need your help, so come on, we are leaving."

"I'm not leaving with you," I said, trying to sound more firm this time.

Slaughter stepped forward, ignoring Riot. "I wasn't asking. The fucking dog isn't invited. I'll take care of him before we leave."

"I'm not going with you, and I'm not helping you steal cars."

"I didn't get you all that computer training so you could sit around on your ass. I told you we needed you for this job, and you ran out. You owe it to me, and you know what? You owe it to your mother to help the family get more money. She has worked her ass off for you and now you don't want to do this for her?"

"For her? How is committing crimes going to help her?" I yelled. I could hear it now. It was so clear to me how he used every word to manipulate me.

"I really wasn't asking," Slaughter said. "Get her." He nodded to Tristan who ran up behind me. His arms came around my waist, pulling me back against him. Fear coursed through me, the world spinning into a nightmare as I realized escaping was slipping further away. I was helpless. This was exactly what I had been scared of.

More engines revved around the block and I knew it was over. If there were more of them, I would never stand a chance. Even now, the odds were not in my favor. Tristan's arms tightened on me as I fought back, a scream ripping from my throat as Riot barked, jumping up onto us as he snapped his jaw. Tristan lowered me, my feet finally touching the ground again. That was one bonus point of being a little heavier. There was no way he was carrying me, while I fought back, all the way to his car.

A sleek black car rounded the corner, two more behind it, and I recognized it immediately.

The Charger. It was Jax.

It was enough to remind me that I wasn't alone. I pulled my arm out of Tristan's grip, swinging my elbow back. In the same moment, Riot attacked, biting down on Tristan's arm and not letting go.

Tristan screamed, dropping me to the ground as I lost my footing, but Riot wasn't done. He lunged at him, biting down on his arm again and pulling. Tristan's screams filled the air.

Slaughter started yelling over him, waving his gun around, as he tried to get it all under control, but his eyes were on the cars pulling up. His resolve seemed to waver as he realized he was now outnumbered. He hesitated, taking a step towards his car as his grip on the gun faltered. I knew Slaughter would assume they all also had guns, even though Jax had told me before that they don't.

Riot, always vigilant, was back to guarding me, his teeth bared at Tristan who was awkwardly holding his arm, and trying to back away. I could see the blood dripping down and pooling at his feet, and grabbed onto Riot, trying to keep him close.

Jax got out of the Charger, walking past Slaughter like he wasn't even there.

"Carly," he said, his eyes searching over me for injuries. I was still on the ground, holding meekly onto Riot. I really had no care if he went after Slaughter or Tristan again, but I was too aware of Slaughters gun, and the threat to kill Riot. Jax grabbed my arms, pulling me up. "Are you okay?"

I nodded, not finding any words.

He nodded back, pushing me behind him, but I stepped back next to him, clinging to his arm.

"Considering you have six other pissed off people behind you," he looked down at Tristan who was almost in tears holding onto his ruined arm, "and your little sidekick is a mess right now. I'm guessing you won't be staying."

"I'm on a deadline. She can't hide forever, and she can't keep my fucking laptop forever. Maybe now that I know where she is, I'll call her in for theft."

"She won't be hiding. You obviously know she is with us, so no need to hide. As for calling in theft, that's pretty rich coming from you. We've figured out how to ruin your life before. I'm sure we can do it again," Jax said with a smirk.

Slaughter stared hard at Jax before his gaze shifted to me, and for a moment, I saw uncertainty flicker in his eyes.

"Tristan, get the fuck up and get her."

I looked over, but Tristan was already stalking back to his car. "That fucking dog just about ripped my arm off. You get her! I need to go get my fucking arm reattached." He slid behind the wheel, slamming his door, and taking off on the sidewalk to get around the crew's cars.

"Fuck," Slaughter screamed. "Fuck, that stupid asshole, running off like that"

He turned to me. "I'm coming back, Carly, and you can expect I will be taking you and that laptop home to finish my job. I have a lot riding on this deal, and you better step up to help your family."

"I'm not your family!" I screamed as he slammed his door and took off.

We all stood, watching as he rounded the corner, and waiting until the sound of his engine faded. Jax turned, grabbing my arms, and looking me over again.

"Are you really okay? He didn't hurt you?"

"No, he didn't have a chance with Riot. He only grabbed me for a minute to try to get me to the car. Thank you," I said, before turning to the rest of them. "Thank all of you for coming."

"Of course," Quinn said. "We will always be here."

Everyone agreed before Jax wrapped an arm around me.

"We are going back to the apartment. Can you guys head to the garage to make sure he doesn't try anything."

They nodded.

"Come on," he said, pulling me towards the car. I went along, not quite believing what had just happened.

"Why are you driving this?" I asked.

"I did have to take it for a test drive," he said, smiling. Riot came over, barking until Jax opened the door before jumping up, crawling over the seat until he was sitting comfortably in the back. I slide in as he held the door open.

"Well, that makes one of you who wants to go for a drive. Could we make it two?"

"We shouldn't be driving this. I don't want to break anything."

"First of all, you won't be breaking anything. It would be me, and I would take the blame. Second, I was short on options and needed to get to you. I'm pretty sure your grandpa would be happy about that."

"Okay, that is fair." He got in, turning to Riot and petting him, telling him how good he was.

I didn't disagree, but I still crossed my arms, watching his eyes light up as he looked at me.

In one beautiful moment, I was falling in love, and in the next, the terrible truth that I had to tell him crashed into me.

I did have to tell him now. Slaughter just told him so there was really no hiding it now, but first, I was going to steal one more moment that I wanted. One more second because there was no stopping the inevitable wreck that was about to happen in my life. Slaughter knew where I was, and I was out of options.

I leaned over, waiting for him to come closer. His hand wrapped around the back of my neck and pulled me in to kiss me.

"Ready?" he asked, putting the car back into gear to head out.

"Yeah, I'm ready."

THIRTY-SIX

JAX

By the time I pulled the Charger into the garage at the apartments, Carly was in my lap, kissing me like her life depended on it.

Which was only fair, since I was pretty sure that mine depended on it now.

"Are you okay?" I whispered, pulling back from her.

"Yeah, I am now."

"Would you like to sit here and talk about it or go upstairs and forget about it for a while?" I asked with a smirk.

"Both," she said, her face falling until she was scowling at me.

"I can give you a lot of things, but I don't know if I can do both of those at the same time."

"You've done enough for me. You've done more for me than anyone." Her tone was so sad that my chest ached at the sound. "I shouldn't ask anymore of you."

"What's going on? Is my little ice witch realizing she actually has feelings like the rest of us?"

She finally cracked, her lips curving into a smile, giving me enough reason to lean in and kiss her again.

"I already had my suspicions," she said, making me laugh. "I'm just realizing that it's going to be hard to leave now."

"You don't have to. I think I've been trying to explain that to you for days."

"But I can't. Look at what happened. I can't put you all in danger because I selfishly want to stay."

"But we're fine. We took care of it. All of us."

"They are going to come back. Ambush me, or all of us, again. Anything they can do to get me and that laptop," she said. Her lips pressed hard together and for a second I was thinking she was going to cry, but she only wrapped her arms around me. "I'm sorry."

"You didn't do anything wrong, sweetheart. Come on, let's go upstairs."

I pulled her out of the car, Riot jumping down and barreling upstairs in front of us. I kept her moving until I moved into the bedroom, pulling off every inch of clothing as we went. The sudden need to be with her, against her, buried in her.

I groaned as a shiver ran through me. I needed her, and more importantly, I wanted her to see that she needed me. Not for anything other than the fact that we belonged together.

I pulled her down into bed, following her back as I kissed her.

Before I could continue, though, she slipped away, rolling over and away from me. She was apparently about to try to freeze me out again. Her little speech that she needs to go and not get us involved only made me more pissed off at Slaughter, and I was about one more fight with Carly about it before I went out and dealt with it myself.

For now, though, I wasn't going to let her shut me out, not after what she just went through.

I moved up behind her, curling around her and moving her hair until I could kiss up and down her neck.

"I'm no longer in the mood for the happy sunshine boy."

"Too bad. You're stuck with him and he wants to kiss every inch of you until you feel better."

She made an annoyed groan but didn't push me away and I took my opening. My lips brushed over her spine before I flicked out my tongue, running it up her neck.

Lips, teeth, tongue. I moved over her, making sure I didn't miss any part as I made my way down her neck and chest and stomach until I reached her hips. I moved back up, mimicking my movements until her hips pushed up into me and she moaned.

"Fuck. You know, you make me cum like you do, and I'm ready to marry you tomorrow," I said, laughing. I knew it was partly a joke, but I couldn't stop myself from saying it. My desperate mind was looking for anything that would keep her here forever.

"Jax, you know I'm —"

"Leaving? Yes, you've only told me a hundred times. While I appreciate the honesty, it does nothing to stop me falling in love with you. I love every second with you, smiling or scowling. Mad at me or happy. I love every minute. I mean, thank you for not leading me on to believe I have a chance, and I wish it did help, but it doesn't. I've already fallen in love with you."

"You shouldn't have."

"It's not like I could stop it. Maybe don't be so perfect for me. Maybe it's your fault for storming into my life," I said with another laugh. I could hear the strain in this one. "And say what you want. I think you've already fallen for me, too."

"I can't."

"You can. You saw that I can keep you safe.. Nothing else is stopping you from staying here until you're sick of me. I would make that really impossible, though."

"But I can't keep you and the crew safe. That isn't fair."

"We can keep ourselves safe."

She was almost snarling at me now. "Is this really the conversation to have while you are trying to fuck me?" I had undressed her the rest of the way, resting myself over top of her until my cock sat against her wetness.

I leaned down, nipping at her ear and pinning her wrists to the bed.

"What are you doing? Are we getting back to sex?"

"No. I just have to hold you down so you don't run when I tell you that I am not *fucking* you. I am one hundred percent making love to you."

Her face scrunched, and she tried to pull away. "Oh eww, Jax. Don't ever call it that again."

I laughed harder, my stomach clenching so hard I wanted to roll off of her. "Fine, but you have to do something for me." I adjusted myself, lifting up and pushing deep into her.

She gasped and then groaned when I stopped again.

"What do I have to do?"

"Keep your eyes on me. Look at me as you cum. Don't look away as you fall apart on my cock."

She gave a hazy nod in agreement before I started to move again, picking up my pace until I was nearly slamming into her, but every time I did she smiled and moaned, encouraging me to do it more.

Her head rolled to the side as her orgasm grew, so I stopped, not saying a word until she looked back at me.

Then I moved again and her eyes went wide until she was clutching at me. Nails dug in and her body tightened, and all I could think about was how I wanted this forever. Then, I was right there with her, my body shuttering as I came hard. Already wishing I could do it all over again. There was never enough of her.

"You're the worst," she panted, but she was still smiling.

"You only say that because you are so insanely in love with me that you can't even stand it. Because you know that I will always take care of you."

She mumbled something as I rolled away, pulling her with me to head to the shower.

She kept up, holding onto my arm as we made it into the shower. I turned on the water, and without another word, she was on me. Her body was flush against mine, reaching up to kiss me. Her hands wove into my hair until she was pulling me down harder. She was giving me everything, and all it did was fill me with dread. After everything that happened today, she was ready to run, and I was starting to worry this was her goodbye.

———

"I'M SO HUNGRY," I whispered into the dark room a few hours later. I pulled myself up and out of bed. "Do you want something to eat?"

"Yes, but there is no possible way that I could get up and cook right now."

"I wasn't even going to ask. And I already know there are leftovers, so we're good." I said, heading out into the kitchen.

Minutes went by before she stepped out, fully dressed, with something in her hand, and looking pissed.

"What could have possibly happened in the five minutes I have been out here to make you look like that?"

She didn't say anything, but came over to the counter and set a laptop down in front of me.

"I'm guessing that's not yours."

"No. This is the one Slaughter was talking about."

"Is it Slaughter's computer?" I asked, opening it up.

My stomach dropped, the words making sense but somehow sounding like nonsense.

"Why do you have his laptop?" I could hear the coldness in my voice, but she had been storing this here, hiding it from me. I had heard him earlier, but had been too preoccupied to ask more about it.

Or I was delusional that it had ever gone away.

"Because I took it when I left."

"This has been here the entire time, and you didn't tell me? I told you that I didn't want to put anyone here in the way of this. And you what? Heard 'bring stolen items into the apartment' instead?"

"No, I heard what you said. At first, I kind of just let myself forget about it, then when you let me put my stuff in the dresser, I realized that I was too scared to bring it up."

"But I never scared you, Carly. I never did anything to make you feel unsafe around me."

"No, but I knew you wouldn't like this. I didn't know if you would kick me right back out at that point and I had nowhere else to go. And honestly, I didn't want to tell you the truth."

"Why? We could have figured this all out weeks ago, and maybe you could have realized you could stay without all of this hanging over your head."

"That wouldn't happen. He still needs my help."

"Why?"

"At first it was because I was too scared to face Slaughter. Then, I didn't know if there was actually enough on it to get him in trouble. I know he needs it to steal these new cars, but I can't figure out why exactly. Plus, a lot of stuff on there might incriminate me, too."

I ground my teeth together, a headache already forming. "Why?"

"Because, for a long time, I helped them with their stealing car operations. I didn't exactly mean to. I was doing the things they asked and keeping the peace. Then something happened, and I woke up to what I was doing. They noticed and told me that I pretty much had one choice and that choice was helping them steal new cars. I was supposed to start hacking into databases to change VIN numbers and make titles, but I couldn't do it. I guess it doesn't matter, though, because my name is all over the files on that laptop. They will assume I had a bigger role in all of it."

"Shit. What the fuck, Carly?" I said, not meaning it nearly as harsh as I sounded.

Then she did the one thing I wasn't expecting, or prepared for. One thing I hadn't seen her do yet.

She started crying.

"Fuck," I said, moving around the counter to her. She didn't move as I wrapped my arms around her. "Don't cry, please, it's okay."

"No, it's not. I'm either going to have to run away like I planned to do, or go to jail."

"Those aren't the only options, my sweet little witch," I said, kissing her head. "We will figure something out."

"We? There is no we? You can't be more involved with this, and I've already dragged it all to your front door. Again, look at what happened today!" she said through tears. "I made this mess, I did some of those things that it shows, I have to be the one to fix it."

"By what? Leaving? I don't want that."

"Of course you do. I lied to you. I hid this from you and put you and the crew in danger. You can't be okay with this."

"I'm not, but I also can't stand you crying. Were you even aware that you had tear ducts?"

That finally made her laugh, the harsh breath coming before she took a deep breath.

"No, I figured they dried up years ago."

"Why are you crying now?"

She pushed harder into me, her arms tightening so much I was going to struggle to breathe soon.

"Because I don't want to leave," she said finally, her voice so quiet I could barely hear it. But I did, and my heart burst at the words.

She was choosing me.

And there was no chance in hell that I was going to let Slaughter and Tristan change that now.

"You don't have to leave."

"I do. I can't bring these problems to you again. I can't let anyone get hurt. and I have already let this go on for too long. I thought I would take care of it sooner, but then everything happened with you and I kept telling myself that I would do it the next day. That I would leave it and take care of it then, but I kept staying. I can't put it off any longer. I don't know what to do, but I have to figure it out."

"No, I don't think you can."

"So then I should leave."

"I never said that. I mean that I agree. We've put it off for too long and we need to take care of this. You can't live your life running from them, and I can't live my life without you here, so we're going to finish this somehow."

"When you found out that I kind of was related to Slaughter and that he was after me, you wanted me to leave. You didn't want to put your friends in danger and make a mess of your lives. Why would you be willing to do that now?"

"Because a lot changes when you fall in love with someone, Carly, including the things you would do for that person."

"I don't want you to do anything for me. I don't want to be your problem."

"I'm begging you *to* be my problem. I want you to stay. I want to kiss you every day, I want to wake up and see you, and sit watching your fucking mean little face until you finish your coffee, and I want to hear about your day. I want Riot to jump on me every time I walk in the door. I want to watch your ridiculous scary movies and try not to make fun of you when I see how much you like the romance ones I put on. I don't care if you have some problems from your past. Would you care if I did?"

"No, but you're not a walking problem. I don't know how to prove that I'm worth being in your life with all of this hanging over my head."

"*Prove* it? What the hell would that mean? You don't have to prove that you are worth loving, you just are. And I mean, you are loveable exactly the way you are. Stop thinking I need you to be some cheerleader in my life. Who you are is perfect for me. We are not exactly the same and I like it that way. We balance each other, and I think we both need that. As for the problems with Slaughter and Tristan, we will take care of it."

"I feel balanced with you. I mean, aside from having all these emotions that I didn't know I could have, the rest of me feels calm, balanced, and I like it. But how could I take care of things with Slaughter without ending up in jail or his prisoner?"

"I don't know, but I don't think we are going to figure that out right now. Come on, you look exhausted. Let's try to get some rest."

She nodded, wrapping her arms around my waist. "Thank you for not hating me. I'm sorry I kept all of that from you. I thought it was the right thing to do at the time."

"I know. I'm glad you finally told me. Now come on. Let's get you into bed."

———

WE WENT TO BED, but I didn't sleep.

I stared at her for another hour before I made my decision.

I was going to fix this.

I had waited until I heard her steady breaths before I got up and threw on clothes. Riot went to move, but I held up a hand. "Stay."

Unmoving, he watched as I crept out of the room, throwing on my boots and jacket quickly before stepping into the hallway. I think Riot was just as worried about her as I was. Maybe more, considering he hadn't been more than a foot away from her since earlier.

Two phone calls later I had Slaughters phone number, dialing quickly before I could worry about making a plan. I need to keep her safe, and wanting to live here, while keeping the entire crew safe from getting jumped. I knew Slaughter would start trying to attack us when our backs were turned. He was a dirty fighter, and we learned our lessons with him before. I wasn't going to put anyone in that position again.

He picked up on the third ring.

"Hey, we need to talk. I don't need you bothering us again, so let's make a deal."

Slaughter was quiet before finally laughing. "Meet me at the empty lot we use for races. Bring her and the laptop and we can figure something out."

"Be there in twenty."

"I'll be waiting."

I looked at the laptop and back at the door. I wasn't bringing either of them, but needed the laptop safe in case we did come to an agreement. I was only handing it over if he agreed to keep her out of this, and erase her name from every single document on that laptop. If he needed it that badly, he would do it. I headed to

Kye's apartment, knocking since it was nearly the middle of the night.

He opened the door in seconds, eyebrows up in surprise.

"You good?"

"Not quite. I have to go meet with Slaughter and need this safe. It's got incriminating evidence for him, but incriminates Carly, too. Can you hold on to it until I figure out what he wants?"

"Yeah, but I think I should come with you."

"No, not yet. I'm meeting him out at the lot we race at. I'm going to find out what he wants and then head back here."

"You sure, though? Wouldn't it be better if I came?"

"No, not now. I don't want him to think I'm up to something and showing up with everyone would definitely make it look like a retaliation attack after today. I'm going to try to talk to him and see if we can come to an agreement. He obviously wants this laptop, but I can't hand it over if it's going to get her in trouble, too."

Kye nodded. "Fine. I get it. Keep texting, so I know what's up and you know we will be there if you need us."

"I know. Hopefully that won't be needed. I'm going to make an offer, and if he refuses, I leave. He wants me to bring Carly and the laptop so once he sees that it didn't, it might be over before it starts."

He nodded, and I headed back downstairs to my car. It wasn't a far drive, but I wanted this over as soon as I could finish it.

The sooner this was over with, the sooner she could live her life the way she wanted. And hopefully, that still included choosing me because I was sure as hell choosing her.

THIRTY-SEVEN
CARLY

I DIDN'T KNOW what time it was when I rolled over, but the moment that I realized Jax wasn't next to me, I was wide awake.

Riot wasn't in the room either, and that made me panic more. I got up, throwing on leggings and a hoodie before heading into the living room.

There was still no sign of Jax, but Riot was at the door, his nose pressed to the crack at the bottom.

I thought it was silent, but as I calmed my loud heart, I heard whispers coming from the hallway. Fear coursed through me until I heard Kye's voice, then Fox's, then Ransom's. I still couldn't figure out what they were talking about, but I crept closer, trying to listen for Jax's.

"He went to talk to him. I don't know what all that means, but it can't be good," Kye said.

"No. It's not," Ransom said. "He should fucking know better. We should at least get closer in case he needs something. You know the guys going to be pissed that his plan failed today"

"Slaughter said to meet him at the lot we raced at the other day. He just left, but I'm guessing he's wasting no time in getting there."

I ripped the door open and stepped out. They were all standing at the bottom of the steps in front of Fox's apartment. Jax wasn't with them, but I guess I knew where he was now. All their heads whipped to me.

"Carly," Fox said.

I ran back in, grabbing my phone off the counter and the keys.

No texts, and no missed calls. He really didn't want to let me know what he was doing.

I raced back out, grabbing the laptop out of Kye's hands, and kept moving down to the apartment garage.

"Carly, wait," Fox yelled again.

"Slaughter could kill him and you three want to stand around waiting to see if he needs help? Why did you let him leave in the first place?" My words were almost a scream as I reached the garage and looked around. The Charger was luckily still here, so he must have taken his car.

I could hear cursing and running around upstairs, but I wasn't going to wait. Jax shouldn't have gone alone, and they should have already been on their way after him. I don't care what reasons he had.

Riot jumped into the car and I didn't have time to pull him back out.

The loud roar of the engine filled the garage as I realized I didn't have a way to open the garage door in this car. Kye was there before anyone else.

"I'll hit the button. Do you want me to drive?"

"No."

He nodded, hitting the button in his car before running back to me.

"I'm riding with you," he said, pulling open the passenger door.

"Fine, but hurry up," I said, already backing up the car before Scout ran down.

"Me too!" she yelled, jumping into the open passenger door before scrambling into the backseat. Kye got in after her, slamming the door shut as I took off.

Scout shrieked and when I looked in the mirror, I could only see Riot pushing into her lap.

"Switch with me!" she yelled at Kye. "Switch with me now! If he sits on me, I will suffocate!"

"Why did you let him go alone?" I asked, not caring to hide my mean tone.

"Because he said that he wanted to go alone until he knew what Slaughter wanted. I can't exactly tell the grown man what to do."

"No, but you can decide to go with him. You jumped into my car and didn't ask. Couldn't you have done the same for him?"

"Listen, I'm not going to win this, but I was already getting everyone ready to go for him. Don't take all your anger for Slaughter out on me. Plus, you don't even know where you are going so you should be glad I'm here for directions," he said with a grin.

"Fine." I huffed, switching gears and speeding up as we hit a long stretch of road. According to Kye, would be there in less than ten minutes, but it still felt like too long.

"Take a breath, Carly. Maybe Jax's got it all taken care of," Scout said, patting my arm. "He might not even need us there."

"He did say that he was only going to make him an offer. He didn't want to get into anything tonight if he could help it."

"And I know Slaughter. He isn't going to let Jax be there and not take advantage of that. You guys see that Slaughter doesn't drop things easily. He is going to do what he can to get Jax involved. Why would he do this?"

"Because he loves you and he would do pretty much anything for someone he loves."

"Well, that can make two of us then. Where's my phone?" I asked.

Scout patted around the seat and I hit my pockets, but neither of us seemed to find it.

"No idea. Why?" Scout asked.

"I need to call Ash."

Scout handed me the phone, and it only rang once before she picked up.

"Hey, we are right behind you guys."

"Great, but I need a favor."

"Alright, anything you need," she said. Her immediate agreement reminded me how not alone I was now. There was a team of people that were ready to jump in and help, even if it was dangerous. Now we needed to figure out how to end all of this with Slaughter, and fast.

***

After ten more minutes of reckless driving while Scout and Kye yelled at me, I finally made it to the parking lot.

I saw Slaughter's car first, Tristan's right next to it, and Jax's in front. There was no one else, but that didn't mean they weren't right around the corner. Slaughter would never come alone like this.

I revved the car, aiming it right at them, but my heart stopped when I saw what was happening.

Jax was about to get into Slaughter's car. The passenger door was open, and he almost slid inside until he saw us.

Anger rolled through me so violently that I yelled. "What is he doing?"

"Pull up next to him and we will find out," Scout said, her

voice calm and even, but I couldn't do it. There was no way that Slaughter was going to get Jax to be a part of his stupid gang. There was no way that I was going to sit by and watch as Jax became anything like them.

I angled the car, heading right towards the driver's side door of Slaughter's car.

Kye swore and Riot barked as I hit it. The door snapped, flinging against the front wheel as I turned the car back around.

"Carly, what are you doing here?" Jax asked, already running over to me. "Why did you tell her?" he asked Kye.

"I didn't tell her! She found out herself and you're welcome for not letting her come alone."

"Don't get mad at Kye. You should be mad at yourself. What are you doing? Why would you come meet with him and not tell me? Not tell anyone basically," I yelled.

I heard the others pull up, their cars idling at the edge.

"Everyone came?" Jax asked, grabbing my arm and dragging me away from everyone. "Why would you bring them all here?"

"They came on their own. I didn't ask anyone. What were you doing getting into his car?"

We both looked over. Slaughter had been screaming since I hit his door and didn't seem to be stopping yet. Tristan was there, trying to help him pull it back with one hand, but it looked ready to fall off.

"Why did you come? What are you doing with him?"

"Trying to make a deal. I want to know what it will take to leave you alone. He was about to ask me to do something in exchange, but you interrupted that."

"I'm assuming these things aren't exactly fixing a few cars or anything. I'm assuming he wants you to help him steal cars for him. Then he has more help, and he knows that I would do what he needs to help you. It's a trick, Jax."

"Maybe, but I've taken cars before, I can do it again if it

makes him leave you alone. Maybe, if I help, he won't need your help."

"First of all, what do you mean you've done it before? And second of all, please don't tell me that you really believe him. Are you going to suddenly be changing VIN numbers and making titles? No. I doubt it. He's going to want your help over and over until you are just like him. He knows you don't want me involved so he will use that against you until you're dead."

"We were all poor kids with nothing and wanted something in our lives. We took some cars to get ahead when we were young. We've righted those wrongs now and I think we made it up to those people, but that shows you that doing this one more time isn't going to turn me into someone else. I will still be me. As for the rest of it, I would rather try than sit around waiting for him to attack you."

"No. Not at all. This isn't the same thing, Jax. This is worse, this is giving Slaughter something to hang over your head. What do you think he's going to do when he gets desperate again and needs help? He's going to call you. He's going to come to me and tell me to help or he will turn you in. He will pit us against each other. He won't stop, Jax. Why would you think you should do this?"

"Because of you. I would do anything for you. I will fight any fight and become any monster you need if it means you're safe. I will still be me, and I will still love you the same."

His hands slid over my jaw, holding my face so gently I wanted to cry.

"It won't change. I'm always going to be me. Exactly who you have come to know, but you should also know that I will never be afraid to get my hands bloody for you. It's not like this is the first time I have had to do something like this and it probably won't be the last, knowing my friends. It does not mean that I won't come home to wrap you in my arms and love you. It does not mean that I will be angry, or violent, or any different to you. I will love you the same way, even if I have to do this. I am doing this *because* I love you."

I was already shaking my head. "I won't risk it. I won't let it happen. They're not going to be my nightmare anymore. I'm going to be theirs," I said, turning and walking straight to Slaughter.

THIRTY-EIGHT

JAX

SHE SLIPPED OUT of my grip as she spun, heading right at Slaughter.

"Carly, stop. Please," I said, trying to catch up, but it was obvious that there was no stopping her. She kept going until she was standing right in front of him. I couldn't see her face, but I could picture the glare all on my own. I was pretty sure Carly wasn't afraid of anything when she was mad, and right now, she was pissed.

I waved at Fox and Ransom's cars that were parked on the edge, having them come over. I didn't think anything was getting better right now and after Carly started whatever she was about to start, this entire thing was going to blow up.

Their cars jumped forward, catching everyone's eyes.

"Why the hell are you having more of them come over here? You think I don't have friends waiting on the side, too?" He waved them over, and I rolled my eyes.

"I'm sure you do, but—" My words were cut off as three more cars pulled up from behind him. I hadn't seen them parked around the corner, but I had already assumed some of them were there. The rest of them were apparently already waiting at the manufacturer lot, where he was planning to steal the cars from. I guess Carly had ruined their original planned date, and Slaughter missed his deadline with his business partner. Who, according to Slaughter, was worse than him, which really didn't seem possible. When I called earlier, he put the plan back into place, calling all his friends to get ready.

I hated that it was such a smart idea. Steal the cars, install a fake VIN plate with fake titles, sell them to random buyers, and by the time anyone found out, it could be months or years later. He could do this with plenty of cars before someone caught on and even then, if he covered his tracks well enough, no one would know it was him.

Unless they had his files.

"What is going to make this stop? What is it going to take to make you leave me alone for good?" Carly said. I stepped closer to her, Riot already at her side.

"We already made a deal. As long as he comes with us, we are good," Slaughter said with a creepy grin.

"That deal is off, because I know it's bullshit. You're going to get him wrapped up in this, so I give in and help."

Slaughter gave a deep laugh. "You stole my laptop, and you're going to start by giving that back. He was here making a deal that he would help in exchange for us leaving you alone."

"I steal the cars, you leave her alone, and find someone else to help you with the rest," I said, repeating what I had already told him.

Ransom stepped closer to me. "Jax, come on. You know better than that."

"If you go with him, he will either kill you or never leave you alone again," Kye said.

"Yeah, well, we are short on options. If any of you have another idea, please tell me."

"It seems you left him in the dark about a few things, Carly, because he really doesn't seem to understand that you and that laptop are the key to this plan working. I couldn't turn down another set of hands that could take another car, though," Slaughter said.

I pretty much already assumed it wouldn't be enough to make him drop it completely, but I hoped it would be enough not to have her randomly attacked again.

"What is he talking about, Carly?" I asked, stepping closer until I could put my hand on her back.

"He can't find someone else," she whispered. "At least not that easily."

"Why?"

"Because I built the program that he uses. No one else knows it like I do, and I never taught anyone else how to use it."

"Shit," I said. "You could have warned me."

"I didn't realize you would be sneaking out in the middle of the night to do this," she whispered angrily.

"What if we give you the laptop back, and then you leave her alone? I'm sure there is someone else that can learn it," I said, wishing she would back up, and let me finish this.

Slaughter laughed. "I don't know. Carly's like my daughter, and I worked hard to teach her what we need her to do. I can't let that investment walk away, and have to start over. And you already agreed to steal a few cars for me."

"Making a deal means you compromise. You want to be paid? Would that end this?"

"That's not happening," Carly said.

"It can happen if that ends this, Carly. I would rather do that than any of the other options."

"I wouldn't. It's already done. The police will be on their way soon, and I'll give them the laptop," she hissed.

"You are not," I said, my heart rate picking up. "You will go to prison for things you didn't do. You said your name was all over that laptop. Unless his name is on there more, he would only be an accomplice."

"I did do them, though, Jax. Maybe not everything on there, but I helped. I created it!"

"And that wasn't your choice or your idea. You can't take any of the fall for that."

"If I take part of the fall, he has to take the rest. That's what I'm doing, Jax. I told you, this isn't something you are going to fix for me. I tried to think of any other way, but there's nothing else. This is the only way, and I should have faced that before."

"Giving the laptop to the police won't be an option for you," Slaughter said, waving Tristan around the car to him.

At his signal, the rest of his friends got out and ran over. One of them stepped a little too close to Carly, and Riot snarled.

"Get back," the guy yelled at Riot, kicking out his foot.

"He only listens to my commands, so save your breath," she said.

I leaned down, my lips against her ear. "Hey, me too." I kissed the side of her neck. "Come on, back up, and get in the Charger. This is quickly getting worse, and if you really did call the police, we need to go before they arrive."

I wrapped an arm around her waist, pulling her back towards the Charger, since my car was now surrounded by Slaughter's goons.

But of course, in true Carly style, she started fighting me.

"I know it's you being you, but you don't have to fix this one for me, Jax. I should have stood up and finished this before. I shouldn't have tried running away, but I don't want to now that I have a reason to stay. You, more than anyone, have shown me who I am and now I know I can fix this. I can face him. For you, for the crew, for myself, I want to fix this."

"One more time, he can come with us and finish this all

tonight or we will take you and the laptop, anyway. Regardless if you fight it," Slaughter said.

The rest of the crew stepped up at that, there was no way any of us were going to quietly watch that happen.

"She's not going anywhere with you, whether she agrees or not," Ransom said. I knew he hated Slaughter, possibly more than any of us, and I knew how serious they all were as they agreed.

She spun to me, anger etched on her face. "Neither are you!" she yelled. "You are not allowed to go with him!"

"Alright both of you shut up," Slaughter yelled. "Tristan, get him in my car. Carly, you're waiting here with my friends because you're obviously going to fuck this up any way you can. We don't need you there, anyway. I need you on the computer later." He turned to Tristan, pushing him forward. "Maybe you can handle him better than the little girl and her dog."

"That's not happening," she yelled as Riot started barking. "You're not involving him."

"He's already involved," Slaughter said, waving his hand again, and everyone behind him descended. This was getting so far out of hand. Now, it was turning into a brawl.

Tristan rolled his eyes, pulling out a gun and pointing it at me. "We need to go, and you're coming with us."

THIRTY-NINE
CARLY

I DIDN'T KNOW exactly what it was, but every time someone threatened Jax, it made my blood boil in a way that I'd never experienced. It seemed absurd to threaten someone who never did anything wrong. Who loved the people around him, and would obviously do anything for them.

"Put that away," I said, stepping between them.

"When he gets in the car, I will."

"No, do it now."

"Carly, relax. Take a breath," Jax whispered behind me.

The only way I could explain it was pure, blinding outrage. I charged forward, punching him in the face and crying out when my hand ricocheted with pain. He yelled out, pulling the gun up, but I hit it down.

His hand must have squeezed the trigger, and the explosion of the gun made me fall back. I squeezed my eyes shut, but I could hear Jax yell and the ground shake as engines started. Out of pure luck, I hadn't been hit, but Tristan had been.

When I finally pried my eyes open, Tristan was yelling out, his foot covered in more blood than his arm had been in earlier.

I looked back at Jax. His eyes were wide, and he looked at me. Before he had a chance to step forward, someone slammed into him, driving their shoulder into his stomach.

All of Slaughter's friends were here now, and for a moment, it was blinding chaos. I looked back for Jax, but Slaughter yanked me away.

"Deal's off. Back to our original plan. Only Carly goes now," he yelled, laughing as he went.

Tristan limped to the car as Slaughter threw me into the side of a car.

"Get in," he yelled, pushing my head down and forcing me in. My sister, Chloe, sat in the driver's seat and my stomach dropped further.

"Chloe? What are you doing here?" The door slammed shut, but I could hear yelling.

I looked out, seeing Jax. His eyes were locked on our car as he punched someone. Part of me hoped that he would save me, the other hoped that he would go home, forget all of this happened, keeping him and the crew safe from more of this.

I didn't seem to have a choice though, because Slaughter had that covered.

"Slash all the tires. We don't need them interrupting us. Then go to your posted places. We are getting this done and solving all of our problems today."

Chloe took off, speeding down the road like a pro. "I didn't know you could drive like this?"

"What the fuck, Carly?" she screamed. "Did you just shoot my husband?"

"Husband? You got married?"

"Yeah, we did, and you shot him. That's *after* you let your stupid dog attack him."

"He technically shot himself," I said, trying not to laugh. I suddenly wished Jax was here, because I knew he would find it funny. "And wait, why are you here? Are you helping them with this?"

"Helping? These guys can barely tie their own shoes. I'm running this one."

I stepped back with horror. "You…You're working with them now? You set this up?"

"Obviously."

"And you're okay with this? You want to do this?" I couldn't believe it. Chloe had always stayed far enough away from all of this that I never would have believed she wanted to be involved.

She shrugged. "Yeah, I like it. I like being in charge and handling things. I like the money it brings, too. We bought a new house, and that's why we got married in the first place. Slaughter said I could take over a few things if we did."

"Why would you do this to me? Why wouldn't you help me and make them leave me alone?"

"Because I don't want to get in trouble either, and we need these cars. Slaughter set up the deal with a partner, and he's breathing down our throat. Some rich guy that needs to get richer. Now, we have to be at the manufacturer lot in twenty minutes to get all the cars out. I can't let my emotions get in the middle of that. I know you're a bitch and you would turn us over to the cops in a heartbeat if you could."

My eyebrows shot up. For all the times I had let my sister walk all over me, I was still surprised that she was saying this right now.

My phone vibrated in my pocket, but I didn't think I could take it now. I already knew it was Jax. He was probably freaking out, and I hoped that Ash was doing what I asked. I told that if things didn't go our way, like this, then she would call the sheriff. I would take whatever blame I needed to if it kept everyone alive and in one piece.

But as much as I was at odds with my sister, I didn't wish this for her.

"Please don't do this, Chloe. Pull over. I don't want you to get in trouble."

"I won't. With you joining us, we have the insurance for you not to call, and we have you back to finish up the VIN plates and titles. No one needs to get into any trouble now. Slaughter has been worried for weeks that you would go to the police, but you never did. I knew you wouldn't. You're a coward, always hiding in your room, and putting your head down. I knew we just needed to get you back, and then you would help."

"Chloe, pull the car over. End this now because it's only going to get worse. I'm not a coward. Maybe I was, but it doesn't seem that way anymore."

Her face flushed with anger and she looked at me. "Why? What did you do?"

"I didn't do anything yet, but you messed with my friends and they aren't going to go down without a fight. Please, stop now and stay out of this."

"Carly," she screamed, yanking the car to the side of the road and pulling to a stop. "What did you do?"

She reached over, and I already knew what she was doing. Chloe was a hair puller and when she was mad, she would rip the hair from my head. I swung up, punching her in the side of the face before she could get a handful. She screamed again, but I was already pushing the door open, falling out as Slaughter's car rounded the corner, his friends not far behind.

Another car came around them, a black 1968 Charger that seemed to keep coming to my rescue. He hit the side of the road, going around Slaughter and his friend, and didn't stop as he pushed to the front, the brakes locking up and skidding to a stop next to us.

Jax was out in seconds, pulling me off the ground and wrapping his arms around me.

"Carly," he said, squeezing me tighter.

"I'm okay. She got a little of my hair, though."

He gave a harsh laugh, kissing my head and keeping me hard against him. I looked over as the rest of the crew came out of the Charger like a clown car. One after another, and I couldn't imagine how uncomfortable it had been. A laugh escaped me, but fear took hold as Slaughter's voice came closer.

"You bitch. You know this isn't done," he said. "Chloe! Get her, we have to go!"

"It actually is, Slaughter. And for you, I think it's over for good now."

I saw the lights, the sirens silent as sheriff cars pulling around, blocking every single one of Slaughter and his friends' cars in. Unless they could somehow navigate the woods, there was no getting out now.

The cops descended, grabbing all of them as Jax held me.

"Carly, what did you do?" Jax said, his arms somehow tightening.

Ash stepped up next to us, Fox holding onto her. "She told me to call the sheriff if things went bad, and I did. He did say Carly would be going to jail with them until I made it clear that she was the one calling him, and not involved. He agreed to work with us on keeping her record clean if we helped him finally get Slaughter locked up for good. He's cost them a lot with all the calls on these stolen cars."

"I didn't know Ash knew the sheriff so well. I've been scared for weeks that I was going to be spending the next ten years in prison if I said anything," I said, smiling even though I felt like crying. "Now, we have to hope I can prove that I wasn't as involved. But either way, it's okay. I don't want to run anymore, and this was the price for staying. Do you think the worst of it is done now?" I asked, watching them grab Slaughter's friends, handcuffing them one-by-one.

"I sure fucking hope so. I just got into another fight and need one of those damn baths. Maybe some of that witch salve for this, too," he said, holding up his arm that had a cut across it.

I reached up to kiss him, seeing the dried blood at his nose, but before I could get to his lips, hands pulled me away, ripping my arms back behind me. Before I could fight back, I felt the cool metal of handcuffs clamp around my wrist.

FORTY

JAX

Apparently, helping the sheriff bring down a huge car theft ring, *again,* wasn't enough to keep you out of handcuffs.

At least this time, none of us were in the back of a car.

Yet.

"Kye, stop fidgeting or he's going to think you're up to something."

"The only thing I am up to is trying to get out of these things. I'm freaking out," he hissed.

"You can't tell me this is your first time being arrested?" Carly asked, handcuffed on the other side of me. I smiled down at her, unable to hide how happy I was to be here with her.

Even if we were handcuffed, it was over. She could stay and not have to look over her shoulder every five seconds.

"He hates the handcuffs part, not the being arrested part. He couldn't care less about that."

Kye jumped back onto the hood of the sheriff's car, moving his legs up and twisting his arms until he was threading the handcuffs underneath him and to the front, smirking into the windshield as he did.

"You know he's going to be pissed, right?"

"Yeah, but at least I can breathe a little better," Kye said, turning to look into the passenger side again as the sheriff came up behind him.

"Kye, what the hell? Do I have to put you in the back of my car, too?"

"Sure, sheriff, I won't mind. Is this 'take your daughter to work' day?" Kye asked, looking into the car. "Go ahead, and put me in the car. Let me see how prom queen is doing at her first drug bust."

That's when I realized what he had been looking at.

"Leave Daisy alone, Kye," the sheriff said, the warning tone serious.

"You're the one that offered to put me in the car with her. I was only trying to be polite."

"Polite my fucking ass," he mumbled, pulling Kye around to the back of the car. "She happened to be with me when I got the call. Don't even look at her."

"She's looking at me!" Kye yelled, somehow jumping himself onto the trunk of the car.

I looked down to see Daisy looking out at us. Kye was right. She was still looking at him, and it was a little funny that he brought his daughter along.

"We aren't the criminals. We did you a favor and you seem to be forgetting that," Ash said, the anger on her face making her turn red. "And I swear I will never let you hear the end of putting me in handcuffs for helping you."

"Sorry, Ashton. I have to keep everyone cuffed until it's all sorted. Don't take offense. I don't need your dad being pissed at me."

"For being treated like a criminal when I was the one to call you? I take a lot of offense!"

Fox leaned down, trying to calm her. I knew Quinn and Ash

had never been handcuffed before, and both seemed pretty upset. Quinn was more upset as Ransom tried to quietly tuck her under his chin.

Carly, on the other hand, looked annoyed, and almost bored.

"You good?" I asked.

"No. I just dealt with Slaughter, and watched a gun be held to your head, and all I would like to do right now is have your arms around me while I kiss you and I can't because of these stupid things."

My heart melted. "That was the most romantic thing I've ever heard you say. My hands are a little tied up right now, but I can still kiss you." I turned in front of her, leaning down as she fell back onto the car for balance while reaching up to kiss me.

Her lips met mine and turned into a frenzy. Suddenly, the people around us didn't matter to her as she whispered for me to come closer, kissing me harder.

"Aww," Scout said. "Look at our little criminals in love."

I dropped lower. "Is she right, Carly? Are you in love with me yet?"

"Mmm, I don't know. Just faced my worst fears, took down a huge car theft ring while shooting Tristan so you were safe and I could stay with you without worrying. Really, what I'm saying is that I'm still on the fence."

I laughed as I kissed her again. "I love you, too."

"I never actually said those words."

"That's alright. I know what you meant."

Her head fell against my chest, and now it was my turn to start getting mad at the handcuffs.

"I do love you, Jax."

"I know, sweetheart, and as soon as these are off, I'm taking you home and showing you exactly how much I love you."

Carly huffed and stepped away. "Alright. Get these handcuffs off of all of us and let us go. It's been two hours now. If you don't, I won't be helping you anymore with this."

The sheriff's eyes narrowed. "You know you all already agreed to help, which includes testifying."

"Consider us all out unless you let us go home right now. I am exhausted, and won't be agreeing to anything unless I get some sleep."

He looked around, eyeing us all up. "Fine. If I have any trouble getting a hold of any one of you, you will all be down at the station for days."

"Deal, just get these off," Kye said.

The sheriff did, un-cuffing us all and letting us go.

I grabbed Carly's hand, pulling her as fast as I could to the car.

It was time to take her home with me again.

This time, forever.

FORTY-ONE
CARLY

<u>2 Days Later</u>

I had barely moved from the bed since we came home that night, choosing to stay safe and cocooned in our own little world.

A new world where there was no guilt, no secrets, no threats.

Just us.

We had only gone out for more food because our plans included staying in bed for a few more days. I walked up the stairs heading to our apartment and froze as I reached the door.

Our apartment.

Jax ran into my back at my sudden stop. "What are you doing? I would carry you, but my hands are full."

"Our apartment," I said, repeating the words outloud.

"Yes, it's the one right there with the dirty paw print on the door now, thanks to Riot," he mumbled. "You okay?"

"In my head, I called it our apartment. Not your apartment."

He groaned and moved around me to open the door. "I'm glad you finally caught up. Does this mean you're done fighting it and planning to stay for good now?"

"Was that an invitation?"

He walked in, leaving me in the hall as Riot came running out to greet us.

"I think I've given you a thousand invitations at this point. Do you need it in writing?"

I smirked, stepping inside and setting my bags down. "That might help, although I don't know how I'm ever going to believe I truly got this lucky in life."

"I agree. I don't know how I got so lucky to find you," he said, coming around to wrap his arms around me. He kissed me hard before I pulled back.

"When did you decide that you liked me?" I asked.

"Do you want the romantic answer? Or the honest answer?"

"Honest, obviously."

"The morning I woke up and saw you there scowling in my shirt. It felt like home, like everything I've ever wanted. I mean, I already thought I did, but at that moment, I knew I liked you."

"That was the romantic answer?"

"No, the romantic answer would be, from the second I met you, I was in love."

"So your honest answer isn't that it was the second we met, but pretty close?"

"Yeah. Might as well get used to the 'second I met you story' because I'll be telling our kids that one like a thousand times."

"Jax!"

"To soon? Fine, I'll only talk about marrying you then."

"Jax!"

"What? That can't be a crime to talk about."

"A crime? No. A little premature? Yes."

At the word crime, I thought through everything we went through. Everything we had to do to get us to this point. There would never be a way I could show Jax how much I did love him. Or even how thankful I was for what he had done for me, but I wasn't mad at the thought of trying to show him what I felt every day.

He laughed, kissing my head. "Fine, then we can leave it at *welcome home*. Your home. Our home. The exact place you belong. Where Riot belongs. I have loved you even on the days you didn't want me to, and I will keep loving you every single day of our lives."

"I want to roll my eyes and tell you to stop with the romantics, but it does actually make me feel better."

"Roll your eyes and give me that scowl. I will still tell you all the romantic things every single day."

I huffed, pulling out of his arms and grabbing his hand.

"What are you doing?" He asked, with a quiet laugh.

"Bringing you to bed."

"What about cooking the food?" He asked.

"It can wait until after," I said.

"After what?"

I looked back at him, watching his smile grow as he tried to fight it.

"You know exactly what I'm talking about," I said.

"Yeah, but I just like hearing all the dirty details from you." I turned, kissing him as we fell back onto the bed. He stopped, his perfect blue eyes staring into mine.

"I love you," he said.

"Love you too, *Sunshine.*"

"Now you did it," he said, pulling off my shirt. "You know what happens now."

And I did.

Jax was going to show me *exactly* how much he loved me.

EPILOGUE

CARLY

A Year Later

I pulled the pan out of the oven, almost dropping it as I cheered. It was perfectly done.

It was the second Christmas I had spent with the crew, but the first one that I was cooking while on camera. At the beginning of the year, Jax had given me all the confidence to upload a video of me cooking, and it had done well enough that I uploaded another one. And then another one, until my videos were doing so well that I was making money from them, surprisingly good money.

Even the crew was getting involved. They liked to call themselves guest stars when they helped me cook something for a video. I didn't mind because viewers seemed to love it when they came on, each one of those videos doing double the views compared to what they did when I was alone. Especially when Jax helped me.

I had grown it enough that I was starting to work on a cookbook, something I always wanted to do, and I hoped it would all continue. The sudden bit of success left me wanting more. The next thing I had on my mind was buying the diner.

I wrapped up the video and laid out the food as Jax's head popped into the kitchen. This was one of my longer videos and they had all taken a turn coming in to help me, but now it was time to actually eat all the food.

"You done?"

"Yeah, I just need this all carried out."

He nodded, grabbing plate after plate of food to bring out to the table before coming back.

He wrapped his arms around me, kissing me hard as he untied my apron and pulled it off.

"This wasn't what you were wearing before," he said, eyeing the low cut top.

"No, I went and changed after the video."

He pulled at the top, sucking in a breath at the red lace underneath.

"I really hope this is the present I get to unwrap."

"It might be one of them," I said. "Have you been good?"

"My best behavior every single day," he said, kissing my neck as his hand dipped in, running over the lace that covered my breast.

"You aren't being good right now."

"Neither are you. You knew exactly what this lace was going to do to me."

I laughed. "Yes, I did, so come on, let's go eat."

He groaned, trailing after me. I knew he would get me back for teasing him as soon as we were alone tonight, and I was already looking forward to it.

We laid everything out on the table as the crew sat down, already deep into a conversation about next week's races.

After everything that happened with Slaughter died down, they all went right back to their lives, moving on like nothing ever happened. They still rarely brought it up to me. At first, I thought it was because they didn't want to upset me, but then I realized that it was because they didn't worry about it anymore. The threat of him was gone, and they were happy to leave it in the past. I was happy to leave it there right along with them. And there were apparently plenty of other warrants for Slaughter's arrest that, on top of stealing the cars that they found in his garage, he wouldn't be out for a long, long time. Which meant that I could live my life in peace.

I sat down as Jax threw his arm around the back of my chair. It was the same place I sat a little over a year ago, scared of these people. I could only laugh now. I couldn't believe I was scared of them for even a second.

"This looks amazing. Good job," Jax said, and I smiled as he started passing dishes. I was pretty sure he complimented every single thing I made, but it never failed to make me smile.

I looked around, waiting as everyone piled their plate and started eating. "I just want to tell you all thank you," I said, trying to keep my voice even. "I wouldn't be where I was with all of this without you all, and I can't tell you how much it means to me."

"Aww, I think this is Carly telling us she loves us," Scout said, jumping up and throwing her arms around me.

"Yeah, that's exactly what I'm saying," I said, laughing as I tried to grab onto her. I might still struggle to verbally tell everyone how much I love them, but I was getting better, and they all seemed to find it more funny than anything.

Except Jax, who would tell me that he loves me over and over until I said it back.

For not having a family, I really found a great family to hang around.

We finished eating and then moved to the living room to

open the mountain of presents. With eight of us here buying presents for each other, the presents piled up fast.

Jax moved them all around, handing them out until everyone had their own little pile, then sat down on the ground, his back against the couch. He grabbed me, sliding me until I was between his legs, and leaned back against him.

Riot sniffed after each box, searching through them until he found the one that held his new chew toy, and getting to work ripping it apart.

From there, I could see one box hidden at the back that he hadn't pulled out yet.

"Did you forget one?" I asked, looking back at him. He grinned.

"No, we can open that one later, alone."

"Oh no, what did you do?"

"Oh no? Are you worried I bought something you didn't like?"

"No, I'm worried you bought something that will keep me tied to a bed all day tomorrow instead of going to my grandpa's house."

He laughed, the rumble of his chest shaking me. "No, it won't keep you tied to the bed. I already have the things to do that. This one will be vibrating against you and making you beg to stay in bed."

I smacked at his hand as he moved down over my jeans, pointing out exactly where he was going to use it.

"You're terrible," I said, laughing. "And calm yourself down. We aren't alone yet."

"Sorry, I didn't know you could feel that."

"Pretty hard not to with the size of that thing," I said, his hard cock now pressing against my lower back. His chest tumbled again, and I laughed. For all the ways Jax liked to be in charge, he loved when I praised him about anything.

"Here," he said, setting a box in my lap. "This is the real present."

I looked at the small box, the horrible wrapping making me laugh. "Did you wrap this yourself?"

"Of course, I did."

"You know the worst part," Kye said from across the room. "He's improved over the years."

I laughed as Jax threw some wadded up paper at him. Kye had also really become one of my best friends over the past year, too. Somehow, our weird talks always made me feel better, and both of us knew that we could end the conversation at any moment by just walking away, and that was somehow my perfect friendship.

Jax kissed the back of my head, reminding me that I still hadn't opened the present. I ripped the paper off and opened the small box, not hiding my smile as I looked down at the necklace.

The small font matched his tattoo exactly. "Forever," I said, reading it.

"I figured we weren't getting matching tattoos anytime soon, so I thought this would be the next best thing," he said, grinning as I looked back at him. "It will at least hang in the exact same place as my tattoo, so we will kind of match."

"That is the sweetest thing you have ever given me," I said, trying to find any words.

"Really? Damn, I just keep outdoing myself, don't I?" he said, kissing my head again. "But you do like it?"

"Yes, I love it. Thank you, and you are right. I wasn't planning on getting matching tattoos, no matter how much I want forever with you."

I had spent days trying to think of something to get for Jax. He was impossible to buy for, aside from parts for his car, and I knew he would be happy with literally anything. He had decided earlier this year that he loved helping the kids with the charity division at Holt Racing, so he had almost taken over running it entirely. Most days he was exhausted, so there was one thing I knew he would love.

"I know you've been going non-stop with the garage, and running the charity at Holt, so I decided to get us a trip away. We are going to our own *private* cabin in the woods for a few days. No interruptions or work."

His chest rumbled and arms encircled me. "That might be the best present I've ever had. I don't know what could be better than a break from everything with my girl, all to myself."

I snuggled back against him, not wanting to move as everyone opened up their presents.

Sometimes, I could still barely believe this life was mine. I woke up every morning in a safe, cozy apartment, had coffee with Jax before either starting my day working, which was really just cooking with a camera in my face, or hanging out with one of the girls. Three girls who had become my best friends after I let my guard down completely.

Sometimes I still struggled with thinking about forever, but I also couldn't imagine wanting forever with anyone else.

I leaned back, turning to kiss him.

"Love you, sunshine," I said, smiling at the nickname.

He groaned. "I still haven't gotten over you telling me that randomly. I love you too, my grumpy little witch."

THANK YOU!

Thank you so much for reading Jax and Carly's story!

If you enjoyed Racing Hearts, please consider leaving a review! Support from readers like you means so much to me and helps other readers find books.

If you loved the crew, make sure to reach Ransom and Quinn's story in **Heart Wrenched.** And Fox and Ash's story in **Wrecked Love!**

Printed by Amazon Italia Logistica S.r.l.
Torrazza Piemonte (TO), Italy

58845897R00218